Praise for *The Exp...*

"This fun romp offers hilarious mor... ...fe issues: the fear involved in becomin... ...vs of one's own upbringing that can da... ...d friends undertake the whodunit." —*First Clue*

"I LOVED this book! Alice is hilarious, the mystery is compelling and fun, and this group of about-to-be moms deserves a sequel, and some cake, obvi! Kat Ailes has written a winner of a book and you'll want to read it immediately!" —Catherine McKenzie, *USA Today* bestselling author of *Have You Seen Her*

"*The Expectant Detectives* is wildly funny, clever, twisty, charming, and unexpectedly relatable. It is exactly the surprisingly heartwarming and uproariously hilarious mystery we all need in our lives. This book is one of a kind and I can't wait for the next installment." —Nora Murphy, author of *The New Mother*

"A gloriously smart and witty telling of the darker side of prenatal groups— this is really funny with edge." —Helen Lederer, author of *Losing It*

"Murdering every mommy cliché with hilarity and heart, this book is a complete triumph. Perfectly plotted, brilliantly observed, and just so much fun." —Lauren Bravo, author of *How to Break Up with Fast Fashion*

"A twisty, turny murder mystery guaranteed to satisfy any amateur detective's cravings, with belly laughs big enough to give you stretch marks." —Fiona Leitch, author of *The Cornish Wedding Murder*

"Kat Ailes nails small-town cozy crime in her debut novel. From the first page, I was hooked. I laughed an awful lot; the writing is so clever and funny." —Chris McDonald, author of the Stonebridge Mysteries

"A humorous, remarkably touching debut. Pacy, funny, with just the right undertones of dark." —Eva Verde, author of *Lives Like Mine*

Also by Kat Ailes

Dead Tired

The
EXPECTANT
DETECTIVES

A NOVEL

KAT AILES

MINOTAUR BOOKS
NEW YORK

This is a work of fiction. All of the characters, organizations, and events portrayed in this novel are either products of the author's imagination or are used fictitiously.

Published in the United States by Minotaur Books, an imprint of St. Martin's Publishing Group

THE EXPECTANT DETECTIVES. Copyright © 2023 by Kat Ailes. All rights reserved. Printed in the United States of America. For information, address St. Martin's Publishing Group, 120 Broadway, New York, NY 10271.

www.minotaurbooks.com

The Library of Congress has cataloged the hardcover edition as follows:

Names: Ailes, Kat, author.
Title: The expectant detectives / Kat Ailes.
Description: First U.S. edition. | New York : Minotaur Books, 2024.
Identifiers: LCCN 2023034625 | ISBN 9781250322708 (hardcover) | ISBN 9781250322715 (ebook)
Subjects: LCGFT: Detective and mystery fiction. | Novels.
Classification: LCC PR6051.I355 E97 2024 | DDC 823/.92—dc23/eng/20230911
LC record available at https://lccn.loc.gov/2023034625

ISBN 978-1-250-32272-2 (trade paperback)

Our books may be purchased in bulk for promotional, educational, or business use. Please contact your local bookseller or the Macmillan Corporate and Premium Sales Department at 1-800-221-7945, extension 5442, or by email at MacmillanSpecialMarkets@macmillan.com.

First published in the United Kingdom by Zaffre, an imprint of Bonnier Books UK: 2023

First Minotaur Books Trade Paperback Edition: 2024

10 9 8 7 6 5 4 3 2 1

For my splendid family and partners in crime,
Jamie, Caleb, Cleo, and Jazz

CHAPTER 1

FOR MY BOYFRIEND'S thirtieth birthday I thought I'd go all out and surprise him with a pregnancy. I mean, I surprised myself too, but it was a broadly good surprise, so Joe and I decided to roll with it. And if you're going to do a thing, you may as well do it properly. So as responsible soon-to-be parents we thought we'd better leave the hive of criminal activity that is London and opt for a safer, more wholesome life in the country. This despite the fact that, in nearly ten years in London, the most heinous crime I'd ever witnessed was a bunch of teenagers running out without paying in a Pizza Express. The metropolitan criminal underworld aside, with neither of us earning a six-figure salary, if we stayed in London we'd be living in a (barely) converted garage and our baby would be sleeping in a drawer. London was out. We were Moving to the Country™.

Our destination was the quiet market town of Penton, nestled among the picturesque Cotswold Hills. As far as it's possible to tell via Google, Penton gave off a certain *vibe* that I would vaguely describe as "posh hippy." When picking our future home, this was something I felt I could get on board with, as despite being neither posh nor hippy I have, more or less successfully, masqueraded as both at various points in my life.

I was ready to embrace the patchouli oil. Maybe I would buy a dream catcher.

As we rolled our cumbersome rental van through the ancient byways of the Cotswolds, I could barely move for the assortment of car snacks wedged around me. I had prepared for the three-hour journey with all the diligence of an excessively snack-oriented Everest expedition. Or so Joe said. But at nearly nine months pregnant, I was taking no chances. If I had to be chronically uncomfortable, radioactively over-heated and need to pee every five minutes, then I wasn't going to add "hungry" to the mix. I opened a pack of Skittles with a contented sigh. I was also wearing my dressing gown because I'd forgotten to pack it, and TLC had just started playing from my Spotify "moving" playlist. If it weren't for the Rolo that had dropped down my cleavage and was slowly melting, just out of reach, I would have had to say life didn't really come much better.

I shared this happy thought with Joe, who merely grunted. He seemed a tad stressed. To be fair, I wasn't driving. Nor had I contributed much to packing the precipitous mound of possessions hovering behind our heads, waiting to take us out with an incautious emergency brake. Being heavily pregnant gives you a get-out-of-jail-free card for lifting anything heavier than a sausage roll. I had directed the packing from the sidelines, occasionally sneaking items back out of the charity shop box when Joe wasn't looking. This was why I was currently sitting with a glittery blue Virgin Mary piggy bank nestled, ironically, between my pregnancy bump and crotch. I knew if I let it out of my sight Joe would gift it to Goodwill faster than you could say "Hail Mary."

I peered out of the van window at the countryside flashing past. It was . . . green. Definitely very green. More so than even Hampstead Heath, which I had previously considered to be pretty damn rural.

"Do you think they have chicken shops in the country?" I asked Joe nervously.

"You probably have to kill and pluck your own."

I nodded sagely. That sounded about right.

At this point Joe took a corner, braked rather abruptly and the Virgin Mary jabbed me sharply in the crotch. I was about to complain when I realized why he had stopped. We had arrived.

Spread out below us was our new home: Penton. Nestled snugly in the valley like the slightly over-warm bag of Rolos wedged alongside the Virgin in my lap. It was small, perhaps a thousand houses running along the valley floor and a handful more clinging to the hills that rose either side.

A dense woodland ran along the crest of the hill opposite, the trees hazed with the almost fluorescent green of oncoming spring. Fields sprawled along the valley sides, liberally dotted with assorted livestock. The golden light of early evening gave it the sort of glow I had previously always put down to light pollution.

Joe hauled on the handbrake until he almost gave himself a hernia. Penton, apparently, didn't do flat. We sat silently for a while and surveyed our new homeland, holding hands across the mound of semi-demolished snacks.

"Nice," Joe said eventually.

"Mm-hmm," I sniffed, a familiar welling sensation behind my eyeballs.

Wordlessly, Joe rummaged through the empty Monster Munch packets to dig out a reasonably clean McDonald's napkin and passed it over, giving my hand a squeeze. Admittedly, it didn't take much to set me off these days—commercials for rehoming dogs, the mere mention of Adele—pregnancy hormones are extremely soggy, it turns out. But, in this case, I felt it was deserved; Penton Vale was rather beautiful.

Never one to miss out on an emotional moment, from the back of the van came the unmistakable sound of the dog being sick, probably over our most precious possessions. The handbrake gave an ominous groan and we set off again, down the winding road and through the heart of our new home.

It took us perhaps three minutes to trundle our van the length of Penton high street and find ourselves heading fieldward again. With alarming rapidity, the trees began to close in.

"I don't think there are anymore houses." Joe squinted up the darkening road ahead of us. It looked suspiciously rural.

I checked my phone. "Stop!"

Joe's sudden braking catapulted the Virgin Mary across the dashboard. It really hadn't been her day.

"Google Maps thinks we're here." This was the level of my navigation skills.

"I can't see anything."

"Well, Google can't be wrong."

"Says who?"

"I don't know. God?"

We reversed, slowly and painfully, and eventually found the house. In our defense, it was easy to miss, what with the *Sleeping Beauty*-esque creepers all but obscuring it from view. It looked like nature was trying to reclaim it—and doing a pretty good job. It was built of crumbling stone, moss and peeling paint, held together by ivy and hope. The chimney pot looked like an endgame of Jenga. I didn't fancy its chances in a strong breeze. The house appeared to be about a thousand years old and definitely infested. I'm not sure what with—spiders, mice, ghosts, take your pick. I made a mental note to call Rentokil, and possibly a priest.

Should we have done more research into Penton before uprooting our lives and moving here? Who's to say. But hey, it had a direct line into London, a couple of pubs with 4-star ratings on Google and an honest-to-goodness stone circle for the local village pagans. What wasn't to like? So we hadn't visited the place before whacking a grand's deposit on our rental house. But I mean, who does actual real-life house visits these days? You just have to trust in Rightmove and remember that wide-angle lenses are a cruel trickery.

Our options had been relatively limited, even in the thriving rental market that was Penton. With Joe working freelance as a graphic designer, his income was both mediocre and sporadic. As a copywriter for an ad agency mine was also mediocre, but at least reliable. For now. But in Penton we were able to rent a *house*. With stairs. And a garden. Which was a hell of a lot more than we could have managed in London. I looked up at my dream home. A small tree appeared to be growing out of its roof.

IT WAS not without trepidation that I pushed open the door to our new home. Part of me was expecting a swarm of bats to burst out, but I was pleasantly surprised. It was unfurnished, so pretty basic, but it had exposed beams, which I very much expected from the countryside, and a genuine fireplace should we ever learn how to lay and light a fire. It was simple—sitting room and kitchen (both small) downstairs, either side of a bizarrely spacious hall, and a dubious-looking bathroom fitted out in peach; upstairs boasted an attic bedroom with a teeny-tiny storage room that would just about work as the baby's room. It felt a bit like a toy house, but then again, it felt like we were playing at being adults, so maybe that was all right.

It was possible, however, that there were some drawbacks to its pocket-size dimensions.

"You said you wanted a place with character," grumbled Joe as he surveyed the twisting and exceptionally narrow staircase, while holding a segment of bed frame that would never in a million years fit up there.

"You said Penton looked 'idyllic,' and just what we were looking for," I replied.

Did I blame him for our move to the countryside? Hard to say. It had definitely been a mutual decision, but potentially one of those mutual decisions where you secretly harbor strong reservations but think you're doing what the other person wants—only to find out they were doing the same.

We bickered the bulkier furniture into the house. By which I mean Joe almost buckled under the weight of all our possessions while I occasionally picked up a shoebox and Joe barked, "No heavy lifting!" The sofa just about wedged into the "cozy" sitting room and the fridge was relegated to the hallway as the kitchen ceiling was about two feet high. The bed stayed in pieces, creating a trip hazard at the bottom of the stairs, and as a temporary measure we dug out the inflatable mattress we'd taken to Glastonbury the previous year. With each slightly too vigorous stamp on the air pump, the soft aroma of year-old festival mattress filled the small attic: essence of unwashed body with undertones of cheap cider. Weirdly, it made me feel quite nostalgic, and then simply nauseous. It made Joe sweaty and then angry.

All in all, as we wobbled precariously onto our temporary bed for our first night in the country, it was with mixed emotions: general excitement mingled with mild apprehension and a side order of barely suppressed panic. In hindsight, it was a beautifully innocent time. Things were about to get a whole lot more complicated.

CHAPTER 2

HAVE YOU EVER slept on an inflatable mattress while eight months pregnant? Here's a tip: don't.

I woke up seriously pissed off. To be fair, this had become quite a default state for me of late, but this time I felt justified. Every time Joe had rolled over, or shifted position, or even breathed, the mattress had wobbled me onto the floor. Then the dog had joined us around midnight, with her signature ignorance of the phrase "three's a crowd."

"And did you hear that weird scratching noise at three A.M.?" I grumbled. "I'm sure it was mice."

"Alice, come over here." Joe was standing by the window, clearly not listening to my complaint.

"Could even be rats," I muttered.

"Seriously, Al, come and take a look at this."

I wrapped myself in the duvet and shuffled over to join him.

OK, so it was pretty nice. The view from the house, that is. In fact, I'd probably go so far as to say it was glorious. Our bedroom window looked out across the valley. Below us, the rooftops and chimney stacks of Penton tumbled down to the valley floor, where the river meandered gently, the early-morning sun burnishing its muddy waters to a bronze glow. Fields speckled with livestock of varying descriptions stretched up the hillside opposite, and off to our right a jumbled mass of woodland glimmered a fresh spring green.

"Not bad, huh," said Joe, pulling me close and wriggling himself into my duvet cocoon, so we resembled a poorly wrapped conjoined mummy.

It's something I loved about Joe from the start—his ability to smooth my sharp edges. Admittedly, of late it had felt as though we'd both been nothing but sharp edges. But right here, right now, we were all golden morning sunlight. Hell, we could be a feature photo in *Home & Country* magazine, or whatever countryfolk read. Closely cropped to hide the outrageous mess behind us, of course, and suitably airbrushed to remove the greasy roots, pregnancy acne and sleepless eyes.

We stood there slightly longer than was wise, until the numb cold of my feet had me hopping back to the sanctuary of the airbed, burrowing my icy toes under the protesting dog. Joe brought up two cups of tea, but they were lukewarm at best, since he hadn't been able to find the kettle and had made them straight out of the hot water tap. This doesn't work, by the way.

THIS BROADLY summed up how the morning passed: we moved stuff about, we discovered things didn't work. The flush fell off the toilet and half a bird's nest fell down the chimney. The Wi-Fi router offered internet at the speed of pigeon post, which played havoc with Joe's Twitter habit. I tried to keep things light, but my jokes were going down increasingly poorly. When Joe started trying to piece together the IKEA changing table, only to discover he'd mixed up the pieces with the new and elaborate spice rack I'd felt was necessary for our new life, I thought it would probably be in everyone's best interests if I vacated the premises.

"I'm going into town," I announced, raising my voice above the hammer blows and swearing. "Do you need anything?"

"Beer," came a muffled voice from under the slats. "And . . ." there was a momentary pause, then, in an ever-hopeful tone, ". . . a pack of Marlboros?"

"Not happening," I declared firmly. Seeing as I'd had to give up alcohol, tobacco, caffeine, unbroken sleep and bladder control, I felt Joe needed to undergo *some* hardships. Although he frequently declared that it was very difficult to enjoy a pint these days with me watching him murderously and drooling like the Hound of the Baskervilles.

It took about seven minutes to walk into town. And calling it "town" was stretching it a bit. Where was I supposed to go when I needed to buy a 99p chicken McGristle burger? I would, however, be able to purchase every conceivable garment in batik, heal myself with a positively dazzling array of crystals and get my chakras aligned at the—I squinted at the poster in a shop window—WOMEN'S INNER GODDESS TEMPLE.

I wanted a supermarket. I wanted Aldi, with its incredible range of rip-off own-brand chocolate. I wanted Lidl with its magical mystery aisle, Middle of Lidl, which one week sold discount vibrators and the next week Christmas onesies (in July). Hell, I'd settle for a Poundland.

What I eventually found was a Waitrose. Of course. Well, I'd probably be able to afford half a loaf of sourdough and a single Gruyère cheese straw.

CLUTCHING MY overpriced and meager purchases, I thought I'd drop by the doctors' office to pick up a registration form. My midwife in London had repeatedly urged me to register *before* moving but, well, there'd been the move to sort, and my last week at work, and saying goodbye to friends . . . I mean, I could list a good ten excuses for why I hadn't done this vitally important task, but the honest reason is that I'm crap at these things and lack the motivation to improve in this area.

The receptionist rather alarmingly told me that the GP could see me in "just a tick" if I was happy to wait five minutes. In London I was used to a six-month waiting list to see the GP for a repeat prescription of the pill (which could explain how I came to be in this particular situation). I nodded nervously and took a seat.

There was another pregnant woman in the waiting room. Half her head was shaved, the rest was a knot of auburn dreadlocks and she was wearing those hippy overalls you see a lot at music festivals. She looked angry, but with that sort of anger that will probably change the world for the better. Her overalls were adorned with a number of enamel pins. I squinted; they seemed to be variations on a theme: a melting earth, THERE IS NO PLANET B, DESTROY THE PATRIARCHY, NOT THE PLANET, and—oh no—a pin shaped like a bag with FUCK NO written on it.

Now, I was yet to find any of our numerous totes with slightly suspect stains, so I'd bought a single-use plastic bag at Waitrose, because I'm a terrible person. This girl looked like she might throttle me with my own carrier bag. I wondered if I might be able to secrete my shopping about my person before she noticed it. But there's a reason shoplifters go for lightweight, expensive items. It's hard to conceal even a small loaf in your underwear. Even the capacious underwear that comes with being eight months pregnant.

Oh well. I gave her my best "hey I'm pregnant too, let's be best friends" smile. She scowled. I hoped her displeasure was aimed at the plastic bag, and not more generally at me.

I wondered if I should just open the conversation with a disclaimer that I, too, thought "fuck no" to carrier bags, and had just been caught short today. But as I opened my mouth to defend myself the doctor's door opened.

"Ailsa?"

I was halfway out of my seat before I realized that this was not, in fact, my name. Dreadlock girl jumped to her feet, cast a disgusted look at my shopping and disappeared inside.

So much for making friends.

I sighed, and ate a luxury cheese straw (cost: one month's rent).

I LEFT the office ten minutes later, having reassured the doctor that I neither drank, smoked, nor took drugs, nor did I regularly partake in shark meat or swordfish (a big no when pregnant). With terrifying efficiency, I was already booked in to see my new midwife the following Tuesday.

As I paused outside to get my bearings, a man in that indefinable gap between middle-aged and elderly pottered past. He looked nice, if a tad eccentric. Head-to-toe green linen is a great look for Santa's elves, not so much on a gentleman of a certain age.

"Congratulations, my dear," he said, pausing and nodding to my bump.

I had heard that this was a thing in the countryside. People just talk to you. It doesn't necessarily mean they're a lunatic, mugger or Jehovah's Witness. They might just be nice. I decided to give him the benefit of the doubt. More fool me.

"Er, thanks."

"And how are you keeping, in yourself?" he asked rather earnestly. He actually seemed interested in my answer, which was a little disconcerting.

"Fine, thanks," I replied automatically. He looked a little crestfallen.

His eyes honed in on the bottle of antacid poking out of my shameful plastic carrier bag. "Oh no!" He looked genuinely shocked. "Oh, that won't do at all!"

"Er, sorry, what?" I asked.

"You mustn't take that!" He plucked the antacid from the top of the bag. "It's full of all sorts of harmful chemicals and nasties. No, if you're having trouble with heartburn you need some slippery elm bark."

A half-laugh, half-snort escaped before I could rein it in. "I beg your pardon?" I tried to turn my snort into a cough. "Slippery what now?"

"Oh yes, slippery elm bark. The inner bark of the elm tree. It's a natural demulcent, marvelous for soothing the inflamed digestive tract. Now tell me, are you also suffering from urinary tract infections? Because it's also an excellent cure for the more stubborn forms of—"

OK, so that was too far. There was no way I was discussing the state of my urinary tract with a strange old man dressed like a retired elf.

"I've actually got to go," I said hurriedly. "I'm late for a . . . pregnancy thing."

"Slippery elm bark," he called after me as I waddled away at top speed. "And chamomile tea—but not if you have a ragweed allergy!"

I waved vaguely over my shoulder, and noticed to my relief that the dreadlocked girl, Ailsa, had emerged from the doctor's and the elf-man was now caught up in conversation with her—presumably pressing various slippery tree products upon her, too. I bet she'd love that. I felt rattled, and also slightly annoyed at myself for being spooked by a probably well-meaning and probably harmless nice old man. Then I realized the nice old man had stolen my antacid. Was the potential embarrassment of another encounter worth the extortionate £11.49 I'd shelled out, paying extra for the slightly more delicious mint version?

Nope.

I STARTED to head for what I supposed I should call "home" now. A creeping sense of dread was coming over me that, perhaps, we had made a terrible mistake. I phoned Maya, my best friend, who now lived a hundred miles away in south London.

". . . and then he asked me about UTIs," I finished dramatically.

"Do you think he was a pervert?" asked Maya interestedly.

"I don't think so. I think he was genuinely concerned for my health."

"Oh God, that's even worse. Give me an honest-to-goodness pervert any day."

"I know, right? Mai, what if everyone in the countryside is . . . you know . . . *weird*?"

"Of course they are," she said brusquely. "That's why they live in the countryside. Normal people live in cities, where we have plumbing and indoor bathrooms."

I sighed, not bothering to contradict her. Maya had been somewhat scathing of our move to the countryside. In fact, we had twenty quid riding on the fact that I'd be back in London before the year was out. I was pretty sure she was predisposed to hate Penton no matter how hard I pushed its charms—The clean air! The charming farmers' market! The rural idyll!—so she was unlikely to be particularly sympathetic.

"I just want to make one normal friend," I complained. "There was a pregnant woman at the doctors' this morning, but I had a plastic bag so I think she hates me."

"Sorry, I think I missed the bit where that made sense," said Maya. "Did you have something terrible in the plastic bag, or—" She broke off with a sharp gasp.

"Is everything OK?" I asked, concerned.

"Yeah," she said. "Sorry, I'm just getting a wax and that one really stung."

"You're getting a wax *right now*?" Her only response was a sort of hissing noise, like she was deflating. "Why did you pick up?" She always did this. I'd had to explain to her multiple times that I didn't feel comfortable talking to her on the phone while she was on the loo. I suspected she still did this, but just lied about it now.

"I thought you'd be a good distraction from the pain," she said through gritted teeth. "With your tales of woe from the pits of the . . . *holy*—"

"Do you want me to call you back?"

"No, no, I know what you're like. You'll call me next April and expect to carry on the conversation about the pervert with the UTI."

"I don't think *he* had a UTI," I countered.

"What about the woman with the plastic bag?"

"No, *I* had the plastic bag—"

"And the UTI?"

"No—well, actually yes, but what's new these days? *Anyway*, I was saying, what if I don't make any friends down here?"

"Good," she said bluntly. "Then you'll see the error of your ways and come back to me."

I sighed—again. Maya was only half joking. I knew our departure stung a bit. She definitely felt it was a personal betrayal. First Joe had arrived on the scene, just over a year ago, and if I was totally honest, I had to admit I'd probably been a bit wrapped up in that. And we hadn't meant things to move quite so fast, but twelve months on and here we were, having a baby and moving to the country.

Maya relented slightly. "What about that prenatal class thing you signed up to? I'm sure you'll meet some nice people there. Some nice, normal people who'll forgive your plastic bag obsession and your UTIs."

"I do not have a plastic bag obsession," I replied hotly. "We haven't unpacked the tote bags yet and—"

"Relax, Greta," Maya chuckled. "Just wear a Greenpeace badge to the meeting or something. When is it?"

"We've got our first meeting tonight," I said nervously. "Oh God, I bet the dreadlocked girl is there. She's totally going to be there. Maybe I *should* get a Greenpeace badge?"

"Well, good luck," she said, sounding a little distracted. "Ring me after. I want to hear all about the pregnant weirdos."

I was about to protest but she was talking to someone at the other end. "Gotta go, she's gone full Brazilian down there which FYI is not what I asked for. And I'm not paying forty quid for that"—her voice moved away—"we said twenty-five for a tidy-up."

I hung up.

CHAPTER 3

THE FIRST CHALLENGE in our new life threatened to derail me at the outset: making new friends as a grown-up. Is there anything more painful, more fraught with pitfalls, more ridden with such potential for deep humiliation? The last time I made friends—nearly a decade ago—I worked in an office crammed with people who shared my interest in HBO box sets, semi-educational podcasts and the kind of wine that comes in those "3 for £10" deals at the petrol station. We were all under thirty, with large career aspirations (hence the podcasts) and small incomes (hence the cheap wine).

Fast-forward a decade and I find myself here. In Penton, population: seventeen people and a cow. I'm thirty-one, heavily pregnant, and largely running on an unstable cocktail of hormones and frosting from a can. Even the dog is sick of my bullshit and has taken to leaving the room as soon as I enter. I am not, at this stage, a socially functional being.

In one of our infrequent planning-ahead moments, we had signed up to an alarmingly named prenatal "crash course"—three sessions over two consecutive weekends, starting the day after we moved. Because why not add to the stress of a late-term-pregnancy house move by finding out exactly *how* unprepared we were for the arrival of this small human? Although the distressing education was more of a by-product; really we were attending the classes for the same reason everyone does—to purchase a new group of friends. Our old friends in London being busy doing unencumbered child-free things like sleeping in till midday, going to the toilet unaccompanied and having a career. Optimistically, we figured that any couples attending a crash course were likely to be a bit like us—disorganized bordering on the chaotic, with a tendency to leave things to the last minute; in short, ill-prepared for parenthood. People we could get on with.

Now that the day had arrived, it didn't seem like the wisest decision we'd made. The house was in a state of unexploded chaos; we'd had to return the rental van this morning, trading down to a miniature car more suited to Penton's horse-width lanes, which had led to a frenzied dumping of our life possessions on the lawn because, obviously, we hadn't bothered to unpack properly last night. Approximately half our belongings hadn't even managed to fit inside yet, so if it rained while we were at the class . . . well, it had just better not rain. The dog was convinced that moving house was a portent of the apocalypse and was dragging herself leglessly from room to room, keening softly. When we left her, alone in the house, to attend our first session, we knew we would be returning to carnage as she frantically took out her overwhelming emotions on every soft furnishing we possessed.

THE SESSION was being held above a small and wind-chime-bedecked shop, intriguingly called Nature's Way. I had spotted the shop on the high street on my stroll through Penton earlier and mentally noted that if I was ever in need of a dream catcher or ten, this was the place. We arrived characteristically late and made this worse by lurking awkwardly outside, assessing the situation.

"It's one of *those* shops," hissed Joe.

"What do you mean?"

"Y'know. Weird hippy shit."

"It's just organic." I tried to defend it, but I knew he was right. Several crystals winked at us from the window, the word "hemp" seemed to feature on every product and the selection of essential oils on display could have drowned a small town. I'd spent most of the last ten years living in Peckham and had thought essential oil was just another name for cannabis oil. To be honest, I still have no idea what an essential oil is or why it's essential. Is it like the Waitrose Essentials range? Because they stock an "Essentials Pheasant" here and I'm calling bullshit on that.

"We could just go home?" Joe suggested, eyeing a fertility idol furtively.

"No way," I argued. "We spent a hundred quid on this course. Let's go make some expensive friends."

I pushed open the door and we entered Nature's Way to the delicate tinkle of wind chimes.

The shop was dark, rural trading generally ceasing at about 4 P.M. The class was being held upstairs, and we had to wend our way between racks of overalls (made from hemp), dream catchers (hemp) and gap-year trousers (probably hemp), to the rickety staircase at the back of the shop. In a small pool of amber light, a man was sitting behind a counter stringing together what looked like necklaces but were probably mystic amulets imbued with the healing power of quartz.

He looked up with a benevolent and slightly unfocused smile.

Oh God, it was UTI man.

And he'd recognized me.

His smile broadened into a beam.

"Ah, it's my charming young friend with the acid reflux. You'll be here for the slippery elm bark!"

"Oh. Oh, no," I fumbled. "No, it's OK, thanks." I wondered if I could ask for my antacid back, but he'd probably burned it by now.

"We're just here for the prenatal class," Joe said, putting a hand on my lower back and steering me toward the stairs.

"Oh." The man looked a little crestfallen and I felt a bit sorry for him. "They're just up—" He broke off, looking at Joe. He tilted his head and stared some more. Joe backed away slightly, edging behind me—the coward. Although admittedly I provided pretty decent cover these days.

"Everything OK?" I asked.

The old man paused, then asked Joe, "Do I know you?"

"Er, nope," replied Joe, looking baffled. "No, can't say I'm a regular customer."

"We only moved here yesterday," I contributed, but the man didn't so much as glance at me.

"We're actually running a bit late." No response. "So . . . we'll just head on up."

We made our way up the stairs. The old man was shaking his head slightly and had gone back to threading disconcertingly shaped beads on a string.

On entering the upstairs room, I did a not-so-subtle scan, assessing for potential friends—although I was temporarily derailed on noticing a side table set out with cookies and an industrial tea urn. Were those Oreos?

There was a woman with a sharp, dark bob, wearing what looked like genuine maternity clothes (as opposed to the misshapen leggings and oversized men's clothes that I favored). Her partner was in a suit. In my experience, only politicians and estate agents wear suits. Hmm, probably to be avoided as I had no intention of joining a political party and no means of buying a house.

And there was the angry girl with the dreadlocks. I just knew she'd be there. Still looking angry. Still wearing the badges. I tried a small smile and one of those awkward little waves where you lose faith in it halfway through and it turns into a sort of limp flap. Great start.

Dreadlock girl sighed.

She appeared to be on her own. I wondered if this was reflective of her relationship status or if her partner had for some reason declined to come. Or maybe they had irritated her by smiling too much or breathing too loudly and she'd killed them and buried them in her plot in the organic community garden. All seemed possible.

There was also a woman with a small afro and a cheerful but worried expression who was clutching her wife's hand so fiercely it looked as though her wedding ring might amputate a finger. Her partner, a smiling woman with very short platinum-blond hair, appeared to be force-feeding her pregnant wife Oreos.

The session leader was easy to pick out. For starters, she wasn't pregnant. She also blended into her Nature's Way surroundings perfectly. Her curly gray hair was swept up in some sort of floral headband and her clothes featured too many clashing patterns, like a chameleon caught in a kaleidoscope.

Everyone was sitting on an assortment of mismatched chairs and pregnancy balls, all looking as awkward as Joe and I felt, but otherwise passably normal. I hoped we looked normal too, because obviously we were being assessed in turn. I had made a real effort: I was wearing actual makeup, a decision I was already regretting as the anxiety sweats beaded the foundation on my nose, and I'd even brushed the overly thick and uncoiffed blond mane that made me look disconcertingly like my dog. I cast a sideways glance at Joe. He had had no such scruples. His unruly dark hair, which always seemed to have just grown out of anything resembling a haircut, was looking on the wild side and there was a hole in his Nirvana T-shirt.

Joe took the last remaining chair (dick), leaving me to balance my enormous and ungainly self on a wobbling pregnancy ball. Given that I was by this point fully capable of overbalancing while standing still, the potential for embarrassment was strong. The whole thing was rapidly taking on the oversaturated tint of an anxiety dream. I rubbed my clammy palms on my leggings, wondering why I had voluntarily put myself into one of those awkward enforced social situations that I normally avoid at all costs. Worse than voluntarily—I'd paid for this nightmare! And *even worse still,* given the one thing we all had in common, there would be no alcohol to smooth the rocky path to friendship.

I was worried that the session leader would ask us to introduce ourselves with an "interesting fact about ourselves." I had nothing. There was a distinct possibility I might get my name wrong when asked.

"Hi, *mums and dads,*" she began. I hated her already. "I'm Dot!" She looked like such a Dot. She beamed. Constantly. "Well, isn't this *exciting*!"

We all stared at her in stony silence.

"I thought we'd start by sharing what we're *most excited about for the birth*!"

More silence. This time tinged with confusion. Were we supposed to be excited for the actual birth? The bit where we squeezed a human being out of our battered vaginas? The bit widely compared to pissing a tennis ball or shitting out a pumpkin?

"Who wants to go first?"

The silence stretched. I was starting to warm to this group.

"What about you, dear?"

Rookie error—I'd made eye contact. Accidentally, sure; I'd actually been staring, unfocused, wondering if there were any Oreos left. But it was too late.

"Er . . . the snacks?" I mumbled. The hospital bag that is meant to sit by the door ready for action was currently eighty percent full of sugary treats and entirely lacking in anything of material use to me or my unborn child.

The woman with the perfect bob snorted. I hoped it was a friendly laugh; it could equally have been pure scorn. But Dot was nodding enthusiastically.

"Yes, yes!" She beamed at me. "And your name, dear?"

"Er, Alice."

Dot wrote on the flipchart in cheerful orange marker: ALICE IS LOOKING FORWARD TO SNACKS.

Great.

THE SESSION didn't improve. Never had I used the word "vagina"—or worse, "vaginal"—so many times in the company of strangers. At least everyone else seemed equally appalled by what we were all facing. When Dot began on episiotomies (if you don't know, *don't* google), the dreadlocked girl in the overalls dashed out. Well, waddled at high speed. Possibly to weep, possibly to be sick, or maybe she just really had to pee.

I learned a lot. For example, that I had, for my whole life, been mixing up the vulva and the uvula. Turns out they are two different things, very much at opposite ends of the body. But when it came to the practicalities, Dot proved herself to be firmly in the aromatherapy and hypnobirthing camp. While I learned a lot about the benefits of Reiki, we barely covered the possibility of a birth that involved painkillers any stronger than a cup of willow bark tea. She also proved herself epically insensitive and borderline racist.

"Of course all cultures have different rituals and practices surrounding birth," she trilled. "What do you do in China, Hen dear?" she asked shiny bob woman.

"Wouldn't know, I'm from Guildford," said Hen flatly.

"Well, yes, but, *originally* . . ."

"Yes, I'm 'originally' from Guildford. And my parents are from South Korea. It's about six hundred miles from Beijing."

Over the herbal tea break we all made tentative small talk, cautiously probing to see if we shared common ground beyond the obvious leaking boobs, swollen ankles and crumbling pelvic floor. The girl in the overalls mentioned that she was some kind of conservation scientist. I perked up. I like nature! Sure, I can't tell a grass snake from a cucumber, but that's just *details*. Hen mentioned that she had briefly lived in Australia. I've never been, I informed her cheerfully, but I used to watch *Neighbours* religiously. This information went down poorly. Her besuited husband, Antoni, looked faintly appalled at this reference to daytime TV. The Oreo couple, pregnant Poppy and blond Lin, used to live in London. *Omg us too!*

I realized I might be coming on a little strong. But when the ex-Londoners mentioned they had dogs, their fate was sealed. I over-enthusiastically explained that the reason Joe had dashed out five minutes into the session was that we remembered we had left our shopping on the kitchen floor and only belatedly realized it contained a bag of grapes—which for some bizarre reason are extremely toxic to dogs. He had rushed home in a panic to potentially do CPR or weep over the lifeless form of our dog. He soon returned with the news that she was fine; the packaging was way beyond her.

By the end of the session I was exhausted. I had learned an awful lot about the terrible fate coming my way and almost immediately filed most of it in the "do not open" section of my brain—which was getting pretty full. I had stress-eaten most of a sleeve of Oreos. I couldn't remember anyone's name or due date. I'd accidentally told the group we were having a girl, which was going to be awkward when our definitely male baby arrived in a few weeks.

And when we got home the dog had popped the airbed, which was now as deflated as my rural dreams.

THAT EVENING Joe and I balanced precariously on the hastily patched airbed trying, and failing, to watch a hypnobirthing video as our dodgy internet cut in and out. I had decided that in our new and improved life we were going to be on point, we were going to get *involved*. And hypnobirthing seemed to be all the rage, according to Instagram—which I had believed to be the last word on these things until Maya told me that all the kids are on TikTok these days.

The hypnobirthing woman annoyed me immediately. I'm naturally drawn to cynics and pessimists, and this woman had optimism shining out of her like a nuclear reactor. Even her *hair* seemed relentlessly positive and excessively glossy. Her T-shirt said POSITIVE VIBES ONLY; I felt my negativity increase a fraction.

I learned that neither Joe nor I should refer to "contractions" during labor. These are "surges"—a more empowering term. The word "empowering" was used a lot. I tutted and skipped to the next section. I learned that "my surges aren't happening to me, they are a part of me." I skipped again. The next video was called *Why Birth Is Like Doing a Massive Poo*. I closed my laptop.

"What did you think?" I asked, turning to Joe.

"Meh. Bit hippy for my liking, a bit"—he waved his hands expressively—"*woo*. Until that last video, and I mean I *never* need to see—"

"I meant about the prenatal people," I cut in.

"Oh . . ." He paused to think. "Pretty much the same, really."

CHAPTER 4

I AWOKE TO the sound of actual birds singing. Not a car engine or swearing drunk to be heard. It was a glorious spring morning, which previously would have had us hotfooting it to the pub for opening time in order to secure a sought-after table in the pub garden before half of south London descended on it. Because we were now new and improved people, we thought we would take the dog for a walk.

For the sheer novelty of it, we decided to take a walk from our own front door. At our old house, this would have taken in such delights as Papa John's, several tanning salons and the taxi company that was definitely some kind of front. Now, we simply had to cross the lane to find ourselves meandering up the hillside along beautiful, albeit treacherously muddy, country paths, through fields with honest-to-goodness hedgerows. There was even a hollow tree you could walk through. Well, Joe could; I couldn't on account of being the size of a tree myself.

All in all, it was delightful. For the first time in weeks Joe and I could talk about something other than the move. It was nice to remember that we actually enjoyed each other's company. We even held hands for a bit. And after a year spent circumnavigating Peckham Rye on a daily basis, the dog was losing her mind. Although, admittedly, this doesn't take much; I'd seen her paralyzed with fascination by a piece of corn on our kitchen floor. But right now, she was absolutely tripping out. She tore from stump to shrub to cowpat and back again, unsure what to chase, what to eat and what to roll in. It was a joy to behold.

A word on my dog. I wanted a dog that looked like a wolf. A lean, shaggy beast of the forests that looked at you with flinty eyes that echoed with the call of the wild. What I got was Helen; the *Legally Blonde* of the dog world. Helen is beautiful. I'm not saying this in the manner of parents everywhere who think that their tiny Winston Churchill baby is the most beautiful child to be born since Jesus. I am saying this as someone who gets stopped ten times on a walk to be told that my dog is gorgeous. She looks like a leggy blond greyhound wearing fluffy pantaloons and a tail wig.

Having said this, I must follow it with a caveat: Helen is also exceptionally stupid. You know the hot blonde in *Mean Girls* who thinks she can predict the weather with her boobs? That's Helen.

The first hour of the walk was delightful. The second, a tad more trying. The novelty was really starting to wear thin, my enthusiasm for all things nature buckling under the weight of my womb, when, lo and behold . . .

"Country pub!"

Joe's delighted shout brought me waddling at top speed—slippery paths be damned. Is there anything better than a country pub? And this one looked perfect. Crumbly old red brick, welly scraper at the door, peeling sign declaring it THE CROSS KEYS—classic. I bet it had ancient beams inside and weird antique farming tools hanging everywhere.

We ducked inside—because country pubs always have bizarrely tiny doors—and breathed a unanimous sigh of satisfaction.

"Open fire," said Joe with a smug smile.

"Farming tools!" I cheered.

"Real ale," breathed Joe, floating toward the bar like a man having a vision. I scowled, but even the prospect of yet another lime and soda couldn't dampen my feelings of well-being. *Of course* we'd made the right decision moving to the countryside. And to think we had this dream pub right on our doorstep, a mere hour's hike away through mud and hedgerow.

As we waited at the bar, Joe nudged me. "Weren't they at the class last night?"

"Who?"

He rolled his eyes. "The super-pregnant woman and her partner in the corner?"

"Oh! Yeah, yeah, they were."

It was Poppy with the afro and her Oreo-enthusiast wife, Lin. The couple from London with the dogs. And that was about all my mental filing system was throwing up.

Social panic set in immediately. Should we say hello? Or pretend we hadn't seen them? Had they, in fact, already seen us and were pretending they hadn't?

"We could sit on the other side of the bar," whispered Joe, reading my mind. "We'd be hidden by the specials board."

I was about to agree when Helen resolved the matter for us. Spotting the two dogs lying peacefully at the couple's feet, she gave a delighted gurgle-bark that sounded a bit like she might vomit, pulled her lead out of my hand and tore across the pub to accost these well-behaved strangers.

"I'm so sorry!" I gasped, crashing across the pub and possibly causing more chaos than Helen in my attempt to restrain her.

Poppy and Lin looked somewhat startled—as you might do if a tornado of blond fur descended on your quiet Saturday-afternoon drink, shortly followed by a flustered pregnant woman. Not to mention that in the commotion one of us knocked over Lin's pint. I'm going to blame Helen.

"Oh!" said Poppy, her face lighting up with recognition. "It's Alice, isn't it? From the prenatal class?"

"Er, yeah. Yeah, it is. I mean I am." *Shut up.*

"Hi, I'm Joe." Joe arrived slightly behind me, looking both normal and casual and managing to effortlessly remember his own name.

"This is Helen," I said, resignedly, as Helen smothered the smaller of their dogs with love. "I'm sorry about her."

"This is Ronnie," said Poppy. "Likewise." She gestured at the small and incredibly ugly dog now lying upside down underneath my dog and grinning up at her. "And this is Sultan." Sultan, a regal-looking greyhound, inclined his head and looked at the two floor-dogs with disdain. He was magnificent. Oh well, at least Ronnie looked like a badger had mated with a croissant, so that evened the score somewhat.

"And I'm sorry about your drink," I said to Lin. "I think Helen . . ." I let the lie trail off. "Let me get you another."

"You really don't need to," Lin said cheerfully. "It was almost done. But hey, I'm not saying no to a free pint. Why don't you guys join us?"

Joe disappeared to the bar to buy more drinks for Helen—or me—to knock over and I tried to fit myself round the table while getting tangled in Helen's lead.

It was awkward at first—how could it not be? Anyone who says they enjoy talking to virtual strangers in a pub is either lying or a conspiracy theorist. But after a while, it wasn't so very bad. Lin and Joe rhapsodized over their pints of real ale, while Poppy and I griped over spending £4 on a J2O, which is frankly unacceptable for a nonalcoholic beverage. It felt kind of normal. I even started to relax a bit.

"So did you know any of the others at the class?" I asked.

Poppy and Lin shook their heads. "Never set eyes on any of them!" said Poppy.

"Actually, maybe I've seen the girl with dreadlocks," said Lin thoughtfully. "I think she protests around town sometimes with the Greenpeace lot."

"Huh," said Joe. "I thought you might know them all. Penton's not a big place."

They both laughed at this.

"It's not *that* small," said Lin. "I know it feels tiny after London, but it's not like some rural backwater with more sheep than humans."

"Feels like it," I muttered into my overpriced juice. I think I sounded grumpier than I intended, which is often the case.

"You've been here, like, a day," said Lin, smiling but unsympathetic. "Give it a chance."

"You guys like it here then?" asked Joe.

Poppy and Lin shared a thoughtful glance.

"Yeah," said Poppy, "we do. A lot, actually. I mean, we miss London, or bits of it at least, but I don't think we'd move back."

"No way," said Lin, rather more emphatically I thought. "I couldn't go back to London."

"Why not?" I couldn't help asking. "What's so great about Penton?"

"The air! The space! The hills, the woods, the commons! Wait till you've seen a whole year turn through the seasons," said Lin, her eyes wide with enthusiasm. "You don't get proper seasons in London, not like in the countryside. Out here, it's a whole new world with each passing month. Everything is just so . . . *more* here!"

I was taken aback. I'd been somewhat of the opposite opinion, that everything in the countryside would be, well, just a little bit less. But Lin was pretty convincing.

"I guess . . ."

"Lin's a gardener," explained Poppy, leaning in. "She's one with nature and all that." She waved her hands vaguely. Lin laughed.

"But seriously," continued Poppy, and her face was very kind, "there's so much to love about living here. Penton's great. It'll feel weird at first, any big change does, but you'll settle into it."

I don't know what happened, but her words unlocked something and it all came pouring out. My uncertainties about leaving London, about leaving our friends. My fear that everyone in the countryside was going to be . . . unlike us. I don't know where it all came from, but Poppy and Lin just seemed so nice. I could see Joe looking slightly shell-shocked at my candidness. I am not an over-sharer by nature, quite the opposite. Maybe it was the J2O going to my head.

Poppy and Lin listened sympathetically. Nodding, and making vague but empathetic noises. Then they laughed. But in a nice way.

"Oh my God, it's like listening to us when we first moved," said Lin. "We felt like complete aliens here. And I mean, I grew up just a few villages away, it's not like I'm a stranger to these parts. But after so long in London, yeah, it felt weird here! Then, after like a year . . . we realized it was home."

"Eh," said Poppy, looking a little more reserved. "Not gonna lie, I still feel a bit of an alien sometimes—I mean . . ." She gestured round the pub, which, I belatedly realized, was entirely white. "It's not the same as London, or another big city, and I don't think you can expect it to be, but, for the most part, people are people wherever you go."

That sounded quite philosophical, so I nodded slowly, trying to look as if I was really pondering what she'd just said.

"Yeah, and some of the people in Penton are crazy," said Joe, clearly less concerned about sounding philosophical. He was on his second pint.

"What did you say you saw in town yesterday, Al? The Inner Woman Goddess Cult or something?"

Lin grinned. "The Women's Inner Goddess Temple?"

"Yes!"

"Home to the Penton Sisterhood. Yeah, they're a bit much," Lin agreed. "When we first moved here I went to a session there called 'Creative Connection to Your Plant Allies.' Turns out they don't know shit about their plant allies. But if you need your chakras realigned, they're your ladies."

Joe snorted into his beer. I was secretly taking mental notes. I had a feeling my chakras might be wildly out of whack. Of course, I'd need someone to explain to me what a chakra was first.

"It's not like you don't get stuff like that in London, anyway," Lin was saying expansively. "Ever been to SoulCycle? It's basically a cult."

I had to agree with her there. Maya had dragged me to a special equinox session, and for a mere forty quid I'd had my soul renewed and my butt destroyed.

"What about that shop where the prenatal class is," I chipped in. "The old guy who works there could definitely be in a cult. I bumped into him yesterday in town—what was it he was trying to get me to take, Joe? Slippery willow or something weird!"

I laughed, but both Joe and Lin, who'd been pretty much dominating the conversation up till now, went quiet.

"That would be Mr. Oliver," said Poppy, shooting a sideways look at Lin, who was spinning a beer mat and watching the dogs. "He owns the place."

Well, that made a lot of sense. I bet he didn't sell Gaviscon there.

"I couldn't believe it when we got to the class last night and he was there in the shop," I barreled on. "And then there was that weird moment . . ." I trailed off.

Joe didn't say anything but downed the rest of his pint. Looked like I'd successfully killed the vibe of that conversation. I felt a stab of annoyance at Joe for leaving me high and dry when two minutes earlier he'd been happily poking fun at Penton.

Poppy came to my rescue. "What about the prenatal teacher? Dot? Personally, I was a huge fan of her knitted uterus."

Everyone snorted at that, and the conversation resumed, discussing Dot's yarn-based approach to female anatomy and dissecting what little we knew about the other attendees, specifically whether Antoni, the only man attending other than Joe, was more likely to be an accountant or an estate agent. It was fun, and I was enjoying myself. We even exchanged numbers with that suitably vague promise that "we should do this again sometime." But I couldn't help feeling I'd somehow made a misstep.

After several hours in the pub, we departed into the fresh chill of the late afternoon. Winter was just tipping into spring and hadn't quite relinquished its bite. Was it colder in the countryside? Or was that, as Joe said, just me projecting?

"Well, we'll see you later then," said Poppy cheerfully.

Ah yes, tonight was class number two. I was ready for another nice, boring prenatal class where I could discuss the height of my cervix with now not-quite-such strangers.

CHAPTER 5

"I'M IN LATENT labor," announced Hen at the start of that evening's meeting.

I looked around, wondering if anyone else knew what that meant. I mean, was the woman in labor or not? And if she was, what the hell was she doing in the poky upstairs room of a wind-chime-and-crystal shop? We've all heard the rumors: if you give birth in Waitrose you get a year's supply of Waitrose food—Essential Placenta anyone? If you give birth on a Virgin flight—oh, the irony—you get free upgrades for a year. If Hen played her cards right, she might get a free supply of dream catchers and a gong bath for two.

"It's probably just Braxton Hicks," said Antoni, whose worried tone belied his words. "You're only thirty-six weeks, it's too early."

"I'm in labor," insisted Hen. "It was probably that clary sage Mr. Oliver sold me before the class yesterday. He said it would induce labor, and I've got to say he knew what he was talking about! This place might look like a joke"—this seemed harsh but fair—"but that stuff packs a punch."

Antoni went completely white. "You took herbs from that *quack*?" He sounded furious. "Hen, this is not a game! You're messing with—"

"Relax," said Hen breezily. "It's just latent labor, it can last for, like, two weeks—"

At that moment her water broke.

The previous day, Dot had repeatedly told us that when your water breaks it is not like they show it in films. It will be a trickle, not a flood. You might not even notice it happening. It can happen gradually over the course of a day. Well, Hen's uterus clearly hadn't got the memo. That woman *gushed*.

Being the supportive and caring group that we were, we all yelled and hid behind our pregnancy balls.

Hen looked briefly shocked. Then the contractions hit like a tsunami of pain and swear words. I don't know if you've ever seen someone in labor, but *dear God*. It is not something you want to witness—especially if you're planning on doing it yourself anytime soon.

"I'm calling an ambulance," I squawked.

"There's no need to overreact, dear," said Dot reprovingly. "Birth is a natural process that society has over-medicalized. Hen doesn't need an ambulance, she needs our *support*."

"Bollocks to that," Hen announced. "I'm going to the hospital."

She heaved herself to her feet and wedged a tea towel between her legs. But she'd barely waddled two steps before another contraction had her on her knees. They seemed to be coming thick and fast.

"I don't think there's going to be time for that, dear," said Dot briskly. "You're in the active stages already. This baby wants to come and it wants to come now. And it looks like it wants to come here. Sensible child," she added approvingly. "I'll pop downstairs and see what Mr. Oliver's got in the shop. Maybe I can find some lavender oil to relax you. Oh, and rose oil, that's good for enhancing positive emotions. I'm sure Mr. Oliver won't mind if we help ourselves." She bustled away to go to town in the shop and honestly, despite her clearly insane faith in lavender oil, it felt like the only adult had left. We all awkwardly avoided eye contact. The elephant in the room has nothing on the birthing woman in the room.

"Shit," breathed Hen.

Her husband, Antoni of the immaculate suit, hovered nervously beside her.

"You want me to get the car, babe?" he asked uselessly.

TEN MINUTES later and things had really stepped up a level.

"Remember your four-eight breathing, dear," trilled Dot, who was fluttering nervously round the sweating Hen, who was on all fours.

When I say sweating, she had a light sheen. Her hair still looked perfect and her mascara wasn't even smudged. She looked like she was giving birth in an episode of *Grey's Anatomy*, with full studio makeup. From the waist up, that is. From the waist down . . . let's just say there was a lot going on. And it was quite . . . messy.

This became increasingly apparent when Hen pulled off her expensive-looking JoJo Maman Bébé maternity jeans, declaring she didn't want to get blood on them. No one knew where to look.

"Do you think we should leave?" whispered Joe in my ear. The poor guy was staring fixedly at his shoes and sweating nearly as much as Hen.

"Can we?" I asked. "I dunno, is that . . . rude?"

"It's not a bloody dinner party," he hissed back. "Look, I'll go and get our coats." And he slipped away.

At this point Dot tried to pin some aromatic herbs to Hen's shirt—the only item of clothing remaining now she'd gone full Winnie-the-Pooh. Hen threw the offending aromatherapy across the room. Privately, I agreed—a sprig of sage ain't gonna cut it—but actually Hen just didn't want pin holes in her Tiffany Rose maternity shirt.

Fortunately, it turned out that Poppy had some basic first aid training—it wasn't much, but it was a damn sight better than the wind chimes Dot kept trying to hang around Hen. Unfortunately, I found myself roped in before Joe could return with our coats and make good our escape.

"You're on mopping duty," barked Poppy, waving a fistful of tea towels at the dreadlocked Ailsa.

"No fucking way." Ailsa shook her head and backed away until she hit the wall.

"Alice!" commanded Poppy, pushing the towels into my hands before I managed to get myself into reverse gear.

"Mopping?" I asked, frankly appalled. Surely this went above and beyond the call of duty to my fellow pregnanteers. I had only met the lady yesterday, and now I was expected to mop her?

And that was how I found myself squatting at what I can only describe as the business end and . . . mopping.

Dot had, somehow, managed to find herself a cushier spot at the head end. "Would you like some positive birth affirmations, dear?" she suggested brightly. Hen didn't say anything; her eyes were closed and she looked like she was concentrating quite hard—presumably on pushing eight pounds of new human out of her vagina. Dot took her silence as consent. She pressed a laminated sheet into Antoni's hands. He looked, if anything, more terrified.

"Go on." She nodded encouragingly. "Read them out to her. And don't just speak the words, really try to *feel* them."

Antoni cleared his throat awkwardly. "I am a force to be reckoned with," he muttered.

Hen opened one malevolent eye.

"My partner and I are the world's best team."

Hen gave him a look that promised to strangle him with the umbilical cord.

"I am overflowing with oxytocin?"

At this point Hen projectile vomited all over Antoni. Then she yelled some more. And then—she had a baby.

IT WAS like some kind of fucked-up nativity scene: Hen, not so much glowing as irradiating, immaculate bob finally in disarray, what looked like an old-fashioned telephone cord corkscrewing up her bloodstained and semi-nude body and ending in what was either a baby or the world's strangest novelty telephone; Antoni, sick-bespattered and nervously loosening his tie; and Dot, hovering like an over-involved Holy Spirit.

And of course us, the witnesses, a broadly useless and horrified audience. Except for Poppy, of course, who had actually brought the child forth and looked like an extra from a horror film set. It's amazing how they always leave the blood and shit out of those cute little plaster nativity scenes. Next Christmas I'll remember to empty a bottle of ketchup over that sentimental mush.

And then, a little on the tardy side, the ambulance arrived. I heard the tinkle of wind chimes as the paramedics entered the shop downstairs.

I waddled to the staircase and shouted down, "We're up here!"

"Huh?"

"We're upstairs! She's already had the baby!"

There was a pregnant (ha) pause.

"Oh . . . we're not here for the chap down here, then? 'Cause I'm pretty sure he's dead and there's not a lot we can do about that."

CHAPTER 6

THAT AWKWARD SILENCE where no one's sure if the whole "dead guy downstairs" thing is a joke.

Well, it turns out it wasn't. There really was a dead guy, slumped forward across the cluttered shop counter. I know, because I saw him. And yes, it is totally creepy that I went downstairs to look. I don't know what came over me, but when the paramedic called up, I just trotted on downstairs—and there he was.

His head had fallen forward and the fringe of white hair around his shiny bald patch made him look like an overgrown daisy.

Oh no . . .

One of the paramedics gently lifted the man's head.

"Mr. Oliver . . ."

It barely came out as a whisper, but the paramedic heard.

"Did you know him?" she asked.

"Er, no. Not really. I mean, a bit," I mumbled. I couldn't stop staring. I'd never seen a dead body before—let alone the body of someone whom I'd spoken with just an hour or so earlier. It was . . . surreal. I can't say I felt sad, not at the time, nor did I feel particularly horrified if I'm honest. In fact, there was a small part of me that felt curious. That's probably a terrible thing to admit, but it's the truth.

The scene was weirdly peaceful. He'd achieved a very clean and tidy death—compared to the scene of new life upstairs, anyway, which was total bloodbath. The worst you could say about down here was that he'd spilled his tea. A mug lay on its side and a small patch of

pale yellow tea had spread across the counter. It was almost definitely
herbal. This was not a shop where you'd find a box of Lipton in the
kitchenette. There were a dozen or so essential oil bottles in a box on the
counter, you know, the little brown ones with grubby labels in spidery
apothecary-esque handwriting, and a handful of these had been sent
scrambling when the man collapsed. There was also a lot of other clutter on the counter, but I got the impression that was probably normal:
one of those old-fashioned receipt books that make a carbon copy of
the handwritten receipt underneath, which is instantly smudged and
illegible; one of those lethal receipt spikes that should require a license
for possession; a calculator; an open packet of CBD lozenges; a pot of
enamel badges . . .

I'd only got so far with my mental catalog when there was a shriek
behind me.

"Crispin!"

It was Dot.

"Is he OK?"

I mean, how to answer that?

The paramedics looked at each other awkwardly.

"No?" said one nervously.

Dot wailed and I took that as my cue to sidle back up the stairs to
where the rest of the prenatal class were still frozen in their tableau of
Nativity 2: The Reckoning. Given the scene downstairs, the amount of
blood everywhere had taken on a slightly sinister tinge. Hen seemed the
least fazed by the situation. With no one around to take charge, she was
cracking on with motherhood and had got the baby firmly attached to
one boob already.

"What's going on down there?" she asked.

I shrugged. "Well, the paramedics are here, but Dot's having hysterics so I think they might be a while. One of them was giving her
oxygen and the other one was looking for Rescue Remedy—on Dot's
orders."

"I *meant*," said Hen impatiently, "is there a dead man or not?"

I really didn't feel qualified to be giving an opinion on the matter. But he had looked pretty dead. And I assumed the paramedics would have been a bit more proactive if there'd been any question around the matter. So I nodded.

"It's Mr. Oliver, the guy who owns this place."

There was a sharp intake of breath from Ailsa.

"Did you know him? Oh!" I remembered suddenly. "You were talking to him outside the doctors' the other day!"

She gave me a cold stare. "So? What are you going to do, arrest me?"

It seemed an odd response. A tad defensive, some might say.

"No, I just . . . I'm sorry. For your loss?" I made what I hoped was a sympathetic face. From her appalled expression I don't think I nailed it.

Everyone stood around, listening to the muffled sounds of Dot's hysterics downstairs. I saw Poppy and Lin exchange a loaded look. I couldn't say what it was loaded *with*, but it was definitely weighty. Lin's normally cheerful face was white and strangely blank. Poppy reached out and grabbed her hand.

More standing around. More hysterics from downstairs.

"So . . ." I said, because I am horribly afflicted with an inability to leave a silence unfilled. "Boy or girl?" I gestured vaguely at the baby.

"Girl."

"Well, er, congratulations!" I said weakly. Hen gave me a look.

EVEN WHEN the police turned up, I don't think I realized anything was wrong. I mean, evidently things were really very wrong for poor Mr. Oliver, but I didn't think there was anything suspicious. I assumed it was a heart attack, which in my limited experience is pretty much the only cause of sudden and unexpected death.

"That'll be the police," announced one of the paramedics, as blue light swept into the room through the window. "I'll go down and talk to them. If you could all just stay up here for now."

"The police?" Ailsa looked startled. "Oh God . . ." She shrank in on herself, no small task at thirty-odd weeks pregnant. Her dreadlocks seemed to wilt.

Well, they kept us waiting long enough. For a while there were scuffles and scrapes downstairs, and muted conversations filtered up through the ill-fitting floorboards. Another car drew up and a woman's voice joined the muddle. Upstairs, we made awkward small talk and Hen's baby fed nonstop; kudos to this child, it really was taking everything in its stride. The paramedics had given both baby and Hen a thorough once-over, declared them to be in perfect health and given the rest of the Oreos to Hen. Lin had made endless cups of tea, apparently unable to sit still, her movements stiff and mechanical.

Eventually, a serious-looking woman appeared at the top of the stairs.

"OK, ladies and gents, I'm Detective Inspector Harris. I'm going to need to have a quick word—Oh for God's sake, Ailsa. What are you doing here?"

Ailsa was trying to look defiant, but unusually it wasn't quite working for her.

"Not murdering anyone, if that's what you're wondering."

And that was the first time the word "murder" had been thrown out there.

INSPECTOR HARRIS and Ailsa had a whispered conversation in the corner of the room that we all eavesdropped on with zero shame.

". . . just trying to do my job and you turn up. *Again.*"

"And I'm just trying to have a goddam baby, so 'scuse me! I can't help it if Mr. Oliver goes and dies in the middle of my prenatal meeting!"

"What are you doing at this thing anyway? I thought you'd be giving birth in the forest surrounded by squirrels and Druids."

"If you mean the commune, then no. Well, maybe, it depends what happens with . . . Look, why are you here?"

"What, the corpse downstairs isn't enough of a reason?"

"I mean, why you?"

"Because I'm . . . qualified."

"I knew it! He was murdered then?"

Inspector Harris's eyes narrowed. "What do you mean, you knew it?"

"I just mean when *you* turned up it was obvious. Anyway, this isn't like last time—I'm not involved and I'm keeping it that way. Can I go home now?"

"Unfortunately not. I'm going to have to speak to you—professionally. And all your prenatal chums too."

"Going to arrest me?"

"Oh, don't be a dick, Ailsa."

At this point Inspector Harris looked round to see all of us watching, hanging on their every word, eyes wide at the mention of murder.

To be fair to her, Inspector Harris almost styled it out.

"Well, I think most of you caught the gist of that." She sighed. "As I was saying before"—she waved her hand to indicate Ailsa, who scowled—"I am Detective Inspector Harris, CID. I apologize for keeping you all waiting this evening. For various reasons that I don't intend to go into now"—she glared at Ailsa—"this has now become a police matter. I'm going to need to speak to all of you individually over the next twenty-four hours. If you could leave names and addresses with the constable downstairs before you leave, that would be very helpful. And, just as a matter of protocol, if I could ask you all not to leave Penton until I've had a chance to speak with you."

Hen snorted. I kinda saw her point—she was unlikely to be disappearing on the run with a two-minute-old baby.

Inspector Harris looked at her somewhat nonplussed.

"Has this all been . . . dealt with?" she asked, this time her gesture taking in the half-naked Hen, the ashen-faced, crumple-suited Antoni, the extremely new baby and the general miasma of bodily fluids.

"Well, 'this' seems happy enough." Hen pointed at the still-guzzling baby with her free hand. "And I don't think I'm about to have another one. So yes, pretty much dealt with."

I couldn't help giving a little puff of laughter. Inspector Harris shot me a look.

"Sorry, sorry," I muttered.

I'd got the impression at the previous day's meeting that Hen was a lady who didn't suffer fools gladly. Not to say that Inspector Harris was a fool, but Hen didn't seem overly impressed with her thus far. Although to be fair, for a woman who'd just pushed a baby out of her vag almost entirely unassisted, only to be upstaged by a murder in the same building, she was taking things pretty well.

"Good," said Inspector Harris, looking awkward. "Well. Yes. Congratulations then." She turned abruptly and left, trying not to look too relieved to be leaving the abundance of pregnant women in favor of a corpse.

CHAPTER 7

"**ARE WE GOING** to talk about this?" I demanded in bed that evening.

Joe didn't look up from Twitter. "Talk about what?"

"That there was a *murder*, like, *inches* away from where we were sitting?"

Joe carried on scrolling. "We've talked about nothing else for the last two hours. What more do you want to say?"

"We haven't discussed the fact that we might be"—I lowered my voice to a whisper—"*suspects*."

That got his attention. Either that or the internet cut out.

"You really think so?" he asked, finally putting his phone down.

I shrugged. "They told us not to leave Penton. That's what they say to suspects. They don't want us doing a runner. Evading justice."

"I'm pretty sure they just want to talk to us. As *witnesses*."

"I don't know. I reckon we're all under suspicion. We'd have heard if anyone had entered the shop—those damn wind chimes would have gone off. Which means it must have been someone already in the building . . ."

"You think we'd have heard wind chimes over the total fucking chaos of that woman giving birth?"

"Hen."

"What?"

"That woman's name is Hen."

"Whatever. My point remains."

Now this made me think. The "total fucking chaos" of birth, as Joe so aptly put it, was the ideal smoke screen for a crime. I could certainly have missed the tinkle of a wind chime, what with all the yelling. And as for the prenatal group, everyone had been coming and going, running around getting towels (always with the towels), hot water, making phone calls. It would be impossible to state for sure whether any one of us had been in the room at any given time. With the exception of Hen, of course. She was pretty much in the clear. Unless . . . No, no need to get carried away. She was a hundred percent in the room. This wasn't an episode of *Jonathan Creek*—in which case the murderer would definitely be Hen, and it would involve mirrors, a secret trapdoor and quite possibly a fake baby.

"I mean everyone left at *some* point," I said out loud. "Even you did. When you went to get our coats."

"Yeah, and I murdered Mr. Oliver on my way back from the hat stand," mumbled Joe absently, his eyes turning back to his phone screen.

I sighed and picked up my own phone. Was it too soon for anything about the murder to have appeared on the internet? This was modern romance for you: sitting next to each other in bed, silent, faces uplit by our phones. Googling murders.

The headline on the local news site, the *Penton Bugle*, was about a pheasant that had got into the haberdasher's—I didn't look any further, assuming that, even in Penton, a murder would knock a beribboned bird off the front page. There was nothing on Twitter. I opened Instagram and a slightly out-of-focus picture of Maya appeared at the top of my feed. She was at a bar, wine in hand, looking slightly wonky—although that could just have been the camera angle. There was a lot of exposed brickwork and an abundance of luxuriant foliage. Shoreditch? Hackney? To be honest, these days it could be any bar in London.

I wondered if a murder might change Maya's concrete opinion that the countryside was boring. I opened my texts.

> Maya, I've got news

> Shit

> Not now!

I'm shitfaced, I am absolutely not in a state to be a responsible grownup

Can you hold it in till tomorrow? Cross your legs or something

Maya was my backup birth partner.

It's not the baby. A guy DIED at class tonight

Literally or metaphorically?

Actually. For real.

Oh shit!

I know right. This place is full-on *Midsomer Murders*

Is that the one where the detective is a vicar?

You're thinking of *Grantchester*

Ugh they're all the same

i.e. crap

But NOT THE POINT

What happened??

Not sure. He was just dead at the shop counter downstairs

I thought it was a heart attack

It's always a heart attack

I know right

But then this police detective turned up

Oh and there was something going on with her and one of the other women

Which one?

The hippy one. Dreads and overalls. Ailsa.

Anyway, they knew each other—like really well

Well, there's like ten people and a sheep in Penton

No seriously!

They were arguing about something

I'm pretty sure she's been in trouble with the police before . . .

Didn't you want to be friends with these people?

Probably don't go accusing them of being crims before you've even had a coffee morning

I'm not getting massive coffee morning vibes off these women

Mind you, hard to tell . . .

Getting murdery vibes off any of them?

Do you think one of them did it??

How would I know?! You're the one that was there!

Fair point

So who was it?

Dunno

Maybe I'll investigate and find out!

Like a youthful, pregnant
Miss Marple in tie-dye leggings

Please don't buy anything tie-dyed

Anyway I *meant* who was
it got murdered?

Oh right

The guy who owns the shop

Owned

eye roll

Sorry. Bit drunk. Too soon?

A tad

I was a little disappointed that Maya didn't seem more aghast at the murder. To be fair to her, I'd approached the subject a little flippantly. But that was probably a defense mechanism to stop myself running screaming through the hills.

Should I run screaming?

Was there a murderer on the loose? Were we witnesses or suspects? Or, the thought trickled through my brain like a melting ice cube, potential victims?

CHAPTER 8

IT'S NOT ENTIRELY surprising that I couldn't sleep that night. In the belly of the night, problems that are, in the cosmic scheme of things, really quite minor—like overdue library books or tax returns—can assume mythological proportions. I would say it was around 3 A.M. that the reality of having been present at a potential murder scene really hit home, and the realization that I was, possibly maybe, living within a few miles of a murderer raised its ugly head. I sat bolt upright, causing the airbed to lurch wildly and Joe to mutter in his sleep. We were living in the middle of nowhere with *a killer on the loose*. London had killers aplenty, but I had never, to my knowledge, been in the same building as one. Earlier that evening, a man had been murdered just a few feet beneath our feet. I'd just been starting to come round to the idea of Penton, with its rolling hills and nice pub, but now it felt like the worst idea we'd ever had. What if it was the *last* idea we ever had . . .

"Joe," I hissed into the dark. "Joe!"

"Hmmmwhuh?"

"Joe, do you realize one of our neighbors could be a murderer?"

I admit "neighbors" was probably stretching it a bit. As Lin had pointed out, Penton was a decent-sized village. It was entirely possible we had never crossed paths with the murderer, and never would. And yet . . .

"What if the murderer was someone at the class?"

"Al, what are you talking about," Joe mumbled and rolled over. "He probably ate a dodgy mushroom or some weird bark or something."

How was he doing this? Who got in a solid eight hours while a murderer stalked the streets outside your very door?

OK, OK, I knew I was getting a tad carried away. And I know people say that your hormones can play havoc with your emotions while pregnant—but in this instance I was more inclined to blame the murder.

"I'm going to check we locked the front door," I stage-whispered. I paused for a moment, waiting for Joe to chivalrously insist that he check.

"Mmm, OK."

Ugh.

The front door was locked. But by this point I was wide awake. And as an added bonus, riding high on a tidal wave of my adrenaline, the baby had decided to throw a samba party in my womb. So I wedged myself in the corner of the sofa, where I had a clear line of sight to the front door—just in case an axe-wielding murderer attempted to break in. Helen joined me, which at first felt comforting, my trusty guard dog who, surely, would defend her beloved mistress to the bitter end. Surely? But as 3 A.M. tipped to 4 and then 5, my terror waned and was replaced with a simmering resentment, most of which was directed at Helen.

As I attempted to find a position that would alleviate the constant pain of my internal organs being elbowed rudely aside, Helen had quietly gathered all the velvet cushions to her corner of the couch, cast me a look of deep sympathy and was now snoring away, upside down, legs akimbo, like a spatchcock chicken.

She gave a grunting snore of contentment. I pushed her off the sofa.

I felt bad about it. But also not.

I was running out of things to worry about, so I turned my attention to my first-ever police interview looming large. To be entirely clear on this from the outset—I did not murder Mr. Oliver. I barely even knew the guy. But that didn't stop me worrying that I had. You know at school when the teacher stands up in assembly and gives a serious lecture about how the kids smoking behind the bike shed are letting the entire school down? And it wasn't you, you've never touched a cigarette in your life, but you feel your face going red with guilt, and that little voice at the back of your head is going, *Are you* sure *it wasn't you? It was you, wasn't it? You're so busted!* Well, that's how I was feeling about this interview. And a little bit of me was worried I might hysterically confess to a crime that I had in no way committed.

ONCE THE sun was fully above the horizon, around 6:30, I judged this to be an acceptable time and woke Joe up with a cup of tea from the hot tap. Then I made him practice police interviews with me for three hours while waiting nervously for my phone to ring.

"OK, what about if they ask if we heard anything? Did we hear anything?"

"Honestly, Alice, anyone would think you're guilty the way you're going on."

"Do you think I'm coming across as guilty? Shit, what if Inspector Harris thinks so too?"

Joe rolled his eyes. "OK, here's a hot tip for your police interview. Chill the fuck out."

He was not helping.

At one point the letterbox clattered and I bolted down the hallway like a water balloon out of a cannon. But it was just a leaflet from a local political candidate for the Penton Value Preservation Party—or some shit like that. I scanned the front page: it showed a headshot of a red-faced man, who almost definitely wore colored chinos, accompanied by a number of deeply obnoxious phrases . . . *seeking to reverse the cultural destruction wreaked by politically correct ideologies and return to our true heritage . . . reinstitute a Common Law based on Christian principles . . . no law or penalty for making so-called "insensitive" jokes or engaging in banter . . .*

Safe to say I am *not* the target audience for this. I ripped it in half and shoved it on the overflowing kitchen sideboard—the designated recycling spot until the mythical future date when we got our heads around the excessively complex recycling system in Penton. In the meantime, I would continue to create precipitous towers of rubbish until Joe cracked and went to the dump.

The distasteful leaflet distracted me from my police interview nerves for all of three minutes before I went back to my phantom guilt.

Around midday my phone pinged. But it wasn't Inspector Harris.

> Hi Alice, it's Poppy from prenatal class.
> I just wondered if you fancied a dog
> walk this afternoon?

Result! I'd liked Poppy, she seemed kind and easy to talk to. Obvs it was important to not get ahead of myself, but she was definitely a friend target. This was big—this was like a *date*. I tried, and failed, not to get overexcited. What should I wear? Casual but stylish. Like I was embracing the countryside, but not, y'know, getting *too* into it. Anorak or denim jacket? Walking boots or trainers? It was important to play it cool.

> Sure, sounds good.
> What kind of time?

> Not sure. Have you had your police
> interview yet?

> No—you?

> Yeah, Harris has just left. Let me
> know when you've had yours and
> we can meet at Stricker's Wood?

> Sounds great. Hope it went well
> with the police!

> I'm sure it did.

> I mean, it's not like
> I think you did it!

This was going horribly. Had I just accidentally suggested she might have murdered someone? Maya was right, I needed to get at least one coffee date in first. I scrambled to delete my last three messages but the three dancing dots showed Poppy was already responding. I waited . . .

Laughing emoji. Thank God.

INSPECTOR HARRIS turned out to be surprisingly boring for a police detective, and initially my first-ever police interview was shaping up to be disappointingly dull. We sat in slightly-too-close proximity in our extremely small kitchen and I gave a blow-by-blow account of the prenatal meeting—possibly in more detail than the inspector really wanted. Was it going to be relevant to the investigation that we had Oreos? Probably not.

I also wasn't able to provide much information on our fellow class members, given that I was still pretty hazy on some of their names let alone their histories. Nor could I say if I'd noticed anything unusual about Mr. Oliver's behavior when we'd arrived. We'd passed him on our way upstairs for the meeting, but we'd exchanged nothing more than a nod and a "good evening," and as much as I wanted to overanalyze that, there's only so far you can read into it.

I did, however, tell Inspector Harris about my encounter with him in town on Friday, blushing furiously as I stumbled through an account of the conversation—which somehow seemed even more embarrassing in the retelling. I would never have imagined that my first police inter-view would include a rambling explanation of how evening primrose oil tablets were just not shifting my semipermanent UTI. Inspector Harris remained stony-faced. When I mentioned the slippery elm bark, how-ever, her eyebrow twitched.

After I tailed off, she continued to sit staring at me.

"And that's it?" she asked eventually.

I nodded uncertainly. Was there anything else? Why did she look like she expected something more from me?

I wasn't sure on the etiquette, either. Was I allowed to ask questions? Because there were a couple of things I just had to know.

"What makes you think he was murdered?" I asked. "I mean, how do you know it wasn't just a heart attack?"

"It could have been a heart attack," Inspector Harris agreed. "We won't know until the results of the postmortem come back."

"But . . . you don't think so. Otherwise why would there be a detective on the scene within half an hour," I pointed out.

Inspector Harris sat back in her chair and narrowed her eyes slightly, clearly reappraising me. "I can't share any details of the case with you, you understand." I nodded, wide-eyed. "And I don't want you wandering around asking annoying questions." Wow, it was like she knew me already. "So all I will say is that Mr. Oliver had been in touch with us the previous day as he had concerns over his safety. He didn't go into anymore details. Unfortunately, we were hoping to speak with him on Monday."

"That is unfortunate," I agreed. Perhaps a really good Ouija board could help? I thought I'd best not suggest it.

"Quite," said Inspector Harris. "And seeing as, according to you, you didn't know Mr. Oliver, I doubt he'd confided any of his worries in you. Or had he? Is there anything else you want to tell me? Alice?"

I stared at her. These felt like loaded questions. I racked my brains, I really did. But I had nothing more to offer. Somehow, a man had been murdered right under my feet, and I'd literally seen nothing. Well, I mean I'd seen *a lot* that evening—some of which might possibly haunt me for longer than the murder—but I didn't think Inspector Harris needed to hear about that.

"Er, no?"

This was clearly the wrong answer. Inspector Harris leaned forward abruptly, her eyes narrowing.

"I just want to be entirely clear on this," she said. "You had one short conversation with Mr. Oliver?"

"Well, two if you count saying hello in the shop, I suppose." I was baffled. Inspector Harris was clearly trying to get at something here. And I had no clue what she was after.

The inspector didn't break eye contact as she reached down into her bag.

"We found this on the counter." She placed a paper-wrapped bottle on the kitchen table. Tied around its neck was a handwritten label. "For Alice. Drink me."

"It's a reference to *Alice in Wonderland*," said Inspector Harris seriously. I side-eyed her. I mean, did she really think I hadn't got that?

"We haven't turned up any other Alices in Mr. Oliver's circle of acquaintances. And given what you've just told me, I'm pretty certain the contents were meant for you."

OK, so this was starting to feel a bit creepy.

"Open it." The inspector nudged the package toward me.

I hesitated. If I touched it, wouldn't my fingerprints be on it? What if Inspector Harris was trying to frame me, I thought wildly.

"We've already processed it for fingerprints," said Inspector Harris irritably, clearly reading my mind. I fumbled to unwrap it, and a small brown apothecary's bottle rolled out onto the desk. Was it . . . poison?

I turned it round to read the handwritten label: SLIPPERY ELM BARK.

My first reaction was to laugh—at Inspector Harris's serious face. At the sheer absurdity of her thinking this was anything other than some quack remedy for heartburn. Then I unexpectedly felt the hot prickle of tears. It was a sweet gesture. He had been a nice old man after all. Weird, sure, but nice.

And now he was dead.

CHAPTER 9

AS I DROVE up to the woods, with the pressure of the police interview now lifted, I began to panic about the upcoming dog walk. I'm not great at in-real-life interactions. Believe it or not, I'm much better over text. And as evidenced that morning, that bar is pretty low. I feared that, with the additional pressure of a murder investigation, my social skills, already limited at best, were going to be under severe strain.

I had invited Joe but he had declined in favor of unpacking the final boxes still languishing in the garden, now lightly rain-damaged. I'd got the feeling he was quite keen on having some alone time, but I was starting to wish I'd badgered him to come a bit more persistently. He was far more socially competent than me, and knew how to make conversation on normal topics, although admittedly with a tendency to default to snooker or nineties rock bands under pressure.

I was also already regretting my outfit choices. When we'd decided to move to the country I'd instantly purchased a Barbour wax jacket. OK, so maybe it isn't *technically* Barbour; those things cost the same as a small car. If you look closely enough at the label it's actually a Barbor. But I reckon it could pass for the real thing in poor light. I hadn't had the opportunity to wear it yet, and when I got out of the car and tried to zip a size 10 jacket over a thirty-eight-week baby bump I realized why.

Poppy was already there, looking casually stylish in a bright red duffle coat that actually did fit over her bump. Having spent several months resenting the phrase "neat bump," largely because it was never applied to me, I had to admit she had a very neat bump.

Spotting Poppy's two dogs, Helen flew into an instant spiral of frenzied joy and threw herself at the rear window like I'd trapped Taz the Tasmanian Devil in my car trunk.

I admit, I was *delighted* when Ronnie also began hurling himself around like a loon. I get real dog-based schadenfreude—I love it when other people's dogs are worse than mine. Helen wasn't done yet, though. As soon as we were out of the car, she threw herself flat on her stomach and belly-crawled toward Poppy as if her legs had stopped working, her tail thrashing the dirt.

I *had* hoped she wasn't going to embarrass me on this walk.

No matter—within five minutes I'd managed to embarrass myself.

As soon as the dogs were allowed off the lead, they all started sniffing around my jacket pocket. Mystified, I put my hand in my pocket and drew out a rubbery yellow mess. I was briefly confused.

"Ah!" I said, comprehension dawning. "Omelette."

Poppy looked at me quizzically. "You have an omelette in your pocket?"

Belatedly, I realized that this was probably not normal behavior—but does explain why I won't spend £500 on a jacket. I opened my mouth to rationalize the situation. I had nothing.

Poppy tried to help me out. "Oh, did you bring it for the dogs?"

"Yeah . . ."

Bringing a pocketful of omelette on a walk as a tasty snack for your dog is borderline odd. But probably not as weird as admitting that the congealed eggy mess in my hand was in fact my lunch, which I didn't have time to eat before leaving. My morning sickness has never quite left and tends to lurk around, waiting to ambush me if I go more than, say, twenty minutes without eating, so I don't like to go anywhere without a hearty supply of snacks. But why oh why had I not filled my pockets with cookies, like a normal person?

Still, the dogs were delighted at my offering—well, Ronnie and Helen were. Sultan looked frankly appalled, and I couldn't blame him. He kept looking from Helen to me, as if unable to decide which of us he was more horrified by. It looked like Helen had made a firm friend in Ronnie, however—although their idea of a friendship appeared broadly based on sniffing each other's butts and leaving each other secret messages by weeing on tree trunks. Still, you've got to start somewhere. I'd probably take a different tack with Poppy.

We set off through the woods. I was still getting to grips with the whole countryside thing. Sure, I had the Barbor, and I had long been a frequenter of London's parks—even the wilder ones like Hampstead Heath and Richmond Park. Although Joe and I once got so lost on Hampstead Heath he had to dissuade me from calling Mountain Rescue. But I felt a little out of my depth walking through woods knowing that I wasn't going to emerge any minute to find a concrete-lined duck pond filled with pedal boats, or a small café selling Frappuccinos.

I had to admit that these were very pleasant woods though. The onset of spring had fuzzed them with a brilliant green, and the shifting branches sent a rippling play of light and shade across the path like sun through water. I let myself relax a little.

We walked in silence for a little way. I thought Poppy seemed distracted. This was fair enough, given the events of the last twenty-four hours. I wasn't sure where to open the conversation. We had two things in common: pregnancy and a murder. As new acquaintance conversation-starters, it was a tough call.

I was just about to go in with a probably ill-advised question about pelvic floors when she, thankfully, plumped for option two.

"So, how'd your police interview go?"

"I think it went OK," I said. "Although, a kind of weird thing happened."

I told her about the bottle of slippery elm bark and the note addressed to me.

She nodded seriously. "Yeah, Mr. Oliver did things like that. It was probably a kind gesture, but he could be a little . . . pushy."

"I'm so sorry, I didn't realize you knew him."

Poppy sighed and rubbed her face.

"I didn't really . . ." She was quiet for a moment. Then: "He was Lin's uncle. But we didn't know him. Not at all, really."

Well, I hadn't expected that.

"I'm sorry." What else was there to say? *I'm so sorry your wife's uncle was murdered while we sat upstairs completely oblivious*?

"It's fine." Poppy sounded tired. "Really, I meant it when I said we didn't know him. There was some sort of falling-out between him and Lin's mum years ago. Lin didn't ever see him, growing up, and then when we moved here she didn't feel the need to get in touch with him. It wouldn't be worth upsetting her mum. So we bumped into him occasionally, but we pretty much avoided Nature's Way. Until the prenatal class ended up being held there, of all places."

"Is Lin OK?" I asked. The murder of even an estranged family member still felt like kind of a big deal.

"Yeah—well, I mean she says she is. But Inspector Harris just wouldn't let it go. Kept asking Lin what her mum had fallen out with her uncle over—and Lin doesn't even know! But she wouldn't let it drop. Ugh, that woman . . . Anyway, Lin went over to the community garden this afternoon, said she wanted to be on her own with her plant allies." Poppy gave a small laugh. "And I didn't really fancy hanging round the house thinking about it all, so I thought I'd see if you were about. I hope you don't mind."

"Not at all! I'm always up for a dog walk." This was a lie; I'm a strictly fair-weather dog walker.

"What did you make of Harris?" Poppy asked.

I thought for a moment. Inspector Harris had disconcerted me slightly. There was a hunger about her, an eagerness that I hadn't liked. I had a distasteful feeling that she was a little bit pleased that there had been a murder, so that she could stretch her detective legs and maybe even make a bit of a splash. I didn't imagine there was much to do as a homicide detective in the Cotswolds, which didn't strike me as a hotbed of crime. But then, what did I know? The evidence would suggest otherwise.

"I didn't like her . . ." I said slowly.

Poppy gave a slight grin. "You don't have to say that just because she gave Lin a rough time."

"No," I countered. "It's not that. I felt there was a ruthlessness to her. Like she was keen to prove how much cleverer she is than everyone else. I mean, she hung on to that bottle of elm stuff until the end of the interview, then produced it as if she was proving me wrong, or even proving me guilty of something. Like I'd lied to her."

Poppy nodded soberly. "I know exactly what you mean. That's what worries me a bit. She was going after Lin with this dogged persistence, like she'd already decided Lin was—well, not guilty, I'm sure she doesn't think Lin's *guilty*—but as if Lin was holding something back from her. As if she was involved somehow and the great Detective Harris was going to prove it."

"I'm sure she doesn't think Lin had anything to do with it," I said, rather lamely. Because that seemed exactly the sort of thing Inspector Harris would latch on to. "Wasn't Lin in the room the whole time, anyway?"

"Well, no, not exactly," said Poppy reluctantly. "She did go downstairs at one point to use the bathroom, and it took her a little while to find it. Harris asked her if anyone could confirm that. I mean, what kind of stupid question is that? No one has an alibi to go to the toilet!"

"Hmm, yeah, ridiculous," I agreed, slightly nervously. Poppy was sounding pretty worked up.

"What about Harris and Ailsa, huh?" I said, trying to steer the conversation away from Lin. "What was all that about?"

"Yeah, that was a bit intense," said Poppy, grasping the new tack gratefully. "Did you hear what they were saying?"

I raised an eyebrow. "I think we all did. They weren't exactly subtle. Sounded like Ailsa's been in trouble with the police before."

"Specifically with Inspector Harris."

"Yeah, well, I bet Harris will be all over her."

"Poor girl," said Poppy.

I didn't *quite* agree. I wasn't sure I liked Ailsa. She'd been spiky and rude and, to my mind, suspiciously defensive—over everything. I felt like I'd annoyed her somehow, but it also seemed pretty likely this was her default attitude toward all humans.

"I reckon she can handle it."

Poppy laughed, but at that point we had to pause the conversation as we labored our way up a gentle incline. Pregnancy gives you the lung capacity of a hundred-a-day smoker and the muscle tone of a jellyfish.

"How was Joe's interview?" Poppy puffed at the top.

"Oh, in and out in about three seconds. I was listening at the door—obviously—and he basically said there was a woman giving birth on the floor in front of him, did she really expect him to have noticed a bloody thing?"

Poppy laughed. "Yeah, pretty convenient for the murderer, wasn't it?"

"I know—talk about fortunate. For them, that is! Not for Mr. Oliver, clearly. I mean, the whole thing is obviously awful." *Cool rambling, keep it up, Alice.* But Poppy made an interesting point. "It was *very* convenient for the murderer, wasn't it? Although, it's not like they could have known that was going to happen." I paused. "Could they?"

She shrugged. "I doubt it. Maybe it was an opportunistic crime? Like, Hen starts giving birth, everyone's running around, they seize their chance."

That sounded plausible. Only, if it was an opportunistic crime, that would mean it had to have been committed by someone who was already there, which pretty strongly pointed the finger at someone within the prenatal group.

Poppy was clearly thinking along the same lines. "I suppose someone could have been passing the shop outside and heard what was going on? Popped in to see what all the fuss was about, bumped into Mr. Oliver and . . . y'know."

"Yeah . . ." I said slowly. "Yeah, I guess. I mean, it's either that or it actually *was* one of us."

Was I genuinely accusing someone in my prenatal group of being a murderer?

"Well, at least you're in the clear." I tried to sound lighthearted. "You were pretty busy the whole time!"

Poppy was still looking thoughtful. "No, it couldn't have been me," she said seriously. "And it couldn't have been Hen."

"Definitely not," I agreed.

"But it could have been pretty much anyone else," she went on. "I mean, people were in and out the whole time. Anyone could have slipped downstairs and done it without the rest of us realizing."

"Is there anyone we're sure *didn't* leave the room?" I wondered aloud. "Other than you and Hen. I mean, I can barely even remember if *I* left the room."

Poppy frowned. "Well, I remember Antoni leaving. He went to the car to get Hen's hospital bag. That was quite early on."

"Yeah," I cut in. "Can you believe they had that with them? I mean I know they say take it everywhere with you at this stage, but who actually does that?"

"Haven't packed mine," said Poppy absently. That made me feel better about the bag of plentiful snacks and a solitary onesie that was languishing in our hallway, frequently getting raided by me and Helen.

"He might have left again," I pondered. "Did he leave to call the paramedics? Or was that me?" I genuinely couldn't remember.

"Couldn't say," said Poppy. "I was pretty busy by that point." She grimaced at the memory.

"And Dot went downstairs to get some essential oils and wind chimes and shit from the shop," I continued. "And she didn't mention anything about a body when she came back up. So either he was still alive when she went down—"

"Or she did it," concluded Poppy.

"Yeah. But I can't remember if she went down before or after Antoni . . ."

"Well, let's say both her and Antoni are possibilities. What about Ailsa?"

I shook my head. "Can't remember. I don't really remember her being around at all. She was pretty quiet."

"I think she was the first person who said it was murder, though," said Poppy thoughtfully. "Even before Inspector Harris did. Which is a bit weird. I don't know, is that suspicious?"

"The one who smelt it, dealt it." I shrugged. This got a small chuckle from Poppy.

"Then of course there's Joe," I went on. "He went downstairs to get our coats at one point . . . We were thinking of making a run for it—before you roped me in to do all that mopping. Thanks for that, by the way."

She grinned, but I was still thinking. "Actually I don't really know what Joe was doing after that. I didn't really see him. I was kind of occupied . . ." I shook myself. "I mean, clearly it wasn't him. But technically I don't think we'd be able to rule him out."

"And Lin went to the loo—without an alibi, as Harris established. But it wasn't her," said Poppy firmly. "I couldn't say where she was the whole time, but while I can see her nicking the rest of the cookies, I don't think she popped downstairs to murder her estranged uncle."

I smiled awkwardly. *Quick, think of something reassuring to say.* "Well, I'm sure Inspector Harris will get to the bottom of it."

Poppy sighed. "Are you? I wish I had your confidence."

In truth, I wasn't sure I believed what I'd said. I'd just said it to fill the silence before it became awkward.

Poppy checked her phone again. She'd been doing this every few minutes since we'd started walking.

"Still nothing from Lin," she said. "I just feel . . . uncomfortable at the way Harris was going after her. I don't think she has a clue what happened, so she was latching on to anything that could be a lead. And for now, that's Lin." She paused. "Or potentially you."

"What now?"

"Oh, I'm sure you didn't do it. I'm just saying that Harris might *think* you did."

"Because of the slippery elm bark? I had *heartburn!*"

Poppy shrugged. I felt slightly sick. Which could have been down to the murder, or could have been the cold omelette in my pocket.

Poppy stopped and turned to me. "Who do you think did it?"

I was taken aback. "I have literally no idea!"

"Just supposing you were Harris. From what we've just been discussing, who would be on your suspect list? What would you do next?"

I cast my mind back to all the cozy crime dramas I'd devoured over the course of my insomniac pregnancy.

"So the major factors are means, motive and opportunity," I said slowly. "We've only really been able to cover opportunity, and even that's been pretty sketchy. From that, I don't think anyone can really be ruled out, apart from you and Hen. I don't think I could even rule myself out. Means and motive would be trickier. Means would depend on *how* he was killed, which we don't know."

"Right," agreed Poppy. "All we know is that it wasn't messy."

"No. Definitely not a stabbing or a shooting or anything." I pictured the scene in my mind. "My money would be on poison—he'd spilled a cup of tea just before he died—could there have been something in it? But that's just speculating. I wonder when the police will know for sure?"

"Do you think they'll tell us?"

"Probably not," I admitted. "So then the last factor would be motive."

Unfortunately, the only thing that sprang to my mind was this family argument between Mr. Oliver and Lin's mum. But I didn't feel it would be tactful to bring this up. Besides, Poppy had already said that Lin knew nothing about it.

Knowing my big mouth and unfiltered brain, I would probably have said something to kill our blossoming friendship. But—and it's not something I can often say—I was saved by the dogs.

From the woods up ahead a frenzy of barking broke out, accompanied by a man shouting.

Simultaneously, we broke into a wheezy high-speed waddle in the direction of the commotion.

CHAPTER 10

WE HUFFED AROUND the corner and straight into an X-rated scene.

Ronnie was enthusiastically humping a young man's leg while the object of his affections tried to prize him off with a stick. Helen was jumping around, clearly cheering Ronnie on. Sultan was standing to one side, trying to look like he wasn't with these two weirdos.

"Oh my God, I'm so sorry!" Poppy rushed forward and dragged Ronnie away. Fortunately, Ronnie caught sight of Helen and made a beeline for her instead.

"It's fine, really," insisted the guy, averting his eyes from Ronnie and Helen.

"I'm so sorry, he's a randy little bastard," apologized Poppy again, now trying to separate the dogs. It was hard to tell who looked more embarrassed—Poppy or the young man. Or possibly Sultan. As for me, I was really enjoying being around a dog that was worse behaved than mine. It was so refreshing to listen to someone else apologizing for once.

"It's fine, it's really fine," the guy repeated.

He was quite good-looking—at least, I *thought* he was, although in truth pregnancy hormones had addled my libido to the point where I could get horny watching an advert for string cheese one minute and be taking a vow of chastity the next. But this guy definitely had something going on, despite many errors of style judgment in my book. He had that curly-top hippy-posh-boy hair that normally looks twattish but was working for him, and was wearing some sort of woven hoody, the sort that you buy in shops called things like Shakti or Moonflower. But I was willing to overlook this because, well, he was hot. And maybe slightly familiar-looking? I squinted, but I couldn't place it . . .

"Are you OK?" Poppy broke in, neatly drawing attention to my prolonged creep-staring.

"Yep! Yep, fine. Yeah."

Oh God, sign me up to the nuns.

"I'm so sorry about the dogs," I burbled. "We were just . . ." I wasn't sure where that sentence was going. Walking the dogs? Duh. Trying to solve a murder? Weird.

"It's fine, really," he said. "I think they're off again though . . ."

I looked around just in time to see Ronnie squeezing under a large padlocked gate marked PRIVATE. Helen's tail was already disappearing out of sight down the (private) path.

"Oh great."

I pressed my face against the gate, trying to catch sight of the errant dogs. Poppy's head appeared next to mine.

"Reckon we can scale this?" she asked, looking up at the six-foot gate.

"You can't climb that!" said the young man, sounding scandalized. "Not in your condition!"

I hate that phrase. My "condition" is a perfectly natural state and does not prevent me from—Well, actually I have to admit it prevents me from doing quite a lot of things. Probably up to and including scaling six-foot gates.

"Got any other ideas?" asked Poppy, already wedging one foot on the lower bar of the gate.

"Yes!" he replied, hurrying forward. "I could unlock it for you!" He produced a key from his pocket.

"That gets my vote," I conceded.

"SO WHAT'S down here?" I asked, as we accompanied the guy, whose name was Rowan, down a lovely woodland pathway lined with beautiful yellow flowers, which might have been buttercups, I wouldn't know, and a fair sprinkling of PRIVATE and KEEP OUT signs, and even one TRESPASS-ERS WILL BE CURSED sign.

"It's my dad's commune," Rowan replied, as if this was as normal as "my dad's garage" or "my dad's embarrassing collection of Cliff Richard CDs."

"Oh. Lovely." I couldn't think what else to say. So, how long have you been a hippy? Or, does your commune dance naked at the full moon?

Rowan grinned, like he knew what I was thinking. "It's not as weird as you think. It's just a community who want to live off-grid. They're just not into things like the internet and mobile phones and capitalism. It's fine. It's nice, actually. I should know, I grew up here."

Which, I thought, didn't exactly make him an impartial observer. But I was intrigued, and willing to withhold my judgment for now—in the full expectation of judging with extreme bias further down the line.

The path ended at another gate, this one set in an arch woven from those thin, bendy sticks. A creeper covered in small star-like white flowers grew across it. I was enchanted—who doesn't love a mysterious doorway that clearly leads to Rivendell? Rowan pushed open the gate, although I thought he hesitated for just a fraction of a second before doing so, and I stepped into my first-ever commune.

My initial impression was that it looked like a really nice glamping site, or a suitably middle-class family-friendly festival. My second was that it was big! This wasn't a few hippies in a tree, this was a sizable settlement. There were several large yurts, maybe ten or twelve, scattered throughout the trees, as well as a couple of permanent stone cottages that looked far less robust than the yurts. There was also a large building nestled among the trees that looked like it was made of the earth itself. Can you build houses out of soil?

The surrounding nature had been tamed into multiple vegetable plots and even a small flower garden around one of the cottages. The overall atmosphere was one of tranquility; brightly colored hammocks swung between trees and a handful of people milled about, gardening, chatting, reading, all sporting variations of Shakti-Moonflower chic. A couple of dogs lazed in the chilly spring sunshine—and there was Helen, licking the strange dogs' faces and generally being ignored. The distant cluck of a chicken had me lunging to clip her lead before she caught on.

It felt like I'd stepped back in time, or onto a set from *Game of Thrones*.

"It's amazing!" breathed Poppy. "Oh shit, Ronnie—" She darted away as she caught sight of a small badger-like shape disappearing behind a yurt.

"It's pretty nice," admitted Rowan. "It didn't exactly prepare me for life at Leeds University though."

I snorted. I'd once visited a friend at Leeds University and the Student Union on a Friday night was a far cry from this peaceful rural idyll.

I noticed an incongruously modern padlock on the door of one of the cottages.

"What's with Fort Knox?" I asked Rowan, nodding toward it.

"Oh, that's the dispensary."

"Medicine?"

He shrugged. "Of a sort. Natural remedies, that kinda stuff. It's mostly harmless, but Dad likes to keep things secure."

I wondered whether the dispensary stocked any slippery elm bark.

"Want to look around?"

But before I had time to take Rowan up on his offer—and yes please to poking round hippy-timewarpsville—a large man barreled out of a nearby yurt and almost took Rowan out.

"Rowan! You came back! Why didn't you tell us you were coming? We thought you were somewhere in Nepal!" It must have been Rowan's dad—there was the same curly-top, but this time in salt-and-pepper, and the same fine bone structure, which was slightly at odds with the broad shoulders.

"I only landed yesterday—bit of a spur-of-the-moment decision." Rowan looked as if he was about to say more, but his dad had spotted me and looked delighted.

"And wait till your mum sees you've brought a *girl* home with you!"

I opened my mouth to correct him, but at this point Poppy reappeared, having tracked Ronnie down from where he'd been, judging by the state of him, rolling in chicken shit. "Sorry, Ronnie had found the chicken pen—oh, he didn't eat any! He might've eaten quite a lot of their chicken feed though, sorry."

"*Two* girls!" The man raised his eyebrows at Rowan and gave him a roguish wink—which annoyed me. Then he caught sight of our telltale bumps and his face went pale.

"Oh, Rowan, you haven't."

"What? No! I mean, well—" For a weird moment I thought he was going to confess to having impregnated both myself and Poppy. And I knew categorically that at least fifty percent of that would be a lie.

"I mean—of course not." He seemed to get a grip on himself, although he looked strangely angry. Wow, this father-son reunion had deteriorated fast. "Not that—ugh. This is Poppy and this is Alice. I met them in the woods just now and their dogs broke into the commune."

I felt this was a little harsh. Neither Helen nor Ronnie had the brain capacity to really *break in* anywhere, which seemed to signify some sort of intent and/or plan. It had been more of a stumbling in. Which, apparently, seemed to have coincided with some kind of prodigal son return with more subtext than a Shakespeare play.

"Poppy, Alice, this is my dad, Camran. He runs the commune." The warmth with which Rowan had previously spoken about the commune had edged away from his words.

"Welcome, welcome." Now he'd established we weren't carrying his grandchildren, Camran was all smiles again. "Come and have a cup of tea. Rowan, your mother will be thrilled you're home. Although why you didn't tell us . . ." He looped an arm around his son's shoulders and swept him away, shaking his head and smiling. Unsure what else to do, Poppy and I bobbed along in their wake like a couple of pregnant balloons.

IF YOU'VE never had tea at a hippy commune, I highly recommend it. Rowan's mother, Hazel, was everything you'd hope for in a hippy mother, from the embroidered waistcoat to the excessively chunky jewelry. She fussed around Poppy and me, bringing us more cushions than were necessary and a whole selection of organic teas, none of which I'd ever heard of but which she assured me would cure all of my many and varied pregnancy-related ills. She also acupressured my wrists—which genuinely made me feel less nauseous, for the first time in months. And she constantly entreated us to have more of her homemade cookies. They were sugar-free and entirely organic, she told us, and made with foraged acorn flour and spruce needles. I was unsure about the advisability of this last—I'm almost certain a spruce is a Christmas tree? And from sustained experiments in my childhood I can tell you with conviction that those are not edible. But actually the cookies were passably acceptable. I had four.

As she overloaded us with cookies and cushions she chattered away—almost entirely about Rowan, who was clearly her pride and joy. I wondered idly whether I would become this sort of mum—baking cookies from grass clippings and regaling total strangers with stories about my son's childhood antics. It seemed unlikely, but motherhood can do strange things to people.

From what I could gather from the ever-flowing but erratic information pouring out of Hazel, Rowan had left the commune about a decade earlier to go to university, and had spent the intervening years as a sort of itinerant man-child on a permanent gap year. I wanted to be scathing, but to be honest it sounded great. I wouldn't mind yak herding in Tibet or running the post office in Antarctica. Were these things people actually did? Like, for real?

"You were never tempted to come back and live in a Cotswolds commune then?" I asked—meaning it slightly jokily. I mean, how does living in a commune with your parents compare to mountain unicycling in Bolivia? But at my suggestion Rowan's face shut down.

"Absolutely not," he said quietly.

"Sorry," I said, although I wasn't sure quite what for (nervous apologizing is a hobby of mine).

He waved it away. "It doesn't matter. It . . ." He paused like he was going to say something more, then he just shrugged.

I glanced at his parents. Hazel's permanent beaming smile had faltered. Camran looked stony.

I tried to rescue things. "Well, I just mean, how can sleepy old England compare to all those adventures you've had! Although saying that, you'll never guess what happened at our prenatal meeting last night." I felt Poppy tense next to me, but crashed on regardless.

"Halfway through the meeting, one of the girls only goes and gives birth! And then it turns out that the guy who runs the shop downstairs—you know Nature's Way?—he's been murdered while we're all upstairs! And none of us heard a thing!"

Hazel dropped her cup. Camran made a sudden gesture as if to grab me, but caught himself. Then everyone just sat there, frozen. I was aware that I had somehow made a bad situation considerably worse.

"Crispin?" whispered Hazel. "Crispin Oliver?"

Shit. I should have realized they might know him. They run the hippy commune. He runs the hippy shop in town. I'd probably just broken the news to them that their best friend had died. And so flippantly, as if it was just a bit of town gossip.

"I'm so, so sorry," I breathed. "I'm so sorry."

The silence stretched like a spider's thread—gossamer-delicate and taut as a steel wire.

"Were you very good friends?" I asked tentatively.

At this, Camran seemed to shake himself awake.

"No," he said briskly. "No, we weren't. We knew him a while back but haven't seen him in—oh, must be ten years now. Knew he had a shop in town, never been though."

"No," echoed Hazel, less convincingly. "No, it's been a while."

"Very sad news though, of course," continued Camran. He started stacking the cups, then unstacking and restacking them in a different order. "How upsetting for you girls. Not the kind of energy you want to be exposed to in your condition." There was that phrase again. "You should put rock salt in every corner of your rooms tonight. It will absorb the negative energy."

We mumbled our agreement.

"How upsetting for poor Mairi," said Hazel. "I wonder how she's taking it. It's going to be very hard for her."

Camran snorted. "Mairi will get by just fine. I always thought it was a mistake, the two of them going into business together. No doubt she disapproved of his little sideline, but that's all that kept that shop of his running." Stack. Unstack. Stack. Unstack. "From what I hear," he added, apparently belatedly remembering that he didn't know anything about Mr. Oliver or his shop.

"Is Mairi Mr. Oliver's wife?" I asked.

"No, just his business partner," said Hazel. "Neither of them ever married. Least of all each other! Lord, can you imagine . . . Of course Crispin was heartbroken when Flora left but then weren't you all." There was a bite to her voice at this last, and she shot Camran a less than friendly look. Wow, we'd really opened a can of worms here.

"Was Flora Mr. Oliver's girlfriend?"

"No. Flora was not anyone's girlfriend. You do ask a lot of questions, don't you?" Camran's tone was light but there was a warning note to it. I'd been about to ask more about Mr. Oliver's "little sideline," but I suspected this would go down poorly, and I had no desire to be chased out of town by angry hippies—they could send some seriously bad vibes my way. I couldn't help thinking, however, that Hazel knew an awful lot about Mr. Oliver's personal life for someone who barely knew the man.

I wondered how we could effect a swift exit from tension city. Clearly they also felt the same way.

"Why don't you show the girls around?" suggested Hazel, turning to Rowan with her best mum-smile. "I think Ailsa was here earlier. You should introduce her to the girls." She turned to Poppy and me. "Ailsa is one of Rowan's oldest friends. She's having a baby too—I'm sure she'd love to meet you both. Such a sweet girl."

I avoided Poppy's eye.

CHAPTER 11

WE FOUND AILSA in the vegetable garden. And, as expected, she didn't appear particularly pleased to see us. Or perhaps it was Rowan she wasn't so keen on. They might have been old friends but you could have cut the tension between them with a knife—or the extremely sharp and dangerous pruning shears Ailsa was wielding.

"Back from your *gap yah* then?" she asked, not really looking at him and focusing instead on the beans she was training round an obelisk of garden canes.

"Well, for now," he said awkwardly. "Not sure how long I'll be in Penton for."

She sniffed. "No change there then."

"It's nice to see you," he ventured.

She sniffed again. "Pass me the string."

"This is Poppy and Alice," he said. "They're pregnant too."

I tried so hard not to laugh at this incredible introduction, but I may have let out a teeny chuckle.

Ailsa didn't look our way. "Yeah, I know. We're in prenatal class together."

Rowan's eyes narrowed. "You were at their prenatal class?"

"Yeah. And?"

"When Mr. Oliver was killed."

Ailsa froze.

"You should have said something," Rowan hissed—like this would mean Poppy and I couldn't hear from all of three feet away. "You should have told me."

"How could I?" she shot back. "It's not like you told me you were coming. You haven't shown up here in like a year."

"Well, fine. And—I'm sorry, I should have told you I was coming back. But still, you could have told my dad—about Mr. Oliver I mean."

Ailsa gave him a look so withering it made my toes curl. "I came to get some beans for Nana Maud. I'm not the damn town crier."

"Soooo," broke in Poppy, presumably growing tired of being the awkward invisible bystander. "You guys are, like, old friends?"

"We went to school together," said Rowan. At the same time as Ailsa said, "Not really."

"Awkward," I said, under my breath. The way things were going, maybe I'd just get "awkward" tattooed on my forehead.

Ailsa sighed and put down her pruning shears. Not gonna lie, I was a bit relieved. She seemed a tad too edgy to be handling sharp implements.

"Hi Alice, hi Poppy," she said in a singsong voice. "So nice to see you, you both look great, let's get coffee sometime."

I had no idea what to make of that. Did she want to go for coffee . . . ? Or was she just messing with us?

"Er," I said.

"Come on, Ailsa, be nice." Rowan sighed. "They just wanted to say hi."

This wasn't strictly true. Rowan's mum hadn't really given us any choice in the matter. There seems to be a certain school of thought that all pregnant women will be instant friends because of this one thing they have in common. But it's total bollocks—I mean, you wouldn't go up to two women in a doctors' office and be like, "Oh, you both have athlete's foot, you'll totally get on!"

"Actually we were just trying to get our dogs back," I corrected.

Ailsa remained unimpressed. "Yeah, the one that looks like a badger pissed on my cabbages and then the fancy one dug them up."

Normally, I'd dissolve into a stream of apologies, but I couldn't really be bothered. Ailsa wasn't very nice, so maybe I didn't need to be nice either.

"Dogs gonna dog," I replied. And she actually cracked a smile. A small and unwilling one, but a smile nonetheless.

"You might as well take one of the cabbages home," she offered. "They were kind of ready for digging up anyway."

"One that Ronnie peed on?"

"So wash it." A dog-pee cabbage was thrust into my hands. As peace offerings go, it wasn't the greatest. But it was clearly the best I was going to get.

"Do I get a pee cabbage too?" asked Poppy.

Ailsa shrugged. "Want some asparagus?"

Unbelievable. I get a pee cabbage and Poppy gets asparagus? I don't know much about vegetables, but I do know there's a hierarchy.

While Ailsa cut the asparagus, Poppy and I made awkward small talk with Rowan. I was very distracted by the asparagus bed—I don't know if you've ever seen asparagus growing in the wild but it is *freaky*. I'm not sure what I'd expected, maybe some kind of asparagus tree? Or maybe that it grew underground like potatoes. But no, it just pokes straight out of the soil like alien fingers. Totally horrific.

"So it sounds like it's been one hell of a prenatal course so far," Rowan was saying.

"Yeah." I dragged my attention away from where Ailsa was decapitating asparagus. "I'm so sorry for breaking the news like that. I just wasn't thinking."

"It's fine," said Rowan with a pained smile. "Like my parents said, I don't think any of us had seen him for a long time. It was just . . . a shock."

"Of course," said Poppy gently. "And we're really sorry. It's not an easy thing to hear, even if you weren't close anymore."

How did she manage to say the right thing like that? I decided I should probably leave the interpersonal side of things to her. But I just had to ask . . .

"How come your parents and Mr. Oliver fell out?"

Rowan shot me a sharp look. "No one said anything about falling out."

"No, I just figured, if they hadn't spoken in so long . . . I mean, Penton's not a big place. You bump into people . . ." I trailed off. Rowan was looking angry—and perhaps just a little scared? Although admittedly that could be my imagination running away with me.

"The commune . . . hit a bad spot," he said reluctantly. "A while back. I guess it must be ten years ago now—Dad would know. My parents haven't really been back into town since then. I mean, why would they, they have everything they need right here." The look he gave me was practically flashing "no more questions" in neon.

I shut up—against my instincts. My brain was turning itself inside out. What had happened here ten years ago? And could it have any bearing on what had happened to Mr. Oliver last night?

"So what now?" Rowan asked. "Have they arrested anyone?"

"I don't think so, not yet. I think they're still trying to work out what happened. We both had visits from Inspector Harris this morning," I said.

Rowan's eyes widened. "Whoa, *Jane* Harris?" He turned to Ailsa. "Your *sister* is the investigating detective?"

Poppy and I swiveled to face Ailsa.

"Inspector Harris is your *sister*?" I asked. "No way!"

Ailsa's face had clammed up tighter than a . . . clam.

"I mean, that's cool," I tried to amend.

"No," she said. "It's not cool. And we're not talking about it."

But I had so many questions! Why did people keep stopping me from asking questions when there were so many intriguing ones just begging to be asked?

I opened my mouth to ask, probably ill-advisedly, what Ailsa had meant when she'd told Inspector Harris, aka her sister, that this murder "wasn't like last time." But at this moment, the voice of Camran broke in, probably saving me from being murdered with pruning shears.

"You all look terribly serious! Rowan, your mum's made scones. Why don't you all come and try some?"

WE MANAGED to escape the commune with a minimum of fuss by Poppy faking some Braxton Hicks contractions—quite convincingly, I thought. There was no way we were sticking around for a tea party that promised to be even more painful than the first. Still, Camran had looked somewhat suspicious as we beat a hasty retreat. Rowan had also made a swift exit, mumbling something incomprehensible under his breath and not making eye contact with anyone.

"So . . . something bleak happened there ten years ago, I'm thinking," I said as we tramped back down the path to the cars.

"Sounds like it," said Poppy, looking troubled. "There's definitely a story there. And probably not a happy one."

"No," I agreed. "Then there's Ailsa and Rowan—possibly a close family friend or possibly a casual school acquaintance, who's to say."

"Yep, I'm thinking there's a story there too."

"Then there's Ailsa and *Inspector Harris.* There's some interesting family history there if I'm any judge."

"Why does it feel like everywhere we turn there are secrets?" Poppy kicked a stone.

I had to agree. And however much we wanted to pretend otherwise, one of them circled around Lin and whatever her mum had argued with Mr. Oliver about. Probably best not to mention that, though.

"Hmm," I mumbled noncommittally. "Where to even begin."

"I'm not sure," she admitted. "But I kind of want to find out a bit more. What about you?"

I thought about it for a minute, not entirely sure what Poppy was suggesting. "I don't want to get in any trouble . . ." I began, cautiously.

"I don't mean anything serious, I just mean maybe we should ask a few more questions," Poppy said hurriedly. "Just in case . . ." She faltered. "Just in case Harris gets the wrong idea about Lin. I think it would be good to just, you know, give her a gentle nudge in the right direction, if she needs it."

I couldn't imagine Inspector Harris taking too kindly to any sort of nudging, gentle or otherwise. But I also couldn't deny my curiosity was piqued.

"I suppose it couldn't hurt to ask around a bit. Maybe find out a bit more about Mr. Oliver. And his argument with Rowan's parents. And if it has anything to do with what happened at the commune ten years ago." I was starting to warm to the subject already, against my better judgment. "That place has a weird vibe. I want to know what's going on there."

"Great!" said Poppy, her natural enthusiasm springing back to the surface. She was like one of those squishy balls that always pings back into shape. "We'll just do some really small-scale investigating, how does that sound?"

"Sherlock Lite," I agreed. "So, where do we start?"

"We should speak to everyone who was at the prenatal class," said Poppy. "Find out what everyone remembers from that evening."

"You know, I was just thinking it would be nice if we called on Hen tomorrow afternoon. See how she's doing with the new baby and all."

"Perfect," Poppy agreed. "We'll take her cookies."

"And pick her brains about this murder. And we need to get Ailsa on board," I continued. "Firstly, because she's in with the commune lot, and I've got a *lot* of questions there."

"And secondly," chipped in Poppy, "because her sister is Inspector Harris."

"Yeah, so the only remaining problem we have is the fact that she appears to hate us. And her sister. Possibly everyone, in fact."

"Speak for yourself. I got asparagus."

I looked gloomily at my pee cabbage.

CHAPTER 12

ON THE DRIVE home from Stricker's Wood I was feeling pretty smug about my first "mum" social interaction. Granted our dogs had broken into a hippy commune, I had clumsily announced a murder to old friends of the deceased and I'd been given a pee cabbage—but I also felt like Poppy and I had got on pretty well. Dare I say it, the beginnings of a friendship could be taking root.

Then I opened the trunk of the car and discovered that Helen had thrown up everywhere. Including all over my Barbor jacket, which I had chucked in the back with her.

It's a pretty grim thing to admit to, but I couldn't help noticing that the vomit smelled . . . different. Over the last year I'd had the pleasure of being introduced to an array of Helen vomits—the time she ate the air freshener, the time she drank Joe's lethal home brew, the time she licked a toad and the approximately 5,128 other times she has thrown up on us, our furniture or various guests for no discernible reason. Anyway, in comparison, this bout was almost—and I know this sounds weird—*fragrant*. It had a piny, resinous tang, slightly reminiscent of Christmas trees. Perhaps she'd been eating trees up in the woods—it sounded like the sort of thing she would do.

Given Helen's extensive back catalog of nonemergency vomits, I wasn't too concerned. However, when I pulled her out of the fetid trunk, she promptly fell over. This was more unusual. I propped her upright. She took a couple of steps, then fell over again. She lay there and looked at me with a faint expression of alarm. I was ten steps ahead of her and already reaching the dizzy heights of panic.

"Joe!" I yelled into the house. "Something's wrong with Helen!"

His reply from the depths of the house was supremely unconcerned. "What's new?"

"No, like *really* wrong!" I looked down at Helen, who had made no attempt to get up again. "I think she's dying!"

It seemed alarmingly possible. Helen was now trembling and pawing at her face in a distressed manner.

There was a scrambling from inside, and Joe half fell out of the house. We knelt beside Helen and I gently pulled her paws away from her face.

"Oh my God," breathed Joe. "What happened to her mouth?"

All around Helen's mouth angry red blisters had sprung up, livid against her black lips.

"We have to get her to the vet—holy shit!" Joe had bundled Helen up in his arms and turned to deposit her in the trunk, only to be faced with the sea of vomit.

"She can go on my lap." I was already in the passenger seat, stretching the belt over my bump.

It was the most stressful drive of my life, cradling the shivering Helen on my lap and expecting her to expire on me at any minute. By the time we reached the vet I was covered in dog sick and shaking almost as much as Helen.

The vet swung into action like a low-budget scene from *ER*. Within minutes, Helen was intubated and on a drip, and the vet turned her attention to me.

"You OK?" she asked. "You need a sedative or anything?"

I wasn't entirely sure whether, as a vet, she was qualified to be dosing pregnant women with sedatives, but I could see her point—I was weeping hysterically and hyperventilating.

"Is she going to die?" I managed to get out, between sobs. I had spent the last year bad-mouthing this beast to anyone who would listen, but the truth of the matter was that I was besotted with her in all her horrendous glory and would be broken if she died.

"Possibly, but then possibly not," said the vet brusquely, pulling back Helen's eyelid to inspect the whites of her eyes. It made her look like a dead fish. "She's young and healthy, she might pull through."

It wasn't quite the reassurance I'd been hoping for, but it did sound cautiously optimistic.

"What's wrong with her?" asked Joe quietly. I was a little surprised to see how shaken he looked. He hadn't always been fully on board with Project Helen, averring that she demanded much more than she gave back. He was right, of course, but it seemed a little churlish to hold it against her, in my opinion. She was only a dog, after all. But perhaps her brush with death had awakened his dormant fondness for her.

"Toxic shock," said the vet. "See the burns and blistering round her mouth? She's eaten something extremely toxic. Do you have any idea what it might have been?"

A wave of guilt washed over me. To be honest, it could have been any-thing. I hadn't exactly been paying close attention to her on our walk that morning, and she'd pretty much run rampant round the commune; who knows what she might have been snacking on up there.

"Could it have been a tree?" I asked tentatively.

The vet raised an eyebrow.

"I mean, I thought I could smell pine trees when she was sick," I clar-ified.

The vet looked thoughtful. "I don't think so," she said slowly. "She'd have to eat about two whole trees to make her this sick. But that's inter-esting . . ."

She looked at Helen again. "We'll need to keep her in overnight to get her fluids up and ensure that whatever it is clears out of her system. We'll also want to keep an eye on her liver and kidney function to check there hasn't been any damage. We could run toxicology bloodwork, which would give us a better idea of what caused the reaction, and whether there might be any further complications to look out for."

"Do it," Joe said quietly.

"It'll be expensive," warned the vet.

"She's insured," I sniffed. In fact, she was insured up to the hilt. We might be incompetents in many areas of adulting, but two weeks living with Helen had made it abundantly clear that this was a dog that needed the full package. We had no life insurance for ourselves, or home insurance—and in fact the best home insurance would have probably been to get rid of Helen, who was responsible for ninety-nine percent of domestic disasters—but Helen herself was insured up to and including breaking a toenail.

WE LEFT Helen to the tender mercies of the vet, who was peering inside Helen's ears when we departed, possibly having a look for her brain. The vet had promised to ring hourly with updates but seemed to think it likely that Helen would make a full recovery. I was less convinced that I would.

"How are we going to raise a child when I can't even walk the dog without her going into toxic shock?" I asked Joe as we drove home.

"It's not your fault," he replied. "You know what Helen's like. We can't have eyes on her all the time. Where were you walking her?"

"Just up in the woods." I realized that in the drama of Helen's collapse I hadn't even told him about our eventful walk. I launched into an account of the day's events. When I started talking about the commune, I saw his hands tighten on the steering wheel.

"Well, she could have eaten anything up there," he said, sounding exasperated. "Honestly, Alice, why do you have to get yourself in these situations?"

This seemed a little unfair—I was pretty sure this was the first time I'd gone on a dog walk and ended up at a hippy commune that may or may not have poisoned my dog.

"So you do think it's my fault?" I asked in a small voice.

He sighed. "No, I don't think it's your fault. But I *do* think you should steer clear of this commune from now on."

"You think she ate something there?"

"I don't know, Alice. Probably. Just stay away, OK?"

CHAPTER 13

I'D EXPECTED TO be collecting a pretty subdued Helen from the vet's the next morning, but she appeared to be full of the joys of life. She threw herself on me in a frenzy of face-licking, ending in turning a full somersault and sprawling on her back at my feet. She then proceeded to start licking the floor.

"That's an odd dog you've got there," said the vet cheerfully. I grimaced; I mean I'd said it myself enough times, but coming from a medical professional that was practically a diagnosis.

"Is she OK?" I asked, hauling Helen back onto her feet.

"Seems fine," the vet said. "In fact, she bounced back remarkably quickly."

"What was it?" asked Joe, who had, unusually for him, taken the morning off work to collect Helen. I chalked this up as further evidence that secretly he had a deep and abiding love for Helen, no matter how many of his socks she ate.

"We won't know until the toxicology report comes in, which will take a couple of days. In the meantime, give her one of these charcoal tablets once a day, which should absorb any remaining toxins in her system. And, of course, if she shows anymore symptoms bring her back in immediately."

We pocketed the alarming-looking black pills, cheerfully asked the vet to send the (whopping) bill direct to our long-suffering insurance company and shepherded our odd dog out the door. I was never letting her out of my sight again.

* * *

"YOU BROUGHT Helen?" Poppy looked appalled when I met her outside Hen's house later that day. I instantly realized I'd made a terrible mistake. Helen is a social abomination, and I can't make friends with people while my dog eats her own shit in the background and then tries to lick their babies. But it was too late to back out now, we were at the gate to Hen's house.

"She's actually pretty well behaved," I said defensively. Poppy looked quite offended by the enormity of this lie. She'd only known Helen forty-eight hours, but Helen can make quite an impression in a very short space of time. Like an unexpected tax bill. Or being mugged.

"Anyway, I didn't want to leave her alone." I changed tactics. "She's been extremely ill."

"All the more reason not to bring her," retorted Poppy. "She is almost definitely going to throw up in Hen's house. And Hen is going to invoice you for the cleaning bill."

This seemed extremely likely. Even the exterior of Hen's house was bizarrely pristine, with those funny little hedges that have been trimmed into balls (seriously, what is the point?) and elegant columns either side of the front door, as if we were visiting a Greek temple, rather than an upper-middle-class residence.

"Are you sure this is her house?" I found myself whispering.

"Absolutely," said Poppy briskly. "Dot gave very precise directions. Also, isn't this exactly the sort of house you'd expect Hen to live in?"

She had a point.

Dot had been criminally delighted to hand over Hen's address when Poppy contacted her saying we wanted to pop by to congratulate her, privacy laws be damned.

Hen answered the door looking remarkably well put together for the new mother of a two-day-old baby. She was wearing lemon-yellow jeans and a white nursing top that was unacceptably crisp and free of sick stains. I, on the other hand, had just noticed a small splash of dog vomit on my left shoe.

"Come through to the conservatory." Hen ushered us through. That's right, she had a conservatory. It was a *nice* house. Not a Greek temple, granted, but very, very nice.

"Banker?" I mouthed to Poppy as we were led through the immaculate house.

"Almost definitely," she whispered back.

Every room we passed looked Instagram-ready. There was none of the clutter you'd expect with a new baby. Joe and I were already living in the eye of the baby storm, and ours hadn't even arrived yet.

The conservatory was, of course, delightful. Charming wickerwork furniture and overflowing with glossy houseplants, not a shriveled leaf in sight. A plate of cookies and tea *in a teapot* materialized before Poppy or I could even offer to make a cuppa, which I believe is the correct etiquette when visiting a new parent.

"It's so nice of you to visit," Hen said, and she actually sounded like she meant it. Like the polite hostess she was, she made no mention of Helen, although I thought I saw her wince just a little at the fine trail of dog hair now meandering through her house, and the miscellaneous particulates that puffed up as Helen settled herself on a rug that looked like it had never been walked on. Hen took the chair next to the bassinet in which, I assumed, the baby lay sleeping. I felt weirdly eager to see the baby.

That might sound like a stupid thing to say—I was about to have a baby, of course I was interested. But the truth is, I'd never been one of those "baby people." When women used to bring their babies into work I'd always been terrified they might ask me if I wanted to hold their child. Because I really, really didn't. Babies scream as soon as I awkwardly hold them and I don't know how to talk to toddlers. I've always worried that this makes me look like a "bad woman" somehow. Thanks, centuries of gender stereotyping and reductionism. I really hoped it was going to be different with my own. But now? I realized I actually *wanted* to see this baby—maybe even hold it, if I got carried away with maternal hormones.

"She's sleeping at the moment," said Hen, catching me craning for a look in the bassinet. "Want to take a look?" She sounded pretty casual, but it was that studied sort of casual. Very similar, in fact, to my carefully nonchalant response of "Yeah, go on then."

We clustered round and looked at the baby in silence for a bit. Part of me wanted to wake her up so we could see her do some baby stuff, but clueless as I may be in the parenting stakes, I do know enough to never wake a sleeping baby.

"Name?" I whispered.

"Not yet," replied Hen, also whispering. "Haven't found anything that fits."

I nodded sagely, as if trying to picture what would fit the wrinkled little doll in front of me. Prune? Raisin? In Penton, I doubted anyone would blink an eye at those names.

"So, how's it going?" asked Poppy, when we'd done our fill of baby staring and retreated to the wicker furniture—which, it turned out, was more stylish than comfortable.

"Yeah, all right," said Hen. "I mean, under the circumstances. Not quite what I expected, but then I doubt anyone dreams of the first twenty-four hours of parenthood involving a visit from the police."

"Oh, you had a visit too?" I was surprised. I'd assumed they'd at least let Hen have a couple of days to recover from the whole giving-birth thing before interviewing her. Although to be honest Hen looked more on top of things than I could ever dream of being, baby or no baby.

"Yeah, that Inspector Harris called round yesterday. Said it was best to get it over with while things were still 'fresh in my mind'"—Hen rolled her eyes—"if I was OK with that. I told her all that was fresh in my mind was the sensation of stretching my vagina wide enough for a bowling ball. She didn't stick around long after that." She smirked.

I laughed. I could imagine the inspector's prim face at that. Hen looked justifiably pleased with herself.

"Also, I kept having to get my boob out to feed the baby, and I think that put her off even more. Plus, it's not like I saw a huge amount from where I was. What about you guys?"

"I mean, I saw a lot, but none of it's going to be of much help to the inspector." I cringed when I realized I'd basically just reminded this woman, whom I barely knew, that I'd spent most of my Saturday night hovering around her nether regions. Fortunately, she laughed—then clapped a hand over her mouth and cautiously peeked inside the bassinet.

"Honestly, it's kind of best when she's asleep," she admitted. "When she's awake I don't really know what to do with her."

"Oh God, I was hoping once you had your own you just sort of magically knew what to do," said Poppy nervously.

"Same. I mean, it's not like we learned a huge amount at prenatal class," I agreed.

"Well, you've still got one more class, haven't you?" said Hen.

I hadn't really thought about it; technically, we had another class scheduled the following weekend. "I don't know. I mean, if we do they'll have to find a new venue. Our old one's a crime scene now. Blue tape, police guard, the works."

"Not to mention that the whole class *and* the teacher are suspects in a murder case," added Hen.

Poppy and I shared a significant look. Which was not lost on Hen. She leaned forward, eyes narrowed. "You think so too?"

"I . . . well, I mean it *could* have been one of us. Well, not you, obviously. And not Poppy. And it wasn't me. And I mean, I know Inspector Harris thinks Lin . . . but we're pretty sure she wasn't . . ." I trailed off as Poppy glared at me.

"Inspector Harris thinks Lin what?" Hen narrowed her eyes.

I went red and didn't say anything. Poppy and I should probably have got our story straight before we'd embarked on this conversation.

"She thinks Lin had something to do with the murder?" pressed Hen. "Why? What's her motivation supposed to be?"

"He was her uncle," Poppy supplied reluctantly.

"Oh!"

"But I mean, that's not a motivation, really, is it?" I cut in hurriedly, feeling Poppy's eyes on me. "It's just, I don't know, genetics."

"Genealogy, you mean?" said Hen.

"Yeah, that." Of course I don't know what genealogy is. I might look it up on Google later, but to be quite frank I don't know how to spell it— and also don't care.

"So Lin's the main suspect—" said Hen thoughtfully.

"Hold up," broke in Poppy. "Lin is *not* the main suspect. Harris has been a bit irritated with her, but if she thinks Lin had anything to do with it then she's barking up the wrong tree. And if she can't see that, then we'll just have to . . . do a bit of digging ourselves."

"So you're investigating the murder," said Hen flatly.

It wasn't a question.

She sat back and surveyed us. "OK, fine, I'm in."

I exchanged a startled glance with Poppy. I wasn't aware we'd been asking Hen to join our . . . whatever this was. But I certainly wasn't about to tell her that. She'd probably kick me out.

"Er, great," I managed.

"Yeah, whatever. So tell me what you've got so far."

We filled Hen in on our visit to the commune the previous day and the questions this had raised. She looked skeptical.

"It's not much to go on," she objected. "So Mr. Oliver used to be friends with Camran and they fell out—people fall out literally all the time. It doesn't mean they *kill* each other."

"We're not saying Camran killed Mr. Oliver," Poppy interrupted. "But what did they argue about that's so bad they haven't spoken for ten years? And why would they try and hide the fact that they fell out? Rowan was really weird about it."

"And, oh, I can't explain," I said, "it's more a feeling than anything concrete that we've found out, and I know that sounds pretty woolly, but there's definitely something a bit off at the commune. They were really upset when they heard he was dead—or maybe upset is the wrong word . . . They were . . . scared." I hadn't realized it before, but as I said it, I realized that it was true. Camran and Hazel had definitely been scared. "But then they tried to cover it up," I continued, following my train of thought. "They acted like it was no big deal to them. In fact, they were a bit too insistent on that. I mean, it's a big deal if anyone is murdered, especially if it's someone you used to know, even if you hadn't seen them for ages."

"Well," said Hen slowly, "ten years is a long time. If they really haven't seen him in that long—"

"And ten years ago is also when Rowan left the commune," Poppy cut in. "And, in his words, the commune 'hit a bad spot.'"

"Yeah, which he was *totally* weird about," I continued. "He wouldn't say anything more about it. But I'm thinking this 'bad spot' was somehow linked to Camran's row with Mr. Oliver. And it was bad enough that they never spoke again and, according to Rowan, his parents have hardly left the commune since."

"Or," Poppy interjected, "could it have been bad enough that they'd commit murder over it? But then, why ten years later? That seems unlikely. In which case, are the two totally unrelated? Is it just a coincidence?"

"In terms of motive, Camran is probably at the top of the list," I said. "Although, I'll admit, it's a pretty short list right now."

"How would he have got in, though?" asked Hen. "I didn't hear anyone come into the shop."

I snorted. You could probably have marched a brass band through the shop and Hen wouldn't have noticed. Birthing a child is pretty all-consuming, as it turns out. Understandably.

Hen looked annoyed when I pointed this out. "Fine, it's a possibility. So there's probably something worth looking into up at the commune."

I shared a frustrated glance with Poppy. There was more than "something"! I had the irritated feeling that Hen's involvement could turn our little investigation into the Hen & Co. show. Anyway, the commune angle was pretty much all we had to work with for the time being.

"What would you do next?" I asked, trying not to sound accusatory.

"Talk to Ailsa," said Hen definitely.

"Oh?"

"Definitely. Didn't you hear her talking to Inspector Harris? There's history there."

"Oh that," I said, feeling just a touch smug at knowing more than Hen about this. "They're sisters."

"*Sisters?*" Hen looked suitably shocked, I was pleased to note. "God, I can't imagine two more different sisters. Ailsa's so spirited and . . . and . . . I don't know, *wild*. And she's beautiful—under all those disgusting dreadlocks!" She pulled a face. "Inspector Harris is so uptight and *plain*."

This description of Ailsa surprised me. I had to say I hadn't thought of her in those terms. And Hen seemed to have formed a pretty strong opinion of her based on one and a half prenatal meetings.

"Anyway, that's all the more reason to bring her on board," said Hen, moving on briskly. "She'll be a valuable asset. First, we should ask her for a copy of the postmortem report. I'm sure she can get that from her sister."

"I'm not so sure, they didn't seem . . . close," Poppy demurred. "And I'm not sure how much Ailsa will want to help us. We saw her yesterday and she was . . . spiky."

"Also," I said slowly, because what I was about to say wasn't something you comment on lightly, "do we need to be a bit careful what we say to Ailsa? I mean, I know Inspector Harris is her sister, and that kind of explains their little row at the crime scene, but Ailsa did say something about it 'not being like last time' and her 'not being involved this time.' I mean, I definitely don't want to sound like I'm accusing her of anything, but doesn't that sound a bit like Ailsa's been in trouble with the police before?"

There was a tense silence.

"You don't think she had anything to do with *this*, though, right?" asked Hen.

"Absolutely not," I clarified—possibly more forcefully than the situation required, because I couldn't help feeling that there was definitely a fair bit that Ailsa wasn't telling us. "I just think maybe it's worth, I don't know, asking her what she meant by those comments."

"Well volunteered," said Poppy bracingly. "And while you're at it you can ask her for the postmortem report."

I had sort of walked into that one.

"Would we understand the report anyway, even if we got our hands on it?" I asked, changing tack. "I pretty much failed biology at school. My teacher said I lacked a proper scientific approach."

"*You* almost certainly won't," said Hen, and her dismissive tone made me bristle a little. "But I will."

"Oh yeah?" said Poppy, clearly feeling a little put out by this slight on our intelligence.

"Yes. I have a degree in forensic biology."

"Well. OK. That should do it," said Poppy, a little stiffly.

"OK, science nerds, let's see if we can get our hands on that report then!" I tried to lighten the atmosphere.

Poppy nodded at me. "You should speak to her about it—she likes you."

"Er, she hates me?" I corrected her. "I got the pee cabbage, remember."

Hen raised an eyebrow.

"Don't ask."

"I don't want to know."

"She invited you round to her house," insisted Poppy.

"I don't think she invited me. She told me I could pick up some rhubarb if I wanted to. And I don't want to. What the hell would I do with rhubarb?"

"Eat it?" said Poppy, rolling her eyes. "Look, just go round to hers, get some rhubarb, butter her up and get that postmortem report."

"I don't think Ailsa responds to buttering. She's more of a vegan spread kind of girl."

Hen was looking annoyed. I could sense I was on the brink of being kicked out of an investigation I wasn't even sure I wanted to be a part of.

"So what else do we know," I said, trying to show helpfulness and move things along. "Hen, what about you and Antoni? Did you guys know Mr. Oliver at all? Or the commune lot?"

"Not really," said Hen thoughtfully. "I'd spoken to Mr. Oliver once or twice in the shop. I bought that clary sage off him the other day."

"Do you think it actually made you go into labor?" I asked interestedly. My knowledge of herbal remedies is pretty much nil. My mum used to burn incense every so often, but I'm pretty sure she got her incense sticks from TJ Maxx, which doesn't feel legit hippy.

"No," said Hen bluntly. "At the very most it might have encouraged things along when they were already starting. Antoni flipped out at me though, told me I was playing Russian roulette with mine and the baby's health." She rolled her eyes. "We can probably strike him off our list of suspects, by the way. He grew up here but he left fifteen years ago and I don't think he's been back since. Not until we moved here last year. Nature's Way wouldn't even have been here when he left. And it's not exactly his kind of place—I highly doubt he'd set foot in there until the prenatal class. I can't see him popping in for a quick Reiki session."

I laughed, picturing the besuited Antoni hanging out with Mr. Oliver at Nature's Way, discussing the merits of Reiki versus reflexology.

"Is it worth asking him about the commune, though?"

"I can try," said Hen. "But I can almost guarantee he won't know much about it. Antoni works in pharmaceuticals—hippy communes and crystal healing are about as far away from Antoni's world as the moon."

"Pharmaceuticals?" I wasn't entirely surprised, given the guy had worn a suit to a prenatal class. "But he grew up here? This place is *marinated* in essential oils!"

"I wouldn't be surprised if that wasn't part of the reason," Hen said, and I could see her point. "He *hates* herbal remedies—and he's an absolute stickler for following the medical guidelines. The other day he gave me a full-on lecture because he saw me wash down my pregnancy vitamin with a cup of tea, when 'the leaflet clearly states you should swallow it with a cold drink.'" Hen rolled her eyes.

"Where is he, by the way?" I asked, realizing I had neither seen nor heard him the whole time we'd been there.

"Oh, he had to go up to London," Hen said casually. "Work."

That seemed a bit off to me. I know paternity leave isn't *great*, but I was pretty sure you were entitled to more than a day.

"He, er, didn't want to be a bit closer to home?" I asked. "What with the new baby and all that?"

"I'm managing perfectly well on my own," said Hen stiffly.

"Oh, I mean, of course! You're doing great! I'm sure on day two I'll be covered in baby sick and weeping into a muslin." I'd just said it to flatter Hen, but my stomach knotted a bit at how true those words were. Not to mention the realization that this was now my very immediate future.

"Mind you, I'm not actually sure how much help Joe will be when the baby's here . . ." I mused. I mean, I love the guy, sure. But there were times when he actually made *me* look competent. And I had to admit I was . . . concerned. I couldn't quite put my finger on it—to be honest I'd tried not to think too much about it—but since we'd decided to leave London, and the imminent arrival had become so much more imminent, Joe had definitely been a little withdrawn on the matter of the baby. Baby nerves were to be expected—my body and brain were one jangling mess of them!—but I just wished he'd say something instead of retreating into his phone every evening. It felt as though we'd only discussed the practicalities of the baby of late—and even that only infrequently.

Haltingly, I tried to say something along these lines to Hen and Poppy, feeling horribly like I was being disloyal to Joe. I barely knew these women, after all—he knew them even less! And here I was coloring their opinion of him before he'd even had a chance to make an impression. I had invited him along today, but he'd opted to work. Being freelance, Joe could technically take all the pat leave he wanted, but being freelance there was always a fear that twenty-four hours without communication would see his clients evaporate, never to be seen again. I worried, though; it was going to be more difficult for Joe to meet people in Penton than me—I had a rather obvious point of connection with Poppy and Hen. And Ailsa, I suppose. The last thing I should probably be doing was complaining about him to virtual strangers. It was so *nice* to see some sympathetic faces though, and hear some fairly baseless (given they knew neither Joe nor me) but still comforting reassurance. And it was a relief to know I wasn't on my own with this.

"Antoni's the same," said Hen, slightly awkwardly—probably suffering the same pangs of disloyalty. "He's just been quieter and quieter as the due date got closer. Not that he was ever a particularly loud person. He's always kept himself to himself, and recently, just more so."

"Yep, sounds like Joe," I said gloomily.

"I think it's difficult for the partners," said Poppy gently. "We go through the whole pregnancy thing, we have this really physical buildup to the main event. But for them? They watch us going through it all, but they're kind of on the sidelines. And then the baby arrives and it's like, BAM, instant parent. No wonder they freak a bit. I know Lin's really worried about it."

"Yeah, but you *know* she's worried about it," I said. "She actually told you."

Poppy nodded.

"Well, Antoni's not said a thing," said Hen. "That's part of the problem. Right now, I've got enough on my plate trying to work out what *she* wants"—she gestured at the bassinet—"without having to interpret his endless silences as well. If something's wrong, can't he just tell me?"

"It's like—just say what's on your mind!" I agreed.

"But you know guys," said Hen. "They won't tell you there's a problem until their arm drops off or something."

"Men," said Poppy, quite unsympathetically I thought.

"I suppose Lin is all sweetness and light?" I grumbled.

Poppy laughed. "Absolutely not. She's driven me mad at times during the pregnancy—so overprotective. But she's all right. To be honest, I'm the one that took a bit of convincing on the whole baby front. Lin was the broody one. But, well, I'm sure we'll encounter more than our fair share of troubles along the way."

This was no doubt true.

"It was pretty bold of you guys, moving house just a few weeks before the baby arrives," said Hen to me. "How did that go? Moves are so stressful; Antoni barely spoke to me for a week after we moved here—something about the kitchen cabinets, I think."

"It was pretty shaky," I admitted. "But better now than a few weeks *after* the baby arrives."

"True," she conceded. "What brought you guys down to Penton anyway?"

"Meh. We wanted to get out of London. We didn't massively fancy trying to raise a child in, like, two square foot of space—most of which is taken up by Helen. So it was pretty much a pin in the map. I think Joe found Penton initially? I can't remember how. But we liked the look of it, so here we are! What about you, Hen—you said you and Antoni moved back here last year?"

"Yeah, when we got married. Like I said, he grew up round here, but his parents moved away years ago, before I met him. I think they're somewhere up in Scotland now?"

"You sound unsure about where your in-laws actually are." I laughed, but Hen didn't.

"It's ... complicated," said Hen. "Antoni's sister passed away—cancer—and his parents more or less shut themselves off. To be honest, Antoni doesn't really talk about his family; we never see them, and that's his decision."

Poppy and I nodded somberly. There was a slightly awkward silence, broken by a knock on the conservatory window. We all jumped a mile as we saw Dot's cheerful face smiling in at us, her curly hair escaping from under an exuberant headscarf.

One hand clutching her chest, Hen opened the conservatory door and Dot stepped in.

"Well, isn't this nice!" She beamed, with truly terrible timing, given what Hen had just been telling us. "I do so hope that these classes will really bring the mums together. Create bonds that you will cherish for life. You are each other's biggest support! You've clearly already formed such a *connection*."

As awkwardness-inducing speeches go it was a pretty good one, really reminding the three of us that we barely knew each other, and that while we may have reached the investigate-a-murder-together stage, we were definitely not ready for sleepovers and brushing each other's hair.

"We were . . . just having tea," I said lamely.

"Lovely!" Dot looked like nothing could have delighted her more. "Decaf of course, I hope!" She gave us a horribly roguish wink. "Well, I won't interrupt your *girly time*"—all three of us winced—"I just wanted to drop this round for you, Hen dear."

She popped a sparkly pink gift bag on the coffee table next to the tea and cookies, gave the chirpiest wave, all wiggly fingers, and breezed off again. It felt like we'd been speed-mugged by a fairy godmother.

Hen sniffed. "She didn't even want to see the baby."

"She has bought you a present, though," I pointed out. "Er, should we have done that? Sorry."

Hen waved this away. "It's fine, I won't get you one either."

This seemed fair.

Poppy and I leaned forward expectantly as Hen dug into the bag, hoping for something truly ludicrous. We were not disappointed. Horrified, scarred, traumatized, yes—but no one could accuse Dot of disappointing. Hen drew out a Tupperware, popped the lid, and—

"FUCK!"

"HOLY SHIT!"

"WHAT THE HELL?"

I shot back from the table so fast I overbalanced and landed on my ass. Hen had dropped the offending article on the floor and it slithered toward me, leaving a bloody trail. I scooted backward on my butt until I hit the conservatory wall.

"Get it away from me!"

Poppy slammed the Tupperware back over it, like it was a spider making a bid for freedom. We all finally drew breath.

"Is that . . . a *human heart*??" I asked, trying not to gag.

"Is it a threat?" asked Hen, looking utterly horrified. "Is Dot the murderer, and I'm next?!"

Poppy lifted the Tupperware and gingerly prodded the lump of flesh.

"It's not a heart," she said. "I think . . . I think it's your placenta, Hen."

HALF AN hour later, we were still reeling. The unexpected delivery of a placenta, or perhaps more accurately our totally legit response to it, had of course woken Hen's baby. She had screeched wildly, in turn causing Helen to totally freak out. But when Helen had poked her nose into the bassinet to work out why this basket was so loud, the baby had unexpectedly shut up. For the last ten minutes both the baby and Helen had been staring at the same blank patch on the wall, apparently transfixed. Every now and then the baby would give a small chuckling sound, and Helen would share a look with her like "I know, right."

"What are they doing?" asked Hen, sounding disconcerted.

"I don't know. Connecting?" I suggested.

"With what?"

"Each other."

"No offense to your dog, but I don't think I really want my baby connecting with her."

This was fair enough. It was only some very quick thinking (and lunging) on Poppy's part that had stopped Helen from eating Hen's placenta. I couldn't blame Hen for not warming to her. That's a weird start to any relationship.

The placenta had been unceremoniously dumped in the bin by Hen, who seemed quite offended by the delivery.

"Don't you want to . . . I don't know, bury it or something?" I had asked, gesturing to the immaculate lawn rolling away from the conservatory.

"It's a garden, not a graveyard for offcuts," she had replied.

Extremely tentative exploration of the gift bag uncovered a card with a cheerful smiling cat on it and the legend CON-CAT-ULATIONS. I mean, it's barely even a pun. Personally, I wasn't sure what was more offensive, the card or the Tupperware of placenta.

The card read:

> Dear Hen,
> Congratulations! What a spectacular delivery!
> It was extremely powerful. I hope you are resting up and feeling
> well. I saved your placenta for you—it will aid your recovery. If
> you need any tips on how to prepare it do give me a ring.
> Best wishes,
> Dot

There was a shocked silence.

"Prepare it?" I asked, not really wanting an answer.

"What the hell is she on about?" asked Hen.

"I think . . ." said Poppy slowly. "I think she wants you to eat it?"

Hen gagged.

"Lots of women do," said Poppy. "I think it's very rich in iron or something. Or you can send it off and some company will make it into little pills for you."

"Isn't that, like, cannibalism?" I wondered.

"I think it's only cannibalism if you eat someone else," mused Poppy. "I don't think it counts if you eat yourself. So if *you* ate it, then yeah, that would be cannibalism."

"No one is eating my placenta," Hen broke in.

"Was your delivery spectacular?" I asked, trying to change the subject.

"I would say so," said Hen, sounding slightly miffed. I wasn't sure if this was because I'd cast shade on her spectacular delivery, or because I didn't want to eat her placenta.

CHAPTER 14

WHEN I ARRIVED home I found a note from Joe saying that he was working from the pub. Freelancing has its upsides. Without him around, I felt a little lost. I tried to distract myself with some enforced nesting. It was my first day of maternity leave that didn't involve packing or moving house, and given the oddness of the past couple of days, I felt like I should do something normal and maternity-ish.

I'd heard a lot about this "nesting" instinct. "You'll know the baby's coming soon when you start to bleach the baseboards and disinfect the light switches," Joe's mum told me confidently. A friend told me how she reordered all her Tupperwares by size the day before her water broke. Another friend spent the week running up to her labor dusting the houseplants and descaling the kettle. To which my only response was, what is this, and should I be doing it?

I had been cautiously looking forward to experiencing this surge of hitherto unfamiliar domestic fervor. And, well, no time like the present. Perhaps I would find myself inspired by Hen's immaculate house. So, I cautiously tried dusting the excitingly named dragon plant languishing in the corner. Most of its leaves dropped off.

I glanced at the pile of unopened boxes in the corner of the sitting room and immediately discounted them. I was sure that would come under "heavy lifting." I opened the cupboard under the sink and a jumble of discolored Tupperwares began a slow and steady avalanche toward me. *Tupperwares.* Oh great. Dot and her Tupperware party had even ruined sensible food storage solutions for me.

I glanced at the clock. Joe wouldn't be home for at least a couple of hours. I supposed I should get used to being home alone without him. Two weeks after the baby arrived his paternity leave would disappear and it would be back to work for him, leaving me to figure out what to do with myself—and the baby—for the next twelve months.

One dreamy day we will achieve parenting equality. Where women's careers don't disappear in a puff of talcum powder and where men aren't treated as though they don't know one end of a baby from another. We're making progress, don't get me wrong. For a start, Joe was actually intending to be present at the birth of his first child. My dad, some thirty years ago, had missed my grand entrance, opting to pop into town and buy a pair of shoes instead, followed by two days' annual leave before his boss started ringing him and asking when he was going to stop messing about and get back to the office. My mum had never worked again. Whereas if I was really lucky, I'd be allowed to go back to my job and continue working there for another decade with no promotion or pay rise due to my "lack of commitment to the company." Joe would almost certainly get a promotion within a year of the baby's birth, as most new fathers do.

I prodded gloomily at a dark corner with a feather duster, and leaped back as an enraged spider, which had probably lain undisturbed for centuries, emerged.

My phone buzzed, and I scrambled for it. "LAURA" was flashing up on the screen—Joe's mum.

"Hi!" I was genuinely pleased to hear from her—and not just because it gave me an excuse to abandon dusting. I liked Joe's mum. She was, in so many ways, like Joe—scatty, haphazard, ever so slightly chaotic—but while Joe always seemed to be fighting against these characteristics in himself, she embodied the phrase "laissez-faire." She also called me approximately fifty times as often as my own mum, who would most likely call me in October to wish me happy birthday (my birthday is in June) and be surprised, and horrified, to discover she was a grandmother. I had told Mum, of course, multiple times, but it always seemed to coincide with some other drama—a broken nail, a spilled cocktail, my dad wearing Crocs—and I wasn't entirely convinced the news had registered. With my parents living out their expat dream on the Costa del Sol (don't ask), they were more than just geographically distant. Joe's mum, on the other hand, had been deeply involved in the whole pregnancy process; she and Joe were a small family of two, and she was delighted to be adding to their numbers.

"I hope you don't mind me calling, love," she began.

"Not at all! What's up?"

After we'd exchanged the usual pleasantries—she asking about the baby, me asking about Cribbins, her elderly (and horrible) cat—she got on to what I could tell she really wanted to discuss.

"I just wanted to ask you about . . . Joe," she said hesitantly.

"Yes?" I felt myself tense up.

"It's probably nothing. It's just, he didn't answer any of my calls this weekend. I'm probably being a silly overbearing mum," she gave a slightly brittle laugh, "but I was just a bit worried. It's not like him. Is he . . . OK?"

I was about to say yes, of course he was, when I realized I was answering without thinking, responding according to thirty years of ingrained social niceties. But the truth was, I was a little worried about Joe, too.

"I don't know," I sighed. "I mean yes, he's fine"—as I heard her sharp intake of breath on the other end of the line—"but he has been a bit quiet recently."

"Has anything happened?"

"No, not that I'm aware of. I think it's just pre-baby nerves, you know?" I was already regretting having said anything. I really didn't feel like rehashing the conversation I'd had with Poppy and Hen earlier, especially to Joe's mum.

"He'll be fine." I tried to sound reassuring.

"You don't think it's the move, do you?" she asked anxiously. "It's a big thing you've done, uprooting yourselves like that just before the baby arrives."

"The move went fine." I tried not to sound too exasperated. Like Maya, Joe's mum had been pretty anti our move to Penton. If anything, she'd argued, we should be moving closer to her in Manchester, so that she could be on hand to help with the baby.

"We're actually really pleased with our move here," I pressed on. "We're settling in really well. We've met some nice people, there's great countryside for dog walking—Helen loves it here!" As if Helen were any sort of arbiter of good taste . . .

"You don't think Joe's struggling with the move?" she was still saying. "It's not the easiest of towns. Or, I don't know, you don't think"—she hesitated—"anyone's said anything to upset him, or anything?"

This seemed like an odd thing to say. As a middle-class white heterosexual cis man, Joe wasn't exactly a target for hurtful comments. And who would have said anything—the monosyllabic bartender at the pub? The elderly lady with the cat basket in the vet's waiting room?

"No? What would anyone say to Joe?"

"Oh, I don't know," she sighed. "I'm probably just being overprotective. A mother's prerogative. You'll learn all about that soon enough."

I wondered. I've never been the overprotective, overinvolved sort. But everything people kept telling me about motherhood seemed to suggest I was going to undergo a complete personality transplant after giving birth.

"I think he's OK," I said. "I think maybe he just needs a bit more time to adjust. But we're looking after each other, don't you worry. And I'll ask him to give you a call this evening."

"Thanks, love." She didn't sound entirely convinced. "Yes, you two look after each other now. I'm so glad you've got each other."

I felt a bit guilty at that—my comment had definitely not been pointed, but she had been a single mum. Joe's dad had left before Joe was born—I wasn't sure of the ins and outs, but his mum never talked about him. I was, quite frankly, terrified about the upcoming baby and how Joe and I would manage; the levels of competence and self-sacrifice required to be a single parent blew my mind.

"We'd love to see you soon," I said, trying to make up for my unwitting blunder. "Maybe you could pop down before the baby arrives."

"Maybe, love, maybe," she said noncommittally. I got the sense she wouldn't be packing her overnight bag anytime soon. I did feel a bit bad; maybe we should have moved closer to her. She'd been so excited when we'd told her about the baby, but since we'd decided to move down here, her desire to visit every five minutes had cooled off. You couldn't exactly pop down to the Cotswolds from Manchester.

"Well, speak soon then!"

"Bye, love, take care."

After I'd hung up I realized I had, somehow, failed to mention the murder. It seemed a pretty big thing to forget, but my mind had been on Joe. Oh well, he would tell her about it next time he spoke to her.

I carried on failing to "nest"—pottering around the house and moving things about aimlessly, just enough for it to be annoying when I couldn't find anything later—but something was niggling at the back of my mind. Someone had said something today that had struck a wrong chord, but I couldn't quite put my finger on it . . .

I DRAGGED Joe out on a dog walk almost as soon as he got home. Helen went predictably mad with joy at being out with *both* her owners. She showcased her delight by rolling in some horseshit before we'd even got to the end of the lane.

On the climb up the hill behind our house, I filled Joe in on PlacentaGate. He was, understandably, shocked and appalled. This seemed to me to be the appropriate response to receiving an actual human organ in a Tupperware. We whiled away the climb inventing wilder and wilder placenta-based recipes for Hen to cook up.

"Parmesan placenta fries," Joe suggested. "Gettit? Like polenta but placenta?" I laughed—even though I do think having to spell out your own jokes detracts from them a bit.

I waited until we were high up on the hillside before mentioning my phone call from his mum. The views out over the surrounding countryside and the brisk spring breeze felt so cleansing. It was the opposite of that tactic beloved by parents everywhere, when they wait until you're trapped in the car with them to have an awkward conversation.

"Your mum rang me," I said casually.

"Oh yes?" Joe was standing with his head tilted back, his eyes slightly narrowed into the wind. Next to him, Helen had assumed an identical position, ears blowing in the breeze. The two of them looked like an advert for Cotswold Outdoor, or *Horse & Hound*. I have to say Joe was pulling it off more, though—the horse manure smeared down her flank was throwing shade on Helen's model looks.

"She's worried you're not settling into Penton life," I continued.

He laughed. "We've been here, like, two minutes."

"I know, right," I agreed. Who knew a single weekend could contain so much drama? "She was being a bit weird, to be honest," I continued thoughtfully. "Said she didn't want you to be upset—but I'm a bit worried that *she's* upset with *us*."

"Why would she be upset with us?"

"Oh, you know, I'm pretty sure she's offended that we moved down here rather than closer to her. I invited her down for a visit, but she didn't seem that keen. She and Maya could form the Hate Penton Society at this rate."

"Probably best if she doesn't come down. I mean, we've got quite a lot going on at the moment. We haven't finished unpacking; the house leaks like a sieve; there's so much stuff still to do before the baby arrives. We don't need more complications."

I was surprised. It wasn't like Joe to put off seeing his mum, or to lump her in with unpacking and DIY as a "complication."

"Is everything OK? With your mum, I mean?" I asked.

"Of course," he said shortly. "Why wouldn't it be?"

I could tell we were heading for confrontation territory, where Joe got snappy and I got annoyed. I decided to retreat.

"Well, maybe you could give her a call this evening," I suggested, thinking I'd leave it at that. "Oh! And I forgot to tell her about the murder! So you can fill her in on all the gory details."

"Don't be ghoulish, Alice," he said, and there was a definite chill in his voice now. "And I don't think we should say anything to Mum about that."

"Seriously?" I shot Joe a skeptical look.

"I just don't want to worry her," he continued. "Like you said, she's not the biggest fan of us moving here. Let's not give her anything to back that up."

"But—"

"Just leave it, Alice."

So I left it.

CHAPTER 15

THE NEXT MORNING I still hadn't got over PlacentaGate. I may *never* get over PlacentaGate. I was also having doubts about our decision to poke our noses into this whole police investigation.

"What else are we going to do until these babies arrive?" argued Poppy over the phone. "I started mat leave one week ago and I'm already bored."

I had to admit I was feeling pretty much the same. While I had a to-do list as long as my arm I also had zero intention of actually doing any of the things on it.

"I don't know," I replied weakly. "What do normal pregnant people do? Pregnancy yoga? Coffee mornings?"

"You can do some downward dogs with Ailsa when you collect your rhubarb, and we're meeting Hen for coffee on Friday—*with* the post-mortem report. And to get our hands on that you need to speak to Ailsa first. Why don't you go and see her this afternoon?"

"I have a midwife appointment at four."

"So go before."

I was silent.

"Oh my God!" Poppy sounded gleeful. "You're scared of her, aren't you!"

"I am not scared of Ailsa," I said, trying to sound dignified.

I was. I was totally scared of her.

Poppy laughed. "Do you need me to come and hold your hand?"

"No."
Yes, yes I do.

IN THE end Poppy did come with me. Not because I couldn't do it on my own. Because I totally could have done. But as Poppy had been at pains to point out, she had nothing to do. So, as I pointed out, she might as well come.

Ailsa's cottage was straight out of "Hansel and Gretel." It had this olde-worlde thing going on, all crumbling stone and a thatched roof that looked like a lot of things lived inside it—much like our new abode. But whereas our cottage looked like a disused cowshed, this one looked like something from a fairy tale. The garden was spectacular, all towering purple lupins and sprays of bright red nasturtiums and a sprawling wisteria climbing all over the face of the cottage—and no, I hadn't recognized the flowers, but Poppy had started my country education by naming some of the "more basic ones" for me.

The door was opened by a woman nearly as old as the cottage.

"Oh, sorry!" I immediately backed away and trod on Poppy's foot. "I think we've got the wrong house. We were looking for Ailsa."

The old woman chuckled. "This is Ailsa's house. I'm her nan. Come on in."

"This cottage is amazing," Poppy said politely, as we were led through the house. And it was, kind of—but I also kept expecting to see a spinning wheel in the corner. On the inside it was still fairy tale, for sure, but possibly because the wicked witch was shacked up there.

"Four hundred years old," said Nana Ailsa. "It's seen plenty, this cottage has. I'm sure these stones could tell a story or two. There's much happened in this place—good and bad."

"Is it haunted?" I asked. Because nothing can be that old and not have gathered a few ghosts. Nana Ailsa looked like she might have a few ghosts haunting her at that rate.

"Terribly haunted," she confirmed. "Mainly the ghosts of old ladies. I expect I shall join them some day."

Well, that was officially creepy.

"This used to be a witch's cottage," Nana Ailsa continued. *Knew it!*

"It's got magic steeped in the stones. Keeps the ghosts hanging about. It can get pretty crowded of an eve, all those old ladies with nothing to do but natter natter natter." She led us down a corridor so dark I had to run my hand along the wall so I didn't trip on the uneven stone flags underfoot.

"You're not telling them about the witch ghosts, are you, Nana?" Ailsa poked her head in through the back window. Her dreadlocks glowed auburn, backlit by the bright sun outside that was glaringly white against our dark-adjusted eyes; her head, haloed in sunshine and floating in the square of the window, did look curiously disembodied and ghost-like.

"She asked," the old lady said defensively. "This one has a good aura, I can sense it. Very receptive." She gave me an approving nod. I felt strangely proud—no one had ever complimented my aura before.

Ailsa sighed. "Come on out into the back garden," she invited us. "The ghosts don't like the sunshine."

Nana Maud, as she told us to call her, also insisted on joining us. And then insisted we shell peas for her while we talked, because "the devil makes work for idle hands," which I presume meant that the only options open to us were shelling peas or being pressed into some sort of satanic labor by the cottage's resident witch ghosts. I was perfectly happy with Nana Maud's company because not only did Ailsa appear to soften like ice cream in the sun in her nan's presence, but also Nana Maud turned out to be a fountain of knowledge (or at least gossip) on local affairs, past and present, including the commune up at Stricker's Wood. Although her memory left some rather frustrating gaps.

"I knew there was something amiss when you said old Crispin Oliver had kicked the bucket," she said matter-of-factly to Ailsa. I enjoyed her use of "old" to describe a man a good twenty years her junior. "I didn't need your sister coming home with all her 'I can't talk about my work.' Of course he was murdered. My money's on that business partner of his. Oh, Mairi and Crispin never could stand each other. Why they wanted to go into business together . . ." She shook her head.

My ears pricked up. This was the second time Mairi had been mentioned, and both times none too fondly.

"How did they end up running the shop together?" I asked quickly.

"It was a rum old do, actually," said Nana Maud, frowning slightly at the memory. "She was his spiritual adviser."

I choked slightly on my homemade lemonade. "His what?"

Nana Maud nodded sagely. "He got himself in a sticky situation, a very muddled aura. I could see it all around him—never cleared, mind you, not in all this time."

"What happened?" asked Poppy curiously.

Nana Maud leaned forward conspiratorially. "No one really knew," she murmured. "But there were some who said he'd got mixed up with a young lady and there were *consequences*." She gave us a knowing look.

"A baby?" I asked blankly.

Nana Maud gave a coy shrug.

"How come you've never mentioned any of this to me?" demanded Ailsa.

"You know I don't like to gossip, dear," said Nana Maud, patting her knee. "Anyway, once he'd been kicked out of that commune of his—"

"Mr. Oliver used to live up at the commune?" I interrupted. I didn't mean to be rude, but—what? Camran had said they used to be friends, but had somehow neglected to mention that Mr. Oliver had actually been a member of the commune.

"Oh yes," she said. "Thick as thieves they were, him and that Camran. They started the place together."

"They *started* the place together?" I realized I was repeating Nana Maud like a stuck record, but this was big. This had implications, surely.

Nana Maud's eyes misted over. "They were going to change the world, those two. They said there was a different way of doing things. All living in tents and eating tree bark and chanting and whatnot . . . Respect the earth, respect the body . . . It was all herbal this and alternative that . . ."

"So, did Mr. Oliver get kicked out because of this woman?" I asked.

"Oh no, I don't think it was anything to do with that. No, there was some big falling-out between him and Camran," said Nana Maud vaguely. "I can't remember what it was about, but there were harsh words said. Very harsh words. Crispin Oliver came down into the town and I don't think he set foot in Stricker's Wood again. Started that shop in town with that woman. Spiritual adviser my posterior, that Mairi Webb's one to watch. Do you know what, my money's on her what did for him. I expect she'll be getting the shop now he's gone." She nodded knowingly.

I wasn't so convinced that claiming sole ownership of Nature's Way was grounds for murder, but Mairi Webb definitely sounded like a Person of Interest, as the police would say. I caught Poppy's eye and she gave a slight nod. Then there was also the question of Camran, Mr. Oliver and the Great Bust-Up begging to be explained.

"You can't remember what they argued about?" I prompted gently. But Nana Maud's eyes were unfocused, looking fifty years into the past: "I do think it's a shame when friends fall out."

"Do you remember what happened?" I asked, turning to Ailsa.

She shook her head. "I would have been just starting uni at the time, in Wales. I barely came back over the three years. When I did move back, Miss Webb and Mr. Oliver had opened Nature's Way, and no one at the commune would talk about him. It was like he'd never been there."

"That must have been strange," prompted Poppy.

Ailsa shrugged. "A bit. I can't say I paid it much attention at the time. I wasn't up at the commune so much then. Rowan left for uni at the same time as me, only he never came back, and the commune felt . . . different. A lot of the old crowd had left, some new people had arrived . . . Most of my friends had moved away, so I had no reason to be up there."

Was my mind just overly suspicious, or was it strange that Ailsa had stopped going to the commune at the same time Camran and Mr. Oliver had fallen out?

"How come you didn't come back much from uni?" I asked, trying to sound casual. Ailsa shot me a look.

"Why would I?" she challenged. "I had my own stuff to be getting on with. I was doing a lot of climate activism around then. It took up a lot of my time. People think it's just turning up at marches and shit—"

"Language, Ailsa," interrupted Nana Maud mildly.

"But if you want to actually make a difference there's a hell of a lot of work to be done behind the scenes."

It was an area I had to admit I knew extremely little about.

"It's very impressive," said Poppy. "I spent most of my uni time either drunk or contemplating how next to get drunk . . ."

I had dropped out of uni shortly after my first unsuccessful lecture (hungover, didn't understand it), but this sounded quite familiar to me from most of my twenties.

"I should have joined Greenpeace or something," I said vaguely.

Ailsa rolled her eyes, but she looked slightly mollified. "You can still do something about that," she pointed out. "No one's stopping you."

"Oh, you young people," sighed Nana Maud. "Always campaigning. I don't know where you get the energy. Camran and Crispin were just like that as boys. Wanted to change the world, those two," she said again, "one solstice at a time."

"Are they Druids?" I asked, with some notion that Druids and solstices went together.

"No," huffed Ailsa disparagingly. "They are not *Druids*, don't be so reductive."

"Well now, Ailsa," said Nana Maud reprovingly. "There was always a touch of the Druid about Crispin Oliver, I thought. With his alternative medicines. He was the apothecary up at the commune, you know," she said. "Dispensing his potions and what have you. Yes, more than a touch of the Druid to him."

"Well, maybe it used to be like that," Ailsa conceded. "But it's not like that now. Camran's not running some Druid cult up there. I mean, some of the commune members are Wicca but they don't make a big deal out of it. It's all very laid-back."

"Wicca?" My memory was throwing up some hazy details from that film *The Craft*, and I kind of wanted to ask if Wicca was the same as witches, but I knew Ailsa would probably curse me if I did.

"*Not* witches," said Ailsa.

My mouth dropped open. "You can read minds. You *are* a witch. Busted!"

She actually laughed. "I can read your face. And it was screaming witches. Wicca are not witches; it's nature-based paganism. Pantheism."

"Like, worshipping the earth?" I hazarded.

"Kind of . . ." said Ailsa slowly. "But for most of the people up at the commune, it's more just a respect for the earth. Treating it like a living being—which it is. But of course that's not how most of our species think of it," she concluded darkly.

"Are you Wicca?"

She shrugged. "Jury's still out for me. But I definitely think a little more respect for Mother Earth wouldn't go amiss."

"You spend a lot of time up there at the commune nowadays?" asked Poppy. After all, she'd looked pretty at home up there the other day, beheading asparagus left, right and center.

She shrugged again. "I pop up from time to time. It's nice up there. And the people are all right."

"Will you have your baby there?" I asked, remembering what Inspector Harris had said, way back on that fateful night: *I thought you'd be giving birth in the forest surrounded by squirrels and Druids.*

Ailsa looked uncomfortable. "I don't know. Maybe. It's . . . complicated."

"But you could do, right?"

"If I wanted to. They know what they're doing up there. In fact, there's a woman, Elowen, she'll be giving birth at the commune any day now. I'll be going up for the birthing ceremony. You guys are welcome to join if you want. Come and see how they do it there—it doesn't have to be hospitals and epidurals and all that shit."

"Don't swear, please, Ailsa," said Nana Maud automatically. I was pretty sure she was fighting a losing battle there.

I wasn't sure what to say. On the one hand, pagan birthing ceremony in the woods? Yes please! On the other hand, I was already terrified of giving birth, and watching Hen's hadn't helped. I wasn't sure I was ready for another one, without any of the marvels of modern medicine to smooth the passage, so to speak.

"Er."

"I'd like to," said Poppy in her usual gentle manner. "I mean, my plan is to go to hospital and have seven types of painkiller, but I'm open to seeing how other people want to do it."

Well, now I'd feel like a right cop-out if I didn't too.

"Sure," I said weakly. "Count me in."

"Wow, no need to sound so enthusiastic." Ailsa rolled her eyes. "Well, she's already past her due date, so I don't think you'll be waiting long. I'll let you know when we're up—just keep your phones off silent, and if it happens in the middle of the night you'll need to bring a torch."

"Yay." I tried to look enthusiastic. How many births was I going to have to witness before getting round to my own?

"Jane's not keen on you having the baby up there, you know," put in Nana Maud suddenly.

Ailsa shrugged. "Well, it's not Jane having the baby."

"No, but she is your sister. She just wants the best for you," Nana Maud said mildly. Ailsa rolled her eyes again. She was very good at it. If I tried it people just asked if I needed to sit down.

"Oh yes, Inspector Harris!" I said. "I can't believe she's your sister!"

"Why's that?" asked Ailsa with a wry smile. "Because she has a proper job and a sensible haircut? Or because of my dark and shady past?"

I went red. Was she actually reading my mind?

"I didn't mean . . ."

"Yeah, yeah, it's fine. I'm used to it. Jane was always Little Miss Perfect. Such a Goody Two-shoes. It was no surprise when she joined the police. Whereas I was always on the wrong side of the force." She pulled a face as she said it.

"You shouldn't joke about it," said Nana Maud mildly. "Jane was very upset when you were arrested."

"You were arrested?" I blurted out.

"Yep."

"What for?"

"Peaceful protesting outside an energy company who are sitting back and letting the world burn while they get rich off the smoke. I didn't do anything illegal and it wasn't a lawful arrest."

"Your sister was very upset. She didn't want—" repeated Nana Maud, but Ailsa cut across her—rather quickly, I thought, as if she didn't like where Nana Maud was going.

"Jane was very upset because it didn't look good for her career if she had a sister in the cells," said Ailsa tartly. "And no, I've never been involved in Homicide, which is where Jane works now, if that's what you're thinking."

Her story checked out, although I couldn't help but wonder if Ailsa had been a little quick to explain away the comments she must have known we'd overheard the other evening. And she'd cut Nana Maud off very abruptly.

"More lemonade?" asked Nana Maud brightly into the slightly tense silence, and she shambled off into the house.

It wasn't exactly the perfect moment, as I'm pretty sure Ailsa thought we suspected her of something, but with Nana Maud out of the way for a minute, I felt I had to seize the opportunity.

"Look, Ailsa, this is going to sound really weird. But talking of your sister . . . What are the chances you might be able to get a look at the post-mortem report on Mr. Oliver?"

Ailsa's eyes narrowed. "And why would I do that?"

It felt embarrassing to say it out loud. "Well, Poppy and I were sort of having a think about Mr. Oliver's murder and we were just trying to work out what might have happened. Sort of like a hobby . . ." I concluded lamely. I had promised Poppy I wouldn't mention Lin—so we just sounded like a couple of pregnant weirdos playing detective.

There was a brief moment, then Ailsa laughed. "Wow, you ladies need to get yourselves a *proper* hobby. Amateur detectives, huh?"

I flushed.

"Well, there's not much else to do at the moment," said Poppy reasonably. "So yeah, I guess we are amateur detectoring. Go on, let us see the report. If you can get hold of it, that is."

"Oh, I'm sure I could get hold of it all right," said Ailsa. "But I'm not sure aiding and abetting your little hobby is worth getting myself in even more trouble with my sister. And *please* don't try the whole 'well, I suppose it's too difficult' tactic to try and trick me into saying I'll do it, because that would just be demeaning for all of us."

Poppy laughed. "Well, if you've got anything better to keep us occupied . . ."

"As a matter of fact, I do. There's a gong bath at the Women's Inner

Goddess Temple on Thursday, midday. I'll see you there and if—*if*—I have the report, I'll bring it then."

"Dammit," said Poppy, "I've got a midwife appointment then. But Alice will be there, won't you, Alice?"

"Whoa, what now? A what? Where?" This sounded like my actual worst nightmare.

"You don't know the Women's Inner Goddess Temple?" smirked Ailsa. "It'll be right up your street."

"I don't think I have an inner goddess, I'm afraid," I said hurriedly. "Anyway, isn't that like from *Fifty Shades of Grey* or something? Are you trying to get me to go to some weird sex dungeon?"

"Would you prefer it if I was?" Ailsa raised an eyebrow.

"On balance, probably yes?"

Poppy laughed. Easy for her; she was well out of this with her midwife appointment—if there even was an appointment, I thought darkly.

"So what's a gong bath then? And what's it going to do to my inner goddess? Are you sure it's not a sex thing? It sounds like a sex thing."

Ailsa rolled her eyes. "It is not a sex thing. Unless you find cosmic vibrations sexy."

I stared blankly. To be honest, it was still sounding like a sex thing to me.

"It's like meditation," clarified Ailsa. "Please tell me you know what that is."

"I know meditation," I retorted. I mean, I know what it is, sure. Never done it. I've taken acid before though (in my misspent youth, I hasten to add, before I was a respectable person with a pregnancy and a dog). That's kind of like meditating, right? I'm pretty sure I'd had some cosmic vibrations at the time.

"Great. I'm sure you'll be a natural. And bring a cushion, you have to lie on the floor."

"Is this like some messed-up way of making me earn the report or something?" I asked petulantly.

"Never. Rhubarb?"

CHAPTER 16

I LEFT NANA Maud's house with more rhubarb than any sane person knows what to do with. I had also, apparently, been signed up for some cosmic vibrating with Ailsa and an aquanatal class with Poppy, which had been her sole concession to my request for some "normal" maternity leave activity. Between all that, plus a baby to birth and a murder to investigate, my rural social calendar was looking pretty full. More pressing right now was the fact that I was also late for my first Penton midwife appointment. I walk-jogged—with a hint of waddle—to the doctors' office and arrived with such an intense stitch I did wonder if I might be going into labor.

Joe was lurking outside looking nervous. I was too out of breath to say anything, but he was a step ahead of me and instantly produced a Lucozade and a bag of Frazzles. God, I love that man. I scarfed them down in a frenzy of faux-bacon crumbs and we headed in.

My new midwife was approximately fifteen years old. I'm not even joking. She introduced herself as "Candy," which *cannot* be her real name. Then again, she had bubblegum-pink hair, a nose piercing and a hand tattoo of a fern (which I actually thought was pretty cool); she did look like I'd expect a Candy to look. But what could she possibly know about birthing a child? I mean, don't get me wrong, I don't claim to be an expert, but I didn't want to have to make small talk about pop music and teen crushes in between contractions. Sorry, "surges."

"I really don't want to sound rude," I began. She raised an eyebrow. "But how many births have you done?"

She grinned. "Enough. Seriously. You're in safe hands." She waggled said hands at me. It made the tattoo on her hand ripple in a strangely mesmerizing way. When did the youth become so confident? And at which birthday had I ceased to include myself in "youth"? At her age I'd still been agonizing over whether hair mascara was a good move. (It wasn't.)

"Have you thought about where you're going to give birth?" she asked.

Yes, every night, in my nightmares.

"Er, not really, no."

"Well, home births are very popular in Penton."

Of course they were. And also: absolutely no way, when hell freezes over.

"I don't think so," I cut in quickly. "We live in a rental. I don't want to lose my deposit over placenta stains on the carpet."

Joe nodded vigorously.

Candy laughed but, I noticed, didn't contradict me. "Well, there's the local maternity hospital," she continued. "That's the midwife-led unit here in Penton. We can cope with pretty much anything there, and it allows you to have a more natural environment than going into the hospital in Bridgeport."

I wasn't sure exactly what she meant by "natural environment." Would I be giving birth in a cave? Or a tree? Like my distant Neanderthal ancestors? Would Joe lurk at the door with a club, ready to fight off the mammoths and saber-toothed tigers and, quite possibly, my mother-in-law?

"Hellooo?" Candy waved a hand in front of my face. I realized I'd glazed over.

"Sorry, yes, the local hospital sounds nice?" I suspected I sounded as uncertain as I felt.

"Could we have a look around first?" asked Joe. Uncharitably, my first thought was that he would want to check the Wi-Fi connection before committing to twenty-four hours in the place. Then I realized he was looking as terrified as I felt. We were heading into uncharted waters here, but it was good to know we were doing it together.

"Of course! Why don't we have your appointment next week there? I can show you round afterward. We've still got a good fortnight before

your due date." She surveyed my chart in what was, I admit, a very professional manner. "So if you want we can book you in for a sweep in, say,
three weeks' time?"

"What's a sweep?"

"Basically, I give you a good old fingering."

I blinked. "'Scuse me?"

She jabbed upward with a couple of fingers. It was a horrifyingly sug-
gestive gesture. Joe's death grip on my hand tightened.

"Oh," I said weakly. "Lovely. You're not even going to buy me a drink
beforehand?"

She gave such a dirty laugh. I was deeply confused. I knew things had
been strained with Joe recently, but was I *flirting* with my midwife? Or
possibly just making a tit out of myself?

"Relax," she said. "It's just to separate your membranes."

I gagged a little. Yeah, not flirting. No dirty talk should ever include
the word "membranes."

"If I can pull the uterine lining away from the—"

"Whoa!" I held up a hand to stop her. "It's OK, I don't need the details." Joe was looking increasingly like the green-faced emoji.

"All right, just making sure you know what's going on," said Candy
with an easy smile. "But so long as you're comfortable with the process,
that's fine. I'll book you for two weeks on Friday."

I was in no way comfortable with the process, but then there was so
much I had not been comfortable with over the course of the last nine
months.

As a case in point, Candy asked me to hop up on the examination
table while she checked my cervix.

I will never get used to this.

As her hand disappeared into my nether regions, I tried to distract
myself from the rummaging sensation down below by mulling over what
we'd learned at Ailsa's that morning. We needed to speak to the unpop-
ular Mairi Webb, that much was clear. Perhaps she could cast some light
on what had caused Mr. Oliver's "muddled aura" and why he had been
kicked out of the commune. My knowledge of hippy communes was as
limited as my understanding of sweeps, but I would have reckoned them

to be a pretty forgiving bunch—what did you have to do to get chucked out of one?

"Al," hissed Joe, and I realized Candy was speaking to me.

"Your cervix isn't ripe yet," she announced, withdrawing.

"I beg your pardon?" Something about having a teenager for a midwife was apparently making me speak like a maiden aunt.

"When you're approaching birth your cervix will ripen," Candy expounded. "Like a peach."

Well, thank you for ruining peaches for me.

"So I'm not giving birth anytime soon?" I asked, wanting to be absolutely clear.

"Not even close," said Candy cheerfully.

I pulled up my pants and took my disappointingly unripe cervix home with me.

CHAPTER 17

BY THE TIME we got home I was utterly exhausted. At least there was a pleasant surprise awaiting me: Joe had unpacked the final boxes while I'd been out at Nana Maud's, the house was passably tidy, and the recycling had been taken out.

"Dinner?" Joe asked as I slumped on a kitchen chair. He'd even been shopping, and had remembered to take tote bags. Joe went through sporadic phases of getting his shit together—which was more than I ever managed—and I really, really hoped this was the beginning of one of his proactive spates.

"Candy seemed nice," he began, pulling fresh vegetables out of one of the totes.

"I don't want to talk about it," I mumbled. The unripe cervix still stung—literally and metaphorically.

He made a vaguely sympathetic noise and turned his attention to the aubergines. Which were probably ripe—the bastards.

I also had another concern niggling at the back of my brain. I had been turning over Ailsa's invite in my mind all the way home. "Do you think I have an inner goddess?"

"Am I supposed to say something like 'You're all goddess to me, babe'?" he asked, slicing and dicing like a pro.

"Am I?"

"Not really, no. What's all this about?"

"Ailsa—you know, the dreadlock girl from prenatal?—has invited me to a gong bath at the Women's Inner Goddess Temple."

"Sounds like a cult. Don't go."

"It does a bit." I brightened; this was making it sound somewhat more interesting. "She's more hippy than culty though, I would say. I thought she was a bitch at first, but she's kind of growing on me."

"That's how they lure you in," he said darkly.

"Talking of cults," I said carefully, "you know the guy that started the commune up in Stricker's Wood?"

"Camran?" said Joe, frowning at me. "What about him?"

I was slightly surprised that Joe had remembered Camran's name. I hadn't got the impression he'd been hanging on my every word when I'd told him about my hippy afternoon tea.

"Did you know that he started the place with Mr. Oliver? But then they had some massive row and Mr. Oliver left and they never spoke again."

Joe bit into a slice of pepper and then added a splash of soy sauce to the wok before replying. "What about?"

"Not sure, Nana Maud couldn't remember. But it was bad. It was like ten years ago, and they've literally never spoken since."

"Ten years ago? Well, that's . . ." But whatever he'd been about to say, he drifted off and turned back to the stove. "And who is Nana Maud?"

"Ailsa's nan. Anyway, we were wondering, what if it has something to do with Mr. Oliver's murder?"

"You're not still messing around with that Poppy girl, playing detectives, are you?" Joe sounded unnecessarily annoyed. "What are the chances of some row ten years ago having anything to do with this guy's death? He probably had a heart attack or something. Why can't you just drop it?"

"The police don't think it was a heart attack. They're doing a full postmortem. That's why I need to go to this gong bath thing—I need to keep on Ailsa's good side," I continued, deliberately obtuse to his increasing bad temper. "Her sister is the investigating detective, and I want to see the postmortem report."

There was a clang as Joe dropped the wok back on the hob. "Why on earth do you want to see the report? You're about to have a baby, Alice! Priorities!"

"I'm just interested," I said defensively. "I've never seen a postmortem report. It might be interesting to find out what he died of, and all that."

"Can't you wait until it's in the papers, like everyone else? Or better still, can't you just leave it?"

"No harm in just asking a few questions."

"Yes, there could be a lot of harm in it, Alice. It's a murder investigation."

He turned back to the stove, holding himself all stiff like he does when he gets angry. He'd not been best impressed when I'd told him that Poppy and I had made a suspect list. Even less so when I'd informed him that he was on it and asked if he could provide an alibi for when he'd left to get our coats. I thought he knew I was joking, but possibly not . . .

I toyed with a couple of scraps of paper on the table, then realized it was the Penton Preservation Party leaflet I had torn in half the other day.

"You missed a bit." I waved it at Joe.

"What?"

"When you took the recycling out. You missed a bit."

"Oh, right, yeah."

I crumpled it into a ball, and noticed Joe watching me do so.

"Sorry, did you want it?" I asked, holding it out and raising an eyebrow. "Planning on joining Fascists Unite?"

"No," he said coldly. "But you shouldn't be so rude about other people's politics. Not everyone has to be a lefty liberal, you know."

"Jeez, sorry for breathing."

"Just saying." He turned back to the stove. "Stir-fry's ready."

I watched his tense back for a moment before hauling myself up to fetch cutlery. I loved Joe, I really did. He was chaotic, kind, intelligent, had an astonishing range of funny voices and, most of the time, was incredibly easygoing. But recently he seemed to have taken a rain check on that last one. Now I know it had been a pretty stressful week, granted, but he needed to lighten up—align those chakras, take a gong bath or something.

CHAPTER 18

"**WHAT ARE YOU** doing today?" asked Joe when I stumbled sleepily into the kitchen the next morning to find him eating peanut butter out of the jar with a knife (Helen had recently taken against spoons and hidden or buried every one we owned). He didn't even wait for an answer before barreling on, "And please don't say you're playing Sherlock Holmes again, that has *got* to stop before you actually do some damage."

"Actually," I said huffily, "I am going to an aquanatal class with Poppy."

Joe looked immensely relieved.

"That sounds wonderfully normal," he said. "Have a lovely time. I'll sort dinner. Any requests?"

"Carbs, please," I said absently. "Swimming works every muscle in your body."

And he actually laughed.

I felt bad for lying to him. Well, it was only lying by omission. I *was* going to an aquanatal class. But after that Poppy and I were going to stop by the offices of the *Penton Bugle*, to see if there had been anything in the local papers about any strange goings-on at the commune, specifically ten years ago and specifically involving Mr. Oliver. I didn't think this would go down well with Joe.

As he left for work, he even gave me a kiss on the top of my head. It felt weirdly like a papal blessing, but it was also the most affection he'd shown me in the last few days, so I'd take it.

* * *

FIVE MINUTES into the aquanatal class it became apparent that swimming works several muscles that, it turns out, I do not have. The class was a torture session of bending and stretching and bouncing. I was regretting two things. First, having agreed to come to the class at all. And second, being such a penny-pincher that I'd refused to shell out for an actual maternity swimming costume. Instead, I was wearing a pair of bikini bottoms that barely fitted, and a nursing bra that had gone very see-through in the water. Combined with the fact that my nipples had recently enlarged to the size of saucers, it was not a good look.

Four other pregnant women were swishing about in the water, looking surprisingly lithe and way more energetic than anyone should be at that stage of pregnancy. We appeared to be a doing a full-on dance routine with choreography worthy of Diversity (all my pop culture references are ten years out of date, which is approximately when I stopped paying for a TV license). And we were doing it *in the water*. I could barely catch my breath.

"Is this meant to be fun?" I huffed at Poppy, who was apparently having no issues at all and had also managed to wear an actual swimming costume to a swimming class.

"It'll get your blood flowing," she replied, bopping around in a circle.

"My blood was flowing fine before," I grumbled.

"It's good for the baby."

"The baby likes naps and chicken nuggets."

"We can go for cake afterward?"

OK, fine, that did cheer me up a bit.

"Any joy tracking Mairi Webb down?" I asked Poppy, trying to sound as serious as is possible when bobbing up and down on one leg while lassoing your arms wildly in the air. We'd agreed that, along with the Stricker's Wood Commune, Mairi Webb was our best lead; we needed to get in touch with her.

Poppy shook her head—although at first I wasn't sure if it was a dance move. "Not really. I took a little diversion past Nature's Way on my way home from Ailsa's yesterday and it was extremely closed—like, police officer on guard closed, so I couldn't even poke my nose in. But I highly doubt Mairi was there. So I googled her when I got home. There's an ancient website for her old spiritual adviser business but it hasn't been updated since 2010 and when I emailed the address listed, it bounced."

"No phone number?" I asked, disappointed.

"No. There was one thing, though . . ."

"Yes?" I prompted.

"It looked like she used to do a lot of work with the Women's Inner Goddess Temple. Workshops, tarot readings, that kind of stuff. Aren't you going there with Ailsa tomorrow?"

"You know full well I am," I said grumpily, accepting a violently purple noodle from the aquanatal teacher. "It's gong bath day tomorrow."

"So have a poke around," urged Poppy. "Speak to whoever's running the gong bath. See if she's still involved there, see what you can find out about her. And a phone number, email or home address would be helpful."

"All this while buttering up Ailsa?" It was starting to sound like an impossible task.

Poppy flipped effortlessly onto her back, like a pregnant floating island. "I have faith in you!" she said winningly.

I sighed and turned my attention back to wrestling the noodle, which erupted from the water like a deranged worm and bopped me in the eye.

I had to admit, however, that by the end of the class I was maybe feeling a little bit of the benefit. I also felt sweaty, though, which I didn't think should be possible, given the whole class had been in the water. But these days my body was finding all sorts of new and interesting ways to distress and embarrass me.

"I think you enjoyed that in the end," said Poppy as we hauled ourselves out of the pool like a pair of beached whales.

"It was tolerable," I conceded. "But now cake."

"Fine, now cake."

"And I don't want any of that prepackaged supermarket cake. We're going into town to find proper cake."

Poppy rolled her eyes and disappeared into a cubicle. I spent another five minutes trying to remember the code for my locker.

*   *   *

WE'D HAD to travel to the nearby town of Bridgeport to find something as metropolitan as an aquanatal class. Bridgeport had all sorts of exciting amenities that Penton could only dream of—like a cinema and a bowling alley and an Indian takeout. It wasn't exactly an urban jungle, but it did at least have a faint buzz to it.

"Helen's toxicology report came back," I told Poppy as we turned onto the thrumming high street (a queue of pensioners outside the post office and a couple of youths hanging out at Greggs).

"What was it?"

"Methyl salicylate," I said, frowning.

"Never heard of it," said Poppy.

"No, neither had we—had to google it. Apparently it's used in some foods as it's kinda minty flavored, but not in the concentrations Helen had ingested. And it's in some painkillers as well, but again, not in such a high concentration. God knows where she got her paws on it."

"Is there any long-term damage? I mean, she seemed OK yesterday?"

"She's bizarrely fine already. Thankfully there don't seem to be any lasting effects—her liver and kidney function tests came back normal. They're probably the most normal thing about her, in fact."

"How the hell did she get hold of this stuff up in the woods?" asked Poppy curiously.

"Unless she found it at the commune," I pointed out. "Although I can't see what they'd be doing with this stuff. It sounds pretty lethal. They think Helen had ingested about one milliliter, and she almost died."

"Could she have found some painkillers there and snaffled them?"

I frowned. "None of the other active ingredients in most common painkillers showed up in her tests, so it doesn't look like that was the cause . . ."

"Something to think about . . ." mused Poppy. "One more mystery to add to the pile!"

"Agreed," I said. "But talking of mysteries, it's already half past twelve, and we told the receptionist at the *Bugle* we'd be there for two, so we need to get a shift on. But first"—I stopped outside a promising-looking café—"cake?"

*   *   *

WE SAT in the window of the café and people-watched, inventing highly plausible backstories for anyone who caught our eye.

"That woman is planning a heist on the school PTA funds and is going to run away to Cuba with her salsa instructor on the stolen proceeds."

"That kid is skipping school and selling poppers. No, for real—I just saw him. The one in the weird burgundy school uniform."

"That woman used to be a conjoined twin but they were separated at birth and she's spent all her adult life searching for her long-lost twin who actually lives in Bahrain and is married to the sultan."

"That guy is—Wait, isn't that Antoni?"

It was hard to tell. After all, we'd only met the guy twice. And the second time there had been a lot going on. This guy was wearing a suit, sure, but he was also with a girl who wasn't Hen. They'd just come out of the Costa opposite.

"Yeah, I'm pretty sure it is," said Poppy slowly. "Who's he with?"

"No idea. Work colleague?"

"Doesn't he work in London? And she doesn't look like a suit." She had a point. In fact, Antoni's "friend" was wearing a Costa apron; she clearly worked there. "Ooh no! Do you think he's having an affair?"

"He seems the type," I said darkly.

"Haven't you met him, like, twice?"

"OK, so I'm judgmental, I'm a bad person. But I'm not the one sneaking around town with my tongue down another girl's throat."

"Alice," protested Poppy, "he's not even touching her."

"For now."

Our accusations had escalated pretty quickly. The poor guy was just having a coffee with someone who would no doubt turn out to be a colleague or an old friend or an estate agent (like that episode in *Friends*).

But at that point, the girl grasped Antoni's arm, hard. It was an emotional gesture. He ran a hand down his face. Then they were hugging, hard. Gripping each other in what a romance novel would no doubt call "the throes of passion."

"Ah," said Poppy. "That's a bit more intense."

"Should we go over and confront him?" I asked, then immediately regretted it. I hate confrontation, and couldn't imagine anything worse than asking a man I don't think I've exchanged two words with whether he's cheating on his wife.

"Er, feels a bit awkward," mumbled Poppy.

"Yeah, let's not," I agreed hurriedly.

We sat in silence for a bit, watching as Antoni and the woman finally separated, the woman heading back into Costa, while Antoni strode off down the street.

"Would you ever have an affair?" I asked Poppy.

She gave it some thought, then shook her head. "No. I think if it started to seem like I wanted to, then I'd probably break it off with Lin, rather than having some sort of secret affair. I can't imagine I'd ever want to, though," she added. "Lin's just about the best thing that's ever happened to me. What about you?"

"No, I couldn't hack it," I said. "Honestly, when people are having affairs in films it makes me feel actually sick with nerves. I'd confess after like one day."

I paused for a minute.

"I sometimes wonder if Joe could, though." It felt horrible saying it. Poppy waited for me to continue. She was good at that, I'd noticed. She would actually wait until you'd got all your words out before she replied.

"I don't think he's having an affair," I clarified. "But I feel like something is going on in his head that he won't share with me. And I probably haven't done a very good job of asking him about it. But there's something going on, and the more I try and ask him the more he shuts himself off."

"Do you think it's about the baby?" Poppy asked.

"Maybe." But I didn't, not really. And it was starting to irritate me how everything seemed to be put down to "the baby." It was possible, surely, that there were things going on in our lives, in our relationship, that didn't revolve around the baby. The previous day's conversation swam through my mind and the idea formed almost as I was saying it: "I'm worried he might be getting into right-wing politics."

"Couples can have different politics," said Poppy gently. "If that's even what it is."

"I know," I said. "I know that. But also, it's quite a big thing to disagree about. It's not so much about political allegiance. It's more about whether or not your fundamental values are aligned." I paused. "To be honest, I think I'd rather he was having an affair."

I was only half joking.

CHAPTER 19

AT LEAST OUR research trip to the *Penton Bugle* took my mind off Joe—in a pretty bleak way. We parked up and strolled along the canal to the newspaper's offices. I say offices—it was a converted water mill that still had the old wooden wheel stuck to the side of the building, paddles turning lazily in the current. Honestly, if this place got anymore picturesque I was going to bump into Miss Marple. A faded hand-painted sign read THE *PENTON BUGLE*: PURVEYORS OF FINE NEWS SINCE 1802.

"Why don't they just get a town crier and be done with it?" I wondered aloud.

"They had one until two years ago," said Poppy.

"You're kidding."

"Totally serious. Budget cuts meant they had to choose between the town crier and the lollipop lady and he didn't make the cut."

I shook my head in disbelief as we climbed the steps into the building.

"We're here to see the archives," I said to the ancient receptionist. "We called ahead."

She smiled. "Oh yes. Lovely to see new residents taking an interest in local history."

I smiled back painfully. Yes indeed, we were very interested in local history, its deepest secrets and darkest corners, please.

Well, the archive had plenty of dark corners, that was for sure. It was down in the basement and I'm pretty sure we were the first people to set foot in there for several years. Strip lights buzzed arthritically overhead, illuminating a room full of filing cabinets labeled by year, stacks of "to be dealt with" paperwork and a veritable fly graveyard.

"Where to begin?" whispered Poppy. It had that atmosphere you get in the presence of a lot of paper, which means you have to whisper. Like libraries and bookshops.

I froze, thinking I'd heard a scuffling sound from among the cabinets. Then forced myself to relax. It was unlikely to be someone listening in.

"I think we should start about ten years ago, when Mr. Oliver fell out with Camran and left the commune. This cabinet is 2020, so . . ." I began drifting along the regimented ranks, the years rolling back as I headed further in.

"Two thousand and fourteen, two thousand and thirteen, two thousand and twelve . . ." I read aloud, and turned into the next row. "Two thousand and—*Shitting hell!*"

I screamed. From somewhere in the darkness there was a bang as Poppy fell over at the sudden cacophony.

"Whoa!" Rowan rose from where he'd been crouched in among the filing cabinets, kicking a drawer shut with his foot. "Whoa, Alice! Chill. I didn't mean to startle you."

"Oh my God, you nearly sent me into labor." I leaned over, one hand on the bump where the baby was about to be hit with an absolute tsunami of adrenaline.

"Shit, for real?" Rowan rushed forward, a hand on my shoulder, a look of genuine concern on his face.

"Give me a minute and I'll let you know."

He looked alarmed.

I took some deep breaths—or would have done if my lungs hadn't been elbowed into my throat by the baby.

"What were you doing hiding down there?" I asked indignantly, straightening up. Poppy's ashen face appeared round the corner of the filing cabinet wall and she squeaked in agreement.

"I wasn't *hiding*," he protested. "I was just looking something up, and then you nearly stepped on me!" He slipped a folded, slightly yellowed newspaper into the folder he was carrying.

"But what are you doing *here*?" I persisted. "At the *Bugle*?"

"I work here," he replied, relaxing now that I didn't appear to be giving birth. "I used to write the odd article for them, back when I was a teenager. When I came back and decided to stick around, I needed a job, and they said I could come on the staff here."

"You do the filing, do you," said Poppy dryly, nodding to the haphazard ranks of filing cabinets extending in every direction, old newspapers sliding off them and accumulating in drifts on the floor.

"Very funny," said Rowan with a smirk. "I'll have you know I'm an extremely talented up-and-coming reporter. Except I can't find my press pass, I must have dropped it somewhere. I was down here the other day looking for some stuff on . . ." He trailed off. "Anyway, I thought maybe I'd left it down here. You haven't seen it, have you?"

"Er, no," I said.

Rowan peered distractedly under a few filing cabinets. "So what are you ladies doing down here? History project?"

"Oh just, y'know, getting a feel for the place," I said vaguely. I instinctively felt that the fewer people who knew what we were up to, the better. "I'm new to Penton and all that."

"You know, most people just look online for Penton tourist information," he said with an amused glance, still groping in the dusty recesses below the cabinets.

I shrugged. "I like old newspapers."

"All right." He half smiled. "Well, if you want a guided tour of the back copies at any point, just let me know. I can talk you through my teenage greatest hits. My coverage of the two thousand and nine Great Penton Jam Off was the talk of the village."

I gave a weak smile.

"I'd better crack on. If you come across that pass . . ." He gave us a cheerful nod and departed, whistling to himself. A textbook example of a man attempting a nonchalant departure.

Poppy and I shared a look.

"Well, I found two thousand and ten," I said lamely. "It's this one. The one Rowan was looking at." The bottom drawer that he'd nudged shut with his foot was slightly ajar still. I pulled it open. May 2010.

"Might as well start here."

I pulled a stack of musty old newspapers out of the drawer, thrust a handful at Poppy and began to read.

It was mostly your classic local news, with what I was swiftly coming to recognize as that signature Penton twist. I flicked past several headlines about the weather, and skimmed a number of articles on subjects ranging from the aforementioned jam competition to a drunk squirrel causing havoc in the fudge shop and a sheep that had sprouted an extra pair of horns.

FURORE AT HARVEST FESTIVAL

IS THIS THE HOTTEST SUMMER ON RECORD?

MAUREEN TATTLE SCOOPS COURGETTE OF THE YEAR FOR THE FOURTH YEAR RUNNING

You'd think these papers were from 1910, not 2010. Time apparently moves slower in the country—by like a century.

I admit I kept getting distracted by the utterly fascinating local news of a decade ago. The scarecrow competitions and the village fetes and the various countryside concerns that I had little to no understanding of, like whether or not it had been a good harvest, and the terrifyingly named "ash dieback" that blighted the local woodlands.

Then Poppy gave a sharp intake of breath.

"Read this."

She shoved an aging paper under my nose, which made me sneeze. Ugh, it didn't bear thinking about how many mold spores we were probably breathing in down here. A few lines into the article, however, I stopped worrying about mold.

It was short and to the point.

TRAGEDY STRIKES STRICKER'S?

There have been unconfirmed reports that a body was removed from the Stricker's Wood Commune in the early hours of this morning.

An unnamed source states that an anonymous call was made to the emergency services some time after midnight. Police and ambulance attended the scene, but we are reliably informed that the victim, believed to be a young woman in her early twenties, was pronounced dead on arrival at St. Mary's Hospital in Bridgeport. The cause of death is as yet unknown.

The police have not yet issued a statement, but we are confident in stating that we believe there to be grounds for suspicion. Investigations are said to be ongoing.

We attempted to contact the founding members of the Stricker's Wood Commune but were told that no one was available for comment.

"Shit . . ." I breathed out slowly.

Poppy nodded somberly.

I looked at her, speechless. We'd been so convinced that something must have happened at the commune, that it was hiding some dark secret, we hadn't paused to think about how upsetting it might be to uncover the truth. Someone had *died*. A young woman. What had happened to her? And was it connected to Camran and Mr. Oliver's big row?

I read the article again. This woman, this girl, had been nearly ten years younger than me. With a start, I realized that meant that, if she had lived, she would have been the same age as me now. She could even have been in our prenatal class.

I shook my head—it was no use going off on flights of fantasy like that.

"Poor girl." It felt a horribly inadequate thing to say. It *was* a horribly inadequate thing to say.

"So . . . what happened to her?" asked Poppy.

I sifted through the rest of the paper.

"There's nothing more in this one. Where's the following week?" I flicked to the front of the paper and noted the date. "We want the last week in June."

Poppy leaned into the filing cabinet, but re-emerged empty-handed.

"It's not in there," she said, grabbing the pile of papers she had already looked through and rifling through them. "Maybe it's got out of order . . ."

I did the same, leafing through the papers stacked beside me. Nothing. My heart sank.

"Rowan took a newspaper," I said heavily. "I saw him slip one into the folder he was carrying. It must have been the one we're after."

We stared at each other.

"But why . . . ?" Poppy began.

"Who knows? Maybe he's doing the same as we're doing. Or maybe . . ." I didn't really want to finish that thought.

Poppy's face was inscrutable.

I grabbed the July newspapers and began leafing through them.

"There's *got* to be something else here . . ." I muttered.

But there was nothing. I grabbed the next week, and the next. How could there be *nothing*? A girl had died!

"Oh wait—"

There was a small notice in among the personals at the back of one of the July papers.

> A tree-planting ceremony will be held this coming Saturday at the Stricker's Wood Commune, to commemorate the return of our sister's life force to her mother earth.
>
> Please do not send cut flowers.
>
> Journalists and rubberneckers not welcome.

And that was it. No name. No cause of death. Just a short, rather terse note about a tree ceremony.

We left the archives without speaking, barely acknowledging the ancient receptionist's bright "Cheerio!," and sat down by the canal outside the *Penton Bugle* offices.

In strict contravention of the archive rules, I had done a Rowan and pocketed the newspaper with the TRAGEDY STRIKES STRICKER's article. We scoured it for anything we'd missed, but it was almost scandalously short on details. We tried googling every variation on "death at Stricker's Wood Commune" but turned up nothing. The commune had extremely little presence online—the occasional mention in a Facebook post, a brief line on the official Visit Penton website referring to it as a "private endeavor not open to the public." The newspaper archives online only went back to 2018, when Penton had presumably discovered the internet. And without a name, or anymore details, we didn't have much to go on.

"In her early twenties," I kept repeating. "She was so young. What could have happened?"

"Well," said Poppy. "I guess you're looking at either natural causes, unusual in someone so young, or some kind of accident . . ."

"Or foul play," I concluded bleakly.

We parted ways rather somberly. Was this detectoring? Digging up unpleasant stories and then hitting a brick wall? If so, I wasn't sure it was for me. What I needed right now was a bag of Doritos (tangy cheese for preference), a bath and a solid hour of mindless internet scrolling.

CHAPTER 20

ALL THAT REMAINED of the Doritos was a thin coating of neon-orange dust on the surface of the now-tepid water, and I had read all of the internet. It was time to tackle the potentially awkward conversation I'd been putting off all evening.

Poppy had nominated me to ask Ailsa what she knew about the death at the commune, because she kept insisting that Ailsa likes me. I kept explaining that Ailsa thinks I am an unnecessary carbon footprint upon our planet. But Poppy was not to be dissuaded. At the very least, however, I could take the coward's route and text Ailsa rather than asking her in person tomorrow, where she would be able to give me that very particular glare.

To be honest, it didn't go much better over text.

Yo!

Excuse me?

Hi?

Better.

How are you?

What do you want?

. . . a chat?

No, you want something. Spit it out.

OK fine

So Poppy and I were just wondering if you knew anything about some girl who died at the commune like ten years ago

It all seems a bit mysterious

Do you know what happened?

Not really.

Like, not really no? Or not really you know a bit?

I mean, I think I remember something like that.

Dunno what happened though.

But people must have talked about it?

Dunno.

I was at uni.

Oh

Right then

That everything?

I guess

See you tomorrow!

Can't wait!

Her only response was the meteorite emoji. What did *that* mean? Sure, I'd been warned to expect a cosmic journey but a meteorite seemed a tad violent. I was more thinking twinkling stars and gentle cosmic rays.

As for her response to the death at the commune, she hadn't really told me anything at all. Maybe she was holding out on me; but then again, maybe that was just Ailsa's way.

With Poppy having wriggled out of it and my fear of Ailsa at an all-time high, there was no way I was taking the path to inner enlightenment without backup tomorrow. It was time to call in the troops.

I rang Maya.

"Can you pull a sickie tomorrow?"

"Why? I've got a very important meeting."

"You hate important meetings. Anyway, I need you to come to a gong bath with me."

"Fuck off."

"It's to do with the murder . . ."

There was silence on the other end of the line. I had her now. Maya had been following our murder investigations with even more interest than she showed in *Love Island*, demanding multiple updates a day.

"Keep talking . . ."

I'll admit I was stretching the truth a tad. All we had to relate the gong bath to the murder was an extremely tenuous and outdated connection between the Temple and the deceased's business partner, but my spidey senses were tingling. Unless that was just sciatica from sitting in the bath too long. Anyway, it was the only way to entice Maya down to the backwater that is Penton, and I needed her there.

Maya and I had previously run away together from a vegan, alkaline, silent yoga retreat to get a McDonald's, so we had a solid history with these kinds of events. I was pretty sure we could handle a gong bath. Plus I couldn't help feeling I was getting drawn into the whole Penton hippy vibe at a slightly alarming rate—I needed a connection with my London roots. I needed to spend some time with someone who could name the entire cast of *The Bachelor* and knew what a Slim Jim was.

CHAPTER 21

"**OH MY GOD,** you're enormous!"

If anyone else had said that I would probably have punched them, but it was OK coming from Maya. She, of course, looked great. Because she was still enjoying luxuries like sleep and coffee and wasn't retaining more water than the Hoover Dam.

"So this is Penton, huh?" She looked around at the sleepy village station. It was a judging look; I could almost see her mentally holding up a four out of ten as she took in the empty platform, the actual field of actual cows on the far side of the tracks, the complete and utter lack of Starbucks.

"Yeah, the next train back to London is in a week," I said.

She looked panicked. "What? Seriously? I have to get back tonight; I've got work tomorrow! What the hell?"

"I'm *joking*. There's like a train an hour. This is the Cotswolds, not the Outer Hebrides."

"I don't know, do I," she grumbled. "I don't know how things work outside London. I never *needed* to know, until you decided to come and be all *Good Life* down here."

It was fair to say Maya had taken our move pretty personally. I had been genuinely worried she might refuse to visit, but the double lure of a murder and the opportunity to scoff at some "hippy shit" had proved enticing enough. I hadn't told her about the gift-wrapped placenta as I'd worried that might scare her off.

"How long have we got before this gongle bath?" asked Maya. "I'm starving."

We picked up a quick bacon sandwich on our way over to the Temple, which made me panic like a teenager who realizes that they've forgotten their Impulse body spray when smoking behind the bike sheds.

"They'll smell the bacon on us!"

"So?"

"They'll know we're not proper vegans."

"We're not any sort of vegans."

"Yeah, but we probably *should* be. Everyone else will be. For sure."

Maya rolled her eyes. "OK, if anyone asks I'll say I'm vegan," she said, in a heavily sarcastic tone that I did not think was good for her chakras.

THE WOMEN'S Inner Goddess Temple had definite village hall vibes. Ailsa was waiting for us outside, tapping her foot impatiently.

I made hurried introductions between Ailsa and Maya, marveling at how different the two of them were. Maya had opted for neon athleisure wear, while Ailsa was in some sort of corduroy overalls. She was also eyeing us slightly suspiciously. She sniffed. "Bacon?"

"The vegan sort," said Maya, straight-faced.

Ailsa rolled her eyes and ushered us into the village hall-cum-temple. A floaty sort of lady in a white gown greeted us in that wispy, ethereal tone of voice that means you have to ask someone to repeat themselves three times. She had glorious auburn hair that seemed far too bold for her barely there voice.

"Have you voyaged before?" she whispered.

"Have I what now?" asked Maya.

"No, we haven't. First-time voyagers," I cut in, before Ailsa could.

She ushered us into a surprisingly packed room. The silky drapes hung all around didn't quite hide the institutional green walls behind them.

We picked our way over the prone bodies already sprawled across the various rugs and pouffes to a small patch of floor space at the back. I tried to assume a position that would be comfortable enough to allow me to reach inner peace, but uncomfortable enough to stop me from falling asleep and no doubt snoring.

The high priestess of the gong began to talk us through what we could hope to experience over the course of the gong bath. My mind (and bladder) instantly rebelled.

"Over the next two hours we will be taking a voyage through a soundscape, during which we will cleanse ourselves from the realm of the mind and attune with our divine essence."

Shit. This thing is two hours long? I'll have to pee at least twice in that time.

"You may experience intense emotions of joy or ecstasy, or even of fear or anger."

Oh no, I need to pee already. And we haven't even started.

"It is important that we embrace these emotions and give them full expression."

Would it be better to slip out now? Or wait until the first gong is rung?

"You will be immersed in the waves of sound, like a child in a mother's embrace."

My baby is kicking my bladder, why is he doing that? Why?

"You may find yourself laughing, or crying, as the emotions seek an outlet."

I need an outlet, like, right now.

"To experience the gong is to experience the universe itself."

I'll go now and maybe hopefully I'll make it through the next two hours without having to go again.

I trod on several hands and feet on my way back across the room. I could tell people were having emotions at me.

THE GONG bath itself was not unpleasant, although I confess I didn't have any particularly strong emotions. But then, I had watched an entire series of *Married at First Sight* over the course of the previous sleepless night so it's possible I'd just used up all of my emotions on that. Plus, it's not particularly comfortable lying on the floor at thirty-eight weeks pregnant, and that had occupied a lot of my mental space, leaving very little room for me to experience the universe.

As the final gong rang out and everyone sat up (or in my case rolled and flailed on the floor until Maya pulled me upright), I was thankful that at least I hadn't had to speak to anyone and there hadn't been any chanting.

"If we could all form a circle and join hands, we'll have a brief session of cosmic chanting to conclude our journey," whispered the high priestess of the gong.

I ended up holding hands with Ailsa on one side and Maya on the other, so at least I was saved from the clammy palms of a complete stranger. Unfortunately, several minutes into the chant one of the women piped up.

"My sister is currently forty hours into a really terrible labor," she said sweetly. "It's been horrific. Could we do a chant for her? She could really use some positive vibes."

What she could probably use, I thought, was her sister being on hand with a bit of support, rather than fucking off to a gong bath.

Nonetheless we all joined hands again and chanted this poor woman's name. "Emmammemmammemma." The chant seemed to be free-form, with everyone doing their own thing. One woman went up so high I reckon the bats could hear her. I felt the baby wince inside me; I don't think he's into cosmic chanting.

At the end, I nervously approached the gong priestess. She gave me a benevolent smile.

"Did baby enjoy the gong bath?" she asked.

"Er, yes. Yes, very much. Loved it," I gabbled, before plunging on. "I was actually wondering, I need a spiritual adviser for my . . . spirit. Someone mentioned there was a woman at the Temple who might be able to help. I think they said her name was Mairi something?"

"Mairi Webb?" The woman's gossamer tone slipped ever so slightly. "I wouldn't waste your time with her. The woman has the spiritual depth of an egg cup. A very *closed* mind. No, if you're in need of spiritual guidance I'd be more than happy to help. Is there something specific you want to be guided through, or are you simply searching to deepen your connection to the cosmos?"

"I, er, thank you. Yes, maybe. I did kind of want to talk to Mairi Webb though, I don't suppose you have contact details for her?"

The priestess pursed her lips. "No. I don't. She works at Nature's Way in town—you could try and contact her there. Now, if it was spiral plane voyaging you were interested in . . ."

I eventually managed to escape with a flyer about astral spirals, and no information about Mairi Webb that I hadn't already known.

"What was all that about?" Ailsa popped up at my elbow; Maya had wandered off to peruse a poster advertising "Bliss Walks." Before I could reply, Emma's sister cornered us.

"It's so wonderful what you're both doing," she gushed, like we were saving starving children from floods or curing malaria or something. I knew what was coming next . . . yep, she put her hand on my stomach. I needed one of those signs from the commune hung around my neck, TRESPASSERS WILL BE COSMICALLY CURSED. I tend to operate a sexual-partners-only policy on any form of touching, and at almost nine months pregnant that was a shortlist of zero.

"I just hope you don't go through what my poor sister is going through right now," the woman continued, making way too much eye contact. "Nearly two days now and still nothing. First the baby was breech, which makes it very hard for there to be a natural birth without *significant* damage to the mother, if you know what I mean."

Being pregnant is like wearing a huge sign on your face saying *"tell me the worst labor story you can dredge up: the more blood and screaming the better."*

"But of course Emma wouldn't have *anything* other than a natural birth. It's so important to give the child the right start in life, isn't it? But it does mean she's already torn—"

"I'm actually on a positive birth journey," interrupted Ailsa at this point. "Any negative birth stories will damage my aura. Sorry." And she dragged me away.

"*Jesus*," I breathed.

"I think you mean Bebinn," corrected Ailsa.

"What?"

"Pagan goddess of safe childbirth."

Honestly, I had no idea if she was joking or not.

"Are you really on a positive birth journey?" I asked her curiously.

She shrugged. "Does it matter? It shut her up."

"Any sign of that woman giving birth up at the commune yet?"

"Elowen?" Ailsa shook her head. "Nothing yet. Want to do a chant for her?"

Maya sauntered over, saving me from having to work out if this was a serious question or not. "Are we done chanting and shit now? Can we go and get a drink? I mean, can *I* go and get a drink? You losers can have a lemonade or whatever pregnant people drink."

To my surprise, Ailsa agreed. "Sure. Let's go to the Asafoetida Café. You can get an organic wine." And she moved off to collect a stack of cosmic yoga posters, gesturing impatiently at us to follow.

"Is she winding me up?" demanded Maya.

I did an Ailsa and shrugged. "Your guess is as good as mine."

CHAPTER 22

MAYA DID HAVE an organic wine. And it seemed to be going down very well. I wished I could say the same for my Karma Kola, which tasted like leather.

"So this café is, what, sponsored by hemorrhoid cream?" asked Maya, tapping a neon-orange nail on the "Asafoetida" logo on the paper menu. "Free butt cream with every fifth latte?"

"You're thinking of Anusol," Ailsa replied, unfazed. "Asafoetida is a spice. It's a type of fennel."

I just couldn't work out if this girl had absolutely no sense of humor or a brilliantly deadpan one.

As vegan organic hippy cafés went, this one was all right. It even did cakes with actual sugar in them. It also did a thriving trade in mums and babies. Everyone in the café seemed to have a pram with them. And, somehow, they all looked like mums. Which I really don't feel like I've nailed yet. Is it to do with the clothes? Or the hair? Or the perpetually harassed and careworn expression? Do I need to start shopping at JoJo Maman Bébé? Which I only recently and embarrassingly discovered is *not* pronounced Beeb.

I looked at Ailsa, with her shaved undercut and dreadlocks, currently pinning her cosmic yoga posters up on the café corkboard. She wasn't exactly on-brand with JoJo either. It felt extremely weird sitting in a café with Maya and Ailsa, like my past and future were colliding. The two eyed each other suspiciously as Ailsa sat down.

"So, how's your boyfriend dealing with the whole baby thing?" asked Maya blithely. "Freaking out, like Joe?"

Ailsa's face went stony. "There's no boyfriend."

"Yep, sorry, your wife, right?"

"No."

"You're thinking of Poppy," I hissed to Maya. "Also, Joe's not freaking out. Also shut up."

"Well, excuse me for trying to make polite conversation," said Maya cheerfully. "Shall we just crack on and talk about this murder then? Seems like a less hazardous topic."

"Sorry, you're involved how?" said Ailsa, pretty rudely, I thought. But then—Ailsa.

"I'm involved because my best friend is a suspect in a murder case," said Maya, looking disproportionately pleased by this.

"Whoa, whoa! I'm *investigating*, I'm not a suspect!"

"Sorry, Al, you don't have an alibi, plus the dead guy left you some bottle of voodoo, so you're definitely a suspect." Maya didn't look that apologetic as she accused me of potentially being a murderer.

Still, it did seem to make Ailsa thaw toward her a tad. Perhaps they could bond over their shared suspicion of me. "Very true," Ailsa agreed. "And the same goes for me. I'm definitely a suspect."

This was a little close to the bone, as we definitely *hadn't* ruled Ailsa out. I coughed awkwardly.

"OK, well, we can both be suspects then," I conceded, as if we were deciding who should be the banker in Monopoly. "And Maya, who definitely isn't a suspect, can be . . . I don't know. Consultant or something." This seemed to satisfy both of them. "I don't suppose you managed to get a copy of the postmortem report?"

"Nope."

I groaned. "And you couldn't have told me this *before* the gong bath?"

"And let you miss out on a chance to discover your inner goddess?"

"Alice doesn't have an inner goddess," chipped in Maya. "She just has an inner Helen."

I glared at both of them. They were equally awful, I decided.

"Anyway," said Ailsa. "I couldn't get a copy of the report because they haven't done the postmortem yet—some kind of backlog at the mortuary. Jane's pretty pissed off about it—doesn't think they're taking her case seriously. She's got ambitions, has Jane." There was an edge of bitterness to her tone.

"Things been busy on the murder front around here lately?" I asked. This really was sounding increasingly like *Midsomer Murders*. In which case we'd be looking at a body count of at least five by the end of the week.

But Ailsa wasn't finished. "I *have* got a copy of Jane's initial report on the crime scene, though," she went on, producing a sheaf of paper from her bag with a flourish.

I was enjoying amateur sleuthing. I mean, what else do you do in that weird dead time between going on maternity leave and actually popping the kid out? But suddenly pinching a police report seemed a bit serious, and reminded me that we had absolutely no right to be doing this. Whatever "this" was.

Ailsa noticed my hesitation.

"You want it or not?" she demanded, waving the report in my face.

"Don't flap it around," I hissed, looking furtively around the café.

"Oh, relax." She rolled her eyes and slapped it on the table in front of me. It was pretty slim, just a handful of pages stapled together. I skimmed them hopefully.

"So . . . what does it mean?" I asked eventually. It was full of words like "myocardial" and "atheroma" and mystifying references to "latent print evidence."

"Pass it here." Maya grabbed it out of my hand.

"Sorry, I forgot that your degree in marketing qualified you to decipher murder reports."

Maya gave me the finger and began flicking through the report with an ostentatiously professional air.

"Haven't the foggiest," she declared two minutes later, skating the report across the table back to Ailsa.

"No, I couldn't make much out of all the forensic bits," agreed Ailsa. "But look here, under the list of items secured from the crime scene . . ."

She opened the report to one of the many appendices that I had, admittedly, skipped past.

"Here." She jabbed at the page and then read aloud: "'One photo showing three individuals, two male one female, handwritten legend on the back reads: 'With Flora and Camran, summer eighty-nine.'"

She looked up at us. "Dunno if it's anything relevant, but it says here under where the item was found that it was underneath his body—"

"Gross," interjected Maya. Ailsa ignored her.

"—which suggests that he was looking at it when he died. A photo of Camran, seems a bit weird, doesn't it? I mean, Camran's a decent guy, don't get me wrong. But why was Mr. Oliver looking at a photo of them together after all this time? With some woman—I don't know who she is. I can't remember there being any Flora at the commune. Although, eighty-nine, well, that was before I was even born . . ."

"Flora," I said. "I know that name . . ." Then it came to me. "Flora! That's the woman they were all in love with!"

"What now?"

I filled them in on what Hazel had said about Flora. Although to be honest there wasn't much to be said—it had been more of a passing comment. Still, Ailsa looked thoughtful.

"Sounds like we could use a bit more info on this Flora . . ."

"Could you ask Rowan?"

Ailsa looked uncomfortable. "Yeah, maybe. If I see him."

This wasn't the go-getting detectoring attitude I wanted to see, but I had already learned that pushing Ailsa had only one effect, and that was that the pusher fell flat on their face. However, I wanted to know more about the enigmatic and magnetic Flora—I filed it away under "to be investigated" in my mind, an already overflowing mental drawer.

"Is there anything else in here?" said Maya, running a finger down the list of items. "I mean, what the fuck even is half this stuff? What's an *athame*?"

"Oh yeah, I noticed that," said Ailsa. "Interesting that it's there, but wasn't used."

"Used how?"

"It's a ritual knife, used in Wicca ceremonies. He sold them."

Maya and I looked aghast. Ailsa just shrugged. "So? If you went into a gardening shop you'd find a hundred things that could be used as weapons. In Nature's Way there's bound to be a few things that you could do some harm with. Anyway, he wasn't stabbed, so it's kind of irrelevant."

"Except," I pointed out, "like you say, it's interesting that it wasn't used. The murderer went for a less violent form of attack, which probably tells us something about them."

Ailsa and Maya continued looking at me.

"I mean, I don't know *what* it tells us about them," I clarified. "But it definitely tells us something. *Psychological*, you know?"

"Sherlock Holmes strikes again," muttered Ailsa under her breath. "Well, I looked through the list, and everything else on there is stuff related to the shop. Either stuff he sold, or like his accounts book. A calculator. That kind of thing."

"Anything else in the science?" I asked.

"Not sure. Didn't you say Hen knows about this sort of thing?" Ailsa said. "I could take it over to hers, see if she can get anything more out of it."

"It's OK, I'm seeing her tomorrow, I can show it to her then," I said without thinking.

"Oh. Fine then."

Belatedly, I realized that Ailsa had gone a little cool.

"Do you want to come? I'm just meeting her for coffee."

"Wouldn't dream of crashing your cozy little crime club. It's not like I'm the one putting my neck on the line and pinching police property for you or anything."

"No really, you should definitely come. We'd be lost without you." But the flattery was getting me nowhere.

"Forget it. Three's a crowd, and all that."

I figured now wasn't the time to mention that Poppy was also meeting us. How stupid of me not to have thought to invite Ailsa. Admittedly, that was probably because we hadn't fully ruled her out of maybe being involved. Although I kind of felt that now she'd pinched the police report for us, we should probably return the favor and stop suspecting her of murder. Then I reminded myself that detective work has to be completely objective and can't be influenced by these things. I really wasn't cut out for this.

"Look, come along. It'll be fun. We can read crime scene investigations and speculate about murder."

But Ailsa was as stubborn as they came.

"Nope. Got things to do. Say hi to Hen from me." She began gathering her stuff together, leaving me holding the report and a whole bag of guilt.

"Is that man taking your posters down?" commented Maya, who had watched this whole exchange with interest.

It was a masterpiece of misdirection. Ailsa's perpetual irritation, never far from bubbling over, was instantly redirected at the portly red-faced man wearing wine-colored chinos who was yanking her posters off the corkboard, not even bothering to remove the pins but simply tearing the paper.

"Oy!" yelled Ailsa.

I cringed a little. Maya grinned, leaned back and stretched an arm round the back of my chair, ready to enjoy the show.

The man turned round, showing one of those faces that just scream heart attack alert—pouchy and ruddy with little broken veins playing across the nose and cheeks.

"Leave my posters alone," snapped Ailsa.

The man's piggy little eyes narrowed. "This is a public space," he snapped. "You can't be advertising your rubbish here."

"You're handing out leaflets," pointed out Maya reasonably, nodding toward the wedge of leaflets in his hand.

Oh dear, I recognized those leaflets. In fact, I recognized this man. His face had been blazoned across one of the very same leaflets when it came through our door.

"You're that guy. From the Penton Whatsits," I exclaimed, unable to keep the note of distaste out of my voice.

"Ronald Pilkington. Founder and president of the Penton Preservation Society," he said pompously, drawing himself up. "Can I interest you in one of our leaflets? We'll also be holding a rally this weekend at the Corn Exchange." His eyes flickered to my bump. "Bring your husband along, make a family day out of it. Unless . . ." Those eyes narrowed again as he took in Maya sitting next to me, her arm still draped across my shoulder. "You're not . . . This isn't your *girlfriend*, is it? Not another—"

"Would it matter?" I asked, genuinely confused, at the same time as Maya said, "Yes," and laid a hand flirtatiously on my thigh.

I thought he might have his heart attack there and then.

"As if . . . I mean to say . . . Never . . ." He genuinely couldn't get his words out. I don't think I've ever seen that happen in real life before.

"Whoa," I said, a little alarmed. "Calm down. She's just having you on. But seriously, you do know this is the twenty-first century, right?"

Pilkington looked, if anything, even more furious on hearing that we had been winding him up.

"I shall be having a word with your husband about this," he fumed.

"Telltale," said Maya under her breath.

"Joe's not my husband, he's my boyfriend," I snapped, sensing this would annoy the man even further.

"Joe? The new chap? Well, rest assured I will be speaking to him next time he comes round."

Word clearly spread pretty fast in Penton—we'd not been here a week yet. "I don't think he'll be coming round yours for tea anytime soon," I retorted, pretty smoothly I thought.

But his eyes sparked with a maliciousness that I didn't like. He muttered something viciously under his breath and stamped out of the café.

"Dickhead," said Maya calmly.

"Totally," agreed Ailsa, repinning her cosmic yoga poster.

I made some sort of noise of assent. I was furious at Pilkington and his hideous bigoted opinions. But I confess my mind was elsewhere. What had Pilkington meant about the *next time* Joe came round?

CHAPTER 23

IT WAS A wrench saying goodbye to Maya at the station that evening. Being around her was just so comfortable it made me ache a little for my old life. But things were changing; my old life wasn't compatible with my new circumstances. And that was a good thing, I reminded myself. For the most part.

As the train carried her away, back to the bright lights of London—or as I was already starting to think of it, "the City," ugh I needed to nip that in the bud—I turned and began to trudge back through the deserted high street. It was only 8 P.M., but all the shops were closed and there was not a soul on the streets.

My heavy footsteps took me past Nature's Way, with half a thought in my mind that perhaps Mairi Webb might have returned to the shop. But the windows were all dark, and blue-and-white-striped police tape formed a large X across the door, although the police guard did seem to have been lifted. I couldn't help but shiver. As I sloped home along the darkened canal, I felt vulnerable, and painfully aware of my responsibility for not just myself but my unborn baby, whom, technically, I supposed I was already looking after right now. As I approached the underpass where the canal dipped below the road, I saw two figures in the shadows under the bridge. I decided to loop up and over the road, rather than pass them. I was probably being ludicrous, but you don't spend several years living in London as a woman in your twenties without learning to avoid certain situations. It shouldn't be that way, but it is.

As I climbed the steps to the left of the underpass I heard them talking.

"Well, that's the last of it."

I frowned. There was something familiar about that voice. But it was hard to tell; whoever it was they were keeping their voice low.

"There must be more. I could go and take a look?" The second voice was also ringing bells . . . Where did I recognize them from?

"Don't be silly, dear, that's a terrible idea."

Aha! One of the shady figures was Dot. I'd taken a detour to avoid the criminal mastermind and archvillain that was Dot. However, I was also going to stick to my chosen path, because I didn't really feel like a conversation on the state of my pelvic floor right now (in a word: poor). I dawdled slightly as I descended back toward the canal on the other side of the underpass, however. What was Dot up to, hanging about in underpasses at eight o'clock at night like some teenage yob? Didn't she have something better to do, like arrange her dream catchers, or detangle her wind chimes?

". . . best to wait until the police have lost interest in poor dear Crispin," Dot was saying as I came back into earshot. I froze.

"That could be months," grumbled the mystery voice.

"Oh, I doubt it," said Dot breezily. "Something else will come along and they'll forget all about it. For now, we should just keep a low profile. And don't do anything stupid, dear."

There was muttered assent from the other party.

"Now I really must get going," said Dot brightly. "I have transcendental meditation this evening, and dear Franklin does get so vexed if anyone is late."

There was a clattering of footsteps and two figures emerged from the underpass, one heading back in the direction I had just come from, toward town, and the other up toward the main road. Neither of them noticed me lurking in the shadows.

Well, Dot certainly seemed to have got over the death of "poor dear Crispin" swiftly. And why on earth did she and her mysterious companion need to keep a low profile? Surely, *surely*, Dot couldn't have anything to do with Mr. Oliver's murder?

As I hurried on home, I wondered who the other voice had been. I knew it was familiar, I just couldn't quite put my finger on it . . .

CHAPTER 24

"AND THEN THAT awful man from the Protection Party or whatever it's called turned up." I was filling Joe in on the events of the day in between shoveling lasagne into my face. Turns out gong voyages make you extremely hungry.

Joe sighed. "'That awful man' has a name."

"Pratface Pilkington, or something."

I really wanted to ask Joe if he knew Pilkington, or why Pilkington had appeared to know of him. But more than that, I wanted Joe to volunteer the information himself.

"Percy Pilkington, I think?" I prompted.

"Ronald Pilkington," corrected Joe, as if without thinking.

"Oh?" I said lightly. "You know him?"

"There was that leaflet through the door, remember," Joe said, a little *too* casually.

"Ah yes, I remember now, you were thinking of joining up," I said, half teasingly. I don't think I pulled off the jokey tone I was going for though, because Joe's face went hard.

"Don't be a dick, Alice," he said grumpily.

I went up to bed.

"I'M SORRY."

Wow, it wasn't often I heard those words from Joe.

"About what?" I asked, not looking up from my laptop. I could think of at least three answers he could give to that.

"For calling you a dick," he clarified. Well, it was a start.

"It's fine."

"No, it's not." He climbed onto the mattress beside me. "I shouldn't have said it, and I didn't mean it."

"Really, it's fine."

The inflatable mattress dipped and wobbled, sliding us together whether we liked it or not. Helen gave a heartfelt sigh at this disruption. It's a hard life being a dog.

Unusually for Joe, he didn't get his phone out for his usual pre-bed Twitter routine.

"It's nearly the weekend," he said.

"Your powers of observation astound me," I said dryly.

"We could do something nice together." He rolled to face me and tried to prop himself on one elbow, but the mattress was having none of it. I couldn't help giggling as he hammed it up, flailing and overbalancing dramatically on Helen, who gave us a long-suffering look and rolled onto her back, all four legs in the air like a dead fly.

But Joe made a valid point. Given the week we'd had—moving house, witnessing a murder, being interviewed by the police, etc., etc.—we hadn't had much time for each other, and it showed. Over the last week we'd rowed, we'd cuddled. We'd sulked, we'd laughed. I'd contemplated leaving him (not, like, *seriously*, but still . . .) and I've no doubt he'd felt the same about me—specifically when I'd announced my intention of attending a gong bath. It would be nice to spend some time together.

"What did you have in mind?" I asked, finally shutting my laptop.

"I heard Penton rocks a mean farmers' market on a Saturday," he offered.

Poppy and I *had* discussed trying to get back into the commune on Saturday, but my instinct told me that sharing this information right now would be a terminal move for our relationship.

Joe's fingers wrapped around mine.

"Yeah, that sounds really nice," I said, and I meant it. It sounded wholesome and rural and the kind of thing I'd imagined we would do upon moving to the country. "We could get some organic chutney and overpriced cheese and go for a picnic afterward."

"Ideal. I've heard you can get a loaf of bread for *under a tenner*."

I laughed and snuggled in a bit closer.

"I feel like I've hardly seen you since we moved here," said Joe, speaking into my hair.

"We had that hot date at the midwife appointment together," I pointed out, knowing how weak that sounded. "And we have prenatal class together tomorrow." Unbelievably, the course was going ahead with its final session, despite the disastrous start.

"Not exactly quality time, is it?"

He had a point there. No one's dream date included Dot and a knitted uterus.

"You're so busy with your new friends," he continued mournfully.

"I'm sorry," I said, feeling guilty, and then a touch annoyed at feeling guilty. "We do have to meet people here though, make new friends." I thought of Antoni and his suit; I couldn't imagine him and Joe hanging out over a pint and discussing snooker anytime soon. Joe had seemed to get on well with Poppy and Lin though, and had been very taken with Sultan.

"You know you're always welcome to join us," I proffered.

"What, at aquanatal class?"

I laughed. "Maybe not that, I wouldn't wish that on anyone. But we're going for coffee tomorrow, why don't you come?" Even as I said it, I knew this was a terrible idea—we were going to go through the crime scene report tomorrow and Joe would almost certainly not approve of this.

"I probably ought to work. I've got a really big project on," Joe said gloomily. "I want to get it out of the way before the baby arrives."

I tried not to look relieved.

"Well, we'll have the weekend together," I said cheerfully.

"Yeah," said Joe.

"And you've always got me and Helen!"

"Yeah . . ."

Helen started to lick her own butt. Joe sighed.

CHAPTER 25

I **WAS BACK** at the Asafoetida Café, which, irritatingly, would probably always now be called the Anusol Café in my mind. I'd texted Ailsa again, trying to persuade her to join us, but she had replied that she had better things to do. Probably involving asparagus.

"Hand it over," said Hen, without much preamble. For all that Hen with her shiny bob and immaculate designer maternity clothes was the opposite of Ailsa to look at, sometimes the two were really very similar. I said as much to Hen and she blushed. I wasn't sure it had been a compliment, but was relieved she wasn't biting my head off.

I filled Poppy in on the gong bath, while Hen perused the report, occasionally making notes in the margin and rolling the pram back and forth while her daughter slept.

"No mystic visions? No deep and meaningful revelations about your sense of self? Or your purpose on this planet?" Poppy sounded disappointed at how mediocre my voyage of cosmic discovery had been.

"I mean, I felt this tingling sort of feeling in my coccyx," I said. "But it turned out my butt had just gone to sleep."

"Your whole butt?"

"Pretty much."

"Didn't know that could happen."

"Yeah, it's a weird feeling. Kind of cosmic, actually."

Eventually, Hen broke up our incredibly deep and philosophical conversation.

"Interesting," she said, tapping the report on the table.

"Well?" Poppy and I leaned forward on tenterhooks.

"Well, actually not that interesting," amended Hen. "There's very little to go on, it seems. There was no evident cause of death, no marks on the body, no biological evidence to speak of—no blood or bodily fluids," she added at our blank looks. "Then when it comes to trace evidence and latent print evidence"—she looked at our faces again and sighed—"trace materials are things like soil or clothing fibers, anything the perpetrator might have brought in with them and might help identify them. Latent print evidence—oh come on, you must know *something*—that's finger-prints, palm prints, boot prints . . ."

I nodded with what I hoped was a knowing expression on my face. "Let me guess—nothing?"

"On the contrary. Too much. Being a shop, the crime scene was con-taminated with all sorts of prints. On the basis of latent print evidence alone they could probably prove that half of Penton did it."

"Ugh." Poppy sat back, a frown wrinkling her forehead. "Is there any-thing actually useful in there?"

"Well, there's this photo found under the cadaver"—Hen's use of the word "cadaver" was both impressive and slightly alarming—"which might be useful if we could actually see it. But somehow I can't see In-spector Harris handing it over anytime soon. And then some spilled tea that's been sent away for testing. You'd already picked up on that, Alice." I allowed myself a small smug smile.

"I'd bet a million pounds the tea was poisoned." I nailed my colors to the mast.

"You haven't got a million pounds," said Hen absently.

"You don't know that."

"Poison seems most likely though, right?" stepped in Poppy quickly. "If they didn't find any marks on the body then surely that's how he was killed."

"*If* he was killed," corrected Hen. "The report says they're treating it as a suspicious death in light of Mr. Oliver's call to the police the previ-ous day. But there's no evidence as yet to suggest that it was in any way unnatural."

"No way," I said, sitting back. "No way did he drop dead of his own accord. There's something so suspicious about this whole thing."

"I'm pretty sure Harris thinks so too," said Poppy gloomily. "She was over in Tattlesworth yesterday, questioning Lin's mum about her relationship with her brother."

"Oh really?" asked Hen, leaning forward slightly. "What was she asking?"

Poppy sighed. "About this stupid family row. I mean, Lin's mum was at a Women's Institute supper club on Saturday night so she has a rock-solid alibi—about twenty respectable middle-aged women will testify that she didn't set foot outside the village hall that night, but . . . I don't know. I just hate the way Lin's family are being dragged into all this."

"Any ideas what the argument was about yet?" I asked tentatively.

Poppy shot me a look that was slightly sharper than her usual gentle expression.

"Apparently they fell out when he left the commune. He wanted to borrow some money off her to start up his shop. She refused. Harsh words were said. And that was that."

Ah, I thought gloomily. Money. That's never good.

"Interesting," said Hen thoughtfully.

"Not really," said Poppy shortly. "People fall out over stuff like that all the time. Anyway, it was years ago."

"I guess the police have to follow up every line of inquiry," I said, not sure whether this was helpful or not.

"Well, they're wasting their time with Lin's family," said Poppy. "Do you know if they've spoken to anyone else? Have they been up to the commune at all?"

"I don't think so," I said cautiously. In fact, Ailsa had said the previous day that her sister was focusing pretty heavily on the family line of investigation. I wondered why. Jane Harris clearly wasn't stupid—she might be lacking in interpersonal skills, and have all the charisma of a spoon, but she *was* a police detective. And she had access to all sorts of resources we didn't. I didn't like it, but I couldn't help wondering whether Inspector Harris knew something we didn't.

Hen and I exchanged a brief look.

"Is Lin . . . OK?" I asked tentatively.

Poppy inspected her nails. "Yeah, I think so. She's been pretty quiet the last few days. Said she's 'busy with work.' I feel like I've hardly seen her this week . . . Still, it's good practice for the next six months I guess, sitting at home worrying while our partners are off working."

Hen nodded. "Tell me about it. Antoni's company have been a nightmare. Absolutely no respect for paternity leave. Apparently, there's some crisis with one of his clients that they can't possibly resolve without him."

"We actually saw Antoni in Bridgeport the other day," I said without thinking. "We would've said hi, but he looked like he was in a hurry."

She looked surprised. "In Bridgeport? When?"

"Wednesday, after our aquanatal class." I was already biting my tongue. Poppy was giving me a slightly despairing look.

Hen shook her head. "Antoni was in London on Wednesday. Work."

"Oh. My mistake. Must've been someone who looked like him." I smiled awkwardly. "Just as well we didn't go over to some total stranger then!"

With a rare attempt at tact, I decided I wouldn't mention the girl he'd been with. Or the embrace. In fact, maybe I'd just shut up for a while.

"So," said Hen briskly, clearly signaling that our brief tea break to discuss our personal lives was over. She was definitely the sort to counter emotions with action. "In terms of the murder, some things will have to be left to the police. The results of the test on this tea, for instance. And the postmortem—once they get their asses in gear and actually do it. Alice, can you speak to Ailsa and find out when they're expecting those results?"

"That might not be so easy," I admitted. "I think she's pissed off with me for not inviting her today."

"Why didn't you invite her?" asked Poppy.

"I did! But only after I'd told her I was already meeting Hen. I think it looked like a bit of an afterthought."

"What are we, thirteen?" asked Hen scathingly. "Just ring her up and say sorry then invite her for ice cream or something."

"I don't think she eats ice cream," I said gloomily. "Too frivolous."

"Too dairy," corrected Poppy. "You need vegan gelato or something."

"Whatever," said Hen. "She'll get over it. Just make sure you invite her along next time."

I felt suitably chastened.

"So what next?" I asked.

"Did you get anywhere with tracking down Mairi Webb at the Temple yesterday?" asked Poppy.

"No joy," I admitted. "The gong priestess just said we should try Nature's Way, but that's still closed—or it was last night anyway."

"We could swing by, just in case," Hen suggested. "Even if she's not there it might be worth seeing what we can find."

"You mean, like a clue?"

Hen looked a bit put out at my simplistic take on the matter.

"If you must," she sighed.

"I can't," said Poppy. "I want to go and surprise Lin at work on her lunch break. Actually, I need to have left like ten minutes ago. I'll see you at class tonight!" And she disappeared in a whirl of brightly colored scarf, like a pregnant genie.

Hen looked at me, and I couldn't help feeling she was very much getting her second choice of detectoring partner. But she just handed me her swanky nappy bag like I was her personal porter. "Come on then, let's go and find you a clue."

CHAPTER 26

THERE WAS, UNSURPRISINGLY, still a CLOSED sign on the door of Nature's Way.

"What do we do?" I asked nervously. "I don't really fancy breaking into the scene of a crime." It was bad enough that Ailsa had stolen a police report.

"Shh, there's someone in there!" Hen pulled me away from the shop window and we ducked down behind the pram—probably not the most effective hiding place.

"Is it Mairi Webb?" I whispered excitedly, peering back round. But it wasn't.

She wasn't wearing her priestess gown, but I'd recognize that auburn mane anywhere.

"Is that . . . ? What is the gong priestess doing here?"

Hen's head appeared below mine. "Don't know, but something shifty by the look of it."

She was right. The priestess was flitting around at the back of the shop, sifting through the crystal display, apparently looking behind each object. As we watched, she moved to the counter and began searching through the drawers. After a few minutes, she moved on to the shelves behind the counter, opening jars and peering inside them. At one, she paused, then slipped something into her pocket. She looked up nervously, and we quickly withdrew into the shadows.

"Is she shoplifting?" asked Hen. "I thought only teenage girls did that."

"Or worse—what if she's pinching evidence?"

"The police will have taken any evidence already, surely."

This was a good point. I paused. "Unless . . . it's evidence that might not *look* like evidence?"

"Let's go and ask her," said Hen.

"What? No!"

But Hen was already reaching for the door of the shop.

Just as Hen was about to rap on the door, there was a cry of "Sandra!" from inside the store. Silently, we pressed our faces to the glass.

A sharp-faced woman, probably in her mid-sixties, was descending the stairs that led to the upstairs room where the fateful prenatal class had been held. She wore a utilitarian linen dress and her iron-gray hair was pulled back austerely from her face.

"What are you doing, Sandra?" The woman's voice was even sharper than her face.

It took me a minute to realize she was talking to the high priestess of the gong. Whose name was, apparently, *Sandra*? Not Rainbow or Willow or Esmerelda. Plain old Sandra.

"Oh, Mairi! I . . . didn't realize you were in." Priestess Sandra could not have looked more guilty. Hen and I, however, exchanged delighted looks. We had found Mairi Webb!

"No?" said Miss Webb skeptically. "You could have tried knocking. How did you get in?"

Sandra looked even guiltier as she held up a small key. "Spare key. Crispin always left it in the hanging basket."

Miss Webb pursed her lips. She did not look best pleased.

"Of course, I might have known. And honestly, Sandra, do you really think *now* is the time?"

"I just thought, if it was *there*, there was no harm in—"

It was at this moment that Hen's baby woke up—angrily. She gave a screech like a banshee. Sandra's and Miss Webb's heads whipped round to where the two of us stood shamelessly eavesdropping. As one, we stepped back from the door. I tried an awkward wave.

Miss Webb's eyes narrowed as she strode toward us. For a spiritual adviser, she had a very intimidating stride.

"Leave this to me," muttered Hen.

"Miss Webb, I'm *so* sorry," she began the minute the door was opened. "I know this is terrible timing, and I'm so, so sorry for your loss. I wouldn't ask unless I was desperate, but I just *have* to get hold of some Roman chamomile for the baby. She's not sleeping at all and I'm just at my wits' end."

She held up the squawking baby: Exhibit A.

Miss Webb looked unconvinced. She glanced back at Sandra, who gave us all a brittle, forced smile.

"I'm so sorry if we're interrupting something," said Hen brightly.

"Not at all," said Miss Webb shortly. "Sandra was just about to help me with a stocktake. Weren't you, Sandra?"

Sandra was eyeing us all nervously. "Oh, I'd love to, Mairi. But I'm so sorry, I'm already really very late for . . . a thing. It was so lovely to see you. So sorry about Crispin. Do pop round for a cup of tea, any time." And she scurried out without meeting anyone's eye.

As she slipped past, I wondered wildly whether I could accidentally bump into her and try and slip a hand in her pocket to see what she'd taken. But I haven't pinched anything since I stole a nail varnish from Superdrug when I was seven, and I don't think I've got the sleight of hand to pull it off anymore.

Miss Webb was still regarding us suspiciously. "Roman chamomile, you said?" She turned to the cabinet of essential oils, selected one and slammed it down on the counter.

"Four fifty," she said, unsmiling.

Hen jiggled the baby while rummaging one-handed in her handbag.

"You wouldn't mind holding her for a sec while I find my purse, would you?" She thrust the baby at Miss Webb, who took her instinctively. The effect was astonishing. Instantly, her whole body relaxed, the harsh lines of her face softened.

"Oh! Oh, she's rather nice." She gazed down at the baby and the corners of her mouth twitched into the hint of a smile. "What a poppet. So tiny!"

"Didn't feel tiny on Saturday evening," muttered Hen, digging around in her bag.

Miss Webb stopped bouncing the baby. Hen and I froze as we realized her mistake.

"It was you, wasn't it?" she asked. "You gave birth here that night." She looked round at me accusingly. "And you? Were you here too, at the prenatal class?"

We nodded mutely.

Miss Webb sat down heavily on the chair behind the counter, still clutching the baby. "You were here . . . when Crispin . . ."

"We're so sorry about your partner, Miss Webb," said Hen. "Are you OK?"

She waved a hand at us, signifying . . . I'm not sure what. That it was OK? That we should leave? But then she spoke. "No wonder Sandra didn't want to stick around," she said, a trace of bitterness in her words. "It was one of your lot who told the police she was here the night poor Crispin was killed. She's been interviewed by the police and everything."

We exchanged glances.

"What?"

"Yes. Some bloke, apparently. Told the police he'd seen Sandra hanging around the shop."

Well, this was news.

"I'm sure she'd just popped by for . . . a chat," continued Miss Webb. Again, there was a hint of something in her voice. "She often does, of an evening. *Did*, I suppose I should say. I don't suppose she'll be around so much now."

She lapsed into gloomy silence.

"Have you heard anymore from the police?" I asked tentatively. "I don't mean to pry or anything. I just, you know, hope everything gets . . . resolved."

"Oh, they don't know anything," said Miss Webb tersely. "They kept asking me if Crispin ever got muddled. I know what they were driving at. As if he'd have accidentally poisoned himself." She snorted derisively. "He was an idiot, Crispin, but he wasn't stupid."

It was an interesting comment.

"You definitely don't think it was an accident then?" I asked—as gently as possible, but let's be honest, there's no "nice" way to ask that question.

"Oh no," said Miss Webb grimly. "And what's more, he knew it was coming."

"What makes you say that?" asked Hen.

"He'd been worried. Something had upset him. For maybe a week beforehand he'd been so on edge. Jumping at his own shadow. Then he kept thinking he'd seen someone in the garden. Well, for all I know he had! And then that day he kept . . . dredging up the past. Talking about Flora. And about . . . *all that*. Well, I don't know what had brought that on. It's dead and buried, I told him. What's happened has happened, and there's nothing you can do about it. But he fretted. Oh, he fretted." She broke off.

The mysterious Flora once again. And . . . something else?

"Who's Flora? Talking about what?" I asked—perhaps a touch too urgently. Miss Webb fixed us with a beady eye.

"You've got your Roman chamomile," she said, getting heavily to her feet. "Is there anything else I can do for you ladies?"

"We just wondered—" began Hen, but Miss Webb cut her off.

"Yes, I can see that. Well, now you can just *wander* on home." She thrust the baby back into Hen's arms and began busying herself behind the counter. "Thank you for your business. I'm afraid we'll be closed a while longer. I'm sure you can appreciate why."

There was nothing we could do but file out, Hen clutching her little paper bag, both of us burning with questions.

WE FOUND a bench on the high street and sat down in silence.

"Here, have this." Hen thrust the Roman chamomile into my hand.

"I'm OK, thanks. I have literally no idea what I would do with this. Drink it? Burn it? Smoke it?"

"You can do what you like with it, but I can't keep it. If Antoni found it he'd totally freak out on me."

I needed to get home. I needed to shower, I needed a cookie or five, I needed a break. But there was an unspoken question hanging between us. Being a coward, I waited for Hen to bring it up.

"Was it Joe? Who saw Sandra?" she asked eventually.

"Not that I know of," I said quietly. "He didn't say anything to me."

"Neither did Antoni."

We were silent for a moment. Joe and Antoni were the only two men who'd been there. It must have been one of them who had seen Sandra and reported her to the police. But in that case, why had neither of them told us?

CHAPTER 27

OUR NEW CLASS venue was, believe it or not, the Women's Inner Goddess Temple.

Joe had been out at a client meeting and said he'd meet me there, so I arrived on my own, and I've got to say, I was feeling pretty weird about the whole thing. After all, last time we'd met as a group one member had given birth and someone had been murdered about six feet away. I *really* wasn't up for a repeat performance.

Dot was, of course, on boundless good form. When was she not? If she had murdered Mr. Oliver, I'm sure she would have done it while humming a jaunty little ditty and apologizing for inconveniencing him.

"Welcome back, welcome back!" she trilled as I scuttled in. She was sorting through a pile of brightly colored nappies and looked like she couldn't be more delighted about it. In fact, did she seem . . . *too* cheerful? Was there a manic edge to that smile? Was she being even chirpier than normal? But then, it's hard to tell when you've only met someone three times, and one of those times they had a Tupperware full of placenta. I mean, who's to say where someone like that sets the bar for "normal"? I edged past her cautiously, just in case she did decide to freak out and throttle me to death with the fake umbilical cord she was holding and appeared to have knitted herself.

At least my fellow students were no longer terrifying strangers. I grabbed a chair next to Poppy and Lin.

"Hey, Alice." Lin smiled at me, but there were shadows beneath her eyes and a tightness to her face that was new. "Thanks for keeping this one out of trouble this week. I wasn't sure what I was going to do with her once her maternity leave started!" She squeezed Poppy's shoulders affectionately and Poppy stuck her tongue out at her.

I grinned nervously. I didn't think poking our noses into a murder investigation necessarily constituted keeping out of trouble. Although I wasn't actually sure how much Poppy had shared with Lin about our recent activities. Then there was the fact that Lin herself seemed to be somehow implicated in the investigation that we were trying to unpick. And, well, I had a few questions there myself, which made me feel like a bad friend.

"It's been fun," I said awkwardly. "Except for the aquanatal class. That was hell."

"Sounded appalling," agreed Lin. "What's the point of being pregnant if you can't sit around eating cake and not exercising?"

"Says the one woman here who's not pregnant," said Poppy, rolling her eyes. "And, for the record, you'd be horrendous at being pregnant. You can't sit still for five minutes."

Lin grinned. "We'll see. I guess it'll be my turn next time round."

"Are you seriously thinking about a second already?" I was alarmed. Joe and I had barely got our heads around the arrival of one; the prospect of a second was about as high on my priorities list as laser hair removal (which is to say, something I would talk about for ten years and never get round to doing because it sounds painful, expensive and unnecessary).

"No," said Poppy, at the same time as Lin said, "Maybe."

At this point Ailsa sidled into the room.

"All right," she mumbled, sinking into the chair next to me.

"How's it going?" I asked.

"Fine. Did you cook the rhubarb?"

It took me a minute to understand what she meant—at first I wondered if this was a slang phrase for something pregnancy-related and probably gross. Then I remembered that she had literally given me some actual rhubarb.

"Oh. No," I confessed. "I did chop it up but then I wasn't sure what to do with it so I put it in the fridge and forgot about it, sorry."

"What about the cabbage?"

"Same."

Ailsa sighed. "My produce is wasted on you."

"Probably," I admitted. "Unless you swap your cabbage patch for Sour Patch Kids. I'm smashing those at the minute."

Ailsa wrinkled her nose. "What the hell are Sour Patch Kids?"

I was so out of place in Penton.

Fortunately, at that moment Joe arrived. Someone who knew, and appreciated, sour candy.

"Well, if that's all of us," Dot's voice rang out, full of good cheer, like a nappy-wielding Father Christmas on speed. "How wonderful to see you all back here. No Hen of course, she's well away in Mummyland." She beamed.

Mummyland? Did people speak like this for real? I tried to keep the horror from my face. Then noticed that Ailsa wasn't even trying.

"Let's get cracking! We've got so much to cover this evening, after last weekend's meeting went a little off schedule."

That was putting it mildly.

And we really did get cracking. For a fluffy-haired, grandmotherly figure, Dot really put us through our paces. In swift succession I was introduced to 4-8 breathing, the joys of colostrum and reusable nappies.

"Sorry—say what?" asked Joe, horrified.

"Reusable nappies, dear," repeated Dot. "As you'll see, we have a number of different styles here. Do come and take a look. This here is your classic terry nappy, with accompanying nappy nippers. And a wool wrap to go over it. Here we have a pocket nappy with bamboo boosters. And this one here is an all-in-one"—she took stock of my and Joe's dismayed faces—"yes, I think the all-in-one would be the simplest for you two."

"So, hold up." Joe was still struggling with the concept. As, admittedly, was I. "After the baby has pissed and shat in the nappy . . . you *reuse* it?!"

"Yes, dear." Dot nodded encouragingly. "You tip any solids down the toilet"—I gagged a little at this—"put it through the washing machine on a hot wash and start over!"

"You weren't going to use disposables, were you?" cut in Ailsa, sounding genuinely appalled. "You do know it takes them five hundred years to break down in landfill, right?"

Well, no, I didn't know that, but now she said it I could understand where her horrified look was coming from.

"And there are three billion nappies thrown away every year in the UK alone," continued Ailsa. "You can't possibly be willing to be a part of that."

"Um, no," I mumbled, realizing somewhat shamefacedly that I had been a hundred percent ready to unwittingly become a wholesale contributor to the problem. Which I definitely did not want to be. Which meant . . . reusable nappies, apparently. But Ailsa wasn't quite done.

"And the nappies that go to landfill, the contents often end up in our water system. Like, the water in your tap. That you *drink*. At least with reusables it's going into the waste treatment system. The stuff in landfill? That's going straight into—"

"Whoa!" Joe held up his hands in surrender. "We get the picture!"

Ailsa glared at him.

"Yeah, and we're on board with it," he clarified. "I just . . . don't need to hear the finer details, OK?"

Ailsa's face relaxed, just a little.

"Any other horrors we need to know about?" asked Joe resignedly.

"Let's talk about baby wipes," said Dot brightly.

"And the monstrous fatbergs they create," piped up Ailsa. "The one they found under London was two hundred and fifty meters long and one hundred and thirty tons. That's like *ten* blue whales end to end."

Joe sighed.

NEXT, DOT had us practicing light-touch massage, which would apparently help with the contractions during labor and act as a natural painkiller.

"Ailsa, sweetheart, since you've not got anyone with you, you can partner with me."

Ailsa looked furious—either about Dot's unsubtle drawing of attention to her single status, or possibly just about being called "sweetheart." When Dot began enthusiastically kneading her shoulders, her expression darkened even further.

Soon, Dot had me leaning against the wall with Joe behind me massaging my hips. Poppy was bent over a pregnancy ball while Lin rubbed her sacrum. The scene looked like it was taken from a particularly niche edition of the *Kama Sutra*.

"Am I doing it right?" Joe asked.

"No idea. But I'll be sure to let you know if you're doing it wrong during the birth."

"So kind."

I was actually quite enjoying it. But personally still felt pretty sure that I'd be reaching for something stronger than light-touch massage and a spot of yogic breathing to get me through labor. Still, I was disappointed when Dot called an end to proceedings and announced we were moving on to sleep and feeding patterns and all the horrors that they entailed.

As the session ended, I was feeling a little subdued, to put it mildly. I had always wanted children. So had Joe. Sure, we'd expected to have a little more than a year of enjoying each other's company before the urge to reproduce had us throwing caution to the wind—but when we'd found out we were having a baby, the overwhelming emotion had been excitement. After three prenatal classes, I was starting to feel like I had entered some sort of Faustian pact with the beast in my womb. It would take my sleep, sanity and youth in exchange for . . . fun? Carte blanche to watch kids' films without feeling like a loser? A comfy care home and fortnightly visits in my old age? All good things, sure, but . . . *so is sleep.*

"Pub?" I suggested as we all filed out, each clutching our sample reusable nappy.

"Hell yes," said Lin. "Let's go to the Rose and Thorn. I need a pint."

"Ditto," agreed Joe.

Poppy, Ailsa and I scowled.

CHAPTER 28

I LINED UP my glass of Coke and my glass of tap water on the sticky pub table in front of me.

"So what are the chances of there being any sort of nappy contents in this?" I asked, holding the water to the light mistrustfully.

"Not unlikely," said Ailsa. This was not reassuring.

"I think I'll just stick with the Coke," I said, wondering whether I could get through the rest of my life without drinking water.

Ailsa opened her mouth, presumably to tell me what horrors my Coke contained, but I held up a hand to stop her. "Whatever it is, I don't want to know."

"So irresponsible," she muttered. "Do you even care about our planet? Or your child's future?"

"I absolutely do," I retorted, "but right now I'm still getting my head around the fact that I'm going to be reusing nappies. One thing at a time."

Ailsa shot me an exasperated look. I shrugged. "I'm new to this, be gentle with me."

I'm not sure Ailsa had ever been gentle with anyone. But she dropped it and let me drink my almost-certainly-toxic Coke in peace—for which I was very thankful.

"You care a lot about this stuff, don't you?" asked Joe, sounding genuinely curious.

"Who wouldn't?" shot back Ailsa. "It's literally life or death—if the planet is poisoned, it isn't a huge leap of the imagination to realize that's not great for us as a species. If nothing else, we should be interested on a purely selfish level."

"So true," chimed in Lin. "It's like we don't think of ourselves as a species though, as if we're somehow separate from all the other species on earth."

"Just because we've overrun the world," agreed Poppy. "And here we all are, contributing to the problem."

"Yep," said Lin. "Having a baby is probably about the worst thing we could do for the environment."

Ailsa looked uncomfortable at this.

"Unless one of our babies turns out to be the next David Attenborough, or Greta Thunberg," I suggested. It seemed unlikely that this would be my and Joe's baby, given our track record, but then our kid was going to grow up in Penton with access to a whole lot more nature than either of us had ever experienced.

"Maybe we should call our baby Attenborough, to sort of kick-start him," I suggested to Joe.

"Or just, you know, David," he countered.

"No, there's lots of Davids. That could turn him into anyone—like, David Hasselhoff or David Schwimmer."

"Seriously, those are the first Davids that come to mind for you?" Poppy asked. "Interesting."

"They're nineties classics," I said defensively.

"What are nineties classics?" A familiar curly-top had appeared at our table. It was Rowan.

"Hey! Join us for a drink." I was probably being overenthusiastic; I barely knew the guy, but he seemed nice, and it would be good for Joe to meet some more people in Penton. I just hoped Joe wouldn't ask him if he followed snooker. No one under fifty follows the snooker. Except Joe. And, I admit, I had a slight ulterior motive. I was pretty sure Rowan had taken that newspaper from the archives—I wanted to see it, and I wanted to know why he'd taken it. Maybe after a few pints he might feel more inclined to discuss the matter . . .

Rowan and Lin disappeared up to the bar to get another round in, and Poppy and Joe were busy comparing their free-gift reusable nappies.

I turned to Ailsa, who had been conspicuously silent since Rowan had joined our table.

"Everything OK?"

"Yeah, why?"

I was going to ask what the deal was with her and Rowan, but I wasn't brave enough. So instead I decided to try and Get To Know Ailsa. I suspected this would be on a par with deciding to understand quantum physics, or running a four-minute mile.

"So, you're from Penton?" I asked. "Born and bred?"

"Bridgeport born, Penton bred," she confirmed. "I moved here when I was fifteen to live with my nan."

"And her ghosts," I added.

Ailsa laughed (ten points to me!). "And her many ghost lodgers. There was hardly room for me and my teenage angst."

"And Jane?" I asked. The laughter shut off abruptly.

"What about Jane?"

"Did she come and live with you and the ghosts?"

"No."

"Okaaaaay."

Ailsa sighed. "God, you're nosy, aren't you?"

"It's one of my better qualities."

"Jane did not come and live with Nana Maud too. Jane was part of the reason I came to live here."

"No need to overshare." I had a stab at sarcasm.

"No, but if I don't tell you, you'll go off and conjure up all sorts of little theories with Poppy."

This was probably true, I thought guiltily.

"Jane had just landed her first job as a detective constable. After I got arrested—which you already know about, you nosy bint—she got a bit intense with me, and I decided to move in with Nana Maud for a bit. And I stayed. Because, well, you've met Nana Maud, she's great. And because Bridgeport is a dump."

"Got to agree with you there." I hadn't been blown away by Bridgeport. It was an in-between sort of place, lacking the vibrancy of a larger town or city, but without the rustic charm (ha) of a Penton.

It was all totally legit—well, getting arrested was the opposite of legit, I supposed. But Ailsa's story checked out, kinda, even if she was pretty cagey. And if she said her arrest had just been for peaceful protesting, well, who was I not to believe her? I decided to pursue the marginally safer topic of Rowan.

"And that's where you met Rowan? At school in Penton?"

"Yep. Final year."

"And tell me, has he fancied you ever since then?"

That caught her off guard. I guess she hadn't expected me to be so blunt. It was worth it for the momentarily flummoxed expression on her face.

"What are you—? Oh my God, you are *so* annoying!"

I grinned. "Yep."

"Ugh. Fine. Yes, he asked me out a couple of times. But he also disappeared on a never-ending gap year and has shown up here like three times in the last decade. So I'm guessing his interest is pretty passing."

I really, really wanted to ask if one of those times was nine months ago. But I was skating on such thin ice I could hear it creak. And that water looked pretty cold.

"Any news on the postmortem?" I asked quietly, casting a furtive glance around the table, but everyone else seemed pretty involved in their own conversations.

"No movement. Jane's losing it."

"Has she got anything else to go on?"

"Said she's following a strong lead but wouldn't say what."

"Dammit." I wondered if that lead had anything to do with Lin and her family. A couple of pints in and Lin was looking less strained, but I couldn't help noticing that she and Poppy held hands tightly, even when they were in separate conversations. I wanted to tell Poppy about what Hen and I had seen at Nature's Way the previous day, but it didn't seem appropriate to blurt it out across a crowded pub table.

I told Ailsa about it in a totally non-suspicious hushed tone of voice. She was skeptical.

"I know Sandra," she said. "She's a bit of an airhead, but I don't think she's a *murderer*."

"I'm not saying she is," I said hastily. "It's just . . . suspicious, that's all. Do you think we should tell your sister?"

"I wouldn't," said Ailsa. "Innocent until proven guilty and all that. Jane doesn't understand the meaning of the phrase."

I wondered if I should be a bit more generous on this front and stop suspecting everyone I came across of some degree of criminality. I'd hoped to corner Rowan and subtly bring the conversation round to the missing *Bugle* paper—subtlety being one of my strong points—but he was now deep in conversation with Joe, and I didn't want to discourage this. On tuning in, however, I heard the name Ronnie O'Sullivan mentioned several times in quick succession and groaned inwardly. Ronnie O'Sullivan, for the blissfully uninitiated, is some sort of snooker god—according to Joe, that is. Now you can erase that information from your memory—it's a waste of good brain space.

I rescued Rowan from a blow-by-blow account of Ronnie's greatest breaks—for which he could thank me later—and dragged a slightly tipsy Joe home with me, it being well past my usual bedtime of 9 P.M.

"A top bloke, that Ronan," Joe said, slightly blurrily, as I drove us home. When this baby was out Joe was going to owe me nine months of designated drivership.

"Rowan," I corrected.

"Like the tree?"

Now that surprised me. I didn't know Joe knew the names of that many trees. And a rowan is, in my limited knowledge, one of the more niche trees.

"Yeah, I guess."

"Huh." Joe appeared to consider this for a while. "Named after a tree. Damn hippies," he mumbled eventually. "Bet he's one of *them*."

"One of what?"

"A communist."

"Huh?" This really threw me. Were my fears about Joe's right-wing leanings about to be realized? Not that I was overly fond of communism either, if it came to that.

"A communal," he corrected himself. "A communite?"

Ah, he meant the commune.

"Firstly, that's not a word. Secondly, yeah, he is. His dad runs the place."

Joe mumbled some choice swear words under his breath.

"Still, stand-up guy though, right?" I said hopefully.

Joe slumped forward till his head hit the dash. End of conversation.

CHAPTER 29

I KNEW I shouldn't have had a Coke. That tiny dose of caffeine into my chronically deprived system was enough to keep me awake for most of the night.

Around 4 A.M. I gave up on sleep long after it had already given up on me and came downstairs. I sat nursing a mug of mint tea.

Four A.M. is a lonely time. Even the baby was sleeping, and for once I'd have quite welcomed one of his swift elbow jabs to the kidneys just to remind me that I had company—of a sort.

I messaged Maya.

> Hey, you awake?

To my surprise, a reply flashed up almost immediately.

> Yeah. Why are you??

> Had a Coke. Can't sleep

> As in—the beverage, right?

> YES. And I'm insulted you'd even ask

> Ha!

> Why are you up?

> It's Friday night bitch! I'm out!

Of course she was. The thought made me feel even lonelier.

Where you at?

Canavans!

I was halfway through typing "Who you with" when I paused, and deleted it. I didn't want to know. Canavans was *our* club. It was the weird little local pool club–cum–dance bar that we'd frequented when we first lived together in Peckham. Pretty much every Friday had seen us playing pool appallingly, dancing even more appallingly or snuggled up together on the ancient beer-saturated sofas, warm Red Stripes clutched in our sweaty mitts. It was where I'd met Joe. Belatedly, I wondered if that had felt as weird for Maya as it now felt hearing that she was there without me.

My phone pinged.

Sorry, bathroom break over

Speak to you tomorrow?

Yeah

Have a great night!

dancing emoji

Yeah you too!

I snorted at that.

Still, I didn't have to spend the night drinking mint tea in my dressing gown. I threw on my Barbor over my pajamas, shoved my feet in my trainers and fetched Helen's lead.

Helen, great lover of the outdoors, the dog who would walk all day, was nonetheless unimpressed at being woken. I had to poke her for a good five minutes and, when she still wasn't getting the message, clipped her lead on anyway and started dragging her to the door. Her choices were to give in and come with me or get throttled by her own lead.

As soon as I set foot in the woods I knew I'd made the right choice.

In the cool, still, pre-dawn morning it was almost like being under-water. It felt so *clean*. I breathed deeply—no small feat at thirty-eight weeks pregnant—and felt myself relax slightly. I realized that it was the first time since the move that I'd been really alone. Helen didn't count; she had already disappeared into the trees and I would only spot her as a blurred streak of blond until we got back to the car. I'm not an alone sort of person—I like to be around people, hence having thrown myself with great enthusiasm into the prenatal group and the subsequent mur-der investigation—but I was also realizing that opportunities to be truly alone were going to be thin on the ground from here on.

In fact, I was probably the only person in this neck of the woods. I had deliberately come to the opposite end of Stricker's Wood to the com-mune, and it was not yet 5 A.M.; even the most ardent dog walkers and joggers would be another hour in bed. I set my Spotify Daily Mix to shuf-fle, didn't bother with headphones, and began singing along at the top of my voice. Because why the hell not. I'd never have been able to do this in London, the city that never sleeps, where you can walk down Peckham High Street at 4 A.M. and have conversations with half a dozen individ-uals ranging from whether the chicken shop is still open to an impassioned debate on Big Data and how Google is planting microchips in all our brains. But here? With no one but the trees listening? I let rip. And let me tell you, I gave that dawn chorus a damn good run for its money.

I was belting out Cher's "Walking in Memphis" (a true classic) and doing a weird sort of boppy walk that I won't even attempt to defend, when I saw him. My audience.

Bloody Rowan from the bloody commune—and the newspaper, and the pub. The guy popped up more often than a game of Whac-A-Mole. He was leaning against a tree and smirking. Who the hell hangs around in forests leaning against trees at five in the morning? Well, hippies I guess. But . . . seriously?

"Morning," he said with a grin.

"You didn't hear that," I said immediately. "I was absolutely not sing-ing Cher, extremely badly."

"Didn't hear a thing," he agreed solemnly.

Normally, I try to blame most things on Helen, but I didn't think I'd get away with that this time. Plus, Helen, sensing a deeply embarrassing situation, had run away. Somehow I felt it made me look even more weird being up here at five in the morning without even a dog as an excuse. Like I'd just come up to give the birds an impromptu concert.

"I was walking Helen." I gestured vaguely at the empty woods around us.

"She's not a fan of your singing?"

"I think we agreed there wasn't any singing."

"Right. And I think she went that way—extremely fast."

He fell into step beside me as I headed Helenward. So much for my alone time. But I felt surprisingly comfortable around Rowan, which is not normally the case with men I have known for all of ten minutes.

"You couldn't sleep either?" I asked.

"No, it's weird being back here." He scuffed the ground with his foot. "Thought I'd get up and visit . . ." His voice trailed off.

"Visit who?" I asked. There weren't a huge number of options in the woods. The trees? A friendly neighborhood squirrel?

"Oh . . . a favorite spot," he said. But I couldn't help feeling that wasn't what he'd set out to say.

"Want to show me?"

He shook his head. "It's nothing special. Let's go this way, there's an amazing view just up ahead."

We diverted down a side path, smaller and overhung with whippy branches and brambles. But a couple of minutes later, the trees suddenly opened out, ahead of us the ground dropped away and we could see out over the valley. The Cotswold hills rose on either side, wooded to our right, rolling fields to our left. Penton sprawled across the opposite flank of the valley, looking for all the world as if it had gently toppled from the crest of the hill and was just sliding its way down to the valley floor, like a drunk leaning against a slippery wall.

I couldn't believe *this* wasn't Rowan's favorite spot. It was definitely mine.

I sat down on the woodland floor and Rowan dropped beside me.

At this point, Helen emerged from the woods with quite a lot of fern in her tail and a slightly manic gleam in her eye. She went and stood by the view, silhouetted really quite majestically against the backdrop. For a total buffoon, she really has an eye for the dramatic.

"That's a good dog," Rowan commented.

"Hmm, Helen?" I was distracted by the view. "Oh, she's only part dog."

"What's the rest of her?"

"Mainly demon with a side portion of cow, I think."

He laughed.

"Have you got a dog?"

"Nah, moved around too much." Ah yes, how could I have forgotten the decade-long gap year? "I briefly had one when I was yak herding but I had to leave him behind when I moved on."

I tried not to roll my eyes.

"Maybe I'll get one now I'm back," he continued thoughtfully.

"You're back for good then?"

He sighed. "Maybe. I'd like to be around a bit more for Mum and Dad. They're not coping so well. But, I don't know, coming back to all this *stuff* going on. I'd rather just run away again, to be honest."

By "stuff" I presumed he meant the death of Mr. Oliver.

"You didn't time your return brilliantly," I admitted. It probably wasn't a particularly comforting thing to say. A little niggle in the back of my mind was whispering, *What a coincidence, Rowan turns up and Mr. Oliver drops dead*. I told it to shut up—I couldn't go around suspecting literally everyone of murder. I'd have no friends. And then I'd probably go mad.

"It must have been nice growing up around here," I said conversationally, trying to drown out the nasty little suspicious voice. "All this nature and stuff."

He grinned. "You didn't have nature where you grew up?"

"Central Reading? Nope, not really. We had Forbury Park where the druggies hung out and the canal by the prison, and that was about it."

"Sounds charming."

"It made me what I am today."

"What, pregnant?"

I laughed. "Not directly. Although it *was* the teen pregnancy capital of Europe when I was at school."

"What a claim to fame."

"We had to take what we could get." I took in the view again, the small cluster of houses that was Penton, dwarfed by the surrounding country-side. "I imagine it was quite different growing up here."

"You could say that," Rowan agreed. "A lot more climbing trees and a lot less shagging in the park."

"Meh." I wasn't sure that was necessarily an improvement.

"And being homeschooled really set us commune kids apart. We didn't mix with the town kids that much when we were little."

"You were homeschooled??"

"Only until I was eleven. Then I rebelled and said I wanted to go to proper school."

"I think I was rebelling *against* going to school around that time."

Rowan laughed. "I guess kids always want what they haven't got."

"True. I spent the first five years of my life begging Mum and Dad for a baby brother. Then I got one. Then I spent the next ten years begging to be an only child."

He snorted at that. "Where's your brother now?"

"He's in Spain, same as my mum and dad, doing eff all. You'd like him."

He laughed again. It was pleasant, sitting admiring the view, listening to Helen snuffle around in the undergrowth, discussing the pros and cons of homeschooling in a hippy commune (pros: almost total freedom; cons: didn't learn anything).

"Do you remember Flora?" I asked, hopefully quite casually.

"Oh, Flora," laughed Rowan. "No, she left before I was even born. Mum whips her name out when she wants to piss Dad off though."

"Oh? Why's that?"

"I think Dad was quite taken with her, you know?" He gave me a sly look. "But then she left under a cloud or something. I don't really know what happened. But Mum likes to drop dark hints about how she was up to no good, and how she had them all fooled." He laughed again. "I think the commune was a bit of a wilder place back then."

Given that he seemed to be in a good mood, I risked pressing the conversation a little more. "When we were in the archives, we came across something about a tragedy at the commune. Someone died?"

Rowan's face darkened; the laughter shut off in an instant. "We don't talk about that."

"I just . . . wanted to know what happened." I tried to keep my tone light, but a spring chill had crept into our sunny little bubble.

"Well, now you do," he said shortly.

But I couldn't quite let it go. "Actually, we don't," I said. "The papers didn't really say anything. In fact, the paper from the week after it happened was missing . . ." I left the rest of the sentence hanging in the air.

"The archives are poorly kept." His friendly tone had completely gone. He was all hard eyes and cold voice.

"It was about ten years ago," I persisted. I was pretty sure I'd pushed my luck over the cliff and out to sea already, so why not drown it good and proper. "You would have been here at the time. Did you know her? What happened?"

"I was at university at the time," he said. "And after what happened to Jasmine I stayed away from the commune. And so should you."

With that he got to his feet, brushed himself down and disappeared into the trees. It was so abrupt I was left a little stunned. I was saddened that our pleasant early morning had soured so dramatically, but above all I felt frustrated. I'd spent the last week running up against brick walls. Everyone here seemed to have their secrets, and they all kept them very close to their chests.

But I had something now. I had a name.

Jasmine.

CHAPTER 30

I MADE MY way back through the woods, which seemed colder now. I'm not going to lie, Rowan's warning chilled me. Clearly we were in over our heads. We'd wanted to know what had happened at the commune ten years ago. Well, now we did. Or bits of it, anyway. But what did it have to do with Mr. Oliver? It couldn't be coincidence that he'd left the commune around the same time that Jasmine had died. Had he been involved somehow? Had he known something he shouldn't have known? Which then begged the question, if we found out whatever it was that Mr. Oliver had known . . . might that bring the same kind of unwanted attention to us? I shivered, despite the warm spring sun.

The woods felt a lot more claustrophobic suddenly, full of noises that my city-bred ears didn't understand. I also realized, belatedly, that I was completely lost.

I wondered if Helen might finally prove her worth and guide me back to the safety of my car. With nothing better to try, I crashed off the path and followed her through the undergrowth.

After five minutes and not a single familiar-looking tree, I heard a noise ahead that cut through the standard-issue birdcall and woodland rustling; clipped blows rang out through the trees, like metal striking metal. Instinctively, I slowed.

Through the trees up ahead I could just make out a small clearing, and a figure kneeling at the base of a tree, their arm rising and falling as they rhythmically struck at something apparently in among the roots. My nerves were already stretched taut like piano wires, and every metallic blow seemed to reverberate along them.

I tried to hide behind a tree, but with my nine-month pregnancy bump I needed a five-hundred-year-old oak with a girth like Queen Victoria. Then I chastised myself. I was being ridiculous. It was probably just another dog walker. Or a . . . tree surgeon? It almost definitely wasn't a murderer. Almost definitely. And I was lost, I needed help.

I stepped out from behind my tree, my knees shaking ever so slightly. "Hello?"

The figure stopped, arm raised, and their whole body stiffened. They half looked round when Helen exploded out of some nearby ferns. She bounded up to the person, who scrambled to their feet and took off through the woods with Helen-worthy speed.

OK . . . so that wasn't your standard reaction to a perfectly reasonable "hello." Although I supposed it was an understandable reaction to Helen.

I wobbled forward into the clearing, toward the tree they'd been kneeling by. Even I could see that this was one fine-looking tree. It had shimmery silvery-white bark and delicate pale green leaves. It seemed to shine slightly, standing apart from the more mundane trees that made up the bulk of the woods.

At the base of the trunk something had been set into the bark. I knelt awkwardly, using the tree for support, slightly worried that I might snap its slender trunk. Nestled between the roots was a bronze plaque, slightly tarnished but yet to acquire that strange green patina of really old bronze.

In loving memory of Jasmine ——
May your spirit long dwell in these woods.

The surname had been scored right through, almost obliterating it. It was a short name, just a few letters. The first looked like a P or an R . . . Or possibly a B. I closed my eyes and ran my hand over the deep gashes, trying to read with my fingers. I could almost feel the anger, like a heat radiating out from them.

I sat back on my butt, ignoring the ground chill seeping through my jeans. My right hand landed on something cold and hard. I looked down to see a hammer, and just a foot away a chisel. The mystery plaque-desecrator must have dropped them when they were mugged by Helen.

Little pieces of information were slotting together in my mind. The death at the commune, the tree-planting ceremony we had read about in the paper, Jasmine . . . But for every question answered there were ten more raised. Who had been up here at dawn, destroying Jasmine's memorial plaque, and why? It felt like such a violent act. Who would want to erase the very memory of this girl?

CHAPTER 31

I WAS IN a bit of a daze when I got home, and was surprised to find Joe already awake and eating Marmite and peanut butter on toast in the garden, which was now miraculously clear of boxes and furniture.

"I was thinking we could build a sandpit out here for the baby," he mused as I wandered over and nicked the remains of his toast. "I always wanted a sandpit as a kid."

It seemed like an achievable dream. And it was nice to hear him proffering ideas for the baby, which had at times felt like a taboo subject of late.

"A pit with a view," I replied, looking out over the rolling vale that virtually shone in the early-morning light. "This is going to be one lucky baby."

"You were up early," he said, pinching back the last morsel of toast. "Couldn't sleep?"

"No, so I took Helen for a walk . . ." I trailed off, wondering how much to tell Joe about my morning exploits, and then wondering why I was even wondering this. At what point had I started curating my version of events to him?

"I bumped into Rowan up in the woods," I began.

"The guy from the pub last night? Wouldn't have pegged him for an early bird. Seemed a nice guy—we said we might try and get a pint in at some point."

I smiled weakly. This was exactly what I'd wanted, for Joe to make his own friends here—only, it did slightly complicate things that his first potential friend appeared to be ever so slightly mixed up in whatever the hell was going on here.

"You OK?" Joe was squinting at me through the low morning sun.

"Yeah, yeah, sorry. Bit hazy, not much sleep."

Joe put an arm around me. "You know what, I think you should splurge and treat yourself to a biodynamic, hand-milked, avocado-bean coffee from the farmers' market. One coffee won't hurt. Come on, let's hit this place up."

IT WAS the first time that Joe had been into the center of Penton—and I use the term "center" loosely for a town where fifty percent of the population are sheep. Let's just say it's heavy on the bunting. And hanging flower baskets. It is probably one of those Britain in Bloom towns. You know, the sort where defacing a flower bed might actually get you lynched. I was exceptionally glad we'd decided to leave Helen at home.

Stalls lined the quaint cobbled streets, selling a variety of wholesome and organic wares at eye-watering prices. We bought a fantastically overpriced falafel wrap each and wandered through the throng, snickering behind our hands at the more ludicrous stalls. It felt . . . nice. It was good to be on the same page for once. Even if that was poking fun at twenty-pound soaps and candles that could "heal your aura." Alongside the crystal and candle stalls were the rural craft stalls, selling hand-knitted socks and hand-painted ceramics. Everything was "by hand" or organic—or both.

Then there were the wonderfully old-fashioned produce stalls from surrounding farms and businesses, selling vegetables and cheese and bread. It was exactly what I'd hoped for in our move to the countryside. I wanted honey made by my friendly neighborhood bees. I wanted cheese from the cow down the road. I even found an organic dog stall and delightedly spent twelve pounds on a slab of yak butter that Helen would no doubt turn her nose up at.

Fortunately, Joe reined me in from spending our life savings on a giant hand-carved statue of two boxing hares that was taller than me and would have scared Helen into next week.

I was inspecting some handmade earrings—the jangly, dangly type favored by Pentonites—when I heard a familiar voice.

"Now, dear, I just think you're being a bit silly about the whole thing."

I peered around the rack of batik scarves at the edge of the stall. It was Dot, and she was chatting to, of all people, Sandra of the Gongs. Neither of them looked particularly happy at the way the conversation was going.

"I'm just saying—" tried Sandra, but Dot cut across her.

"Let's not do anything we'll regret later. Just sit tight for now and I'm sure something will come along."

"Well, I actually went to Nature's Way just yesterday and—"

"You did *what*?!"

"I just popped by and—"

"Honestly, Sandra, sometimes I think you haven't the common sense you were born with. What on earth possessed you to do that?" It was strange hearing Dot angry. She was like an enraged guinea pig; very squeaky but you knew there was no fire there.

"I just wanted to check if it was still there," Sandra said insistently.

"And was it?" Despite herself, Dot sounded curious. Possibly even . . . a bit eager?

"Yes! So of course I—"

I leaned forward, as eager as Dot to hear what Sandra had found—and with a crash sent the rail of batik scarves flying.

Dot shrieked and Sandra uttered some very un-cosmic swear words.

"Oh my God, I'm so sorry!" I gabbled. "Dot, Sandra! Fancy seeing you both here!" I was pretty sure I was fooling no one. Dot looked incredibly flustered, and Sandra's look of alarm was tinged with suspicion. Although by rights I reckon I was the one who should have been looking suspicious right now.

I ended up buying three batik scarves in order to extricate myself with the minimum amount of awkwardness.

Joe raised an eyebrow as I rejoined him, flushed, disheveled and clutching my three new scarves.

"Really embracing the Penton look, huh?"

In an undertone I began to tell him what I'd just overheard, but he cut me off.

"Why were you listening in on their private conversation in the first place?"

"Because it might have something to do with the murder," I hissed. "Dot's up to something, I'm sure of it, and—"

"And *I'm* sure it's none of your business," snapped Joe. "Look, are we going on this damn picnic or not? Let's just get out of here before you buy anymore tie-dye crap."

"It's not tie-dye, it's batik," I said with dignity.

"And the difference is . . . ?"

That stumped me, as I really didn't have the foggiest. But at that moment I spotted a suit through the crowd—and only one man would wear a suit to the Penton Farmers' Market.

"Look, it's Hen and Antoni, let's go and say hi. You can meet the unnamed baby." I dragged Joe after me to where Hen and Antoni were standing with their incredibly swanky pram, one of those ones that probably has a heated seat and seven gears.

To be fair to him, Joe showed more than a passing interest in Hen's baby. He peered in at where she was lying cocooned in a lovely fluffy sheepskin. He proffered his opinion when Hen filled us in on their current dilemma—whether to serve just tea or offer champagne at her somewhat after-the-event baby shower the following weekend. He even made polite conversation with Antoni, which allowed me to drag Hen to one side and hastily fill her in on the argument I'd just heard between Dot and Sandra. Unlike Joe, Hen agreed that this was very suspicious.

"So whatever Sandra took from Nature's Way yesterday, Dot knows about it," she said thoughtfully.

"It's got to be something to do with the murder," I said. "Some evidence that the police missed. Why else would they be so keen to remove it?"

"Except that Dot doesn't think Sandra should have removed it," pointed out Hen.

"No, well, it was a bit stupid, wasn't it," I countered. "I mean, she's not exactly a master thief—she was spotted by Miss Webb *and* by us."

"Well, I don't think Sandra's going to win brain of Britain," said Hen acidly, which I thought was a bit mean.

"Think she's smart enough to get away with murder?" I asked.

I'd been half joking, but Hen looked like she was giving it some consideration. "I wouldn't have said so. But it's best not to jump to conclusions. I mean, we don't know her at all. What if all the airy-fairy gong-bashing is just a front . . . ?"

"Worth digging?"

"Worth digging."

Hen looked at me sideways, as if unsure how her next comment would go down. "It would be kind of handy if it turned out Sandra was up to something, wouldn't it?" she said, biting her lip.

"What do you mean?" I asked, genuinely confused.

"Have you spoken to Poppy this morning?"

"No, why?"

Hen look troubled. "Ailsa rang this morning. Harris has taken Lin in for questioning."

Ah. That didn't sound good.

"What about?"

"Ailsa didn't know. Her sister isn't exactly the sharing type."

"What should we do?" I fretted. "Should we tell Inspector Harris that we saw Sandra taking something from the crime scene? And about the conversation?"

Which would take the heat off Lin a bit, I thought, but didn't need to say.

"Why is she so convinced Lin is involved?" asked Hen thoughtfully.

I shrugged, but didn't reply. I'd been wondering the same.

Hen took a deep breath, looking faintly troubled. "We probably ought to let her know about Sandra."

I nodded.

I didn't feel great about it either, to be honest. I had nothing against Sandra; I'm sure she was a lovely woman with a wonderful aura. It was just that, if someone had bumped off Mr. Oliver, I'd much rather it was gong-bashing Sandra than Lin. And yet, I just couldn't believe Sandra, high priestess of the gong, was involved in *murder*.

I want to clarify at this point: I had every intention of going to the police, I just didn't like it. It's not that I didn't want to help Lin. Of course I did. But I felt uneasy about suggesting, to the police or anyone else, that Sandra was in any way involved—we were swiftly getting an idea of what Harris was like, and once she had her claws into someone there was no helping them. I wasn't entirely convinced that we wouldn't simply be shifting the blame from one innocent individual to another.

There was so much more I had to tell Hen, but at this point I felt duty-bound to rescue Joe from what appeared to be an increasingly strained conversation with Antoni. The two couldn't have looked more different. Antoni's charcoal-gray suit was in distinct contrast with Joe's SKITTLES: TASTE THE RAINBOW T-shirt that he loved with a misplaced passion and had washed so many times the rainbow was looking rather sucked dry.

"Oh"—Hen grabbed my arm as I went to break up the awkward chat of the year—"maybe don't mention any of this in front of Antoni," she whispered. "He's not a fan of our detectoring."

"No, nor is Joe," I admitted, although I felt a small thrill that Hen had referred to our activities as such; it felt so official. "We'll keep it among ourselves for now. But we should have another meeting. Are you free on Monday?"

Hen gestured to the baby in the pram. "Alice, I'm literally always free now."

Fair point.

Hen raised her voice to draw Joe and Antoni back into the conversation. "Lovely to bump into you! We'll see you both at the baby shower?"

Joe and I reassured her that we wouldn't miss it for the world.

"Oh, and Alice," Hen called back to me as we left.

"Yeah?"

"Don't bring Helen."

I did my best sweeping-away walk.

"Never leave me with that guy again," grumbled Joe as we made our way homeward. "He asked me if Ronnie O'Sullivan is a *singer*."

This actually slightly raised my opinion of Antoni. But I thought that the beginning of our wholesome date-day shouldn't be marred by a Ronnie-based row. Still, I needn't have worried about that; just then we turned the corner and walked straight into something that gave us all the ammunition we needed for an absolute belter of an argument.

CHAPTER 32

WE HAD ENTERED the little square in front of the Corn Exchange. My previous experience of corn exchanges had been purely as gig venues, but it turns out that these are places where people used to quite literally exchange corn. In Penton they probably still did.

Well, either it had been a bumper harvest that week, or there was something going on—the little square was full of people. And placards. And a man with a megaphone.

"Is it a protest?" I asked Joe, squinting at the nearest placard. Unfortunately, the plaintiff had quite a lot to complain about, and subsequently the font was quite small—and from the look of the man (tweedy, glasses) he'd probably included footnotes.

"I think it's a political thing," said Joe. "Come on, let's get out of here."

But my eyes had fixed on the man with the megaphone and brought him into hazy focus.

"Oh no, it's that Pilkington dickhead," I said quietly.

"OK," said Joe, taking my arm. "Let's just head off, yeah? We don't need to get involved."

A placard swam into focus: BRITISH JOBS FOR BRITISH PEOPLE. The one behind it was even less veiled: GO HOME followed by a list of nationalities. Another behind that proclaimed: WE WILL NOT KNEEL TO THE MARXIST FORCES CONTROLLING THIS COUNTRY.

I shook off Joe's arm. "No, this is outrageous. No wonder everyone thinks the countryside is full of racists and bigots—oh my God, maybe it is!"

"It's just a few people giving the place a bad rep," muttered Joe, tugging on my arm again. "Come on, let's just go."

"But we *live* here now," I protested. "We can't just let it go. Then we just become part of it."

"Look, let's talk about this at home—"

I wrenched my arm back again. Some of the placard-bearers were watching with interest now. One of them even flourished a leaflet at us—the same leaflet that I had torn up just days before. In fact, oh no, Pilkington was making his way toward us. He raised a hand in greeting—had he forgotten how unpleasant our encounter in the café had been? Then I realized that he was, in fact, waving at Joe.

"We're going." Joe grabbed my elbow and forcibly steered me back through the crowd.

"Ow, Joe! Get off!"

But he kept up the pressure until we were clear of the square, when he finally let go.

"What the hell, Joe?"

"We're well out of that," he said shortly, striding off in the direction of home.

"Really? Because it looked to me as if Pilkington was waving at you. And you were running away."

"I wasn't running away."

"But Pilkington *was* waving at you? Why?"

"How the hell would I know?"

"I don't know, you tell me!"

Joe gave an exasperated sigh and didn't reply. I hated it when he did this. Like I didn't even merit a response.

"Why would you keep a leaflet from his horrible party?" I pushed him. "Why would you stick up for him when I called him a prat—which he is, by the way."

Joe stopped and turned to face me. "Alice, you do realize you're being totally ridiculous over this, right? Yes, I forgot to put his stupid leaflet in the bin—*I just forgot.* And no, I didn't stick up for him, you're blowing that totally out of proportion. It's like you're trying to pick a fight. Well, I don't want to fight, and definitely not over this. OK?"

With that he turned and stamped off down the street without a backward glance.

After a few seconds of sulking, I shuffled after him, because what else was I going to do?

I'D ALMOST caught up with Joe when I saw her. Emerging from the police station, her perpetual frown in place. Inspector Harris.

"Inspector!"

Her frown deepened when she saw me—which seemed unfair; I hadn't even said anything yet!

"Have you just been speaking to Lin?" I asked.

"That's classified information," she said tersely, breaking into a fast stride. I waddled alongside her; she couldn't shake me off that easily.

"I need to speak to you," I puffed.

She barely acknowledged this with a "hmph."

"It's about the case. I have information." Why was I suddenly talking like an informant in a bad B-movie?

"Really."

"Yes! I was at Nature's Way yesterday with Hen . . ." I paused here, realizing we had no justification for why we had been there.

"Of course you were," sighed Inspector Harris. "And might I ask *why* you took it upon yourselves to revisit the scene of a crime? A *serious* crime, I might remind you."

"Hen needed Roman chamomile for her baby," I offered unconvincingly.

"And you could not think of any other shop in town that could have provided you with that?" asked Inspector Harris coldly. "Or, failing that, you have heard of the internet, I presume?"

Ouch.

I had kind of walked into that one.

"Anyway." I decided my best route was to simply plunge on. "We saw—"

"I hope you know that wasting a police officer's time is a criminal offense," cut in Inspector Harris. "And if this is some half-baked attempt to get your friend Lin out of trouble then I will consider that a perversion of the course of justice and there will be consequences."

This was hopeless. She didn't want to believe me and so she wouldn't. End of.

"Look. I've known Lin a week," I said, exasperated. "I wouldn't lie to the police for her! I'm about to have a baby, and I'm not an idiot. I wouldn't get myself in trouble for the sake of a woman I barely know."

That seemed to hit home. Inspector Harris tilted her head and looked at me as though she could assess my level of honesty with her X-ray glare. Perhaps she could. I tried to look as trustworthy as possible, while feeling deeply guilty—for what, I couldn't say.

"Fine," she said eventually, pulling her notebook out. "Tell me what you saw. But be quick."

BY THE time I was done with Harris, who had, to her credit, taken copious notes and asked some pertinent questions, most of which I'd been unable to answer, I expected Joe to be long gone. But to my surprise, when I turned to begin trudging up the long hill home, I saw he was perched on a bollard.

"Couldn't leave you to walk home on your own," he said a little sheepishly. "It's a big hill. What if you went into labor or something. What were you talking to Harris about?"

"Saw Sandra pinching something from Nature's Way yesterday," I said shortly, really not in the mood to rehash the whole thing yet again, not after he'd cut me off so rudely last time.

"Who's Sandra?"

"The high priestess of the gong."

Joe shook his head as we began the climb. "This place just gets weirder and weirder."

I had to agree with him there.

We climbed the hill mostly in silence—because breathing. And also because, while Joe clearly wanted to make nice, and I was glad about that, I was also sure that something was amiss here. Something was up with Joe—and Pilkington had a hand in it.

CHAPTER 33

JOE AND I decided to have our picnic anyway—and by unspoken consent not to mention Pilkington again. After all, we had just spent nearly a month's rent on various edible delicacies and it seemed a shame to take them home where they would come within the purview of Helen.

We found a beautiful spot down by the River Pen. A meadow just beginning to bud with wildflowers ran down to where the river bubbled shallowly over water-smoothed stones. It was too early in the year to be plagued by insect life and, if a tad chilly, I was more than happy with the compromise. We spread out our feast and made ourselves comfortable. Or at least marginally less uncomfortable, in my case.

In a surprisingly short time, there was nothing left but crumbs and a smudge of chutney on Joe's chin that I hadn't told him about.

"We should think about baby names," I suggested, to take my mind off the shooting sciatica pains radiating out from my left butt cheek.

Joe raised an eyebrow. "I thought we were settled on Jack?"

We had been. But since moving to Penton I was anxiously aware that we needed to seriously up our stakes. Names like Apollo and Indigo and Rook were all the rage here.

"What's Hen's baby called?" Joe asked.

"Still no name," I admitted. "She's waiting for a name to manifest or something, I'm not quite sure."

"What if our baby manifests as a Jack?"

"I'm not saying he *won't*. I'm just saying we should be open to the possibility that when he arrives he might look more like a . . . Quail, or a Euripides."

Although what a baby Euripides looks like I have no idea. Presumably they're born wearing a toga.

"Are we planning on having a particularly posh baby?" Joe asked.

"I'm not sure those are posh names, just weird ones," I admitted. "*These* are posh names."

I showed him a *Tatler* article I'd been reading during my sleepless night, citing the poshest baby names this year, but when we got to Npeter (pronounced "Peter"—it's a silent "N") Joe looked like he might actually explode and we had to stop reading.

I'm not entirely sure if my intention had been to wind him up, but I'd definitely managed to. So it probably wasn't the best timing to ask what was going on with him lately.

"What do you mean?" he said defensively, when I asked him if he was feeling OK about the whole baby thing.

"I just mean, you've been kind of weird and distant this week," I pressed.

"I don't know what you're talking about."

"I feel like whenever I try and talk about the baby you just sort of shut down."

"We've literally just been talking about the baby."

"Yeah, and you shut down."

"You wanted to call him Quail!"

It was going poorly, and I probably should have just left the whole thing there. But obviously I didn't.

"It's OK to feel weird about becoming a dad," I said. "I mean. I know you didn't know your dad, which must make it difficult. But you're not going to be anything like him. You're going to be a great dad." I was going for reassuring and supportive, but I'd tragically misjudged.

Joe went very still.

"Alice?"

"Yes?"

"I know you're playing at being a detective or something, but don't start trying to psychoanalyze me or any of that bullshit, OK? I'm not in the mood."

His words stung—almost physically. I wanted to fight back, I wanted to shout and rage and tell him it wasn't fair of him to hold out on me like this. But there was also something vulnerable in his face; he looked like he might crack open. So I bit back my angry words and I reminded myself that being family didn't mean forcing confidences, it meant listening and it meant respecting boundaries.

I sighed. "You've got chutney on your chin, by the way."

THAT EVENING I sat, alone, in our untamed new garden, envisaging it complete with sandpit and mud kitchen, maybe even a swing, and a chubby-cheeked but faceless baby rolling around on a rug laughing. It felt a million miles away. I contemplated my current situation. How the hell had it come to this? I was nearly nine months pregnant, investigating a murder that I really shouldn't be involved in, and my partner, the father of my child, was barely speaking to me and, whatever he said, had got himself mixed up in something unsavory.

I hoped it was just politics.

I really hoped it was just politics.

Joe's unfinished beer sat on the table in front of me. It couldn't hurt . . . could it? Half a beer? I picked up the bottle—it was only 3.5 percent. Some women drank all through pregnancy and their babies were *fine*. French women had *perfect* babies!

The first sip tasted like fucking nectar. God, I'd missed this. I leaned back in my chair and took another long sip. It felt as though the alcohol was waking up dormant parts of my brain while allowing other parts to blissfully shut down. I tried to consider my position dispassionately.

The murder really had nothing to do with me. I'd just been dragged into this out of, well, boredom, a lack of anything better to do on my maternity leave. And then, of course, because the police kept harassing Lin, and I liked her and Poppy. I didn't think Lin had anything to do with the murder, though I had to admit I didn't exactly know her that well. Hardly at all when I came to think about it. I'd met her, what, four or five times, although from hearing Poppy talk about her, it felt as if I knew her better than that. If I was honest then yes, I felt a little uncomfortable at the way we'd totally shut down that line of inquiry. I mean, our whole investigation was pretty much an exercise in disproving Harris's pet theory regarding Lin.

Ugh, this was just making me feel worse. Did I really think Harris might be on to something? Not really. But my point was, proving Lin's innocence—or otherwise—wasn't in actual fact *my* problem. Joe was right—what I should really be doing was focusing on my baby. And him.

Just suppose it wasn't politics.

Just suppose it was something else. Something worse.

I didn't really fancy following that train of thought. I delved into my rucksack in the hope there was still a doughnut in it from our less-than-successful picnic, and instead drew out a folded-up newspaper. It was the copy of the *Penton Bugle* that first mentioned Jasmine's death. I started flicking through it, sipping on my guilty beer.

I paused at a disturbing article that showed a beefy red-faced man holding up a dead fox by its tail under the headline LOCAL MASTER OF THE HOUNDS SAYS HUNTING BAN CAN STUFF IT. I made a mental note to bin the FOXES DESERVE IT T-shirt that Maya once made for me as a joke. It had seemed funny in London. It was less so out here, where people actually think that.

I peered at the photo.

"Ugh. Ronald Pilkington—*again*," I muttered. "Master of the Hounds. God, I bet he loved that title."

I had a swig of beer and settled down to read the article and get myself really worked up.

> Local huntsman Ronald Pilkington is a pillar of the local fox-hunting community and has served as Master of the Hounds for the local hunt since 2004. But Mr. Pilkington's involvement in the community was once of a very different nature. I asked him about his time at the now infamous commune up in Stricker's Wood and his relationship with its controversial leader, "Camran."
>
> He was reluctant to discuss his younger days at the

commune, where he was one of the founding members, and he gave me short shrift.

"I was under the impression you wanted to discuss the ban on fox-hunting, not harass me about decisions made in my sadly misplaced youth, which I deeply regret and have no wish to talk about."

I asked him if he could comment on the unexplained tragedy that appears to have befallen the commune, at which he became somewhat riled.

"I haven't set foot in that place for twenty years and I intend to keep it that way. And what with that recent nasty business, I couldn't be more pleased to be well rid of the place. If you want to talk about hippy nonsense, go and badger Camran."

I told him that the commune had closed its gates to all members of the public. He declined to comment any further.

Our talk turns to the recent motion in the House of Lords which declared public fox-hunting to be "an important part of rural culture, with value in the areas of conservation and pest control . . ."

The newspaper drooped onto the table. Pilkington had been one of the founders of the commune? *Pilkington?* How the hell had that happened? Pilkington, Camran, Mr. Oliver. The unholy trinity. My head was spinning, and not just from the few mouthfuls of beer.

CHAPTER 34

THE NEXT MORNING I was tired. Not just physically, but with the whole thing. With trying to second-guess my boyfriend. With trying to build a new life that I wasn't even sure I wanted. With trying to get him onside when I was almost certain it wasn't what *he* wanted. And I certainly wasn't going to bring up the newspaper article's revelations: both Pilkington and the commune seemed to be trigger topics with Joe, who apparently lived on a hair trigger as it was these days, and I was pretty sure if I brought the two of them up together he would implode.

Joe, however, seemed in a slightly brighter mood. "I was thinking we could go to IKEA today," he suggested over breakfast.

Ah, that explained the cheerfulness. Joe, inexplicably, loved IKEA. Its Scandinavian minimalism and emphasis on tidiness and efficiency were the absolute antithesis of Joe, but perhaps this was why he felt so repeatedly drawn to the place.

"We can get a cot for the baby's room," he said hopefully.

I recognized this as both a bribe to get me IKEA-bound, but also an olive branch offered for yesterday's irritability. And we *did* need a cot, in fact quite urgently. Plus IKEA sold that incredible Daim cheesecake . . .

Of course, it turns out that buying a cot isn't as simple as just rocking up to IKEA all "I'd like one of your finest cots, please." I googled "best baby cot" on the drive down, which was my first error. One of the top articles was "39 types of crib for your baby." Thirty-nine? The article went on to describe why I would need at least three of these cribs. Why? I only have one bed (well, inflatable mattress, currently), which I have to share with a boyfriend and a dog. Why does the baby get three all to himself?

The article wasn't lying. It turns out there are more types of cot than there are species of bird. All of which have their own dedicated internet forums explaining in detail why this cot is the best/worst/only way of ever getting your baby to sleep. There are co-sleeping cribs, and snooze pods, and next-to-mes. There are convertible cribs, portable cribs, cribs that double up as storage and changing tables and probably intergalactic rockets. There are cribs on rockers, cribs on wheels, even cribs that *vibrate* to help your precious little one get to sleep.

"If we buy a changing table maybe the baby can just sleep in the box?" I suggested, only half joking.

Then I had a sudden attack of conscience, that buying a new cot from IKEA wasn't ethical and was a result of us being brainwashed by a consumerist society into thinking that this baby needed everything to be new and shiny, despite the fact that nothing stays that way around babies for more than three minutes. I started looking up secondhand cots on Facebook Marketplace, but was soon put off by the fact that every single cot advertised had variations on a theme of "significant tooth marks to headboard." Some had pictures and it was not pretty. Was I going to be birthing a baby piranha?

This of course led further down the Google rabbit hole of doom . . .

"One in two thousand babies are born with teeth?!" I informed Joe, horror-struck. "Like a full-on set of gnashers! Joe, what if our baby has TEETH?"

"Our baby won't have teeth."

"It might."

"OK, so if our baby is born with teeth, that's fine. If it's as common as you say it is, then clearly it's not a massive problem."

"Easy for you to say, you won't be the one breastfeeding the little freak!"

Joe sighed. "Can you just go back to googling IKEA cots?"

"Fine. There are thirteen pages to choose from. Would you rather have a Sniglar or a Gonatt?"

IN THE end we got neither. We got a Solgul because it was the cheapest. It looked like a small wooden prison.

"I'm worried the baby's not going to be happy in there," I fretted as Joe tried to wedge the flat-pack box on the trolley, balancing it on top of the sundry other items I had gathered on our journey round IKEA. Because everyone knows a trip to IKEA isn't complete until you've spent several hundred pounds on furniture that will either have pieces missing, or not fit into your room, or which you'll decide you hate within a week.

"It's fine. The baby will be happy because it will have its"—he reached into the trolley and poked around—"Klappa caterpillar to keep it company"—more poking—"its Titta Djur squashy to squash and, oh yes, its Gulligast mobile to look at."

He rummaged some more. "What is Bygglek?"

CHAPTER 35

I TEXTED POPPY to see how many types of cot she had bought for her baby, and also for an update on how Lin was getting on.

> Fine. So she says

> Harris let her go

> You think Harris will drop it now?

> Do you?

> Fair point

> God, that woman's a twat

> Fancy a dog walk?

> Sure. Where?

> Meet me at the Clayton Estate

Upon googling I discovered this was a different sort of estate to the one I had grown up on. They speak a different language in the countryside.

I parked up at the gatehouse, which was larger than any house I had ever lived in. While I waited for Poppy I wikipediaed the old Clayton Estate:

"The Clayton Estate in Gloucestershire, England, is a modest country estate but not without its charms. The current incumbent, the Rt. Hon. Ronald Pilkington—"

What now? I had to google "incumbent" to make sure I was reading correctly but yep, Ronald Bloody Pilkington lived on the Clayton Estate. I couldn't get away from the man.

I read on, quietly fuming. It had been the local manor house back in the day when the aristocracy ruled the countryside. Of course, in many ways they still did, in the guise of people like Ronald Pilkington, but these days their influence was less ostentatious, confined to political bullying and aggressive land purchases, rather than literally owning (read: enslaving) the entire local village.

The Clayton Estate had been broken up several decades earlier, the family having "fallen on hard times." Meaning they could no longer afford the upkeep of the fleet of vintage cars, the stable of racehorses or the small army of domestic servants and had to slum it with a mere skeleton staff in their five-story Kensington town house like the rest of us. The majority of the estate had, it appeared, gone to the Pilkingtons.

From where I was standing, a driveway stretched away past the gatehouse, presumably leading to the main house. Personally I felt that calling it a "drive" was stretching it a bit. A drive is a ten-by-eight-foot patch of gravel where you can park a Ford Fiesta, not a mile-long private road. The grounds of the Clayton Estate were so extensive the drive disappeared out of view among the sort of trees often described as "mature." As far as I can tell, this just means "big."

So this was where Ronald Pilkington lived. My mind boggled at the idea that people still live in country estates like this. What does one do with two hundred acres of British countryside? Or seventeen bedrooms? What, exactly, is the purpose of a drawing room?

"Planning to put in an offer?" Poppy had pulled up and was leaning out of her car. Ronnie started throwing himself against the back window and Helen went ballistic in response; Sultan was a regal shadow in the back seat.

"What?"

"The gatehouse. It's up for sale."

I laughed. "Meh, it's a little nouveau riche for my tastes."

In all seriousness, though, Joe and I would have loved to buy a house. We'd never imagined we would start a family while still living in rented accommodation—what would we do when the baby drew all over the walls? Or puked on the carpet? Or poured paint all over the lawn? But life doesn't always care that you're still waiting for your lottery win, and we'd just had to resign ourselves to losing our rental deposit (which, to be honest, Helen had already taken care of) and hoping to get on the housing ladder at some point in our fifties.

"Are we allowed in?" I asked, as Poppy pushed open the small gate beside the gatehouse.

"Oh yeah, it's all public access land. It's only the house and immediate grounds that are private these days."

I'd like to have "immediate grounds."

Reassured that Helen wasn't going to bring down a pheasant belonging to the local lord and earn me a thousand-pound fine or a short spell in the dungeons, I let her off the lead to tear around the estate at will. Ronnie tore after her and attempted to mount her at every turn. Ah, young love.

"So what are we doing at Pilkington's place?" I asked.

"I just want to check she's OK."

"Who?"

Poppy looked surprised. "Lin!"

"What's Lin doing here?"

"She works here."

"Hold up." I stopped in my tracks. "Lin works for *Ronald Pilkington*?"

"Didn't I tell you? I could've sworn I told you. Yeah, she does the gardens here. I told her to take the day off sick, after the shit Harris pulled yesterday. But she insisted on coming in—said it would take her mind off things."

People did that, I knew. For me, any excuse to wallow at home and watch Netflix, but each to their own. Lin had that sort of restless energy about her that I often envied in other people, the sort who genuinely *want* to be getting shit done. I cannot understand it.

"Anyway, she forgot her lunch. So I thought I'd drop it off." Poppy brandished a brown paper bag that suggested Lin's lunch had been made by Enid Blyton.

"Lin is Pilkington's gardener?" I was still trying to get my head round this.

"Yep." Poppy's smile faded somewhat. "When we moved down here, she needed work. Beggars can't be choosers, and all that . . . Anyway, the mutual dislike runs both ways. Pilkington isn't a huge fan of Lin's life choices, shall we say, but he's generously willing to overlook that in return for not having to deal with the hassle of hiring another gardener." Her usually cheerful tone had soured a little. "I mean Lin's basically the best gardener there is. He's not going to sack her just because she married a *woman*. Even a Black woman." She pulled a face. "I bumped into him in town last week. He said he supposed I was happy now. As if I'd got pregnant just to trap her. I mean, she's my wife, for God's sake. And I don't know how he thinks that works with IVF anyway—that would be one hell of a complicated baby trap."

"Wow, the more I hear about Pilkington . . . I mean, what a stand-up guy," I muttered. "I was going to let Helen loose in his flower beds, but if they're Lin's handiwork I'll have to think of a Plan B."

This reminded me. "You're not going to believe what I found out about him," I told Poppy, as we made our way up the tree-lined drive.

I filled her in on the article I'd read, citing him as one of the founding members of the commune. At first she flat-out refused to believe it, but I had a photo of the article on my phone.

"I genuinely can't think of anything more out of character," she said thoughtfully. "Mr. Oliver, Camran and . . . Ronald Pilkington? You don't suppose he's got anything to do with Mr. Oliver's murder, do you?"

"Or whatever happened to Jasmine," I chipped in.

"Hmm. God, I'd love it to be Pilkington . . ." said Poppy distantly.

I felt uneasy. Of course, I'd like it to be Pilkington too—you really hope that whoever is responsible for committing any atrocity, particularly taking someone's life, is going to be a really nasty individual. You certainly don't want to think it might be anyone that you like. If nothing else, what does that say about you? But I was also wary of how blinkered that desire could make us.

There was so much to fill Poppy in on, it took the length of the extensive "drive" to get her up to speed. I was just wrapping up on my interaction with Harris the previous day when we rounded a large hedge and walked straight into Lin's handiwork.

I gaped for all of two seconds, before lunging to clip on Helen's lead before she dug up the picture-perfect scene in front of me. The house and gardens were beautiful—but not in the way I'd expected. I'd been anticipating a large and forbidding manor house, with all the warmth and coziness of Downton Abbey. But while Clayton Manor wasn't exactly cozy, it was definitely welcoming. Now don't get me wrong, it was *big*, but in a "wow, that's a big house" way, rather than a "holy shit, it's Versailles" kind of way. It was a warm red-brick building, with a mere three stories, and it looked slightly old and crumbly, which made it seem a lot more approachable.

But it was the flower garden surrounding it that made it truly stunning. A sprawling creeper climbed all over the red-brick façade of the building, its fresh green leaves tinted with bronze and broken up with creamy white clematis flowers. Along the front of the house the flower beds exploded with color—and I'm afraid at this point my meager flower recognition skills gave up and lay down in admiration. All I can say is, there were a *lot* of flowers, and they were really pretty. It was one of the liveliest gardens I have ever seen. The thick scent of hyacinth hung heavy in the air, and bees zipped back and forth, getting busy with the blooms.

"Nice, isn't it," said Poppy, with evident pride.

"It's amazing!"

"We'd better go round the side," she said, leading the way through the profusion along a worn flagged path.

"Tradesmen's entrance," I agreed, and she laughed.

The path brought us to a couple of greenhouses tucked away behind the main house. Lin was just visible in one of them, almost obscured by some kind of triffid. She waved her pruning shears at us.

"Oh my God, it smells incredible!" I exclaimed as I entered.

Lin laughed. "They're just tomato plants!"

"Tomatoes don't smell like this," I protested, shoving my face in among the leaves and inhaling deeply.

"Not the heavily sprayed, imported across two thousand miles of ocean and artificially ripened ones, no," said Lin, with a wry smile.

I suspected this was another ecological nightmare that I had been comfortably oblivious to, and I would now be obliged to boycott tomatoes—or at least rely on Ailsa to grow me some.

"I brought your lunch," said Poppy, handing Lin the brown bag.

Lin sighed. "Any excuse to check up on me! I'm *fine*, Pops. You really didn't need to come all the way out here."

"You're not eating properly," insisted Poppy, and I saw a glimpse of the mother she would soon be. "You hardly had any breakfast. And it's a tiring job!"

Lin rolled her eyes. "You'd better at least have brought me a pack of Quavers."

"Like I'd forget."

"In that case, you're forgiven." Lin peered inside the lunch bag, extricated the Quavers and shoved the rest onto a cluttered workbench.

"Well, I'm actually busy, because some of us still have jobs." She prodded Poppy. "And I need to keep it that way, all right? So bugger off before Pilkington sees you."

I winced slightly at the forced jollity in her tone.

Poppy leaned forward and gave Lin a tight hug, whispering something in her ear. Lin buried her face in Poppy's neck briefly before pulling away.

"Get out of it," she said gruffly. "Alice, keep this one out of trouble for me, yeah?"

I wasn't really paying attention, having been distracted by exploring the tomato plants. Now I looked closely, I could see clusters of small green tomato fruits tucked away among the leaves.

"Huh? Yep, sure."

Poppy snorted.

We hadn't made it halfway down the garden path, however, when we were stopped short.

CHAPTER 36

MRS. PILKINGTON WAS not what I expected. For a start she was wearing gardener's coveralls—I'd been picturing more twinset and pearls—and a ratty old straw hat full of holes. She had dirt on her face. And, unlike her husband, she seemed delighted to see Poppy.

"Poppy!" She rose out of a flower bed, brushing soil off her coveralls. "Lin said you'd be popping round—the silly old duck left her lunch at home. You really didn't have to come all the way out here, you know I'd have fed her! Anyway, how are you, dear? You look positively glorious! I'd hug you but I'm covered in soil."

Poppy laughed and went in for the hug anyway. "I've had Ronnie's grubby paws all over me anyway, so what's a bit of soil?"

"And who's this? Another one about to pop!"

I felt oddly shy as Poppy introduced me. Mrs. Pilkington was little, beneath the enormous coveralls, and white-haired. She looked like perfect grandmother material. I kind of wanted a hug too.

"Come inside, girls." She fussed around, shooing us toward the house like errant chickens, despite our protests that we were just leaving. "It's too hot for you to be out here on your feet in your condition." Somehow the phrase was less annoying coming from her than it had been from, for example, Rowan. It also wasn't even that hot, but then I wasn't gardening in coveralls.

We waved at Lin as we were hustled back past the greenhouse. She shook her head at us resignedly and went back to tending her triffids.

The side door of the manor led directly into a large kitchen, which again felt more farmhouse than stately home. Mrs. Pilkington insisted we pull up seats at the large and scarred oak table in the center of the room, while she bustled around making tea.

"Now nothing with caffeine in it, of course," she chattered away. "But I must have some decaf tea knocking around . . . yes, here we go. And water for the dogs of course. Let me just see . . . yes, they can drink out of this." She set an enormous saucepan of water in front of the dogs, seemingly unbothered as they drooled and slobbered all over the shining metal.

As she boiled the kettle and fetched mugs, she bombarded Poppy with a steady stream of questions on whether she was sleeping, how her back was holding up, if she'd had anymore Braxton Hicks. She seemed to know more about Poppy's pregnancy than Joe knew about mine. Poppy replied with her usual calm and smiling demeanor.

"Is your husband around?" she asked casually.

"No, he's in town today." Mrs. Pilkington paused. "I heard you ran into him the other day," she said eventually, a worried frown creasing her forehead. "I do hope he wasn't too rude?"

In the face of her genuine concern, Poppy was diplomatic to say the least. "He wasn't *friendly*," she said guardedly.

I kept my head down and slurped at my tea. I'd rather not let Mrs. Pilkington know that I'd also encountered her husband recently, and hadn't been at my politest. I certainly hadn't been expecting to take tea at the manor anytime soon.

"Oh, I am so sorry." Mrs. Pilkington looked distressed. "I really don't know what to say to him to make him understand. It's these wretched political types that he's all mixed up with."

I wondered if Mrs. Pilkington was as naive as she sounded. Ronald Pilkington wasn't dabbling on the fringes of the Penton Preservation Society, he was the founder, president and standing as its candidate in the local elections. The man *was* the Preservation Society.

"He just gets so swept up in these things." She was shaking her head sadly.

"Mmm, it can happen. It's so easy to be swayed by the people around you. I mean, didn't he used to be quite into the whole hippy scene?" said Poppy, deftly steering the conversation.

"Oh well, you're going back a few years there," laughed Mrs. Pilkington. "Must have been thirty or forty years ago now . . . But back in the day, oh absolutely! I mean, we all were back then; it was all the rage. Long hair, bare feet, being one with nature and all that."

"Isn't that when the commune up in Stricker's Wood was started?" I asked innocently.

"Oh yes, that was Ronald and his friends," she chattered on happily, her eyes misted with nostalgia. "I only spent the one summer there, but it was just lovely. They were so idealistic, those boys. Camran, Crispin and Ronald. Or Ronnie as he was back then. Just like your lovely dog."

I tried to turn my snort of laughter into a cough. I loved the thought that Ronald Pilkington shared his name with the pig-dog that is Ronnie.

"How did they come to start the commune?" asked Poppy encouragingly.

Mrs. Pilkington settled back in her chair. "They were dreamers, those three. But radicals too. They thought there had to be a better way of living. We were just beginning to realize the level of destruction we were all wreaking on the planet, you understand. We didn't grow up with that knowledge in the way you children did. Plastics, air travel, fast food, they were the miracles of the modern age. But when we were about your age, we started to heed the warning signs. Ronnie and Camran, well, they were some of the earliest to say we had to turn our backs on so-called modern life. Of course they went quite extreme, they wanted to eschew all modern technologies, go back to a simpler way of living, more connected with the earth. So they did."

She made it sound terribly simple.

"Still, it's a huge undertaking," I said. "They must have been very proud of what they created."

"Oh, well, of course it was all made much easier by the fact that Ronald's family owned this place and all that land," admitted Mrs. Pilkington. Presumably the fact that one owns vast acreages *can* tend to slip the mind. "Otherwise they wouldn't have had anywhere to start their project. But Ronald's father was quite happy to let them set up camp in the woods. Of course he rather indulged Ronald. I think he always knew that it was a bit of a phase as far as Ronald was concerned. I don't think he would ever have dreamed that the commune would still be going thirty-five years later. But, well, the family have more land than they can possibly use anyway, so what's the harm in letting the commune use that little corner of the woods, I say."

"Your husband owns the land the commune's on?" I interrupted, unable to stop myself.

"Oh yes," said Mrs. Pilkington, nodding several times. "That's all Pilkington land. The land deeds are still in Ronald's name. Of course he wouldn't dream of charging them a penny's rent."

"Even after he left the commune?" I asked, intrigued. I'd been under the impression it had been something of an acrimonious falling-out, although now I came to think about it no one had said as much.

"Oh my dear, he and Camran may have argued but Ronald's not a bad man. He doesn't believe in what Camran stands for anymore, but he wouldn't take away Camran's dream. No, the commune will stay where it is as long as Ronald's around."

This did not sound like the Ronald Pilkington I knew.

"What did they fall out over?" Poppy asked. I held my breath. She was so good at this, asking what felt like terribly loaded questions with a casualness that suggested she was merely making conversation.

"A girl, of course," said Mrs. Pilkington breezily. "It was all terribly romantic. Must have been thirty years ago now. Such a beautiful girl she was too. We were up at the commune at the same time, Flora and I."

Poppy and I exchanged an electrified glance. Flora—again!

"Yes, a beautiful girl," said Mrs. Pilkington nostalgically. "Hair down to her waist, and a figure to die for. I'd have been terribly jealous, but she was such a lovely girl I was really rather fond of her. All the boys at the commune were half in love with her. It broke all their hearts when she left."

"Why did she leave?" I asked.

A glint came into Mrs. Pilkington's milky eye. She cast us a sly look that didn't suit her grandmotherly air.

"Ooh she was a wild one, Flora was," she chuckled. "Wild as they come. And very *in tune with nature*, if you know what I mean."

Hadn't the foggiest.

"She was one for gathering nuts in May," Mrs. Pilkington continued, nodding sagely.

Excuse me? Did she mean what I thought she meant? Was this some kind of old-person code?

"She knew her birds and bees."

Ah.

"You mean," I channeled my inner Mrs. Pilkington, "she got herself 'in the family way'?" Ugh, what a phrase.

"She got herself in trouble all right," said Mrs. Pilkington, nodding emphatically. "She was off as soon as the baby started to show. Didn't want to stick around."

"Why not?" I asked. I mean, I know things were different back in the days of yore, but we're talking about a hippy commune here. I mean, if *they* couldn't handle a rogue pregnancy . . .

"I think there was . . . a little confusion," said Mrs. Pilkington delicately, "over the paternity of the child."

Ah. Well, that would do it.

"So who were the candidates?" I asked eagerly, and perhaps a little bluntly.

Mrs. Pilkington's mouth went thin. Clearly I didn't have Poppy's aptitude for this.

"Well, Camran was absolutely smitten with her," she began cautiously. "But he'd just started seeing Hazel and it was all rather awkward. Then there was Crispin, following her round like a lovesick puppy. They used to go out foraging together in the early mornings." She shot us a meaningful look. I tried so hard to keep a straight face.

"Foraging, yes," I agreed. "And Crispin meaning Crispin Oliver?"

"Yes, Crispin Oliver, dear, there weren't any other Crispins around," she said a touch waspishly.

"Sorry, of course."

She gave a big sigh. "Sorry, dear, I don't mean to snap. But, well, people *did* throw Ronald's name about back then. As if he would have been the father," she scoffed. "I mean, yes, he was a bit infatuated with Flora that summer—weren't we all! But he's a gentleman, Ronald.

Never laid a finger on her. No, it was all flowers and sunset walks from Ronald."

God, old people can be so naive. Sunset walks.

"So it was Camran's or Mr. Oliver's child," said Poppy tactfully—I could hear the unspoken "or almost definitely Ronald Pilkington's" dropping into the end of the sentence.

"Most likely," said Mrs. Pilkington. She sighed. "Poor Flora. I often wonder what happened to her."

"You mean, that was it?" I asked. "She just left and none of you saw her again?"

Mrs. Pilkington smiled rather sadly. "That's how it was back then. There was none of this social media. You couldn't just look someone up on Facebook. There was no email. We didn't even have mobile phones. People really could just walk out of your life and disappear."

It was an odd thought. It would be so very difficult these days to simply disappear. There had been that Channel 4 program about it—*Hunted*, I think it was called—where people had to try and go off-grid for a month, and it had proved almost impossible. But thirty years ago? All you had to do was refrain from leaving a forwarding address.

"Have you tried looking her up since?" I asked. "She might be on Facebook now. What was her surname?"

"I doubt I'd be able to find her, even if I wanted to," said Mrs. Pilkington thoughtfully. "We didn't use surnames at the commune—they are the product of a patriarchal system, after all." I refrained from commenting that she was married to the living embodiment of all things patriarchal. "And, well, I wouldn't be surprised if Flora wasn't even her real name. We were all using silly names back then. Of course, Camran still is." She gave a little laugh. "And, well, what would be the point in looking her up after all these years. We'd have nothing in common; just the memories of a shared summer thirty years ago. Things change, people change."

Her husband certainly had, I thought. Best not to say it out loud, though. The mood of the room had definitely shifted.

"So Flora just disappeared," I mused.

"We all moved on with our lives. I was there to pick up the pieces of Ronald's heart and here we are, thirty years later." She smiled indulgently, like it was a charming story, but it made me feel slightly sad for her. No one likes to feel they were the runner-up prize.

My gaze drifted over to the fireplace and the three dogs. Oh wait . . . Sultan was there, sitting regally upright by the fire. Ronnie was sprawled out like a seriously budget fur rug. And Helen was nowhere to be seen. Great.

"Did anyone see Helen leave the room?" I asked. For an extremely loud and tactless dog, she could be an absolute ninja when she wanted to be. Poppy and Mrs. Pilkington shook their heads, Poppy looking a little alarmed—probably fearing that Lin was going to be fired because Helen had buried all the Pilkingtons' spoons. I lumbered to my feet. "I'm so sorry, Mrs. Pilkington, I shouldn't have brought her into your lovely house. I'm sure she hasn't gone far . . ." I wasn't sure at all. Hopeful, maybe.

"Not at all," said Mrs. Pilkington. "I'll help you find her."

"I'll wait with these two." Poppy gestured at her two dogs, neither of whom looked like they had any plans to move ever again, but then you never did know with Ronnie.

For once, Helen had *not* gone far. We found her in the hallway. Unfortunately, she was harassing one of the Pilkingtons' coats that hung on a coat stand by the door. An actual coat stand. It was wobbling precariously, and I lunged forward to grab it before she toppled the whole thing.

"I'm so sorry!" I gasped, detaching Helen from the sleeve of the coat. Then I looked at the coat.

"Really, don't worry," said Mrs. Pilkington. "I remember when I was a child we had a black Labrador called Charlie and blow me if he didn't . . ."

I wasn't listening. I was still staring at the jacket. At the familiar rip in the lining near the collar.

". . . and one time, someone came round for tea, I think it was the vicar, actually, and Charlie—"

"Is this your husband's jacket?" I interrupted—probably rather rudely.

Mrs. Pilkington looked a little taken aback. "Goodness no, dear," she said with a little laugh. "It's far too young for Ronald! No, that was

left here the other evening by a young man who popped round to speak
to him."

"What did he want to speak to him about?"

"Oh, politics, I think," she said vaguely. "I don't really get involved.
They disappeared into Ronald's study and I left them to it. *MasterChef*
was on and I know you can get these things on rerun if you miss them
but I do prefer to watch it live."

I stared at her blankly.

"I'm sorry, Mrs. Pilkington, I'm not feeling too well. I think I need to
go home."

I DIDN'T tell Poppy I'd seen Joe's jacket at the Pilkingtons' house. I needed
to think about it. Instead, I came out with some garbled excuse about
Braxton Hicks contractions, forgetting this was the exact excuse Poppy
had used to escape the commune the other day.

"Are you sure you're OK?" she asked, as we made our way back down
the never-ending "drive."

"Yeah, sorry," I lied. "Just a few twinges. I probably just need to go
home, have a lie-down."

She shot me a skeptical look. I couldn't blame her; I've always been a
terrible liar.

"That was all very interesting, wasn't it?" Smooth conversation change
from me there. Thankfully Poppy rolled with it.

"Why does this Flora keep cropping up?" she mused. "What's the deal
there? For a woman who spent one summer at the commune, she seems
to have made quite the impression."

"Well, even in a hippy commune I reckon a three-way paternity mystery is gonna cause a bit of chat," I pointed out, grasping gratefully at the
new topic. "It's like the shit version of *Mamma Mia!*, isn't it? Only in a
shady Cotswolds hippy commune, rather than on a Greek island. Any
minute now Pierce Brosnan is going to step out from behind a tree and
serenade us."

"It's the only thing that could make this situation worse," Poppy said.

I laughed, pleased to have moved the conversation into the safer territory of shit romcoms (by which I obviously mean really excellent romcoms).

"I always liked the Swedish one with the butt tattoos," Poppy continued thoughtfully. "He's kind of hot."

"Firstly, he is not hot *at all*, he's all leathery. And secondly, you're gay."

"You're so binary, Alice," said Poppy with a condescending grin. "Just because I'm married to a woman doesn't mean I can't find guys attractive."

"OK, fine, but does it have to be seventy-year-old men with butt tattoos?"

"He is not seventy!"

"Whatever—your weird taste in men is getting us off-topic."

"Yes, absolutely—which is deciding which of the mysterious Flora's potential lovers is the hottest."

I pulled a face. "It's hard to pick between the hippy Druid, the racist politician and the dead guy."

Poppy snorted. "Yeah, she really knew how to pick them."

"It always comes back to those three, doesn't it," I mused. "Camran, Mr. Oliver and Ronald Pilkington. The three guys who started the commune and fell out—apparently over a girl. Ronald Pilkington leaves and becomes a right-wing politician, and Mr. Oliver and Camran carry on Druiding around for another twenty years, before *they* fall out and Mr. Oliver leaves."

"At roughly the same time as Jasmine died, in questionable circumstances, at the commune," completed Poppy. "And then ten years after *that*, Mr. Oliver is murdered halfway through our prenatal class. How does it all fit together?"

"It might not," I pointed out. "They might be totally unrelated events."

"Yeah right," said Poppy, and I have to admit I shared her skepticism. "That's a hell of a lot of coincidences."

"There's just too many gaps," I said, kicking at the ground in frustration. "There's too much that we don't know. What happened to Jasmine? Who was Flora, and what happened to her and her kid? And why does any of this mean Mr. Oliver had to die? And we don't even know *how* he died! Ailsa said they still haven't done the postmortem—what the hell's taking them so long?"

"No . . ." said Poppy slowly. "We don't know how he died. Except . . ." She was watching Helen with a strange intensity.

"Yes?" I prompted.

"I've had a thought," said Poppy.

"Yeah?"

"I'm probably jumping to conclusions . . ."

"Extremely slowly . . ." I hinted.

"I don't want to say anything rash."

"Oh, come on."

"I was just thinking about Helen."

"Helen?"

"About when she got poisoned," explained Poppy. "What if this stuff, this methyl—what was it?"

"Methyl salicylate."

"What if this methyl salicylate was used on a person . . ."

"Pretty much what happened to Helen, I should think—Oh!" The penny dropped. "You think Mr. Oliver could have been poisoned with it?"

Poppy grimaced. "I think it's a possibility. I mean, we think he was probably poisoned, and I just think it's odd that the day after he's poisoned, Helen gets poisoned too . . ."

"Which would mean," I continued, "that where Helen found it could be a matter of extreme interest . . ."

Poppy nodded grimly. "And if she *did* get hold of it at the commune, that significantly narrows our pool of suspects."

I nodded in agreement. And, I thought, crucially, that would more or less remove Lin from the pool entirely.

"We need to get back up to the commune and have a poke around," said Poppy enthusiastically. "See if we can find any traces of the poison. Didn't you say there was a dispensary there? We need to get inside!"

"Yeah, sure," I said absent-mindedly. I wanted to share her enthusiasm, I really did. But we were back at the cars now, which meant going home, which meant asking Joe what the hell his jacket was doing on Ronald Pilkington's coat stand.

"So, we need to work out how we're going to get back in there," continued Poppy. "We could let Helen loose up there again and accidentally have to follow her in?"

"She almost *died* last time," I said, affronted. "We are not using her as bait!"

"Sorry."

"We could use Ronnie?"

CHAPTER 37

I CHICKENED OUT of asking Joe about his jacket. At least in any grown-up confrontational manner. Over dinner that evening I casually dropped in, "What happened to your blue jacket? You know, the one with the rip in the lining?"

Joe looked nonplussed. Then, was that a flicker of guilt?

"I don't think I've seen it since we moved." He shrugged. "I might have put it in the charity shop box."

My brain instantly latched on to this. Perhaps some local lad had picked it up at the Sue Ryder in town and left it at the Pilkingtons'. Perhaps Joe had never set foot there! Then I remembered that the charity box was still in the spare room/baby's nursery/general dumping ground of doom. Nice try, Joe.

I didn't push it though, because a) it would have only led to another row, and b) I'm a coward. In all seriousness, though, I didn't want to argue it out of him. I wanted him to tell me. Whatever the hell was going on inside his head, I wanted him to share it with me, not because I forced him to, but because he wanted to. Unfortunately, that seemed about as likely as Helen solving the murder of Mr. Oliver.

But perhaps there was no harm in just letting him know that I knew . . .

"Poppy and I went up to the Clayton Estate this afternoon," I said casually, forking at my baked potato. Did Joe tense? Or was it my imagination?

"Oh yes?"

"Yeah, Lin works there. She's Pilkington's gardener."

Joe didn't respond for a moment. Then: "Off with Poppy again, huh?"

"What's that meant to mean?" I bristled.

Joe sighed. He looked tired. "I just meant, I've barely seen you since we moved here."

"We spent all of yesterday together." Admittedly not really talking to each other, but we'd both been physically present—that had to count for something, right?

"We spent half a weekend together. Then as soon as we got home from IKEA you disappeared off to the woods with your new friend."

"Actually it was the Clayton Estate," I muttered, very much aware that this was not the point.

"You just seem very . . . swept up in everything here," Joe continued as if I hadn't spoken. "I thought part of the idea of moving here was that we'd have more time for each other. More time for the baby. But instead, it's like you're more unreachable than ever."

Well, that sucker-punched me. Because yes, that was exactly why we'd moved here. And Joe kind of had a point; here I was, running off round the countryside trying to solve a murder, when I was supposed to be building a home—I don't mean in a 1950s "a woman's place is in the home" kinda way; it was something we were supposed to be doing *together*. On the other hand, he hadn't exactly been easy company since we'd moved here.

"It's not just me," said Joe, not looking at me, focusing on sliding a melting pat of butter across the surface of his potato. "Maya called me this afternoon."

That threw me.

"What? Why?"

"Because you haven't been answering her calls or messages."

I felt a sharp pang of guilt.

"Was she angry?" I asked Joe.

"No," he sighed. "She was worried. About you."

Well, now I felt even worse. I'd been horribly neglecting Maya. Just as she'd joking-not-joking said I would, once I moved and had the baby. And I hadn't even had the baby yet! There was really no excuse. Well, apart from the murder. But that wasn't fair at all—you don't neglect your oldest and best friend to mess about playing amateur detectives.

And the thought of Joe and Maya talking made me feel weird. It's not that they didn't get on—they did. They both made an effort to, certainly; it's just that Maya had been my best friend since we were eleven, and I hadn't met Joe until just over a year ago. Maya had, a little reluctantly, made space for him in her life, just as she was now doing with the baby. But they'd never been close. And the thought of them talking about me, and probably not in the most complimentary light, made me feel a bit wobbly inside.

"I'll give her a call," I told Joe. "In fact, I'll go and call her now."

"Just a sec." He grabbed my wrist as I went to stand. "Was she right to be worried about you?"

"What do you mean?" I asked, genuinely puzzled.

"I mean"—and he sounded slightly frustrated—"are you OK?"

"Of course, why wouldn't I be?"

"Well"—he appeared to be choosing his words carefully—"you keep asking me if *I'm* OK, but you're being kind of . . . not yourself."

I sat back down. "What do you mean?"

"All this 'investigating'"—he actually made air quotes, which immediately irritated me—"what are you doing? It's not a game, Al! It's serious. And it's not something you know anything about. Nor, frankly, is it anything to do with you. I guess part of me wonders if you're doing it to—I don't know—distract yourself from what's coming up. From how things are going to change."

"I'm not distracting myself," I argued. "But the baby's not here yet, and there's not a whole lot I can do until it is."

"That's not quite true," said Joe. "There's all that IKEA furniture waiting to be put together. There's a nursery full of stuff you've bought and then shoved in there and forgotten about. There's that hypnobirthing course we never finished."

"Hypnobirthing wasn't for me," I said defensively.

His voice softened. "I know. It's just, you keep telling me that it's OK to be nervous, but I wonder if you're giving yourself the same luxury."

I didn't know what to say. Was I nervous? Hell yes. Did I think I'd got involved in this investigation to distract from those nerves? Well, it wasn't impossible. In fact, now I came to interrogate it, I had almost definitely got involved out of a need for something to do, something to give me some purpose that wasn't just waiting around for my life to change forever. I could tell myself that it was to help Lin, to prevent a miscarriage of justice, or something similarly noble, but really I'd got involved because I was nosy, I quite enjoyed crime dramas and I wanted to be friends with Poppy.

"I guess I am a *bit* nervous."

Joe gave a small smile. "You'd be a fool not to be."

"Thanks for the motivational speech."

"You're welcome. And I'm sorry about yesterday. I was in a foul mood."

"Yeah, me too."

It was a truce, of sorts. And it felt a lot better than fighting.

"Friends?"

"Friends."

Talking of friends, I headed upstairs to text Maya.

> Sorry I've been a bit shit lately

That's OK, you're having a baby and solving a murder

> I don't know which terrifies me more

Ha

Yeah well, I know you're busy with your new mum pals

> It's not like that!

> I barely know them!

> And I think two of them hate me

I was only kidding you loon

> Which two?

Hen and Ailsa

> Oh I haven't met Hen (stupid name though I don't think I like her)

> I liked Ailsa though

Why? She's so mean!

> I think that's why

> If you have to have new friends can it be her please

It's a strange thing, female friendship. Possibly because while there's always the doubt lurking at the back of your mind that your romantic relationship could just be temporary, you very much expect certain platonic friendships to be a lifelong commitment. That makes you a hell of a lot more protective of them. These bitches have got to see you through a lifetime. After all, even if I married Joe I could still divorce him, but I knew it would take a damn sight more than divorce to shake Maya off.

It's very hard to share female friends, in my experience. There's always a hint of suspicion when they start talking about "other women," new colleagues at work that they seem to be spending a lot of time with or, even worse, a woman they met at "the gym." On balance, I think I'd probably rather share my boyfriend than my friends.

Was I cheating on Maya?

I'd do something nice to make it up to her.

I went on Amazon and ordered her a Toblerone. In fact, I ordered her six, because there was a significant bulk discount.

I went to bed confident in the knowledge that I was a good friend.

CHAPTER 38

I CAME DOWNSTAIRS the next morning to find a large box sitting on the kitchen table. It was full of mismatched jars containing an assortment of homemade jams and chutneys, a bottle of fancy elderflower cordial, some cozy-looking woolen socks and a big Tupperware of homemade cookies. I got going and ate one—then two, then three—while reading the accompanying postcard.

> *Dear Joe and Alice,*
> *I hope you're both well, and the move went OK.*
> *I know the first week in a new place can be rather chaotic, so*
> *here are a few bits and pieces to keep you going while you settle*
> *in. Alice, the socks are for you—that cottage sounds chilly! Make*
> *sure you're keeping warm—and leave all the heavy lifting to Joe.*
> *Give me a ring when you can.*
> *Lots of love,*
> *Mum*

As was becoming pretty commonplace these days, my eyes welled up. How kind of Joe's mum! (There were *so* many reasons why I immediately knew it wasn't from my mum.) How thoughtful of her. We really should try and get her down for a visit. Then I frowned slightly; it sounded as though Joe still hadn't called her back. I shoved another cookie in my mouth and went to find Joe—and, if necessary, dial her number and hold the phone to his ear.

I found him lurking in the sitting room, peeking out furtively from behind the curtains.

"What are you doing?"

"Our new neighbor's moving in, want to spy with me?"

I budged him aside and peered through the gap beneath his armpit.

"You need to call your mum," I whispered, accidentally scattering cookie crumbs along the windowsill.

"You need to learn to use a plate," he whispered back. Not to worry, a giraffe-like tongue sneaked up over the sill—Helen was on cleanup duty.

"Seriously, though—" I began, but Joe interrupted.

"Ooh, is that a hookah?"

So far a bell tota had been hung in the front window and a string of Tibetan prayer flags had been draped around the front garden. What's the bet the new neighbor was neither Indian nor Tibetan? For an incredibly white village with a not inconsiderable sideline in racist politics, Penton had a thriving trade in cultural appropriation.

Eventually, a hyperactive Helen forced us away from our lookout. As part of our new wholesome lifestyle, we were supposed to walk Helen *before* breakfast every day. A bold move that was so far less than fifty percent successful.

I was bent double on the doorstep trying to access my feet in order to get my shoes on—but nearly forty weeks of baby kept getting in the way—when I heard Joe say something vaguely welcoming to the new inhabitant.

"Thank you," a familiar, floaty voice replied. "I'm so pleased to have bumped into you. I wanted to let you know, I do take a gong voyage every evening, but never after nine P.M. I hope the cosmic vibrations don't disturb you."

I looked up, startled. Holy shit, Sandra, the high priestess of gong, potential criminal mastermind, was my new next-door neighbor.

She looked equally startled when she recognized me.

I knew I should say something neighborly and friendly, but what do you say when you ratted out your new neighbor to the police a mere forty-eight hours earlier? What I really wanted to ask was what she'd been doing snooping around Nature's Way the other day, and what had she pinched from that jar? I decided the best option was the coward's way out. I would pretend that particular episode had never happened.

"Hi," I said brightly. "I came to your gong bath the other day."

Her face relaxed as she went along with the charade. Oh good, I had a mutual understanding with a potential criminal.

"That's right, of course. And how was your voyage? Did the baby respond well?"

"Er, yes, thanks. I think he enjoyed it." This was a total lie. He'd spent the whole voyage with one foot rammed in my ribcage in protest. Every time the gong had banged it felt like he'd had a minor panic attack.

"And what about your friend?" she pressed.

"Maya? Oh, er—" Maya had done a lot of very loud sighing throughout the voyage, no doubt upsetting the cosmic vibrations of everyone in her vicinity.

"I don't wish to be judgmental"—began Sandra. I braced myself for extreme judgment—"but I was sensing a very negative aura around her. A very *repressed* spirit."

Now Maya is many things, but she is not repressed. Her self-expression just comes more in the form of dancing on the bar than channeling the vibrations of the universe. But Sandra hadn't finished.

"Would I be right in thinking she's an Aquarius? They tend to be very introverted. Often quite *closed* to the larger forces."

"I couldn't say for sure, but I'm going to hazard a guess at no," I replied, thinking of the time Maya had streaked the length of Greek Street in Soho for a dare. She'd been channeling some pretty large forces that night.

Sandra looked a little crestfallen. "Well, if she ever wants some one-to-one work, I think she'd definitely benefit from some individual Reiki sessions. I'm a fully trained Reiki master and would be very happy to help guide her."

"I will definitely pass that on," I promised, with full sincerity.

"Well, I'd better get on with unpacking," she said, and with the gentlest of smiles, Sandra disappeared, probably to feng shui her new house.

Later, she invited Joe in to see her gongs. He had to admit they were pretty impressive.

CHAPTER 39

I WAS GOING to put the nursery furniture together that afternoon, I really was. I had thought long and hard about what Joe had said the previous day and had decided to really knuckle down to some serious parenting prep.

I was contemplating slot A and tab B on the Solgul, and wondering how the two might ever be compatible, when Poppy called.

"Want to go into town?"

"Dunno, what are we doing in town?"

"Shopping for paper pants."

"Say what?"

"Didn't your midwife tell you about the paper pants?"

I sighed. "No, Candy did *not* tell me about the paper pants."

I wondered what else Candy had forgotten to tell me about.

"You're going to love this," said Poppy, with what I considered to be an evil cackle.

FOR THE record—not loving the paper pants.

They turned out to be max-strength disposable incontinence pants. Just in case I was feeling a bit too sexy at thirty-nine weeks pregnant. These were apparently for the twenty-four hours immediately following the birth when a tsunami of blood and bodily fluids would be exiting my battered vagina. FUN.

The packaging had a big padlock logo that reminded me of the old Shreddies cereal advert. "Keep incontinence locked up till lunch!"

"Like a chastity belt," I grumbled to Poppy, as I shelled out twelve whole pounds for the pants of shame.

"They probably double up as that too," said Poppy, pulling a face at her own pack of monstrosities. "I doubt Lin will be coming anywhere near me while I'm wearing these. And do they have to be *beige*?"

The pants were indeed a disconcerting shade of peach, like a seventies bathroom.

"They're nude," I said, without thinking.

"For white people, yeah," pointed out Poppy.

"Oh. Yeah."

"Maybe I'll start a petition for non-discriminatory incontinence pants."

"Someone's got to."

We were heading out of the shop when Poppy nudged me. "Isn't that Rowan?"

I followed her gaze. Rowan was sitting in the window of the Dog and Duck pub.

"Should we . . . go and say hi?" I asked uncertainly. I'd last seen Rowan at about 5 A.M. in the woods when he'd flipped out about Jasmine and warned me away from the commune. To be fair, I hadn't been back to the commune since, but this was only because we hadn't yet worked out how to worm our way back in to search for poison . . . A plan that I suspected would go down poorly with Rowan.

"Should we go and ask him what he's not telling us about Jasmine?" countered Poppy. "And whether he fancies sharing that article with us, the one he pinched from the *Bugle*?"

"Er . . ." It wasn't exactly what I'd had in mind.

But it was too late—Poppy was already striding across the street with a purposefulness that I'd come to know and dread. I hastily shoved my multipack of beige incontinence pants as far down in my bag as they would go and scurried after her.

Rowan looked underwhelmed to see us, but he politely gestured for us to join him. His laptop was open on the table in front of him and I happened to glance at it as I pulled up a chair—not meaning to be nosy, just out of habit. He casually pushed the lid down—also probably out of habit.

"Out shopping?" he asked.

"Yes," I muttered, clutching my bag closer, in case the pants made a bid for freedom and clawed their way out in the middle of the pub.

"You?" asked Poppy.

"Trying to write up an article." He sighed. "It's proving . . . tricky." He gestured to the half-empty pint, which I had already been longingly eyeing up.

"What's it on?" I asked.

"Oh, nothing interesting."

"That's your problem right there then," said Poppy dryly.

Rowan gave a brief forced laugh.

"I, um, wanted to say sorry about the other day," he said, turning to me and running his hands through his hair distractedly.

"That's OK," I said awkwardly.

But Poppy wasn't letting him off that lightly. "Want to tell us what that was all about? The whole 'stay away from the commune' thing?"

"Look, I shouldn't have said that; I wasn't thinking straight. It was, what, like five in the morning?" He tried for a disarming grin, but it wasn't quite working for him today.

"So . . . you're fine with us going up to the commune, asking what happened to Jasmine?" I said, in what I hoped was a lightly antagonistic manner. He blanched.

"I don't think that would be a good idea," he said quietly.

"Really? Why not?"

"They don't like people asking questions. Especially not about Jasmine."

He paused, spinning a beer mat between finger and thumb. Neither Poppy nor I said anything. We waited for him to go on. We might not expect the full story, but he'd barely given us the opening credits.

Eventually, he sighed and, still staring at the spinning beer mat and avoiding our eyes, continued. "The commune was my home. It's where I grew up. Damn, it was my whole world, pretty much. And I thought it was perfect. I mean, it *was*. It was the best place in the world to grow up, I still believe that. But what happened to Jasmine—what happened that year—it changed everything. It was like it ripped the heart out of the place. It was never the same after that. My dad was never the same."

The silence stretched uncomfortably. That couldn't be all he was giving us.

"So what did happen to her?"

He looked up and there was a strange helpless look in his eyes. "I don't know."

There was a pause.

"Seriously?"

He met my eyes. "Seriously." When I looked disbelieving he elaborated. "I honestly don't know what happened. I wasn't there. I left home the summer she joined the commune. I was away, not even in the country, I was in France with—" He broke off. "Anyway, when I came back the following summer everything had changed, like I said. Jasmine—this girl—had died and the commune was broken. Dad was broken."

"Why?" I asked. "I mean, why was your dad so cut up about it?"

I realized that might sound a tad heartless. "I mean, I know it's awful and everything, but if he'd only known her less than a year . . ."

Rowan spread his hands on the table and looked at them. "I'm not sure. He was fond of her, I think. She was about my age, and she joined the commune just as I left. I think she kind of filled the gap for him that I left. I was a bit sore about it at the time actually," he said with a rueful grin. "I'm just guessing, of course. He's never spoken about her since—since, you know. But that's the impression I get from Mum."

I didn't say anything. It seemed to me that there were a whole host of reasons why Jasmine's death could have rattled Camran—and none of them were good. But I didn't feel it would be particularly tactful to point this out.

"So you never knew Jasmine then?" I asked instead.

"No. Never even met her." He said it too quickly, and he didn't meet my eyes. I felt a sudden flush of anger—he was telling us a patchwork of truth and lies, I was sure of it. And I was so done with all these Pentonites and their secrets. I opened my mouth to say something that I would no doubt later regret when, with probably quite fortuitous timing, Poppy broke in.

"Is that Antoni?" She was peering out through the slightly grubby pub window. "*Again?*"

I sighed with frustration and squinted in the direction she was pointing. "Got to be. Suit."

"Other people do wear suits, you know."

"Not in Penton."

"Don't be so stereotyping."

"What! It's true. Do you see any other suits out there? Anyway—"

But this time I was cut off by Rowan.

"Antoni?" He sounded oddly tense. "Who's Antoni?"

"He's the husband of one of our prenatal class friends," I said. "The one who gave birth during the class. He loves a suit."

"Yeah I—" Rowan broke off.

"Oh, he's coming in," said Poppy. "Weird. He doesn't look like a Dog and Duck kind of guy. Maybe he saw us and is coming to say hi?"

I was about to say that this was unlikely—I don't think Antoni had exchanged more than a couple of words with any of us—but an exclamation from Rowan cut me off.

"Oh shit."

He'd been shoving his laptop back in his rucksack, and in his haste, the corner of it had caught on his pint glass and beer had gone everywhere.

"Don't worry!" said Poppy brightly, ripping open her pack of paper panties and beginning to mop.

God, those things are absorbent.

Rowan stared in horror. Then without a word he turned and disappeared—out through the beer garden, rather than back onto the high street.

"Ughhhh," I groaned in frustration. "Another dramatic exit from Rowan. What is *with* that guy?!"

"Just when it was getting interesting, as well," mused Poppy.

"Yeah, well, if you hadn't interrupted I was about to try and get some answers out of him," I snapped. I was feeling . . . well, snappish.

"He wouldn't have told us anything he hadn't already decided to tell us," said Poppy calmly.

"What do you mean?" I grumbled waspishly.

"He'd already decided exactly how much he was going to tell us," she said shrewdly. "Enough to try and shut us up but not too much."

I hated to say it, but she was probably right. Rowan had already calculated how much he would say when he decided to wave us over.

I sighed. "Yes, I think you're right." I poked the mess of beer and incontinence pants on the table. "I think things went a little off-script for him at the end there though. What was he so scared of? Was it Antoni? Or the beer pants?"

Poppy inspected the pants, which had swelled to the size of a small sheep.

"There's something not right about Rowan," she said. "Wow, it looks like these things hold literally a whole pint."

"What do you mean?" I asked defensively.

"Oh, come on, Alice." She sounded slightly exasperated. "The guy turns up the day before Mr. Oliver is murdered, he's hiding something about what happened all those years ago and now he's running away from a potential witness?"

"Witness?" I asked blankly.

"Antoni!"

"What makes you think Antoni's a witness? To what?"

"Well, someone saw Sandra at Nature's Way the night Mr. Oliver was killed and told the police about it. My money's on Antoni."

I had to agree with her there—the only other option being Joe, and surely he would have told me. Surely.

"So what if he saw Rowan there too that night?" Poppy continued.

I snorted. "So now you think Rowan and Sandra are in on it together? Partners in crime?" The idea was beyond ludicrous, but Poppy wasn't laughing.

"This case is such a mess, anything's possible. Anyway, there's one way to find out," she said, standing up and waving at the bar. "Antoni! Hi!"

I sank lower in my seat. Why did she have to be so *proactive* all the time? It was exhausting.

I could see the gears clicking in Antoni's brain as he tried to work out why these two strange women were waving at him. Then his eyes picked out the big old bumps (not hard to spot) and the penny dropped.

"Hey, Poppy, isn't it? And Alice?"

I was impressed. He seemed like the kind of guy who wouldn't bother to remember the names of his wife's friends. But maybe that was just me being judgmental.

He was tapping out a message on his phone as he wound his way between tables toward us.

"What can I get you both?" he asked. "They do a decent nonalcoholic beer here."

I was surprised, to say the least. Was he . . . joining us?

Apparently so! He disappeared to the bar in search of nonalcoholic beverages. Maybe that would scratch the itch. As he left, he slung his bag down on the chair next to me. It was slightly open and I could just see the lit screen of his phone. The message he had just sent was still visible on the screen.

> Don't come. Bumped into some of Hen's friends. I'll call you later.

I groaned silently. Well, that seemed pretty incriminating. Of course, there *could* be a perfectly reasonable explanation. Or, if I permitted myself to jump to conclusions as per usual, had he been planning to meet someone here whom he didn't want us to see him with? Someone blond, perhaps? Someone who worked in Costa?

I just had time to whisper this to Poppy before Antoni returned with three pints of the to my mind inappropriately named "Playground IPA."

"Pregnant too?" asked Poppy, raising an eyebrow at his Playground.

"I don't drink," he replied. "Anyway—cheers!"

Again—not in line with my image of him. I really had to stop making such snap judgments. He actually seemed a pleasant and attentive chap who was now asking polite questions about our due dates. Although in hindsight, I wish we'd cleared the beer-sodden incontinence pants off the table before calling him over. Throughout the conversation his eyes repeatedly strayed to them, and who could blame him.

"So, were you meeting anyone, or just popped in for a drink?" I asked casually, taking a sip of my nonalcoholic beer. It was all right, actually. Either that, or I'd forgotten what real beer tastes like.

"Oh, just popped in on a whim," he said—was that a nervous glance at the door? "I was in town getting some ice cream for Hen and thought I had time for one."

"Not in London today?" Poppy asked.

"No." He looked surprised. "Why would I be in London?"

"Don't you work there?" I asked curiously.

"Oh, yes. But I'm on pat leave at the moment. We had the baby, remember?" He looked faintly puzzled, clearly surprised that I could have already forgotten his baby's dramatic entrance into the world.

"Oh right, of course, it's just—" I wasn't sure where I was planning to end that sentence. Fortunately, Poppy rescued me.

"What is it you do?" she asked.

"I work for a pharmaceuticals company." He gave a small smile. "It's very dull. And probably not that popular around here." His smile turned into something of a grimace, but Poppy and I laughed.

"I know, right," I agreed. "I haven't dared tell anyone I work in advertising. Far too corporate."

"You work in advertising?" asked Poppy, sounding surprised. "I can't believe I didn't know that."

I shrugged. Somehow it had never come up. Since I'd become pregnant I'd often found that what I now did was "pregnancy," just as I suspected (and feared) that in years to come my label would be "mother." Of course the onus was, in part, on me to resist this. But the truth was it had happened in my head almost as much as in other people's.

"Yeah, I write ad copy," I expanded. "Need a tagline for incontinence pants? I'm your girl."

Poppy laughed—Antoni gave an embarrassed chuckle and tried to look anywhere but at the pants.

An hour slipped past extremely pleasantly, as we sank not one but three pints of Playground IPA and made twice that number of trips to the bathroom. It was the closest thing I'd had to a session in months. Antoni was surprisingly good company, and I was beginning to think I really had judged him too quickly.

He wasn't too keen on discussing the events of the night his daughter was born, however.

"Hen has a ghoulish fascination with this murder too," he said, looking irritated.

"I'm just a bit concerned," I said, deciding to play the frightened pregnant lady card. "My next-door neighbor was questioned by the police about it. Apparently, someone saw her at the shop that night. What if I'm living next door *to a murderer*?"

I don't think I'm a very good actor, but Antoni seemed to be buying it. He relaxed a little.

"The woman with all the scarves and the red hair?"

"That's her. Was it you who saw her?"

"Yeah, that was me. But I told the police about it and that's an end to it. Look"—he laid his hands on the table and looked at us imploringly—"we're not involved. I keep telling Hen this. Just . . . leave it. You have much more important things to deal with right now."

Wow, he sounded like Joe.

I glanced at Poppy. The problem was, we *were* involved now, especially Poppy. Inspector Harris had let Lin go, of course, but it seemed to be the only line of inquiry she was pursuing with any vigor.

"You didn't see Rowan there that night, did you?" asked Poppy bluntly.

"Who?"

"He's the son of the guy who runs the commune up in Stricker's Wood," Poppy said. "We think he might have been there that night . . ."

I frowned at her—this was definitely "leading a witness."

Antoni frowned, thinking. "You know, it's possible I *did* see someone else . . . I went out to the car to get the birthing bag—I was in rather a rush, I can't say I was taking much in, but there was someone just outside the shop when I came back. Loitering. I hadn't really thought about it."

"Do you remember what they looked like?" I asked, slightly skeptically.

He shook his head. "It was so dark. I think it was a young man though, now you mention it . . ."

Poppy gave me a meaningful look, but I wasn't so sure. I had a feeling if we'd suggested there might have been a one-eyed woman with a peg leg Antoni would also have cordially agreed that yes, he may well have seen her.

But it looked like Antoni had had enough of our detecting. He began making his polite excuses, and departed to purchase the specific brand of dairy-free ice cream he'd originally come into town for. Poppy and I took a gentle amble along the high street in the general direction of home.

"Well, he actually seemed quite nice," I admitted.

"I know," replied Poppy. "I've got to say, I didn't expect it."

"No, me neither."

We walked on in silence for a bit.

"Do you think he *is* having an affair?"

"I don't know," I sighed. "Why else would he text whoever he'd been meeting and tell them not to come just because we were there?"

"And combined with his little Costa trip the other day . . ."

"It doesn't look great."

"Do you think we should tell Hen?" Poppy asked, sounding nervous. I didn't blame her. I really didn't fancy having that conversation with Hen. I wouldn't put it past her to take a pretty literal stance on shooting the messenger.

"We have no proof . . ." I said slowly.

"No," said Poppy. "Maybe we should just leave it."

"Yeah . . . After all, we don't actually *know* that he is."

"Do you think it was Rowan he saw?" Poppy changed tack abruptly. "The night of the murder?"

I frowned. "Who knows? He was pretty vague about the whole thing. And if he saw someone hanging around the shop just before a murder took place, how come he hasn't told Harris about it?" I was feeling annoyed, and I didn't know why.

"Give the guy a break," said Poppy mildly. "His wife *was* giving birth at the time."

"Yeah, yeah, I know."

"If it was Rowan, though—and he did leave pretty abruptly when we said who Antoni was—then it's really not looking great for him," went on Poppy.

"I know," I said heavily. "We need to add Rowan to the list of suspects." I don't know why it sat so badly with me, but I liked Rowan. And I didn't want to think I was *that* bad a judge of character that I could have started to befriend a murderer. But then, I was also facing some uncomfortable questions about the man I'd chosen to start a family with. Perhaps I *was* a terrible judge of character. I looked at Poppy and wondered briefly what dark secrets she might be hiding. Then I shook myself—if I started mistrusting everyone I met, I'd drive myself mad. Besides, it wasn't like I was a totally great person myself. We all have our secrets.

"You all right? You look weird," said Poppy anxiously.

"I'm fine," I said abruptly. "Just thinking."

Both our phones pinged simultaneously.

> When you've finished hanging out at the pub with my husband, Ailsa is here and she has an update.

Damn. We were supposed to be at Hen's half an hour ago!

"If we run we can be there in fifteen minutes," said Poppy, looking worried.

Our phones pinged again.

> Don't bring Helen.

CHAPTER 40

ANTONI SMILED GUILTILY when he opened the door to us twenty stressful minutes later.

"I didn't realize the ice cream I was supposed to be buying was for you ladies," he said. "I'd have offered you a lift if I'd known."

"Is Hen cross that we're late?" I asked anxiously.

"She's not best impressed," he said, ushering us inside and taking our coats. "But her and the girl with the dreads seem to be getting on like a house on fire."

It was true: from down the hallway I could hear the unfamiliar sound of Ailsa's laughter.

Hen and Ailsa were in the conservatory, tickling the baby and laughing at the faces she was making. It was a scene of domestic bliss—really set off by the pristine background foliage and crystalline windows, although I thought I detected a nose smudge at about Helen height. When we'd initially arranged to meet today I'd suggested we gather at mine, but Hen had asked if it was baby-safe and I had to admit it absolutely was not. It housed Helen, for a start, who had all the hallmarks of a dog that would eat nappies and pee on the baby. This was mildly concerning, given that I was planning on introducing a baby to the house imminently.

"Hen said you found a clue," I said excitedly, dropping into a wickerwork armchair.

"I did not say that," interjected Hen. "What is it with you and clues?"

"So what is the non-clue?" I persisted.

"It's not even that interesting," said Ailsa. "But after you spoke to Jane

on Saturday, Alice, she did actually order a new search of Nature's Way."
I felt a small swell of pride—Inspector Harris had genuinely listened to
what I had to say. I had influenced a police investigation!

"What are you looking so pleased about?" asked Ailsa suspiciously.

"Oh, you know," I said, grinning. "Just thinking about how the inspector would be lost without me. I'm like the Holmes to her Lestrade."

Ailsa gave me a blank stare. I wilted a little and downgraded my expectations. "Watson?"

"I'm not sure what you are."

"Can we hear what they found?" cut in Hen testily. "I presume they
found something?"

"Yep, they did and Jane is hopping mad they missed it the first time
round. Said it makes her look like an incompetent prick. I told her she
managed that on her own and—well, you don't need to know about that."

I'd love to be a fly on the wall for one of Ailsa and Inspector Harris's
rows.

"And?" pressed Poppy.

"It's probably nothing," continued Ailsa. "But they found a *Penton
Bugle* press pass on the floor. It had slid underneath Mr. Oliver's desk.
No name on it, just one of the temporary ones they hand out to freelance
reporters. I mean, it could be nothing, it could have been lying there for
weeks—you saw the state of that place, I don't think Mr. Oliver was giving it a thorough tidy every night. Still . . ."

I felt myself go very still.

"Worth thinking about," said Hen thoughtfully. "Any prints on it?"

"Yes, they picked up one set of prints. Not Mr. Oliver's and nothing
came up on the system. I guess they'll take the prints of all the staff there,
but if it was a freelancer then it might not turn up anything."

Hen looked at me and narrowed her eyes. "What do you know about
this?"

Before I could reply Poppy had jumped in.

"Rowan!" she exclaimed. "Remember, Alice? He told us he was looking for his press pass when we saw him in the *Bugle* archives! It's got to
be his!"

"It could be," I said.

"Oh, come on! It's not like there's a massive staff there. And the report said it was a generic one, with no name. Permanent staff members would have their own proper ones, but if Rowan had only just joined . . ."

She was right, of course. We all paused to consider the implications.

"Maybe he just bought something there, and dropped his pass," I suggested. "Like Ailsa said, it could have been there for weeks."

But Poppy shook her head. "No, remember when we first met him he told his dad he'd only landed the previous day—the day Mr. Oliver was killed."

"That's true," I admitted. "But still, he might just have been visiting Mr. Oliver." But we all knew that was odd in itself—if his parents hadn't spoken to Mr. Oliver for ten years, what was he doing paying the old man a visit on his first night back in Penton? Added to the weird conversation we'd had in town with him that morning, I hated to say it, but Rowan was looking more than a bit suspicious.

"I don't know," said Ailsa. She looked uncertain. "I've known Rowan since we were teenagers. And God knows I don't want to defend the guy, but I can't see him as a *murderer*."

"It must be his," insisted Poppy, looking more than a little put out by our lack of reaction. I could see it from her perspective—here was a piece of hard evidence that pointed firmly away from Lin. Of course we should be excited.

"I mean, it definitely looks bad," I tried to muster a bit more spirit. "What should we do?"

"Tell Inspector Harris, of course!"

I had known that was the correct response, I just didn't like the thought of it. God, what was wrong with me, did I want to protect a potential criminal?

"Yeah, yeah we should," I said, trying to sound decisive. I wondered if I was supposed to volunteer to do the deed, but I'd already dumped my next-door neighbor in it with the police. And there were only so many people I could accuse before Harris totally lost patience with me—if she hadn't already.

"Ailsa?" I suggested.

"Nuh," she said firmly. "Like I said, I've got mixed feelings about the guy, but no way is he a murderer."

Poppy scowled.

"Fine, I'll do it," I said quickly, before things flared up. Poppy gave me a small smile. Ailsa inspected her fingernails. Hen picked up my teacup and moved it onto a coaster.

"OK, so who else is in the frame?" she asked briskly. "Rowan's not the only one who was, potentially, at Nature's Way the evening of the murder. We know Sandra was there too. *And* she went back and pinched something. The question is: what?"

"We could just ask her," suggested Poppy. "Didn't you say she's just moved in next door to you, Alice?"

"Yeah, this morning," I agreed. "But somehow, if it's something suspicious she took—which I think we can agree it is—I can't see her just telling me about it. Plus, if she is the murderer, I don't really want to go telling her that I'm onto her. I've seen enough episodes of *Morse* to know how that ends."

"*Morse?* What are you, a seventy-year-old man?" snorted Ailsa.

"I appreciate classic crime," I said in a dignified voice. "Can't you just ask your sister if she spoke to Sandra?"

"What do you think?" retaliated Ailsa, which seemed fair enough. "Let's assume we're not going to rely on Alice's interrogation skills," she continued. "And let's definitely assume I'm not going to be asking any favors from Jane. So where does that leave us?"

"We could . . . break into Nature's Way?" I suggested. "Sandra was interrupted by Miss Webb, so what if she didn't actually get everything she was after?"

"Keep your voice down," hissed Hen. "Antoni would kill me if he even heard me *talking* about breaking into a crime scene. And I have a daughter to think about now. I can't be smashing windows and jimmying locks." I was mildly impressed at the thought that she might actually know how to jimmy a lock.

"And given her track record, Jane will probably have me executed if she catches me at it," said Ailsa darkly.

"Hmm. Yeah, maybe it should be Alice and me who actually do the breaking in," said Poppy thoughtfully.

"Wait, what?" I yelped. "When I said we should break in, I assumed you'd all talk me out of it!"

"Oh, I thought you were volunteering," said Ailsa mildly.

"We're not breaking in anywhere," I said firmly. "Unless we have to," I added, a little more weakly.

"Good, that's clear as mud then," said Ailsa.

"Look, just . . . Fine, give me a chance to talk to Sandra and I'll see what I can get out of her," I said. "Even if it means going gong voyaging again or, I don't know, solstice dancing naked through the woods or something."

"It's March," said Ailsa.

"What?"

"It's March. You're about as far from either solstice as you can get."

"You know what I mean," I said through gritted teeth.

Great, well, that was two fun conversations I had lined up. What to tackle first—handing Rowan over to the formidable Inspector Harris? Or accusing my next-door neighbor of possibly being a murderer, and getting clubbed to death with her gongs?

I FILLED them in on my encounter with Rowan and the mysterious tree desecrator in the woods that weekend, which was generally agreed to be suspicious but also entirely baffling. Eventually, the conversation drifted from murder to the marginally more terrifying topic of parenting.

Hen was soon listing every parenting book she had read—which appeared to be every one ever written.

I leaned over to where Ailsa was eyeing Hen in horror. "Have you read any parenting books?" I whispered to her.

"Yeah. *Let's Pretend This Never Happened*."

As ever, not sure if she was joking.

"I'm so not ready for this," I muttered, watching Hen latch the baby onto a boob for its fifty-millionth feed of the day while holding forth on the merits of *Parenting the Danish Way*.

"I suspect no one ever is," said Poppy sagely.

"Not true," I argued. "Some women are natural mothers. They know how to talk to kids. They don't break out in a cold sweat when someone asks them to hold a baby for two seconds."

"Yeah, I'm with you on that," agreed Ailsa. "And I'm definitely in the cold sweat camp. Honestly, if this little surprise hadn't come along, I'm not sure I would have had kids."

"A surprise, huh?" I asked. "Me too."

"At least you've got Joe to be surprised with together," said Ailsa quietly. No one said anything. Ailsa had studiously avoided all mention of her baby's father.

"The dad's . . ." I began, not sure how I was planning to end that sentence.

"Not around," said Ailsa shortly.

"It's not Rowan then?" The question popped out of my mouth honestly before my brain had a chance to register it.

Ailsa gave a bark of laughter. "I *knew* that's what you thought. You're so transparent, Alice. But no, the dad is not Rowan."

I was genuinely surprised. I'd actually been pretty certain about that. But then, Ailsa was full of surprises.

"You don't need the dad around," said Hen brusquely. "You'll be more than enough on your own. The kid will be lucky to have you."

Ailsa gave a small smile. "Thanks."

"It's not like Antoni's been around much since this one arrived." Hen's shoulders drooped. "I really thought it might bring him home more. But if anything, since she was born he's been more absent than ever. Even when he's at home, it's like he's not really there."

Poppy and I exchanged an awkward glance.

"I'm really sorry we held him up at the pub earlier," I offered.

Hen flapped the hand not holding the baby. "Oh, that, I don't mind *that*. To be honest I was quite pleased—and surprised. It's nice he wanted to hang out with you. It's him disappearing off to work that bothers me."

This time I studiously avoided catching Poppy's eye.

"I can feel you two not looking at each other," said Hen with a hint of the old impatience in her voice. "And yes, I know what you're thinking.

You think you saw Antoni in Bridgeport last week and you think I'm being horribly naive in insisting that he was in London."

"Er . . ." I said. Because that was exactly what I'd been thinking, and I could tell from Poppy's face she had been too.

"I don't care if he was in London or Bridgeport, or at work or with some girl or whatever," continued Hen. I stared fixedly forward, determined not to make eye contact with Poppy. We hadn't told Hen about the girl Antoni had been with, or the embrace that was way too passionate for a Wednesday afternoon Costa stop.

"I just wish he'd be home a bit more," concluded Hen, in a horribly small voice.

No one said anything, but Ailsa slid over and wrapped an arm around Hen's shoulders.

"Who needs men?" said Poppy in a falsely bright tone.

CHAPTER 41

WHEN I GOT home that evening I decided to be strong, turn my back on the evening of Netflix I had lined up and do some parenting shit.

"We should decorate the nursery," I announced to Joe.

"Mhmm," he replied noncommittally, his attention very much on the snooker match playing in the background.

"I'll take that as a yes." I pulled up Pinterest on my phone. "What's our theme?"

He groaned. "Do we have to have a theme?"

"It's like you've never even been on Instagram."

"OK, fine, how about baby-themed?"

I rolled my eyes. We spent the next hour debating back and forth over jungle versus space themes and ended up spending too much money on a mishmash of items across both themes, meaning that our child will spend his formative years sleeping in a sort of intergalactic zoo.

Did I ever worry about the impact Joe and I would have on our as yet unborn child? Sure. Joe had gone the duration of our first year of dating without, to my knowledge, ever changing his bedding. Even now I thought that a meal involving more than one vegetable was a bit fancy. I had zero practical skills and very few interpersonal ones. It wasn't a lot to bequeath my child.

To be fair to us, we didn't have a lot to work with. Joe's dad had been notably absent from birth—although his mum had done a pretty kick-ass job of raising him herself, from what I'd seen. My parents had been . . .

present. Physically, at least. But my mum had seemed only fleetingly aware of my existence and hazy at best when it came to actually identifying me; she had repeatedly tried to take my best friend home at primary school pickup. My personal experience of "parents" consisted of a pair of well-meaning but distracted faces atop aggressively floral outfits, sporting faintly bemused expressions at discovering I was, in fact, still there.

Sometimes it felt like I was just waiting for some kind of parenting gene to kick in, like I'd wake up one morning and just feel responsible. That I'd suddenly understand all those grown-up things that parents (by which I mean other people's parents) seem to inherently know—like how to bleed a radiator or how often curtains should be washed.

It hadn't happened yet. I was starting to fear it never would.

As in all times of need, I texted Maya.

> Will Joe and I be terrible parents?

Hard to say

I don't think I'd want you to be my mum

> Why not?

I don't think you have boundaries

It would be a bit intense

> Oh

Thanks for the Toblerone btw

> Don't mention it

All six of them

> All good things come in sixes

What was it in aid of?

To say sorry for cheating on you with
the mum friends and the murder

You're a twit

Have you solved it yet?

No . . .

Get a move on

Before someone else snuffs it

CHAPTER 42

IT HAD NOT been a good night. At about 3 A.M. Joe and I had been dramatically woken by the sound of a small brass band and Helen screaming. It appeared she had sat on the toy piano some good-hearted colleague of Joe's had gifted the unborn baby, setting off one of the preset synth tunes. It had scared the bejesus out of Helen, and she had then scared the living hell out of us.

By the time everyone had stopped screaming and the tiny piano had been ruthlessly disabled by Joe, we were all wide awake.

I wondered if now might be a sensitive time to bring up the subject of Joe's visit to the Pilkingtons. I hear these conversations go excellently at 4 A.M. when everyone's nerves are stretched like a tightrope. But as if he could sense my intentions, Joe made a swift exit to watch some cricket match taking place in Australia, muttering something about making the most of being awake at this time. I decided to go out into the back garden and watch the sun rise. It seemed like the kind of thing you should do in the countryside. Maybe I'd actually hear the famous dawn chorus. I'm sure the birds had one in London, but it was always drowned out by the night buses.

Well, as it turns out, our new neighbor wouldn't have been out of place in our old back garden in Peckham. Sandra was sitting out in her dressing gown smoking. The distinctive fragrance of weed wafted across the hedge and into our garden. Ah, that took me back. I drew in a deep sniff, then remembered the baby and tried to cough it out of my nose. This alerted Sandra to my presence.

"Alice, hi. I didn't think anyone was up." She sounded even floatier than normal, like her voice might just drift away with the marijuana smoke. "Sorry, you don't mind, do you . . . ?" She waved the joint carelessly.

In her richly embroidered silk dressing gown, her auburn curls caught up in a hairnet that glinted silver in the first rays of the morning sun, wreathed in wisps of herbal-scented smoke, she reminded me of the hookah-smoking caterpillar from *Alice in Wonderland*. I wondered if that made me Alice—it was my name, after all, and I was changing size from day to day. And things felt mad enough that a game of flamingo-hedgehog croquet sounded pretty par for the course to me these days. So long as no one started screaming, "Off with her head!"

"I don't mind at all," I assured Sandra, settling myself tentatively on the ancient garden furniture that had come with the rental property. It was only a matter of time before I went through the seat of one of these chairs.

"Didn't expect to come across much weed in Penton," I said conversationally across the hedge.

Sandra cackled with laughter. It was not in keeping with her usual ethereal demeanor.

"Oh, you city people," she said, waving her joint. "You think the countryside is all picking flowers and woodland foraging. You have no idea."

"No, apparently not," I agreed.

"I mean, there is quite a lot of that," she conceded. "Foraging and the like. Especially around here."

"And gong baths," I added.

Sandra cackled again. "And gong baths," she agreed. "Which, I might add, are considerably more spiritual after a joint."

I knew it. The woman was permanently high. And, well, a stoned gong bath did sound much more appealing.

"Give me six months and I'm all over that," I said. Before realizing that probably wasn't responsible parenting. I'd need to wait till I was Sandra's age before I could get stoned again.

"I mean, there's fuck all else to do around here," mused Sandra.

"To be honest, it doesn't sound that bad," I said. And I meant it. I could probably get into a bit of light foraging and the occasional herbally enhanced cosmic journey.

We sat in companionable silence for a while. I could, as suspected, hear the dawn chorus. It was hard not to—those birds are bloody loud! It sounded like there was a whole army of them out there. But it was an enjoyable racket, preferable to the rumble of the N67 night bus, anyway.

"D'you come out here every morning?" I asked Sandra. She sat with her head tilted back to the sky, blue smoke trickling from her nose.

"Most days," she sighed. "Not for much longer, I suppose. Unless I can find a new supplier."

"Oh? What's happened to the old one?"

She opened one beady eye and looked at me with more focus than I might have expected.

"Dead."

I was about to offer some vague condolences when the penny dropped.

"Mr. Oliver?"

"That's right." She took another deep drag. "Crispin Oliver. Serving the community since nineteen ninety-seven."

I snorted. I liked Stoned Sandra quite a lot more than the High Priestess of the Gong.

"He used to keep his stash in the shop—mainly to piss off that moody old bag he ran it with." Sandra had been musing airily to the stars, but now a scowl creased her face. "Mairi Webb never approved. Caught me pinching the last of his stock last week. And then the cow only goes and drops me in it with the police! Told them I'd been snooping around the shop. Can you believe it? I had that Inspector Harris round here yesterday asking me about it."

Ah. I decided not to mention to Sandra that it was in fact me who had ratted her out. That was one quite significant mystery solved, though! Although it was also something of a dead end for that lead.

"What did you tell Inspector Harris?" I asked curiously.

"Told her I was retrieving an erotic letter I'd sent Crispin, and that now I'd burned it." Sandra grinned evilly. "She didn't like that one bit."

I couldn't help laughing. Poor old Inspector Harris didn't realize what she'd come up against in Sandra.

"Of course it was all purely transactional," clarified Sandra. "Although we would have a lovely chat of an evening. Sample a bit of his wares. Heart of the community, that man." Her eyes unfocused again as she reminisced—or possibly as the weed took over. "Everyone bought from Crispin Oliver."

"Including Dot? She was another one of his customers, wasn't she?" Pennies were dropping like an arcade game now. It had been Sandra I'd heard Dot talking to under the bridge that night after the gong bath. No wonder I hadn't recognized her voice at the time; I'd only ever heard her in wispy high priestess of the gong mode. Sandra looking for her next hit was a different beast.

"That's right." Sandra tilted her head back and blew a stream of smoke at the stars. "Pretty much everyone over the age of fifty around here was on Crispin's books. Except that stuck-up partner of his, of course. Mairi never did like us."

"And the folk up at the commune? Do they—sorry, did they buy from him too?"

"No," said Sandra shortly. "He wouldn't have anything to do with that lot."

"I heard he used to live up there. That he was one of the ones who started it all up."

"You did, did you? I don't know about that, it was before my time, but I know he steered well clear of Stricker's Wood, and that was his business. I used to sneak a bit up to them from time to time. That Hazel's all right. And their son's a good lad, when he's about. But for the most part they're too busy communing with nature to actually enjoy any of nature's delights."

She blew a perfect smoke ring into the air. I was impressed.

"I was round Crispin's every week," she mused, "sneaking in the back gate like a teenager, trying not to wake Mairi . . . She could hear a mouse's fart, that one."

"Is that what you were doing there the night he . . . died?" I asked tentatively—it was a risky strategy, but I figured Sandra was too deep in her own thoughts to wonder how I might know this.

"Yes, making my weekly pickup."

"And . . . did he seem OK?"

Sandra fixed me with a stare for slightly too long. "No, actually," she said eventually. "He was upset."

"Oh? What about?"

"He didn't say. But he was all a-quiver. Something had bothered him."

"What time was that?"

"Couldn't say for sure. Probably around eight. Normally I'd stay for a chat, but that young man with a stick up his ass—you know, The Suit— came down the stairs, just as Crispin was handing over my supply. Gave us a proper stink eye, he did. And poor old Crispin was in even more of a state after that. And there was no need, there's no harm in a spot of weed here and there."

I made a vague noise of agreement.

"I was *questioned*," said Sandra, puffing agitatedly on her joint. "By the *police*. Twice in one week! All over a dab of weed—what's the world coming to? There was no reason to drag me in, no reason at all."

Arguably, she had been questioned over a murder, which seemed legit given she'd been at the scene of the crime, but I thought I wouldn't mention that, not when my incisive detective questioning was going so well.

"And . . . did you see anyone else there that evening?" I asked, hoping I sounded more casual than I felt.

"No"—she puffed—"I didn't stick around. It was all kicking off upstairs by that point. To be honest, I didn't want to get dragged in. You know what Dot's like."

I did know what Dot was like.

Was I relieved that Sandra hadn't seen anyone else there? It didn't really make much difference—I was pretty sure Rowan had been there and—

"Have they got anywhere with the case?" Sandra asked, interrupting my train of thought. "The police, I mean."

"I don't think so," I said. To be honest, I suspected we'd found out a damn sight more than the police had. I'd not heard anything about them being up at the commune, and Ailsa didn't seem to think Jane was making much headway. They were still pursuing the Lin's-family-argument line of inquiry with great enthusiasm. Although no doubt if Harris found out about Mr. Oliver's little sideline she'd try to pin it as some sort of drug-based gangland murder. Which was ridiculous. Middle-aged hippies didn't go around murdering each other over a bit of pot. Did they?

Sandra sighed. "Poor Crispin. I suppose we'll never know . . ." She stubbed the last of her joint out in a flowerpot and hauled herself to her feet.

"Righto. Lovely talking to you, Alice."

"You too," I replied, as she disappeared into the house in a whirl of silk dressing gown. "Most informative," I added quietly.

I couldn't wait to tell the others that my incredible interrogation skills had indeed solved the mystery of what Sandra had taken from Mr. Oliver's shop. Well, I mean I hadn't done a huge amount of interrogating. In fact, she'd pretty much had to spell it out for me . . . But I didn't need to tell them that.

CHAPTER 43

JOE WAS STILL watching the cricket when I came in from the garden. Seriously, those matches go on forever—literally days.

He sniffed as I sat down beside him. "Is that . . . weed? Alice, you haven't!"

"Relax, it's from the Lady of the Gong next door."

"Sandra's a pothead?"

"Are you surprised?"

He thought for a minute. "No, not at all."

The gentle shimmer of a gong reverberated through the wall. Sandra's stoned gong bath was beginning.

"Fancy a free gong bath?"

Joe looked appalled.

"People pay good money for this," I said. "Come on."

I awkwardly laid myself on my side on the sitting room floor (you're not allowed to lie on your back when pregnant, because that would be too comfortable) and gestured for him to join me. With a sigh so loud I expect it sent some cosmic vibrations back through the wall to Sandra, Joe lay down beside me.

"Now what?"

"I don't know, just . . . zen out or something." Why was I suddenly the gong expert after one pretty mediocre gong bath?

We lay there for a while. It was actually quite soothing. The gong had a shimmering, coppery sound to it that I could almost taste. All the questions tumbling about in my mind slowly shook out and settled. There was so much I needed to ask Joe, so much that was unsaid between us at the moment. But when I opened my mouth, what came out wasn't the question I had wanted to ask. Or, I don't know, perhaps it was.

"Do you still love me?"

"Absolutely."

The answer came without pause or hesitation. Joe rolled on his side to face me, but I pushed him back.

"You have to lie on your back."

"Gong rules?"

"Gong rules." Also it was easier to talk to his profile, somehow.

"Do you still love me?" he asked back.

"I do." And I meant it. I still loved him. But I worried that the "him" that I loved was slipping away.

There was a moment's silence, filled only with the dissolving ripples of the gong. I felt Joe's hand grope for mine and hold it.

"Why do you ask?"

I didn't know how to answer him. "I just . . . What's going on?" I wasn't sure if I was talking about the murder, or about me and him.

"I don't know," he said simply. And I was pretty sure his answer would have been the same to either question.

You can have a whole separate conversation through a handhold. Right now, Joe's hand felt relaxed, despite my bombshell question, and his thumb was gently stroking the back of my hand.

"It's all been a bit full on, hasn't it," I ventured.

He gave a short laugh. "You can say that again. The baby, the move . . ."

"The murder."

"That too."

His hand twitched, ever so slightly.

"Joe, is there anything you want to talk to me about?"

His hand went very still in mine.

"Yes," he said eventually. "Yes, there is. But not yet, Al. I'm sorry, but I just need time."

It wasn't exactly what I wanted to hear. But it was better than an outright denial, which I would have known for a lie. And as luck, or perhaps I should say ill luck, would have it, I wouldn't have to wait long for that conversation. Events were about to take a rather unfortunate and extremely dramatic turn.

CHAPTER 44

WE FELL ASLEEP on the sitting room floor, still holding hands. Despite a crick in my neck, and my back, and my hips—pretty much every joint in my body, in fact—I woke feeling slightly lighter. Joe and I would work things out. The situation between us, first of all, and then together we'd figure out this parenting lark. People have been doing it for millennia. How hard could it be?

While I waited for Joe to wake up I googled "educational baby toys" and stared, disheartened, at the myriad of articles that filled my screen. "The 100 top educational baby toys"; "Ten toys your baby genius NEEDS"; "The essential 50 toys to ensure your child's natural and healthy development." Essential fifty? I'd had a pet rock for a week when I was a kid—we'd really been scraping the barrel. No wonder the world is so fucked, it's being run by people who had to navigate childhood without the guidance of the Fledglings Digitech Playsmart Interactive Magnetic Easel. Of course they think they can fix the world's problems by hitting it with a big stick.

For a while I contemplated purchasing a Bopping Beaver (apparently essential for my child's sensory development) before deciding I couldn't countenance giving my child something that sounded quite so much like a budget sex toy.

I let my mind spin idly over the case. We were missing something. There was something wrong at the commune, that was for sure. Ten years ago Jasmine had died, and Mr. Oliver had left the commune—*because* of her death? What had actually happened? And could it be linked to his death, all these years later?

I scrolled down the Beaver's reviews. Poor battery life—well, that would never do.

And how did the mysterious Flora fit into all of this? If she did at all.

Would the baby prefer Bim Bim the Vibrating Squirrel?

By this time Joe was awake.

"I nearly bought a Bopping Beaver for the baby," I announced.

"I think you can get arrested for that." He yawned as he began pottering round the kitchen doing his breakfast routine. I was pleased to see he had jumped to the same conclusion as me. Either the manufacturers were hopelessly naive, or perverts.

We spent an aimless but enjoyable ten minutes coming up with names for new baby toys. Perhaps we should go into business together.

"What are you doing this morning?" Joe asked as he slid a fried egg expertly onto a piece of bread. I tried not to gag. My nausea, never far from the surface, was rebelling against the greasy sunsplat of fried egg. I shoved some muesli in my mouth to quash it.

"It's nearly afternoon," I said through a mouthful of wholesome and tasteless grains. The gong bath had sent Joe and me so deep under, we'd slept through until nearly midday.

"What are you doing this afternoon then?" he asked.

I had a vague idea that I had plans, but my head was feeling pleasantly empty. At that moment the reminder that I still needed to phone Harris and tell her about Rowan's press pass jabbed me uncomfortably in the brain. I would definitely do that. Later.

"Not sure. Maybe I'll take Helen out," I mused. This was what maternity leave should be about. Gentle pottering in the woods with my faithful hound—not attempting to break into suspicious hippy communes or crystal shop–cum–murder scenes.

"You're raising Helen's expectations too much," said Joe unsympathetically through a mouthful of egg. "When the baby's here you're gonna regret it when she wants to be walked five miles every day."

Out of respect for our "moment" on the sitting room floor in the early hours, I tried not to get annoyed. Instead, I got out the dustpan and brush. Helen had tipped up her food bowl, and kibble was scattered across the kitchen. I laboriously got to my knees and swept it up. It is a measure of how low the bar is set for cleanliness in our household that I felt a tiny rush of pride in doing this, and wondered briefly if there was a small trophy for responsible adulting that I should be given. Or at least a badge.

"I would have done that," said Joe distractedly, as I huffed back to my feet.

"Yeah right," I muttered darkly. Joe's approach to housekeeping is even more lax than mine, a sort of "leave it till it grows legs and crawls away" policy. Our child will either have the immune system of a superhero, or cholera.

MY MISPLACED plans caught up with me later that afternoon as I was halfway through an epic Netflix binge, Helen watching me balefully, very much un-walked. When I got a call from an unfamiliar number at 6 P.M. I considered screening it, before deciding that was irresponsible.

"Hey, Alice, just checking if you guys were still coming!"

The voice was younger and chirpier than anyone I knew.

"Sorry, who is this?"

"It's Candy! I was just checking we were still on for that tour of the maternity hospital?"

Shit.

"I am so sorry, Candy! We're running a bit behind—I should have called. We'll be there in ten."

This was optimistic of me, as I still hadn't googled where the maternity hospital was, but Penton was tiny—how far could it possibly be?

THE LOCAL hospital was a good half-hour drive away. We arrived flustered and I was having cramps that might possibly have been from speed-eating a Subway on the drive over, or could perhaps have been the onset of labor. At least if it was the latter then I was headed to the best possible place.

On the drive over we'd realized that we probably needed to put on some semblance of a display of semi-competent prospective parenthood, and had tried to compile a list of questions we should ask that would make us sound like responsible parents-to-be. We'd come up with:

- what level of painkiller can you give me? Is morphine on the table?
- do you provide food, and if not where is the nearest food?
- does takeaway deliver to the hospital?

We were aware that there were other things we were supposed to be asking. But to be quite honest food and painkillers were foremost in our concerns.

The local maternity hospital was . . . more rural than I'd expected. More rural than I'd have liked, to tell the truth. It was only a single story, and there were houses around Penton that were bigger than it. At least it didn't have a thatched roof.

Candy met us at the door.

"Cervix ripened yet?"

I gave a weak smile. Would I actually know when it ripened, I wondered.

We began the tour with the birthing suites. I perked up considerably. They were fancy! For a start, each one was probably bigger than our old flat in London. Each one had a bed, an assortment of birthing paraphernalia and an enormous Jacuzzi-esque bath in the corner. This was the real showstopper for me. I was, of course, familiar with the concept of a water birth. But I'd envisaged a sort of inflatable paddling pool. These were like huge free-standing hot tubs, with steps up and underwater lighting. Sweet, birth was going to be like a day at the spa!

"I'm having one of these!" I breathed.

"Nice! Would I be allowed in?" asked Joe.

"Absolutely," said Candy. "Although we do have to ask you to keep your clothes on—at least underwear, please."

Joe looked rather taken aback. "I wasn't planning on getting naked at the birth."

"You'd be surprised how many times I've walked in here to find a naked man in the tub," said Candy, politely disagreeing.

"What about me?" I asked.

"You can be as naked as you like."

Win.

"I thought it would be more like a sort of blow-up pool thing," said Joe—echoing my thoughts exactly.

"The ones you have at home are," said Candy. "They're basically giant paddling pools. This one is fully plumbed in, so you don't have to mess about with a sieve or a colander or anything."

"Sorry, what?" Joe looked as confused as I felt. What did kitchen utensils have to do with birth?

"You know, to *sieve*."

"Still not with you."

Candy sighed. "Do I have to spell it out?"

"Yep."

"If you do a shit in the pool during labor you want to have something on hand to fish it out."

I went right off water births.

THE REST of the tour continued with its theme of "making me think about things I had successfully ignored for nine months." I learned that the cottage hospital would be able to provide me with limited pain relief, but did genuinely seem an extremely pleasant place to give birth. There was mood lighting. There was a mural of a forest on the wall. There were fresh cut flowers. And, of course, an abundance of aromatherapy and essential oils. The midwives were lovely, a combination of competent, supportive and friendly. But all of this couldn't detract from the fact that, ultimately, this was something *I* was going to have to do. And I really, really didn't feel ready for it.

Joe seemed to pick up on what I was feeling. He slipped an arm around my waist (or at least, where my waist used to be) and gently but firmly cut Candy off in mid-flow about the benefits of low lighting in the birthing environment and how this would help stimulate my oxytocin.

"This is all great, it really is, and thank you so much for showing us round, but I think we need to go and mull things over for a bit."

I nodded mutely and allowed myself to be steered toward the door.

As I was leaving, however, we passed the dispensary and I caught a glimpse of a familiar head of curls. I opened my mouth to say hi, before noticing the flecks of gray. It wasn't Rowan, it was . . . his dad? Who, apparently, hadn't left the commune in ten years. He was taking a pre-scription bag over the counter.

I paused and bent down to fake-fiddle with my shoelace—a classic delay tactic—only to realize partway down that I was wearing slip-ons. Damn.

"Are you OK?" asked Joe, sounding worried as I paused, hunched over in the middle of the corridor. "Oh God, are you going into labor?"

"No, no, fine, just a . . . minor cramp?"

I straightened up again just in time to see Camran pull a box out of the prescription bag. He gave it a cursory check, pocketed it and shoved the paper bag straight into a bin near the exit. Then he left, swiftly and without a backward glance.

My little piece of amateur dramatics had slightly unforeseen conse-quences in that Joe insisted on marching me straight back into the unit to be fully checked over. Candy declared my cervix as unripe as ever, and confirmed that the baby was doing just fine in there, but hooked me up to the monitor for half an hour to check the baby's heart rate just in case.

An hour later, we were finally leaving. Just as we got to the car park, I paused.

"I need to pee. I'll meet you at the car."

"Again?"

"Yuh—*pregnant*?"

I slipped back into the unit and headed straight for the bin. The phar-macy bag Camran had shoved in there was still sitting at the very top. I grabbed it and shoved it in my coat pocket. Then I hurried back to Joe.

"You're sure you're OK to go home?" Joe asked for the thousandth time.

"Yes, I'm fine. It was a tiny cramp. Candy said there was nothing to worry about."

"OK. If you're sure."

"I'm sure."

It pained me to be keeping secrets from Joe, but he was self-confessedly keeping secrets from me. And he was so anti my involvement in the in-vestigation that I couldn't face telling him what, or rather whom, I had seen.

I felt particularly bad, however, as Joe was so damn nice to me all the way home.

"Shall we talk about the birth plan?"

"I'd rather eat a placenta."

That got a chuckle. "In all seriousness, though," said Joe. "I know it was a bit overwhelming in there. The birth is important, I get that. And I realize it's far more important for you than it is for me, and I get that too. But the most important thing is that the baby arrives safely, and that you're safe. And I don't want you beating yourself up because it doesn't go exactly how you think it *should* go. It's only the first microscopic section of our baby's life. If it's wind chimes and natural pain relief and lotus flowers then great; if it's an epidural and morphine and whatever else you want to take, also great. The baby won't hold you to account! And neither will I."

"No, but I might," I mumbled. "Or the Penton Sisterhood."

"Yeah, well, the Penton Sisterhood can go take a spiral leap into the great cosmic abyss."

He'd really picked up the local lingo; I was impressed. He reached out and put his hand over mine.

"Want to go via McDonald's and get a McFlurry?"

"But you'll miss the start of the snooker."

"Some things are more important than snooker."

Now that was true love.

I'D ACTUALLY forgotten about the pharmacy bag I'd taken from the bin. It was only much later that night, when I was digging in my coat pocket in the hope of finding an abandoned snack, that my hand closed around the scrunched-up ball of paper.

I smoothed it out and read the label.

Name: Camran Pan.

Address: Stricker's Wood Commune, Nr Penton.

Camran Pan.

Pan.

CHAPTER 45

I'D CONVENED AN emergency brunch meeting of the prenatal mums, although for some reason it felt weird to think of them like that—what with everything that had happened over the last two weeks, the prenatal classes felt like the least defining aspect of our friendship.

Unfortunately, Penton was still at the "avocado on toast is terribly foreign" stage of civilization development, but I was working my way through a passable cheese and ham croissant—which of course started life as "foreign" but had been solidly anglicized. The waitress had asked if I wanted pickle with it.

"So what's so important you had to drag us all out here?" asked Ailsa, who was eating a vegan omelette (wtf is even in that?) and glaring at me like I had personally slaughtered the pig to make my ham croissant.

I glowed.

"Well . . ."

I laid my piece of evidence reverentially in the middle of the table, smoothing its crumples out. I'd contemplated ironing it, but had worried that the ink might run. I had also considered that ironing evidence was possibly illegal and definitely insane.

"A paper bag," said Ailsa flatly.

"Ugh, did you get this out of a bin?" asked Hen. Admittedly there was a slightly suspect stain on one corner.

"Yes and yes," I said. "But look at the name!"

"Camran?" said Poppy. "You stole Camran's medicine? Isn't that illegal or something?"

"Jane will have you for this," said Ailsa with, I felt, an unnecessary amount of satisfaction. "Speak of the actual devil . . ." Her phone vibrated itself off the table and she disappeared after it.

"Camran Pan. *Pan*," I said excitedly. "Do you remember I told you about the tree in the woods? Jasmine's tree? And the mysterious creepy figure scoring out her name? Well, I'm *sure* the surname was Pan!" I gabbled. "I'm sure of it!"

Hen remained skeptical. "Really? Before, you said it was completely illegible."

"I'm sure," I said definitely—although I privately determined to get back up to the woods as soon as possible to check.

"So does that mean . . . ?" said Poppy slowly, and I could see she was drawing the same conclusion that I had.

"I think Jasmine was Camran's daughter. And what's more, I bet I know who her mother was."

They stared at me.

"Flora."

I sat back in triumph. I probably looked a bit smug. I felt it.

"Explain," said Hen.

"It all adds up," I elaborated. "The mysterious Flora gets knocked up and disappears thirty years ago, according to Mrs. Pilkington. Twenty years later a young woman, about the right age to be her daughter, turns up at the commune—and what was it Rowan said? Jasmine 'filled a gap' for his dad when he left home. Well, of course she did—she was his kid too. No wonder he was so cut up when she died—she was his daughter."

"You know what, it kind of works," said Hen, with a grudging respect.

"It more than works! It makes perfect sense," said Poppy excitedly.

Ailsa returned to the table and sat down. "What did I miss?"

"Jasmine was the daughter of Camran and Flora," I summed up triumphantly.

Ailsa spat out her drink. Like, actually spat a mouthful of it onto the table. It's an expression you often hear, but a thing you seldom see in real life. It's more gross than it sounds.

"Ugh!" Hen dabbed at a bead of cordial/spit that had landed on her baby's forehead.

"What was that for?" I asked.

"No way," Ailsa said.

"No way what?" I asked.

"No way can that be true."

"Why?"

"I'm just saying, that cannot be true."

"What makes you so sure?" Because, I mean, she seemed pretty damn certain.

"Please tell us, the suspense is killing me," begged Poppy.

"But no more spitting, please, it's undignified," added Hen.

"Jasmine is not Camran's daughter."

"You know that?"

"OK, so I don't *know* for sure. But . . . Look, I really didn't want to go into this . . . but you know you've been obsessed with Rowan being the father of my child?" Ailsa directed this at me—unfairly in my opinion.

"I asked you once," I objected.

"Whatever. Well. Fine. Rowan and I did date, back in high school. We were *supposed* to be staying together when we went to uni, only he went and cheated on me."

"Dickhead," I said sympathetically.

Then the penny dropped.

"Oh my God! With Jasmine?"

Ailsa nodded grimly. "With Jasmine."

"But she's his sister!"

"Do we have any proof of that, or is it just wild speculation?" broke in Hen.

"It is a theory based on the available evidence," I said. I heard Hen mutter "guesswork" under her breath. She'd been in a foul mood all morning—my hunch was that it had to do with Antoni, but I wasn't about to get drawn into anymore "guesswork."

"For the record, I think it's bonkers," said Ailsa.

"Just supposing Jasmine was Rowan's sister—well, half-sister," put in Poppy. "Would either of them have known that? I mean, it's grim, but it happens, doesn't it? Half-siblings who don't even know the other one exists, they meet when they're older and have a weird sort of connection . . . and end up shagging?"

"Can we not discuss this in front of the baby?" broke in Hen.

"Hen, she's got the comprehension levels of a mollusc," said Ailsa, a little brutally I thought. "We're not going to scar her for life."

"They're very absorbent at this age."

"When it comes to fluids, maybe. When it comes to murder inquiries and incest, probably less so."

Hen frowned. But her only other option was to leave, and she clearly wasn't going to miss out on such a scandalous conversation.

"Anyway, this is nuts," continued Ailsa.

"So what happened with you and Rowan?" prompted Poppy.

"If you must know, when I found out I went to France, he followed me, et cetera, et cetera. It's your classic story: boy fucks up, girl runs away, boy chases girl, except that there was no happy ever after and we didn't get back together. I went back to uni, he went off to chase yaks or something, and ages later Nana Maud told me Jasmine had died. End of story."

"Wow," I said when Ailsa paused for breath. She glared at me. Then she went back to picking at her egg-free omelette.

It's hard to know where to go with a conversation that's already covered cheating boyfriends and potential incest. But I was a bit bothered. I kept glancing at Ailsa. Eventually, she looked up and raised an eyebrow at me. "Something you want to say?"

"OK, I'm just saying, you did kind of lie to me when you said you didn't know Jasmine."

"No, I didn't."

"You kinda did."

"No. You asked if I knew her, and I didn't. I never met her. You didn't ask me if *Rowan* knew her. That would have been a different matter."

"That's quite the loophole."

She shrugged. "What, and now you think I might have bumped Jasmine off because she slept with my boyfriend?"

I went red. "I didn't say that." I paused, then added, "It's a classic motive, though."

Ailsa sighed. "Alice, people get cheated on all the time. They hardly ever end up murdering someone over it. Not in real life."

It was a fair point. But if this weren't real life, Ailsa would definitely have to go on the suspect list. As it was, I was probably gonna give her a free pass, because I liked her. This was definitely poor detective practice. Plus, I wasn't sure I was the best judge of character—I also liked Rowan and he was at best a cheat and a liar, and at worst an incestuous murderer. Then of course there was my own boyfriend who, by his own admission, wasn't telling me everything.

AS I was leaving, Ailsa grabbed my elbow and drew me aside.

"Got a minute?"

"Is it about the rhubarb? Because no, I still haven't cooked it. I found a recipe on BBC Good Food, but it needed this thing called—"

"It's not about the bloody rhubarb."

"Oh?"

Ailsa went quiet as Poppy passed us on her way to her car. Then she turned back to me.

"Jane thinks she did it, you know."

"What? Who?"

"Lin. Jane thinks she did it."

"Yeah well, Jane's a . . ." I trailed off. Could I call Inspector Harris a bitch to her sister's face? I mean, to be fair, Ailsa said it all the time.

"True," said Ailsa. "But she's also a detective and she's not always wrong."

"You seriously think Lin might have done it? Harris hasn't got anything on her. Some stupid old family row? That's hardly evidence."

Ailsa looked sideways at me. "Did Poppy tell you about the phone call?"

I felt unease coil in my stomach, slippery and unpleasant, like an eel.

"Phone call?"

"Lin called Mr. Oliver the day before he died."

"But they didn't speak," I said dumbly. "They were, what's the word—estranged?"

"Maybe," said Ailsa tersely. "But Lin tried to call him. She left a voicemail on the Nature's Way machine, and it's not so pretty."

"And you know this how?" I knew that what I should really be asking was what was in the voicemail, but I was stalling.

"I looked through Jane's desk," said Ailsa, waving a hand dismissively. "I found the transcript."

"And what did it say?" I asked cautiously.

"I took a photo . . ." She held out her phone.

> Voice: Mr. Oliver. It's Lin . . . your [throat cleared] niece. Look I—OK so not that it's any of your business but my wife and I are having a baby. That's not why I'm calling. But our prenatal class tonight is at your shop and—Look just don't talk to us. Don't talk to me. And definitely do NOT talk to Poppy. If you go anywhere near her . . . And I know you called Mum the other day. LEAVE HER ALONE. If you call her again I'll . . . Seriously. I'm warning you. Don't you think you've done enough damage there? She told me what you did. And it'll catch up with you one day.

OK, so it didn't look great. And I could see why Harris might perceive this as a threat made to the victim the day before his death. I got that. But at the same time . . .

"She's just being protective of her pregnant wife, and her mum," I said defensively. "Mr. Oliver could be pushy sometimes, we know that. Lin didn't want him hassling people she cares about."

"It's a bit full on, though," said Ailsa grimly. "And then twenty-four hours later, he's dead?"

"So you think she did it?" Poppy's voice, uncharacteristically harsh, made us both jump. We spun around. She was standing there, her face hard.

To be fair to her, Ailsa barely flinched.

"I'm just saying, I know you think she's—"

"I don't *think* she's innocent," Poppy cut across her ruthlessly. "I *know* she's innocent."

Ailsa met her gaze skeptically.

"How?" she asked, bluntly.

"Because there are some things you just know. And I know Lin. There is no shadow of a doubt, there is no *question* . . . I'm willing to believe people are capable of some pretty terrible things. I've had some pretty terrible things said to me. Even done to me. People are awful. But not Lin. There is no conceivable universe where Lin did something like this. I. Just. Know."

With that she turned and left.

To my surprise, I found myself welling up. I didn't know whether the tears were for Lin and Poppy, whose world was being beaten and battered from every angle, but who were so *sure* of each other. Or whether the tears were for myself. Because I saw in them something I wanted. And I knew I didn't have it.

I thought about going after Poppy. But I didn't. Because right now, I wasn't sure what I would say. Why hadn't she told me about Lin's phone call? And, crucially, what did Lin mean by "I know what you did"? Had Mr. Oliver done something terrible to Lin's mum? And if so, was it bad enough to merit . . . revenge? The more I thought about it, the worse it seemed for Lin. And if we carried on investigating, trying to clear her name, there was always the possibility that we would find out something we might not like.

CHAPTER 46

I HATE ARGUING with people. I don't do it often—practically never in fact. Bickering with Joe doesn't count. And strictly speaking, Poppy and I weren't technically arguing. But it felt wrong nonetheless. When my phone pinged that afternoon and her name popped up on the screen, I felt a flash of relief.

I'm sorry

I want to explain

Dog walk?

Yeah OK

Stricker's?

Where else?

Well, there were probably plenty of other places, I thought—this was the countryside after all. But something about Stricker's Wood kept luring me back, like a bad relationship. I couldn't quite put my finger on it, but I knew, somewhere in my bones, that the place held answers.

And today I was determined to get some.

POPPY WAS already there, waiting for me. We set off through the trees, a tension between us that was new and extremely unwelcome. The dogs, fortunately, were unaffected. Helen and Ronnie appeared to have struck up some kind of doggy romance. I was hoping it meant that even after this whole murder thing was over, Poppy at least would still have to be my friend so that our dogs could have a weekly hump in the woods.

As we headed deeper into the woods, Ronnie was incessantly trying to mount Helen. She was blithely oblivious, and if anything appeared unsure as to the rules of this new game. In between sporadic humping, Ronnie rolled in shit and disappeared behind trees. He is the only dog I've met who is worse behaved than Helen. Between the two of them it's probably quite good training for parenting. Needless to say, Sultan spent the whole time maintaining the maximum possible distance from both Helen and Ronnie, and also Poppy and myself, which I found rather insulting.

"Dogs are awful, aren't they," I observed, finally breaking the silence. "Do you think children will be any better?"

"Fifty-fifty."

"I don't like those odds."

She gave a small laugh. Then took a deep breath.

"So . . . I should have told you about the voicemail."

"Yeah. Why didn't you?"

There was a moment's pause.

"I'm not sure. I think I was worried you might think there was more to it than there is."

"So enlighten me. Exactly how much is there to it?"

"I know it sounds bad. But it was just words, Alice. Nothing more. Lin freaked out a bit when she realized where the prenatal class was being held, and she just wanted to make sure there wasn't a scene or anything if we bumped into her uncle."

I couldn't help a wry smile at that. Our prenatal class had been the epitome of "a scene"—what with the birth and the death and the ensemble cast of pregnant women, paramedics and homicide detective.

"What did she mean when she said something about knowing what he did? What did he do?"

Poppy scuffed at the leaves on the floor with her foot. "First of all I want you to understand that Lin didn't know about any of this until, like, two weeks ago, when she told her mum where the class would be."

I kept quiet—surely, if anything, the timing of Lin finding this out was a mark against her, given what had happened so soon after.

"So you know I said Mr. Oliver asked Lin's mum, Sal, for money to start up his shop? Well, when Sal wouldn't lend it to him, he went to their mother, Lin's nan, who was sick at the time. Dying, in fact. And told her all sorts of lies about Sal, and she was cut out of the will. Mr. Oliver inherited all the money, and used it to open Nature's Way."

I drew in a breath sharply. That was not good.

"Does Harris know about this?"

"Yeah."

"Are we talking a lot of money?"

"A fair bit. Six figures. But for Sal, it was more about the betrayal than the money."

"Of course . . ." I trailed off. We watched Helen lick a nettle in silence. Then, "I wish you'd told me."

"Yeah, me too."

"How can we investigate this together with you if you're holding stuff back from me?"

"I know, and I'm really sorry. I swear I've told you everything now."

I wanted to ask if she thought Lin had told *her* everything. But I reckoned even the hint of accusation in that question would shatter our tentatively patched-up friendship. It was good to have cleared the air. But I feared a little bit of that trust had been broken.

"You know this doesn't exactly look great for Lin, right?" was the best I could manage.

"Of course I do. But I meant what I said. I *know* it wasn't Lin. You have to believe me."

I didn't have to believe anyone. And increasingly, these days, I didn't. Which made me slightly sad.

As we walked, our footsteps had unthinkingly led us toward the commune. We stopped outside the gate.

"We have to get in there," said Poppy, with a quiet but fierce determination.

I sighed. What were the chances of finding something there that would exonerate Lin? Although actually, when I put it like that, it was probably the best lead we had. And talking of leads . . .

"OK, fine. *One* break-in. But I need to put Helen on her lead—last time she went wandering round the commune she almost died."

I spun on the spot. Then did another rotation. There was Sultan, looking majestic and slightly bored. No Helen, no Ronnie.

"Have they already gone in?" asked Poppy, squinting through the bars of the gate.

"I doubt it." I pointed to the brand-new chicken wire that had been nailed across the bottom of the gate, presumably in response to the dogs' previous break-in. Wow, these guys *really* didn't want visitors.

"Last I remember seeing them they were heading that way." I pointed farther into the woods, toward the old quarry. As I cast my eyes across the worryingly barren landscape I caught the faintest whiff of smoke.

"Can you smell burning?"

Poppy sniffed the air, much like Sultan was currently doing. "Yeah . . . It smells like bonfires."

"How much do you bet that's where Helen and Ronnie are?"

"I mean, they can't have started a fire. What are they going to do, rub sticks between their paws to create a spark?"

It seemed unlikely. But at the same time, entirely possible. I tried to remember if Helen had been in the room when I was watching Bear Grylls the other day.

We broke into a gentle trot.

The smell of burning intensified and a bluish haze of smoke began to seep between the trees like a nineties disco. Just as the smoke became thick enough to sting our eyes we heard the crackle of flames and emerged into a clearing. Despite the quantity of smoke, it was only a small fire, and it was, thankfully, entirely under the control of an adult human.

"Camran?"

He turned to look at us, and in the instant that he turned there was pure fury on his face. But it faded quickly to a sullen resentment.

"Oh, it's you two."

"Good to see you too," I muttered.

He ran a hand down his face in the universal gesture for "I'm too tired to deal with you right now."

"Sorry, girls. It's just . . . you've caught me at a bad moment."

"We can see that," Poppy said.

"What's with the forest fire?" I asked.

Camran bridled. "If you think I would *ever* put the forest at risk, you are sorely mistaken. I have an understanding with fire, it is fully under my control. The trees are safe with me."

Spoken like a true arsonist, I thought. But I held up my hands in surrender. "It was just an expression. Sorry."

My eyes slid to the fire crackling in the middle of the clearing. To be fair, it did look to be a pretty professional job. It was ringed around with stones, which were starting to blacken, and all the dry leaves and general flammable forest debris had been cleared for a good meter radius. The actual kindling was interesting, however. It looked like Camran had just had a bad teenage breakup. He appeared to be burning several sheets of cramped handwriting—a diary?—a handful of photos and what looked like a sweater. I had once done something similar when I found out my boyfriend had made out with Rachel Mitchell at the school disco while I was off with mumps.

I felt this comparison would go down poorly, so exercised some unfamiliar restraint and didn't comment. Besides, anyone making a publicly dramatic gesture such as this wouldn't need any encouragement to tell us why.

Sure enough . . .

"That sniveling, capitalist *leech*!" burst out Camran, without prompting. "That conniving, scheming son-of-a-taxman. Just because he's sold out like the spineless cretin he is, he expects the rest of us to do the same!"

"Sorry—who are we talking about?" asked Poppy.

"Sir Ronald Rich-as-sodding-creosote Pilkington," fumed Camran. I was pretty sure creosote was what you painted fences with, but, again, showed admirable restraint in not mentioning this. Besides, maybe the guy who invented creosote was super rich. I mean, there are a lot of fences in the world.

I tuned back in mid-rant.

". . . and then he has the cheek to call it *his* commune! Because it's on 'his land.' As if the land can be owned! I told him, 'The paperwork may be in your name, brother, but the land does not recognize deeds of sale— you capitalist shit.'"

Poppy was nodding along with a sympathetic expression.

"Not to mention that we had a gentleman's agreement," went on Camran. I'd always thought this was a euphemism, but apparently I was wrong. Unless I really *was* witnessing a traumatic breakup right now.

"So what was it he wanted?" Poppy made a valiant attempt to steer the conversation.

"He was asking"—Camran paused and drew in a deep breath—"for *rent*."

I tried to connect the dots.

"So you burned his sweater?"

Camran looked down at the smoldering knitwear, jumped and swore. Then he dragged it out of the fire and began beating the flames out. "No," he said ruefully. "No, that was mine."

Were we to believe that he had genuinely accidentally burned his own sweater in the middle of the woods?

"And the paperwork?" I asked curiously. A half-charred photo had been dislodged by Camran's sweater rescue mission and had landed by my foot. I flipped it over with my toe and the singed face of a young woman stared up at me.

"Some nonsense my son came home with the other day," said Camran brusquely.

I gazed into the flames and saw the familiar masthead of the *Penton Bugle*. The missing edition! I leaped forward and pulled it out of the flames, mildly scorching myself in the process.

"Hey, leave that! Put it back!" Camran swiped for the newspaper but I jumped back, clutching it to my chest.

"Why are you burning these?" I asked accusingly. "Where did you get them from?"

"It's Rowan's rubbish," snapped Camran. "I don't know what he was thinking, coming home with all this drivel, upsetting everyone. Upsetting the balance. So I told him enough was enough."

Right. Destroying evidence, in other words. I looked down at the fire and wondered if I ought to try and stamp it out, but to be honest everything else looked pretty far gone. And I didn't fancy accidentally setting fire to the woods in order to save some of Rowan's scribbled notes.

I looked down at the newspaper in my hand. It was singed around the edges, but some of it was still legible. The headline read DEATH COMES TO PENTON. The rest of the page had been given over to a large photograph showing a young woman. She looked . . . nice. She looked normal. Beneath the photo was a brief caption: "Jasmine Pan, aged 21, found dead at hippy commune."

Jasmine Pan. I *had* been right. Which meant . . .

I was staring down at the article in my hand, trying to skim-read through my smoke-reddened eyes, which felt like they'd been sandblasted. Words leaped out at me in a jumble. I took a deep breath to clear my head, but got a lungful of smoke and papery ash. I coughed violently. Camran thumped me on the back, which nearly jolted my streaming eyeballs out of my head.

"All right there, girl?" He didn't wait for an answer. "You'll want to be on your way, I expect. You don't want the smoke getting to the baby."

The way he said it was hard to read—possibly concerned, possibly threatening.

But his attention was really on the newspaper, held limp in my hand. With a deft movement he snatched it and tossed it back into the fire, stamping it in with one heavily booted foot for good measure. Poppy gave a small cry and darted forward, but the scorched paper had scattered to ash under his boot. I knew what she was thinking—had a potentially crucial piece of evidence just gone up in smoke?

I looked back into the flames and watched the remains of the newspaper blacken and curl. A few phrases from the article danced across my mind.

"You can't just burn evidence like that!" Poppy was crying.

"Evidence?" snorted Camran. "Evidence of what? It's a load of crap my son's been dredging up."

My eyes were on the ground, where the semi-burned photo of Jasmine was staring up at me, half her face obliterated. I remembered the angry slashes scoring through her name on the memorial tree. Someone wanted her very memory erased. But Rowan, was he trying to dig her up from the past?

"Rowan is looking into what happened to Jasmine?" I asked.

Camran looked up sharply at the name. "What do you know about Jasmine?"

That she was your daughter. Dare I say it? I didn't like the intensity of his gaze. For the first time it occurred to me to feel scared. I caught Poppy's eye and could tell she was thinking the same. We edged closer together. The movement wasn't lost on Camran.

"Not a lot," I said, annoyed to hear the slight tremor in my voice.

"Right. Well. There's nothing *to* know," he said gruffly. "A terrible tragedy. That's all it was."

"I'm sorry," I said rather timidly. "I'm sorry she died." It felt like the kind of thing Poppy might say. But also, I realized, with Jasmine's eyes fixed unblinkingly on mine, it was true.

Camran threw another stick onto the fire, which was dying down now. "Tragedies happen."

"And what *did* hap—" began Poppy, but he cut her off.

"It was nowt to do with me," he said abruptly. "And what's more, I'd have put a stop to it if I'd known. Now if you don't mind . . ."

"You've got things to burn," I completed for him.

He gave a short bark of laughter. "You're an odd pair, you two. I like you." Well, thanks. "But best not to poke your nose too much into things that don't concern you. People might get the wrong idea."

Was this another threat? Like father, like son?

"Your dogs went that way, by the way, after Ronald." Camran gestured into the woods and I remembered with a jolt that we'd been looking for Helen and Ronnie. How long had they been missing now?

"And if they're feasting on his bloated capitalist corpse, they're welcome to it," Camran growled.

It wasn't that funny, even at the time. It was even less so five minutes later.

CHAPTER 47

WE HEARD HELEN and Ronnie before we saw them. They were standing too close to the edge of a sheer drop, where the earth had been scooped away, as if with a giant spoon. They were barking frenetically at something lying at the bottom.

That something turned out to be the body of Ronald Pilkington.

"Shit," I said. Because, really, what else can you say?

"No kidding . . ." Poppy and I stood next to our dogs and stared down at the rather horribly mangled figure at the foot of the drop.

"Should we . . . go and see if he's OK?" It was optimistic to put it mildly, but I felt like we should at least check. Poppy nodded grimly, and we began picking our way along the edge of the drop, to where the ground sloped down to the bottom of the quarry face.

He was dead all right.

I won't go into details because, well, gross. The guy had fallen, like, fifty feet and, by the look of things, hit a few bumps on the way down.

"We should phone an ambulance," I suggested. They weren't going to be able to do much for him, but they'd be more use than us.

"And the police," said Poppy. She got her phone out. "Shit, no signal."

In crime dramas, the moment where they find the body never involves hiking up and down through woodland for twenty minutes holding your phone above your head to get reception. Nor does it involve having to physically restrain your dog from peeing on the corpse. There could have been at least three commercial breaks before Poppy remembered that you can make emergency calls on any network provider. We called the police.

The wait for the ambulance and the police was pretty bleak. We tried turning our backs on the corpse, but somehow that was even worse.

Death is an uncomfortable thing to come face to face with. Twice, now, that had been my misfortune. It felt doubly strange to look down on a life that had just ended while inside me the baby kicked merrily, surfing on a wave of my adrenaline.

THE POLICE were extremely efficient—once they eventually arrived. Within minutes a small white tent had been erected over the mortal remains of Ronald Pilkington. A blue-and-white police cordon had been wound in and out of the trees, sectioning off the scene of the crime on one side from the real world on the other. We stood on the real-world side. It felt better there.

"Well, isn't that interesting."

I turned and saw Inspector Harris striding through the trees, her eyes fixed on me and Poppy.

"Don't let them go anywhere," she barked to a uniformed officer. "And control those dogs."

She kept us hanging around for a good ten minutes as she inspected the corpse, spoke in low tones to a number of professional-looking people and signed various bits of paper. The uniformed officer stood slightly too close to us, unspeaking and watchful. Poppy and I didn't dare say a word to each other about what had just happened.

For the first time, the presence of the "establishment" felt less reassuring and more concerning. Was Inspector Harris going to arrest us? This was the second time that we'd turned up next to a dead body. If I were watching this on TV I'd be yelling at the screen, "Arrest the pregnant women! They know something!" But the truth was, we didn't know anything. We'd been messing around playing detectives, but right now I'd be the first to admit we were in over our heads.

Finally, Harris stopped in front of us. She gave us an appraising look that I didn't like at all. As though she was summing us up. Passing judgment.

"You. And you." She pointed at me and Poppy. "Follow me."

CHAPTER 48

INSPECTOR HARRIS HADN'T arrested us. Yet.

"Let me guess," she said, before we had a chance to say anything. "You just happened to be out walking in the woods, and you just happened across the body of Ronald Pilkington."

I didn't know quite how to respond—after all, that was more or less exactly what had happened.

"I know what you two have been up to," continued Harris. "Poking around, asking questions, playing detectives."

Ouch. I mean, sure, I'd been thinking the same thing myself just a moment ago. But when Harris said it, it sounded like a crime.

Poppy opened her mouth to speak, but Harris raised her voice and continued to speak over her.

"I know you think you're going to catch the murderer, or clear your wife's name, or some such nonsense, but you won't. That's not how it works. So let me tell you what happens now. You will stop messing around and getting in my way. You will leave the police work to me. You will leave it to me to ascertain how guilty, or otherwise, your wife is."

"But you've got it all wrong," burst out Poppy. "Lin hasn't got any-thing—"

"Well, it doesn't look great for her, does it now?" interrupted Harris silkily. "First her uncle, now her employer found dead."

I started; I'd forgotten that Lin worked for Pilkington. But really . . . Harris was clutching at straws here. My face must have said as much.

"You think that's far-fetched? It's no secret that Lin and her boss didn't see eye to eye."

"Sorry, and you think Lin is going round killing people she doesn't like?" It sort of slipped out of my mouth. I could tell Harris wasn't impressed—but she also didn't have an answer for me. People commit murder for money, for revenge, out of genuine deep-seated hatred, or to protect themselves or someone they love. They don't bump off their employer for disapproving of their marriage choices. OK, I'm sure somewhere, sometime in history you could find a case where that has happened, but my point is it's not your standard murder motive. But then it was motivation that we'd been struggling to pin down all through this case. Pilkington might be killed for his money, which would make *his* wife the primary suspect, I supposed, and it turned out Mr. Oliver had a small inheritance, but surely not enough to merit . . .

". . . and keep your smart mouth closed," snapped Harris, her professional cool slipping a little. I stared at her blankly; I'd completely zoned out of what she'd been saying, but by the sound of it, it hadn't been massively complimentary.

"Do you want us to tell you what happened?" said Poppy coldly. "Or can we go now?"

The bluntness of the question seemed to remind Harris of her duties.

"I'll need to ask you some questions," she said formally, getting out her notebook. "Did you see anyone else in the woods prior to discovering the body?"

We began telling her about Camran and his little bonfire. Her face grew redder and redder.

"And you didn't think to mention this sooner?" she exploded.

"Sorry, you were too busy bad-mouthing my wife," said Poppy stonily.

Harris looked like she had swallowed her own tongue. "What was he burning?" she choked out.

"It was paperwork," began Poppy. "Old newspapers and photos—"

"His sweater—although that was an accident," I chipped in.

"His clothes?" snapped Harris.

"Just his sweater," I repeated. "And he said it was an—"

But Harris was grabbing at her possessions—her jacket, her police radio, her phone—then stormed off without even a farewell glare. We could hear her barking orders at some poor lowly subordinate as she went.

It was unclear if we were now free to go or whether anything further was required of us. I suspected Inspector Harris would be quite pleased if she never had to set eyes on us again. Everyone looked quite busy and no one appeared interested in us. We left, before one of the dogs befouled the crime scene.

As we made our way back through the woods we passed Camran being escorted toward the quarry by a uniformed policeman. His eyes were wild and he seemed slightly manic, a look not helped by the streaks of black soot smeared down his face.

I wondered if there had been anything left of what he'd been burning.

"He could have done it," said Poppy in a low voice once we were past.

I had been very much thinking along the same lines. "We've only got his word for it that Pilkington had just left him when we arrived. He could've pushed him over the edge, nipped back to his campfire and pretended he'd been there all along."

"And then burned his clothes to dispose of any evidence," finished Poppy. "That's clearly what Harris thought."

And yet . . . would Camran leave a fire burning unattended in the woods? I might not struggle to see him popping off for a spot of murder, but I just couldn't see him taking risks with his beloved woodland. And there was that look on his face just now . . .

"He looked afraid," I said thoughtfully.

"Of being found out?" asked Poppy.

"I don't know . . ." I said slowly. "Could be. Or he could be scared for his own safety. After all, that's two of the three founders of the commune dead within a fortnight."

Poppy looked surprised. "That's true. God, it always comes back to the commune, doesn't it."

It really did.

"We have to get in there." There was a determined look on Poppy's face that slightly scared me. I nodded, because that's what friends do, right? And, for better or worse, I appeared to be very much involved by this point. But at this precise moment, I wasn't so sure this was a great idea. I couldn't help feeling that Inspector Harris was going to be *very* interested in our movements over the next few days. So when Poppy turned onto the path that led toward the commune, I grabbed her arm.

"We're not going to the commune right now," I said firmly. "No"—as she opened her mouth to argue—"we've just witnessed a murder. *Again.* Harris is all over us. And I need a cheeseburger, or fries, or anything that's carb-loaded and would make Ailsa punch me. Tomorrow we can talk about breaking into the commune. If we really must. But right now I'm getting a Happy Meal and not thinking about murder."

TWO HOURS later I finally had my Happy Meal.

It had been a weird couple of hours. And not particularly happy ones.

"You smell of smoke," Joe had declared as I walked in the door.

"Yeah," I'd said, feeling kinda spacey. "Yeah, Camran was burning stuff."

"Who was what now?"

"Camran, the guy who runs the commune. He was burning stuff. And then we found Ronald Pilkington."

"Alice, if you've been—"

"Dead. He was dead."

I should probably have thought a bit more about how I was going to tell Joe. But I suspect that by that point I was in shock.

Joe froze.

"Who's dead?"

"Ronald Pilkington. He's dead. We found the body."

Joe remained motionless for slightly too long. He was facing away from me, still at the sink where he'd been washing up when I came in, so I couldn't see his face. Then, abruptly, he turned and strode out of the room without even drying his hands. Seconds later, I heard the front door open and close.

He hadn't even stopped to dry his hands. This little detail kept bothering me. He also hadn't asked if I was OK, which bothered me even more. Because I wasn't. Not remotely.

He hadn't taken the car, so I had. Straight to the nearest McDonald's drive-thru.

I sat in the car in the dark and ate my cheeseburger.

CHAPTER 49

WHEN I WOKE, Joe was next to me in bed. He hadn't come in until late last night and I, coward that I am, had pretended to be asleep.

There were a few tiny fronds of fern in his hair. I picked them out gently and he didn't even stir. Had he been up in the woods? That was a hell of a walk from here. But then, he'd been gone hours. Why?

It was only 6 A.M. and I'd barely slept, but I felt restless. My nerves were fizzing against my skin, probably fired with residual adrenaline from finding a dead body the previous day. I needed to get outside, I needed to move.

Minutes later, I was leaving the house with Helen. I hadn't showered—it was only Helen, after all, plus our shower played a vicious Russian roulette where it would turn ice-cold on you without any warning.

Minutes after that, I was turning the engine off at the gate to Stricker's Wood. I had come to the opposite end to the quarry, sure, but still, I knew it was a bad idea. A man had been killed up here the previous day. I was not implicated perhaps, but certainly more involved than I should be. It felt as though the further I tried to pull myself away from this goddam investigation, the tighter it sucked me in, like being slowly eaten by a kraken. The woods drew me back time and time again.

They should have felt menacing—the site of at least one murder, possibly two. But they didn't; they were soft, damp and warm, like the coming of spring; I could feel the tension dissipating, seeping out of my pores and being absorbed by the mossy trees.

I wandered aimlessly, losing the path within minutes. I was vaguely following Helen, which, of course, is never a good idea. But she seemed to have a sense of purpose, which was something I was distinctly lacking. In life, as much as on this walk. But that was probably a problem for another day. Periodically, I would glimpse a flash of blond fur among the trees and crash through the undergrowth in that direction.

My phone rang, making me jump out of my skin. It was Poppy. I hadn't asked her to join me. Partly because it was brutally early, and partly because I just needed the space. It felt good to walk through the woods on my own. I don't know if it was the hormones, or the move, or the murders, or what, but I realized that for the last week I'd been getting more and more wound up until the pressure was unbearable. I felt like a shaken bottle of Prosecco, the cork liable to pop at any second and take out an unfortunately placed light bulb.

Nonetheless, I answered the phone. It felt only polite—after all, we had discovered a body together the previous day.

"How you doing?" She sounded surprisingly chipper.

"Oh, you know . . ." *Scared as hell about what the crap is going on here. Terrified that the father of my unborn child is involved somehow. Due to give birth any day now and absolutely shitting it.*

"Yeah," said Poppy, and I had a feeling she was vibing at least two of the three fears that were gnawing on my brain right now. Possibly all three.

"So," she barreled straight on, "have you had any thoughts about Pilkington's death?"

So many.

"Yeah, maybe, I don't know."

In truth, I'd been trying to avoid thinking about it. I'd turned the page on the calendar the previous night and had been confronted with my due date, which I'd ringed in glittery gold pen and decorated with various emoji stickers a good six months earlier. The smiley face with heart eyes. The party-hat-wearing dude blowing the weird paper tube that no one knows the name of. The red-dressed salsa lady. Right now, they all felt wholly inappropriate. Why had I inexplicably missed off the green-faced vom emoji? The exploding brain. The one that looks like Munch's *The Scream*.

It was nine days away.

Not gonna lie, I was having second thoughts about this whole "investigation." In fact, I'd had second thoughts about a week ago. I was currently probably on seventh or eighth thoughts.

At that point Helen thundered past at top speed, presumably chasing a squirrel or a rabbit or her own sanity.

"What was that? Where are you?" asked Poppy.

"I'm in the woods. With Helen."

"Great! Are you anywhere near the commune? Do you think—"

"I thought I might take a day off detectoring," I said weakly.

"Not now!" She sounded horrified. "The first twenty-four hours after a crime are the most crucial. I wrote down a list of our priorities." I heard a rustle of paper. She'd written an actual physical list? Did she not know her phone had a Notes app?

"First, get inside the commune."

"Easier said than done," I muttered.

"Sure, but there's got to be a way in. We'll speak to Ailsa about that today, she's our best bet. So that's our top priority." She rushed on. "Second, find out what happened to Jasmine. I'm sure it's linked to what's going on now. And again, that links back to the commune."

I didn't say anything. The half-read phrases of the burning article swam through my brain like slippery little fish, offering flashes and glimpses, defying capture.

"And third, find out who the hell Flora is, what happened to her and her baby, who may or may not be Jasmine, and how she's mixed up in all this."

"If she even is," I countered.

"True," admitted Poppy. "That's why that's only our third priority. But if you're in the woods, I think you should at least check if the gate to the commune is open."

She sounded bright, in a slightly manic way.

"Is everything OK?" I asked. It felt like a stupid question, in the face of everything. But sometimes you have to ask anyway.

"Of course," she said, sounding surprised. "I just think we're at a crucial stage in the investigation—"

No shit, I thought. The body count had doubled yesterday. Which, in my opinion, was exactly why we ought to leave this to the police.

"—and the police are on *completely* the wrong track, so really it's down to us."

Ah.

"Have you spoken to Harris since we left the woods yesterday?" I asked gently.

There was silence.

"Poppy?"

"She took Lin in this morning under caution."

Oh shit.

"It's not the same as being arrested!" continued Poppy hotly, although I hadn't said anything to the contrary.

"No, of course," I said quickly, although in all honesty I had no idea of the difference.

"It's voluntary," persisted Poppy. "She's *agreed* to go in for questioning. To, you know, help the police with their inquiries."

"Oh right, yes." *Helping the police with their inquiries.* It was a hollow euphemism. "But, back up, what is she being questioned about? Is this about Mr. Oliver or about Pilkington?"

"Both," said Poppy. "Which is frankly ridiculous. The problem is, Lin was at work yesterday, over at Clayton Manor, when Pilkington was— you know. And there's no one to corroborate that, but she's a gardener, she works on her own, in a garden. What does Harris expect?"

"Has Harris got any evidence?"

"For Pilkington? No. And for Mr. Oliver it's only the stupid voicemail."

That we know about, a little voice whispered in my head. Harris's evidence seemed a little thin to me, but perhaps she felt they'd reached the tipping point where the circumstantial evidence had built up enough. Lin had been at the scene of the murder of her estranged uncle, and had left the room without an alibi, and, of course, there was the incriminating voicemail. Now her employer had turned up dead and, again, Lin had no alibi.

Poppy was still talking.

"Anyway, it doesn't matter," she plowed on. "If the police can't sort this mess out then we will. We're so close to working it out, I can feel it."

Could she? Because I really couldn't.

"So, today—"

"Poppy," I interrupted gently but firmly—or at least, that's the tone I was going for. "Poppy, chill."

I was trying to channel my inner Joe. After all, he'd been right the whole time. We *should* have left this well alone. All our meddling had been to what end, exactly? Nothing. Another dead body, a load of unanswered questions and a fuckload of suspicions aimed at our nearest and dearest.

"Today you should stay at home. Stay with Lin. Do something nice, watch a film, bake a fucking cake. I don't know. But just chill. Lin needs—"

"Lin's at the station being questioned."

"Oh right. Yeah."

There was a pause. Then, in a slightly less manic tone: "Alice, I *have* to do this. You understand, right?"

I sighed. I did understand, I really did. The huge question mark over Joe's recent behavior burned in the back of my mind like mental heartburn. It's just that my preferred method of dealing with these suspicions was to stick my head in the sand; Poppy was somewhat more proactive.

"Please?"

"OK, fine." God, I was a pushover. "Fine. But this morning, at least, take some time out. You need it. I'll be back in an hour or so. For now, I don't know, go and see Hen. Hold a baby. That's always nice."

"Hold a baby?"

"Yeah."

"That's your advice?"

"Yep."

She made a rather curious high-pitched sound that was somewhere between derision and laughter.

"I'm serious, Poppy. Right now, I think the most important thing you can do is look after yourself and look after your baby," I counseled wisely. "We're probably both still a bit in shock after yesterday, and you've got a lot on your plate right now. It's not the time to be making rash decisions or doing anything we'll regret. We can talk things through this afternoon, we need to fill Hen and Ailsa in—if they haven't heard already. But right now, you need to take five."

"Yeah, maybe." She sounded a lot calmer already, and I hung up the phone feeling a warm glow. I had been a good friend. The glow dimmed a little at the realization that I hadn't told her about Joe's weird reaction to the news about Pilkington. I justified it to myself by thinking it would have been insensitive when Poppy was so worried about Lin. But there was also a dark little part of me that feared how Poppy might react—would she throw Joe under the bus to divert attention from Lin?

It was at this moment that I realized I hadn't seen Helen for a while. The last remnants of the warm glow chilled and congealed into a sense of rising dread. The last time this had happened, less than twenty-four hours ago, it had gone poorly.

I tried calling her, but either she couldn't hear me, or was ignoring me. They're funny like that, dogs. On the one hand, you are their whole world. If I have been out of the house for, say, fifteen minutes, the greeting I get from Helen on my return is almost disturbingly joyful. Her whole doggy being lights up. It is absolute balm to the ego. On the other hand, she will pointedly lick her butt when she knows I'm trying to get her attention. Between humans, it would be considered an emotionally abusive relationship.

I called again. The woods remained empty and silent. Not so much as a rustle.

I started pushing my way through the soggy bracken, calling Helen's name.

Eventually, I caught a glimpse of golden fur through the foliage. I stamped my way over, glancing around me in confusion. Did these woods look . . . familiar? Was I becoming a true country dweller, able to navigate by the trees—and possibly even the stars? Although that was probably getting ahead of myself.

I emerged into a clearing and was brought up short. I *had* been here before. In front of me, almost glowing slightly in the pre-morning dawn light, was that ethereal silver tree. Jasmine's tree. It was probably quite a magical scene, but also a tiny bit creepy, the gouge marks across her name thrown into sharp relief by the low sun.

And there, adding to the magic, was Helen, in a patch of bracken opposite the tree, doing her ass-in-the-air-rubbing-face-on-the-ground thing. Normally, this means she has found some fox poo, aka dog perfume. But rather than the distinctive odor of smeared shit, the woods actually smelled extremely pleasant here, almost extra foresty, as if we were in a particularly concentrated area of trees.

I pulled Helen upright and inspected her head for grossness. Nothing. I looked down into the flattened bracken where, at the bottom of a shallow, muddy hole, lay a couple of little brown bottles. I picked them up and there it was again—a whiff of forest. Accompanied by a swoop of déjà vu. Where had I smelled this before?

They were those little glass bottles you get in chemists and whole-food stores, full of essential oils that cost six million pounds per milliliter. I turned one over in my hand.

"Wintergreen oil," I read aloud.

I peered at the small print on the label—98 percent methyl salicylate.

CHAPTER 50

HELEN WASN'T SICK this time. Presumably she'd managed to yum up all the poison last time. I did let her sit in the front seat on the way home, just in case she started convulsing or something and I had to pull over for some roadside CPR. She was fine. In fact, she was loving life in the front seat, pressing her snout to the windshield and occasionally hoovering up the crumbs from my many car snacks.

I called Joe but he didn't answer, so I tried Poppy, who did.

"You'll never guess what," I began.

"You gave birth?"

"What? No!"

"You met Keanu Reeves?"

"What? No, why would I have met Keanu Reeves? I've been at Stricker's Wood!"

"I don't know, you just sound quite excited, and you talk about Keanu Reeves a lot."

"I do not."

"You do."

"Look, he seems like a nice guy."

There was a muffled voice in the background.

"I'm with Hen," said Poppy. "And she says you've mentioned Keanu Reeves at least twice to her."

"Keanu is not important right now. Listen, I found the poison. Well, Helen did."

That got her attention.

"You found the methylene . . . that stuff?"

I heard Hen correcting her in the background, so I didn't bother.

"Yep, up in the woods. Look, where are you? I'll come and join you."

"At the garden nursery. You know, the one on the Bridgeport road."

"The nursery? Seriously?"

"Seriously."

"What are you, eighty?"

"They have a very good café," said Poppy in a dignified tone. "And you're the one who told me to chill out this morning."

It was a fair point. "Well, I'm glad you took my advice. Maybe this afternoon we could play bridge and watch *Antiques Roadshow*."

Poppy ignored this. "Anyway Hen needed to buy some nipplewort."

I paused.

"That's an issue for the nursery, is it? Wouldn't a gynecologist be more help?"

"It's a *plant*. Although she does want to put it on her nipples. Apparently it helps with breastfeeding."

"OK, not gonna ask, don't want to know. Is Ailsa with you?"

"No, she's doing cosmic yoga. She tried to make us join her."

"When you put it like that, nursery café does sound quite appealing. I'll be there in ten."

I FOUND Hen and Poppy at a table in the nursery café, the youngest people there by at least three decades. Hen's baby was asleep. I tried to remember if I'd ever seen her awake. Awake and not feeding, that is. I peered into the pram, surreptitiously checking if she was real. She opened one eye and stared malevolently at me, but seemed to decide I wasn't worth the bother and closed it again.

Helen made straight for Hen's cake.

"If your dog eats my cake," said Hen coldly, "I will wear her like Cruella de Vil."

"Never mind about that," said Poppy excitedly, casually disregarding Hen's threat to skin Helen. "Tell us about the poison. What did you find?"

"I can do one better than that," I said. "I've got it with me."

Hen and Poppy looked appalled.

"You brought *poison* to a *nursery*?" Hen hissed, looking around furtively. Clearly this was the height of bad manners and even worse than the fact that I'd brought Helen.

"Well . . . The thing is, it's not exactly poison," I said. I pulled the bag with the bottles in it out of my pocket.

"Is that a dog poo bag?" asked Hen, wrinkling her nose. "Gross."

"A clean one," I said, feeling slightly offended; I'd been rather pleased with the idea. "I'm afraid I didn't have any police-grade evidence bags to hand."

"Good idea," said Poppy. "Stops the evidence from being contaminated."

"Er, about that . . ."

Hen rolled her eyes. "You touched them, didn't you?"

"I didn't know they were going to be evidence at the time," I protested.

"What are they anyway?" asked Poppy, tipping the bottles out onto the tabletop. Hen immediately grabbed a napkin and used it to set the bottles upright, although I could already see a crumb of cake sticking to one.

"Essential oils," Hen said, carefully using the napkin to rotate one and read the label. "Wintergreen oil?"

"Wintergreen oil," I confirmed. "Which, as anyone knows, is ninety-eight percent methyl salicylate."

Hen raised an eyebrow.

"Says it on the bottle," I admitted.

"Oh my God," breathed Poppy. "He was poisoned with *essential oils*."

I nodded. "It's so Penton, isn't it?"

"That's still conjecture," cut in Hen. I decided to ignore this attempt to put a downer on my brilliant detectoring. Which had left me starving, I realized, so I wiped Poppy's coffee spoon with a napkin and took a big spoonful of her cake. "This is so good!"

"I told you—nursery café cake. It's the best."

"What is it?"

"Hummingbird cake."

"Sounds fancy—what's that then?"

Hen rapped the table like a teacher trying to control a rowdy class. "Can we try and focus for five seconds?"

"Yes, Miss," I said meekly. Poppy laughed. Hen rolled her eyes.

"So what does this tell us?" she went on persistently. "And I don't mean speculation or jumping to conclusions."

"It looks like Mr. Oliver was murdered with essential oils from his own shop," I said doggedly.

"Hen's right though, we can't be sure of that," said Poppy, pinching back the rest of her cake and hissing at me to buy my own. She seemed, bizarrely, in an extremely buoyant mood, if a tad highly strung. Then again, it felt like the kind of enthusiasm that is flirting with the possibility of tears at a moment's notice.

Hen turned to me and snapped her fingers (which annoyed me). "Do you still have that Roman chamomile I gave you? The stuff I bought at Nature's Way?"

I smiled, slightly smugly I'll admit. "Way ahead of you." And I pulled the Roman chamomile out of my other pocket and placed it next to the wintergreen bottles.

"They're the same," breathed Poppy. The spiky handwritten labels were identical.

"They *look* the same," corrected Hen, cautiously.

"Oh, come on," I argued. "The handwriting's identical!"

"You'd need a graphologist to confirm that."

"Unfortunately we haven't got one to hand," I snapped.

"No, but the police will," said Hen with an exaggerated patience that I found deeply patronizing. "I presume you were intending to hand over this potentially crucial evidence to the police?"

Oh yes, the police. I'd forgotten that I probably ought to hand this in.

"Do you want to take it in?" I asked Hen hopefully. But she shook her head.

"You ought to, they'll want to ask you where you found it."

I sighed. Once again, she was right. It was an extremely irritating habit of hers.

"Have you spoken to Harris about Rowan's press pass yet?" asked Hen.

"No," I said and sighed.

Poppy looked up, confused. "Why not?"

"Well, mainly because of the whole finding a dead body thing," I said. "And also . . . things have been weird with Joe, it kinda threw me off."

"How so?" asked Hen.

Haltingly, I told them about his bizarre reaction to the news of Pilkington's death. I hadn't planned to tell them, but I felt put on the spot.

"And your immediate reaction was to go and get a McDonald's?" asked Hen disbelievingly. I probably should have missed that bit out of my retelling.

"Not really the relevant point here, Hen," said Poppy gently.

"We all have our coping mechanisms," I said.

Hen sighed. "Sorry. And I mean, yeah, that is weird on Joe's part. But then, men are weird. Antoni seemed quite upset about it too. And then just wandered off to do some exercise biking. I mean, it's like three minutes of emotion wears them out and that's it, they've had their emotion quota for the week."

I felt mildly irritated that Hen had brought this back round to her. I mean, Joe hadn't wandered off to do some exercise biking, he'd friggin' disappeared for half the night! Poppy gave me a sympathetic look.

"I can come with you to the police," she volunteered, once again keeping the peace. "And we can tell Harris about the press pass while we're there."

I hesitated. Poppy wasn't exactly flavor of the month with Inspector Harris, and I did wonder about the advisability of her turning up at the police station when her wife was actually in the station being questioned. But then again, I was definitely more likely than Poppy to say something that would land us in trouble, so who was I to judge? And I really didn't want to go on my own.

"Yeah. Thanks."

"We should try and get some info in return," mused Poppy. "Like an information exchange. I'm sure that's what private detectives do in films."

"We are not private detectives," said Hen firmly.

"Amateur detectives?" suggested Poppy.

I tried not to weep.

"We want to know if there's been any movement on the postmortem," continued Hen.

"Or the analysis on that tea," added Poppy.

"What I want to know," I said, and they both turned to me, "is how long are we staying here? Because if it's more than five minutes I'm gonna get myself a piece of that cake."

I DON'T want anyone getting the impression I wasn't taking this seriously. I was. One hundred percent. I was also pregnant and hungry and tired. And had seen more bodies in the last fortnight than was good for anyone's mental health.

I got my cake. Like I said: coping mechanisms.

Then Poppy and I set off to brave Inspector Harris in her den. Just as we were leaving, however, my phone rang. It was Joe.

"Hey." He sounded a bit nervous. Which gratified me slightly. After all, he had a lot of explaining to do.

"Where were you last night?"

"I went for a walk to clear my head."

"Oh, right. Well, I hope it helped. It's not like I needed your support or anything. After finding a dead body. At thirty-nine weeks pregnant. No biggie."

"Al, I'm so, so sorry . . ." And he did actually sound it. "Look, let me make it up to you—"

"I don't want you to make it up to me," I interrupted. "I want you to explain."

"Yes, yes, you're right. Totally." This was unusual. "Look, let's go out for lunch and I'll explain everything."

"Can't, sorry," I said abruptly. "I took Helen up to the woods this morning and she found the poison that killed Mr. Oliver. Probably. I have to take it to the police station."

"Whoa. OK. Shit, that's big. Look, I'll meet you there," he said. "And after that, we'll talk. I promise."

JOE WAS hovering outside the police station. He gave me a nervous smile. I nodded to him.

Poppy looked between us, at a bit of a loss.

"Hey, Poppy," he said weakly.

"Yeah, hi. Everything OK?"

"Er . . ."

"Let's just get this over and done with," I said brusquely, striding into the police station with more confidence than I really felt, Poppy right behind me and Joe lagging at our heels.

I had about three seconds to take in the lobby of the police station before everything went horribly wrong. I suppose I should have expected it by this point.

The door to the left of the duty desk swung open and we heard Inspector Harris's voice.

". . . appreciate you doing this. I know how difficult it is, but the formal identification is an essential part of the process of finding out what happened to your husband. And we *will* find out."

Harris stepped into the lobby. Followed by Mrs. Pilkington. She had, it appeared, just been to identify her husband's body. And, as we know, she had actually liked her husband, possibly even loved him. She was sobbing gently into a scrunched-up tissue.

And then she saw Joe.

Her eyes, puffy and swollen as they were, narrowed, and a livid wave of rage suffused her usually grandmotherly features.

"You," she hissed. "YOU!"

She made as if to fly at him, but Inspector Harris caught both her arms and had to physically restrain her.

"He did it! He killed him! He killed my Ronnie!" She was shrieking, demented, clawing as if trying to get at Joe, wanting to shred him.

Joe was a rabbit caught in the headlights. He had frozen, terrified and confused.

Mrs. Pilkington was really going some. There was screaming. There was crying. There was denial and rage and pain. She appeared to be going through all five stages of grief simultaneously.

"A little help here!" barked Inspector Harris.

Two other police officers appeared and joined her, surrounding Mrs. Pilkington.

"Calm down now, madam."

"Arrest that boy! He killed my Ronnie!"

That cold dread that can drown you from within was filling my chest, my lungs, my throat. What was she talking about? Joe hadn't killed Ronald Pilkington. Not my Joe! She had to stop saying these awful things.

"Mrs. Pilkington . . ." began Poppy, hesitantly, her eyes huge, flickering from Mrs. Pilkington to Joe to me. "Mrs. Pilkington, what are you talking about?"

The fight was going out of the woman. She was starting to sag against one of the police officers, although her eyes were still shooting daggers at Joe.

"That boy has been sniffing around my Ronnie. Bothering him. Upsetting him," she spat. "Filling his head with lies. Lies about Flora. Lies about him."

"About Flora? Joe—what?" I stared at Joe. He was still staring at Mrs. Pilkington, apparently appalled.

"Oh yes, you're just like her," snarled Mrs. Pilkington, her eyes still fixed on Joe. "Just like your mother."

CHAPTER 51

I TOLD JOE to walk home. I couldn't face sitting next to him for even that short a journey. He was lucky he was going home at all; Inspector Harris had been reluctant to let him go. She'd questioned him, of course. When you're accused of murder in a police station that's the least you can expect. But there was no actual evidence against him, and after she'd been calmed down with several cups of tea and a digestive biscuit, Mrs. Pilkington had not made a formal criminal accusation. Thank God.

Poppy and I were probably also pretty high on the inspector's list of people to speak to, but I think even Inspector Harris's rudimentary people skills had picked up on the fact that I wasn't in a fit state to answer any questions. I had driven Poppy home, which I think had worried her a little as I had, let's face it, other things on my mind beyond the road.

Joe was Flora's son.

I pulled into Poppy's street.

Flora, the mysterious, beautiful, enigmatic Flora, was in fact Laura, my cheerful, scatterbrained, motherly mother-in-law.

And into her driveway.

Unless, of course, Laura wasn't in fact Joe's biological mum at all . . .

Engine off. Eyes still straight ahead.

Either way, Joe's dad was . . .

I groaned and leaned forward until my head hit the dashboard.

"Do you want to stay at mine?" Poppy asked anxiously. "We can make up the spare bed. Helen can stay too."

It was a mark of how concerned she clearly was that she made that last offer.

"No. I'll go home."

As messed up as this all was, I still wanted to see Joe. His parents were . . . not who I had thought they were. Did that mean *he* wasn't who I thought he was? Was this better or worse than him visiting Pilkington because he was interested in his politics? Why hadn't he told me about this?

But I wanted to see him—I *needed* to see him.

I DIDN'T drive straight home, though. I needed to sit and think. I drove to the Co-op, bought a Chocolate Orange and bit into it like an apple. It wasn't as pleasing as I'd hoped. I sat, my mouth filling with cloying chocolate that tasted like the smell of potpourri, staring unseeingly ahead through the windshield.

I needed to speak to Joe. I needed to speak to his mum. Should I phone her? I toyed with the idea but discarded it. What would I say?

Hi, Laura, weird question but are you sure you're Joe's biological mum?
Not a great conversation opener. And if she said yes, then what?

Great, in that case would you mind telling me who you were shagging at the Stricker's Wood Commune thirty years ago, and also why the fuck you didn't mention this before?

No. I was close to my mother-in-law, but there are limits.

Automatically, my fingers found Maya in my contacts and I rang her. Straight to voicemail. Shit. But then, it was a Thursday afternoon; two weeks into mat leave and I'd forgotten that people work nine-to-fives.

Maybe, and it was a controversial thought, I should phone my own mother.

I dialed, before the unfamiliar urge left me. Rather shockingly, she picked up.

"So sorry, darling, I will be there in literally five minutes. I couldn't find those earrings Graham bought me for our anniversary and I just *had* to wear them with this dress. Could you get me one of those minty ones? Is it the mint tulip? The mint Julie? You know the one I mean—"

Ah, she hadn't looked at the caller ID. That might explain why she'd picked up so quickly.

"It's me, Mum."

There was a brief silence.

"Alice! *Darling!*"

Oh my God. Why had I called?

"Hey, Mum, how are you?"

Wrong question. She was off. My parents' life on the Costa del Sol was a succession of cocktails and pool parties. And probably swinging, who the hell knew? Who the hell cared? I let her frothy monologue wash over me. In a weird way, it was kind of soothing. It was so far removed from my current life.

Eventually, she came up for air.

"Anyway, what's your news, darling? Keep it brief, though. It's been a lovely natter, but I'm supposed to be meeting Carol for cocktails and I'm already terribly late. I misplaced my earrings, you know, the ones your father got me for—"

"I heard, Mum. Look it's nothing really . . . It's just this murder that happened. You know I texted you about it." *Not that you texted back*, I recalled. "Well, there was another one yesterday and—"

"Gosh yes, how terribly exciting!" she interrupted. "Have they caught anyone?"

"No, not yet. Anyway, this man who was killed yesterday, well, it kind of looks like he might have been Joe's dad."

"And is Joe the boy you've been seeing? The one with the earring?"

Was she for real?

"Yes, Mum. Joe is the guy I've 'been seeing' for over a year. We're having a baby together, remember?"

Joe does not have an earring; that was a guy I'd dated about five years ago for about a week.

"Of course you are, darling. Remind me, when's the baby due?"

"Seriously? Next week, Mum." I was trying not to sound exasperated. Really I was.

"Lovely, let me put that on the calendar. Oh wait, your father's taken it somewhere—I'll make a note—or wait, I'll do one of those voice memo thingies on my phone when you've rung off—*there* are my earrings!"

I hung up. She probably wouldn't notice until her third mint julep.

I was almost out of Chocolate Orange.

Well, this was a disaster.

I'd just started the engine to reluctantly head for home when I saw Antoni. He'd just emerged from the Co-op clutching a bottle of wine.

Lucky Hen, I thought miserably. Her husband about to arrive home, wine in hand, ready for a cozy evening in while their newborn baby slumbered peacefully in her Moses basket.

But at the car park exit he indicated left, whereas Hen's house was just two minutes down the road to the right.

I don't know what made me do it, and part of me wishes I hadn't, but on the spur of the moment, I decided to follow him.

I ACCELERATED after Antoni, then immediately decelerated and panicked. I had never tailed anyone before. Did I just . . . drive along behind him? I didn't really have any other option. I knew that if more than one car came between us I'd be screwed; I get confused if there are more than three lanes of traffic, so I'd never be able to follow a car half a street ahead.

I went for a haphazard combination of driving pretty close behind him and then occasionally dropping back. There was no logic to it. Welcome to my life. And there was no way to know if he suspected he was being followed.

As I had half expected, Antoni drove to Bridgeport. He wound his way through the suburban backstreets—his silver BMW thankfully easy to spot in the gathering dark—eventually pulling up outside a nondescript terraced house. I parked a couple of hundred meters farther down the road. After an unsuccessful attempt to angle the rearview mirror so that I could see what was occurring behind me, I gave up and twisted awkwardly in the driving seat so I could peer out the back window.

I saw Antoni's besuited form approaching one of the identikit houses, his light gray suit shining faintly in the half-light of dusk, making him look like a particularly formal ghost. The door to the house opened, spilling warm yellow light into the street. At first the figure in the door-way was just a silhouette, but when she stepped out onto the doorstep to greet Antoni I recognized her. It was the blond Costa waitress.

Antoni disappeared into the house without a backward glance.

An affair then. Another man with his secrets and lies. The small, hor-rible part of me felt a vindictive pleasure that it wasn't just my boyfriend who was at it. The larger and better part of me felt awful for Hen. And it left me in something of a moral conundrum. How could I possibly tell Hen about this? But, equally, how could I possibly keep it from her?

Perhaps I should go home and face my own demons first.

CHAPTER 52

JOE WAS SITTING on the sofa when I finally got in. I sat in the armchair facing him, my arms wrapped around my bump.

"So," I said eventually. "Same question as last time, really. Anything you want to tell me?"

Joe rubbed his hands through his hair.

"Alice, I'm sorry—" he began. But I cut him off.

"I don't want to hear apologies. Not right now. I want to hear an explanation."

Joe spoke into his hands. "My mum used to live here. Up at the commune."

I wondered if he was going to tell me anything I hadn't worked out for myself.

"She knew Pilkington and Camran and that lot . . ." he went on haltingly.

"And you didn't at any point think to tell me?" I winced at the hard edge I heard in my own voice.

There was a ringing silence.

Then I realized Joe was crying.

In all the time I'd known him—which, admittedly, right now wasn't feeling like that long—I had never seen him cry.

I wanted to go and sit next to him, to put my arm round his shoulders, bury my head in his neck. But I stayed where I was. Cold and unmoving. Because I also didn't want to touch him. I felt bad for him, but I also felt betrayed. And scared. What the hell was going on, and how deep in was Joe?

"Let's start from the beginning," I suggested. Then a strange thought struck me. "When did you find out? That your mum used to live here? Did you know before we moved?"

He didn't say anything, just looked at his hands.

I gaped. "I don't believe it."

"Alice—"

"I thought we moved here at random. Oh, a nice town in the country-side, it's as good as any other . . . But it was you who found Penton, wasn't it? It was you who suggested we take a look here. Because you knew all along. You knew your mum used to live here."

"Look, Alice, it's not as big a deal as you're making it out to be."

I was stunned into silence. Because, honestly, it felt like a pretty big deal. Our big move to the country, our fresh start with the baby—it was all tainted now with this ulterior motive.

"So, you came here because you wanted—what?"

"Because I wanted to find my dad, all right!" Joe suddenly sounded angry. Angry and upset.

I was quiet for a moment. Because I knew where this was going—of course I knew. And it was somewhere very uncomfortable. So I stalled. "But still . . . why didn't you say something? If you were thinking of try-ing to track him down even before we moved here? Why didn't you tell me? We could have done it together."

I tried to hold it back, but part of me was angry. Joe had been so anti my "detectoring," but had been carrying out his own secret investigation the whole time?

Joe sighed and ran his hands through his hair again. "Because it was all too much," he said eventually.

It was an answer—of sorts. But I wasn't sure it was good enough.

"Since we found out about the baby," Joe continued haltingly, "it's just all been so intense. I didn't know how I felt about becoming a dad—still don't, if I'm honest. And I don't have any kind of role model, just some anonymous sperm donor who fucked off before I was born. And I know that's not important, loads of people don't know their dads. But . . ." He trailed off.

"It is important," I said abruptly. "Or at least, if it matters to you then it's important—for me as well. But even if your dad was a shit"—I pictured Ronald Pilkington—"that doesn't mean you won't be a great dad."

He snorted at that.

"Don't get me wrong, I'm not saying all my"—he flapped his hands vaguely—"emotions, or whatever, are tied up with my dad. I can't blame it all on him. But it seemed a good place to start. I knew he was probably from around here. I mean, Mum's never really spoken about him, but I've picked up bits and pieces, here and there, and I can do basic maths . . . And when we started talking about moving to the country—it felt like it was the right time, you know? If I was going to get in touch with my dad, it suddenly seemed important to do it before I became a dad myself. It's like that parenting book says, you know, the one with the really long title?"

"*The Book You Wish Your Parents Had Read (and Your Children Will Be Glad That You Did)*?" I haven't read the book, but I had memorized the title.

"Yeah, that one. Well, it says you've got to understand your relationship with your own parents before you can work out what kind of relationship you'll have with your kid."

I was more than a little stunned. Mainly because I'd had no idea Joe felt like this about his dad—or rather absence of. But what I blurted out instead was, "You read that book?"

He actually cracked a small smile. "No, I didn't. But you left it in the bathroom and I read the blurb. Did you know the author is the wife of that artist guy? The one who wears bonnets and stuff?"

"Don't change the subject."

"Fine. Anyway, the blurb makes a good point—for me, anyway. I do need to understand my dad and why he did what he did. And that means finding out who he is, to start with."

"What if he's a bonnet-wearing artist?"

"Now who's changing the subject."

"Just trying to keep it light." But my next question felt weighted. "So . . . you think Ronald Pilkington is your dad?"

Perhaps it would have been more accurate to say "was," but it felt insensitive to correct my use of the present tense right now.

"I think . . . he might be," said Joe heavily.

"Why? What put you onto him?"

"That stupid dog of Poppy's," said Joe. "I mentioned him on the phone to Mum, and she started reminiscing about a Ronnie that she used to know down here. She said they were . . . close. So I did a little digging."

"So it wasn't his politics you were interested in." I didn't know whether to feel relieved or horrified.

"What? No!"

"I just . . . I had been wondering why you seemed so interested in such an awful guy." Belatedly I wondered if I shouldn't be bad-mouthing his dead potential dad.

"I'm sure he was different back then," said Joe, a little defensively.

"Oh, apparently so," I agreed. "Very different."

I thought of the young "Ronnie" Pilkington that had helped found the hippy commune alongside his great pals Camran Pan and Crispin Oliver. Which raised a whole other question.

"What makes you think it was him?" I asked thoughtlessly. "Why not the others?"

"The others?" Joe looked up sharply.

Oh God, he didn't know about the others. Wow, this conversation was going from bad to worse. Although, with a little sting of pride, I reflected that, as critical as Joe had been of our investigation, it seemed we'd uncovered a whole lot more than he had.

"I think," I said, picking my words with care, "that Ronald Pilkington might not have been the only . . . candidate."

Joe's face had gone blank.

"Tell me," he croaked.

I took a risk and scooted over to the sofa to sit next to him, our shoulders touching. This seemed to be the way of things between us recently, swinging between closeness and a horrible estrangement in the blink of an eye. But just maybe we were finally getting to the bottom of why.

"Well, there's Camran," I said. "The leader up at the commune. Mrs. Pilkington seemed pretty sure he had something going on with your mum."

Joe looked confused. "You were talking to Mrs. Pilkington about my mum?"

I realized how little we had been sharing with each other since we moved here. "Kind of. Except I didn't know she was your mum at the time. There's been quite a bit of talk about 'Flora' recently."

Joe looked a little green at this so I didn't press the matter.

"You've met this Camran guy?" he asked, and with a jolt I realized that Joe had never so much as set eyes on Camran. I also recalled that the last time I had seen Camran had been the previous day. Shortly after he had argued with Ronald Pilkington. Shortly before we'd found Pilkington's dead body.

"Yeah . . ."

"Well, what's he like?"

"He's . . . interesting," I said. I was still forming my opinions on this.

Joe snorted.

"Then, there is a third possibility . . ." I said, still not sure I wanted to bring this up.

"Oh yes?" Joe's tone was brittle. I had a feeling he knew what I was going to say.

"Mr. Oliver."

Joe went very still. As though if he breathed he might shatter.

"What about Mr. Oliver?" he echoed.

"It's just something someone said. Camran's wife, or life partner, or whatever. She said he knew Flora when she was here. That he was . . . interested in her. And the woman he runs—ran—Nature's Way with said he'd been talking about Flora just before he died."

"And?"

I didn't like how still Joe was, or the fact that he didn't seem surprised by what I was saying.

I had to ask him. It was like ripping a Band-Aid off—sometimes you just had to suck up the hurt. "Joe, did you know? Did you know Mr. Oliver knew your mum?"

Joe said nothing. A horrible hard, cold lump formed in my chest. I grabbed his hand. "Joe. Did you know Mr. Oliver?"

"No!" But he wouldn't meet my eyes.

"What aren't you telling me?"

"I didn't *know* him. But I did speak to him."

"When?"

Joe cleared his throat. "The day we had our first prenatal class."

"The day before he died?"

Joe nodded.

"The day we moved here? I mean what . . . when?"

Joe took a deep breath.

"Do you remember I had to leave the meeting like ten minutes in, because we realized we'd left grapes on the floor and Helen might eat them and die?"

I nodded mutely.

"When I left, he was in the shop downstairs. He kept trying to talk to me, saying I looked familiar, did he know me—but I was in a bit of a hurry in case Helen was dying so I kind of brushed him off. But then when I came back like twenty minutes later he said he'd remembered who I reminded him of. He asked me if I was Flora Grisedale's son. Then it all got a bit confusing, I said did he mean Laura Grisedale because yeah, that was my mum. And he said no, her name was Flora. And I said I was pretty sure of my mum's name, and it was Laura; did he know her or something? And then he just looked at me for a bit too long and said no."

I let out a long breath. "And that's it?"

"Alice, I swear that's it."

"Did you tell the police?"

"It wasn't relevant."

I nodded. It wasn't relevant. Of course Mr. Oliver wasn't Joe's dad. And I believed Joe. Of course I did.

CHAPTER 53

I WASN'T ON sparkling form when Hen called bright and early the next morning. To be fair to her, she didn't know I'd had a late night stalking her partner and then interrogating my own. Nor did she know that she was one of the last people I wanted to speak to right now—not because of anything she'd done, of course, but I resented starting my day with a moral struggle over whether or not to tell her that her husband was a cheating bastard.

"It's seven A.M.," I groaned.

"Is it?" said Hen unsympathetically. "I've been up since five with the baby. You might as well get used to it."

"I might as well have my last few lie-ins of the decade," I corrected her.

"Well, you're up now."

And before I could explain to her that, if I tried really hard, I could probably still manage to get back to sleep, she barreled on.

"I called Inspector Harris—"

"Did you wake her up too?"

"—*yesterday*. And arranged for us to meet her at the Penton station at ten. Poppy and Ailsa are meeting us at half past for a debrief. Get a shift on."

"Hold up . . ." My brain was sluggishly kicking into gear. How did Hen know we hadn't given the evidence in yesterday?

"Poppy called me last night." Clearly Hen's brain was working somewhat faster than mine and had anticipated what I was thinking.

"Oh God." I rolled over and buried my face in the pillow.

"Yeah, I heard about what Mrs. Pilkington said to Joe." Was it my imagination or was there a slightly kinder note in Hen's voice? Insofar as her regular scorn was softened with an edge of pity. Great.

Then: "Look, we'll talk about *that* later," she said dismissively, as if Joe's terrible lineage was a minor distraction from the business at hand. Maybe I'd imagined the pity after all. "But first of all we need to get this evidence into the right hands. Ten A.M. Police station."

"Fine," I mumbled into my pillow, wondering how many cups of de-caf coffee I could consume before then, before realizing miserably that it wouldn't make the slightest bit of difference.

"Don't be late," bossed Hen.

"I won't," I lied.

"And don't bring Helen."

AS A small act of protest, I brought Helen. And I was late.

It was petty, and largely backfired on me, because Helen *loved* the police station. So many interesting smells to investigate in the waiting room, so many potential criminals to crotch-sniff. Perhaps she'd missed her calling as a sniffer dog. I wondered idly whether Helen felt horribly thwarted in her career, if she could have reached the dizzy heights of Chief Canine Olfactory Officer had she not been lumbered with caring for the likes of Joe and me. I looked down to see her chewing a Talk to FRANK card ("Feeling pressured to take drugs? Talk to FRANK") and decided it was unlikely.

Eventually, we were called into Inspector Harris's office. I confess I was a little disappointed. My expectations of a police station were almost entirely formed from watching a lot of *Death in Paradise*. There are a lot of palm trees. The main detective lives in a beach shack and has a pet lizard called Harry. The main features of Inspector Harris's office were framed certificates on the wall (always a sign that someone takes themselves too seriously) and those big leather-bound books that all match, although I've always secretly suspected they contain nothing more than a complete run of *The Beano*, leather clad. There were no palm trees, and there was a distinct lack of reggae music.

Inspector Harris appeared even less impressed by my decision to bring Helen along than Hen.

"Is that a dog?" was her opening question.

I bit back a retort that if she had to ask, then I didn't know how she'd ever made detective inspector.

"This is Helen," I said, going for cold and dignified. It didn't work, in part because Helen still had quite a lot of chewed card hanging from her mouth and her ear was inside out. In fact, she really looked like she could use a call with Frank.

Inspector Harris sighed. "Take a seat." She gestured to the solitary uncomfortable-looking chair in front of her desk.

"You don't mind, do you?" asked Hen, sliding smoothly onto the chair and immediately beginning to unbutton her shirt. Within seconds, the boob was out and the baby was feeding.

For nine months you get to be pregnant and turf people out of chairs when you want to sit down, only to find you still get trumped by breast-feeders.

Inspector Harris averted her eyes.

"So what did you ladies want to see me about?" she asked. But before allowing us the space to answer, she continued. "And by the way, it is not acceptable to phone the police station and demand to speak to the investigating officer. I'm sure whatever you have to say could have been dealt with perfectly well by one of my constables."

I could see why Ailsa didn't get on with her sister. Jane Harris had gone straight into telling us off without even waiting to hear what we had to say. I would have been tempted to not tell her now, except I suspected that would earn us a lecture on wasting police time and quite possibly a caution to boot.

Hen remained unruffled. "We are key witnesses in your murder investigation," she reminded Harris.

"As far as I'm aware," rejoined Harris, "none of you actually witnessed anything. Of use," she added not quite under her breath.

"Well, now we have found something that I think you'll find is . . . *of use*," said Hen, still refusing to lose her cool. She gestured at me, that sort of "hurry along now" gesture that mothers make to their children. I stepped forward and tripped over Helen's lead.

Inspector Harris sighed. "Yes . . . ?"

"I found something, up at the woods. Stricker's Wood," I began, faltering already. Inspector Harris had this intimidating vibe that took me right back to school, you know, to that chilling moment when a teacher would ask why I thought it was funny to flick a pig's eyeball across the lab in biology, and suddenly I'd be at a loss for an answer.

"And . . . ?" she prompted impatiently.

"We think it might be evidence in the case of Mr. Oliver's murder. It's—actually I should start at the beginning. Sorry, I'm making a bit of a hash of this. So the other day my dog was very ill." I gestured at Helen, Exhibit A, who was staring fixedly at an apparently blank point on the wall.

Inspector Harris put her head in her hands. "Please tell me you haven't brought your dog in as evidence."

"No! I'm just trying to explain—"

"The dog was poisoned from something she ate up in the woods the other day. It turned out she was poisoned by essential oils from Mr. Oliver's shop which someone had thrown away up there," cut in Hen. "The oil of wintergreen has a high methyl salicylate content, around ninety-eight percent, which is extremely toxic to both dogs and humans if ingested. In large quantities, anything over ten mil, it can cause instant convulsions and seizures which can lead to death within minutes, leaving little to no external mark on the body. Although in the interim as you wait, apparently indefinitely, for the postmortem report, I suspect the briefest of inspections of Mr. Oliver's body would reveal slight reddening to the inside of the deceased's mouth and lips."

I had to hand it to her, she was extremely efficient. I'd have taken a good month to explain that—plus I didn't actually know most of it. Turns out a degree in forensic biology or whatever it was gives you certain insights.

Inspector Harris said nothing. Her eyes drifted back to Helen.

"And you're basing this on the dog being ill."

"Her name's Helen," I chipped in, wanting to contribute *something*.

Hen shot me a "shut up and leave this to the grown-ups" look.

"Well, if you put it like that, it sounds tangential," said Hen. Inspector Harris snorted. "But if you consider the confluence of evidence," Hen continued calmly, "the bottles on Mr. Oliver's desk, the spilled tea at the scene and the apparently rapid onset of death, then the presence of two bottles of highly toxic oil of wintergreen, from his shop, found several miles away in the woods. A reasonable working hypothesis would be that he was poisoned with the oil in his tea, and the murderer disposed of the bottles in the woods."

I winced; we'd learned most of that from the report Ailsa had nicked. Had Hen given away too much? Inspector Harris had narrowed her eyes.

"You seem to know an awful lot about the scene of the crime."

Hen shrugged, nonchalant. "Mere observations."

"Incredible observations, I would say," corrected Inspector Harris, "coming from someone who was giving birth at the time."

"I saw the body," I butted in. "I went down to fetch the paramedics and saw everything. And I'm extremely observant."

I saw Hen close her eyes briefly. Inspector Harris rolled hers.

"And I suppose it was your incredible observation skills that helped you spot two small bottles in the vast acreage of Stricker's Wood?"

"Oh no, that was Helen," I said, beaming at my sniffer dog extraordinaire. "Well, first time she just ate the remaining oil. But the second time—well, actually I think she was trying to see if there was any left. She never learns. But I spotted her and—here."

I produced the dog poo bag containing the evidence again. Inspector Harris took her time snapping a pair of those latex dentist gloves over her hands before removing the two bottles.

"So what you're telling me is that this evidence, which might not even be evidence, has been quite comprehensively contaminated by your dog licking it clean of any incriminating fingerprints or other useful marks."

"Oh, except for my fingerprints. I picked them up *after* she'd been licking them, so my prints are probably pretty intact."

I actually thought Inspector Harris's eyes might disappear into the back of her head.

* * *

I **HAD** to have my prints taken as "exclusion" prints, which was quite exciting, but mainly messy. A uniformed constable took me off to a very functional room at the back of the station, where they made me press my fingertips to an ink pad, like the ones you use for finger-painting when you're a kid. Then I was given a sheet of paper and had to do a single print in a square for every finger—both hands, because I couldn't remember which hand I'd picked the bottles up with. Rather irritatingly the police officer insisted on doing this for me, holding my hand and pressing each finger down in turn. I explained that I was perfectly capable of doing this myself, to which she responded, "They all say that, and then they go and fuck it up." Fair enough.

They didn't offer me anything to wipe my hands with afterward, which felt quite rude and rather pointed. So when I came out into the corridor where Hen and Inspector Harris were waiting, I looked like I was fresh from filming *Art Attack*. Helen, who had stayed in the corridor as she presented a further contamination risk, went predictably insane and threw herself at me, swiftly becoming covered in inky finger smears which stood out rather dramatically on her blond fur. It looked like she was in fancy dress as a leopard.

We returned to Inspector Harris's office, me trying surreptitiously to wipe my hands clean on my jeans. This time, Inspector Harris didn't offer us the chair. In fact, she hovered in front of it quite protectively, as if keen to ensure we didn't try and sit down and make ourselves comfortable.

"Anything else?" she asked, picking up a sheaf of paper and rustling it, almost definitely just to give the appearance of busyness.

Hen shot me a glance and raised her eyebrows. I presumed this was my cue to bring up the press pass.

"Er, kind of . . ." I began. But by this point I wasn't so sure I wanted to drop Rowan in it. The guy was a liar, for sure, and there was a lot about him that didn't quite add up. But we had no evidence that he was involved in *murder*. Well, only circumstantial evidence anyway. And Inspector Harris didn't seem the type to hang around; I was sure she would have no qualms about arresting Rowan the moment she had our statement.

Not to mention the fact that we couldn't involve the press pass without Inspector Harris asking how we knew about it. And it wouldn't take a detective's mind, even one as incisive as Inspector Harris's, to realize where that leak had come from.

"In your own time," said Inspector Harris bitingly. I realized I'd been standing there, probably gawping, for a good minute.

I made up my mind. I would give Harris something, not least to prevent her arresting me for wasting police time—but not Rowan. Not until I'd spoken to him and given him the chance to explain himself.

"Do you know about the girl who died up at the commune ten years ago?"

I was gratified to see that Harris looked momentarily baffled.

"What? What are you talking about?"

"Ten years ago a girl called Jasmine Pan died at the commune. You must have heard about it at the time."

Inspector Harris gave me the side eye. "I think I do remember. Ten years ago? I would have been serving my apprenticeship in Sheffield, but I remember Nana Maud mentioning it."

"You weren't here?" I asked, slightly surprised. In my mind, Harris *was* the Penton police department.

Harris gave a thin smile. "Ten years ago? I'd only just left university. So no, I was not here."

This slightly brought me up short. I looked at Jane Harris again and realized that, if you looked beyond the permanent frown lines and severe clothing, she wasn't very old. In fact, she was probably about my age (and I am extremely young).

"Don't you think it might have something to do with Mr. Oliver's and Pilkington's deaths?" I pressed on. "Are you looking into it?"

Harris's face closed down.

"Rest assured, we are investigating all lines of inquiry."

So she *hadn't* been looking into it.

"There's something weird going on there," I said, a touch desperately. "First Mr. Oliver, now Pilkington, two founding members of the commune! Don't you think it's worth—"

"With all due respect," cut in Harris, "I think I am considerably better qualified than you when it comes to deciding what is worth investigating."

With all due respect, I disagreed with this statement.

Hen, meanwhile, was looking at me disbelievingly.

"Anything else you want to share, Alice?" she asked pointedly.

"No, no, I don't think so," I said, giving her my best "don't say anything" face. She gave me her best "you're a moron" face. As unspoken conversations go, I think we did fairly well.

Inspector Harris gave her biggest sigh yet—a real guster.

"Then that's everything? You're quite done now, are you? Or are there any other crime scenes you've decided to frequent? Any other evidence you've contrived to contaminate?"

I thought this last one was pretty rich—after all, she only had the evidence thanks to us. Would a thank-you be too much to ask?

There was a crash from the corner. Helen had knocked over a potted plant.

We left.

CHAPTER 54

"YOU CAN'T BRING that animal in here."

I looked down at Helen, who was still disguised as a leopard.

"She's my emotional support animal," I said. And to my horror I realized it was probably true. However, while this might have got her through the door in some of the more woke cafés in London, in Penton it was met with a stony glare.

"Garden's round the back," the pub landlord said with a sniff.

Hen rolled her eyes and went inside to fetch Poppy and Ailsa while I dragged Helen round into a charmingly picturesque beer garden full of delightful flowers that Helen would no doubt dig up and eat.

"How did it go?" asked Poppy eagerly, the minute they appeared.

"Well," said Hen, "Alice lied to Inspector Harris, withheld evidence from the police and will probably go down for perverting the course of justice."

I felt pretty green at that. "Do you really think so?"

Hen sighed. "No, probably not. But honestly, what happened in there?"

And so I explained my irrational thinking, while trying to avoid looking at Poppy, who I knew would be feeling pretty betrayed by my decision. "And I just felt like if we told her about the press pass she would go out and arrest Rowan there and then," I concluded.

"So?" countered Hen, looking exasperated. "He might be guilty. He probably *is* guilty!"

"We don't know that," I argued. "And I don't think he'd get a fair hearing. *We* didn't get a fair hearing, and we were there to provide evidence. We were the good guys."

"I think you did the right thing," declared Ailsa suddenly. "I wouldn't put it past Jane to arrest Rowan. Anyway, if we do find more evidence pointing to him, *then* we can go to Jane. But for now, I think you're right."

"You seriously think your sister would do that?" asked Hen skeptically.

"Oh yes," said Ailsa, a steely glint in her eye.

"What makes you so sure?" pressed Hen.

"Because she was perfectly happy to arrest me, when I wasn't doing anything to warrant it."

Well, that explained a number of things.

Hen gasped. "Your own sister arrested you?"

"Yep. I technically have a criminal record thanks to darling Jane."

"That makes me feel better about my decision not to hand Rowan over to her," I said. "What? It does!" As Ailsa shot me a glare. I probably should have been more sympathetic about her sister's betrayal.

"We all know Harris has no qualms about pointing the finger without a shred of evidence," said Poppy bracingly, not meeting my eye. "And what's done is done—for now. But like Ailsa says, if we do uncover anymore evidence against Rowan . . . Then no excuses, it goes to Inspector Harris. And Ailsa, I'm sorry about your sister . . . that's rough."

Ailsa nodded curtly but looked somewhat mollified. Once again I was slightly jealous of Poppy's ability to actually think before she spoke.

"I got my fingerprints taken," I ventured. "Did they do that when you got arrested?"

OK so it wasn't exactly smooth. I was pretty sure Hen was doing an Inspector Harris–worthy eye roll behind me.

"Yes, they took my fingerprints when I was arrested," said Ailsa in a singsong voice. "Any other questions?" Then she appeared to actually take stock of what I'd just said. "Why did they take your prints?" she asked, sounding more curious than pissed off for once.

"She contaminated the evidence," said Hen bracingly. "They were just exclusion prints so they could discount her grubby little mitts being all over the bottles. She's not in any sort of trouble."

Yet, I thought gloomily. Knowing my luck, my prints would turn up all over Mr. Oliver's face.

"Anyway, the police will be looking into that. Ailsa, I'm really sorry but we might need to ask you to get some info out of your sister. I told her to check Mr. Oliver's mouth for slight burn marks. And who knows, now they've got our evidence they might even get their asses in gear and do the postmortem, or the test on that tea. If they do, we want to know about it."

Ailsa nodded, her face set, like a general receiving marching orders.

"And when she gets the coroner's report for Jasmine's death," added Hen, "if you could let us know what it says, that would be great."

"Wait, what?" I looked at her in confusion. "She didn't say anything about a coroner's report?"

"No, she didn't. But while you were in the loo as we were leaving I told her I'd left the baby's pyridoxine in her office, so I nipped back to get it."

I was impressed—but also sidetracked by a new concern. "What's pyridoxine? And do I need to get some for my baby?"

Hen smirked. "No—it's just a fancy name for vitamin B_6, but it sounded medical enough to freak her out. Anyway, I had a quick rifle through her desk. There wasn't much there—she's a real neat freak, your sister," she added to Ailsa, who nodded with a grim expression. "But she'd scribbled a Post-it to get hold of the coroner's report for Jasmine. Ailsa, we need to know what it says."

Ailsa sighed and nodded.

"This could be huge," I said excitedly. "If the coroner's report says Jasmine was murdered—"

"Oh, come on," cut in Ailsa. "She wasn't *murdered*. I'm pretty sure it would have been a bigger deal in the village if she'd been murdered. And it would have made national news—there would be stuff about it on the internet. You know what people are like."

"OK, so it's unlikely to say she was murdered, but it could be, you know, a *suspicious death*. I bet loads of murders get passed off as suspicious deaths." I wondered again about the article Camran had been burning; there had been a strange turn of phrase that had caught my eye. I opened my mouth to mention it, but Hen cut across me. "So there's the postmortem, the report on the tea and the coroner's report we're waiting on. We should decide on next steps in the meantime."

"I still want to have another look around the commune," said Poppy firmly. "Ailsa, you know them. You can get us in there."

Ailsa looked uncomfortable. "What do you want to do in there? We know the poison didn't come from the commune now."

"I know, but something's still not quite right," replied Poppy. "I want to have a look at what's going on."

"See if there's anymore poison knocking around," I chipped in. Poppy shot me a "you're not helping" look.

"We just want to have a look around. We won't upset anyone, I promise," she said. I wondered if she had her fingers crossed beneath the table; I was already pretty sure that was a promise we wouldn't be keeping.

"I'll . . . think about it," said Ailsa uncertainly. I couldn't blame her for her reluctance. After all, she'd only known us two minutes and we were making some pretty big demands of her. I could see Poppy opening her mouth to argue the point, and was pretty sure it would have the opposite effect.

"So . . ." I broke in. They all turned to me. "We are getting lunch here, right?"

HALFWAY THROUGH lunch I was surprised to realize that I was actually having rather a nice time. The somewhat unusual events of the last fortnight had gone some way to breaking down the usual social barriers, and it felt very natural, sitting around with these women, talking about heartburn and sciatica and murders. And babies. Of the various topics, it was the latter that scared me the most.

"You've just got to keep them clean and fed, right," Poppy was saying, with a worried expression.

"Like a pet," chipped in Ailsa.

I looked down to where I had been sneak-feeding Cheetos to Helen under the table—I'm pretty sure that said a lot about the kind of parent I would be. Had I given her any actual food that morning? Or had her meals that day consisted of a Talk to FRANK card, a potted plant and some cheesy snacks? As for the clean bit, I could see some bits of dried cowpat still stuck in her fur from the previous day. I definitely needed to up my game.

Hen's baby, on the other hand, was wearing an immaculate pale yellow dress with tiny ladybirds all over it and woolly white tights. She looked like she'd been picked straight from the Baby Boden catalog. With a small sigh, the baby detached from Hen's boob and wriggled with satisfaction on her lap, tiny eyes screwed shut, small pink mouth still open as if unsure where the nipple had got to. Hen popped the baby on her shoulder and began patting her expertly on the back.

"So what's the purpose of this?" I asked, gesturing at the baby draped over her.

"Burping," said Hen. "Honestly, were you listening to anything at the class?"

"Excuse me. *You* were causing a bit of a distraction at the time."

"We did this on the first evening, you have no excuse. Anyway, it's in case they swallow any air while feeding. They need to burp it out."

"Gross."

Perfectly on cue, at that moment the baby projectile vomited, neatly clearing the cute elephant-patterned muslin Hen had carefully placed over her shoulder for such an eventuality, and squarely hitting Helen, who was lying on the floor behind us.

Helen gave the baby a look that broadly seemed to say, "We'll say no more about this for now, but should it happen again, you and I will be having words." Then she began to lick it off.

"Oh grim! Oh, make her stop doing that!" squawked Hen. "That is disgusting."

This seemed a little unfair to me—after all, Hen's baby had just thrown up on my dog, and yet somehow Helen was getting the blame. But then some of us are destined to be Hens in life. And some of us are destined to be Helens.

"I'd better get this one home," said Hen, tucking the baby back in its pristine pram. "Nap time."

The baby appeared to do nothing but nap—well, with the odd feed or vomit to mix things up occasionally—but who was I to comment? I was still blissfully clueless at this stage.

"Let us know how you get on with your sister," Hen called to Ailsa over her shoulder as she left.

Ailsa scowled. "I'm not asking Jane about the coroner's report," she said firmly. "I don't mind trying to get a peer at her notes if I get a chance, but she won't tell me anything, so I'm not even trying to talk to her."

I had to say that sounded fair enough. I don't like to be mean about people's families, pot, kettle and all that—but *God*, Jane Harris was a drag.

"How's Lin?" I asked. Poppy had been noticeably quiet throughout lunch; her interest in the baby chat had lacked conviction, although her determination regarding our own investigation had taken on a rather manic edge.

"Oh, you know," she said with a rather bleak smile. "Hanging on in there."

Ailsa cleared her throat slightly awkwardly.

"I, er, made this." She pushed across the table what looked like a brick wrapped in that fancy wax paper Pentonites like. "It's for Lin."

"Ailsa, that's so nice of you," Poppy said, with a slight catch in her voice.

"What is it?" I couldn't help asking.

"A courgette cake," said Ailsa. "The courgettes are from my garden."

"How nice." It was the best I could manage. And, actually, it *was* really nice of Ailsa. I could say that safe in the knowledge I didn't have to eat the thing.

"I just wanted to say, I'm really sorry I told Alice about the voicemail. It wasn't my place. And also, just for the record, I really like Lin. So—yeah, I made her a cake."

It wasn't *quite* the same as saying she didn't think Lin had done it, the cynical part of me noted. But the sentiment was there. Although I felt slightly awkward at being name-checked in all this.

"And about the commune," continued Ailsa. "I'll have a think. I'm sure I can get you guys in there. Just bear with me."

Ailsa departed in a hurry, her embarrassment palpable, leaving behind her a rather glassy-eyed Poppy and a cake you could probably build a house with.

CHAPTER 55

WHEN JOE GOT home that evening I was wearing my glasses, which always makes me feel more serious, and reading the hideously titled *All Joy and No Fun: The Paradox of Modern Parenting*, which Hen had dropped round that afternoon (unasked). She seemed to think I needed to read it.

With a sigh of relief, I carefully placed Hen's fancy silver bookmark on page nine and closed the book.

"Good read?" asked Joe.

"Meh. Plot's a little predictable. Characters are a tad one-dimensional."

I realized belatedly that I should probably have been making dinner, rather than plowing my way through nine whole pages of parenting gold.

"Takeout?"

Joe paused for a second. "Actually, we could go out for dinner? That might be nice."

The hesitancy in his voice made my heart break just a little.

"Sure." I wondered if he could hear the hesitancy in mine.

We drove to our nearest Pizza Hut. Because I wanted pizza, and because one of the joys I have discovered in my thirties is that although you *can* do grown-up things like eat in fancy restaurants and go to art galleries and watch Fellini films, you can also eat ice cream for breakfast and watch Nickelodeon all day and no one can stop you. Then your options are either to take the judgment of your fellow adults on the chin, or lie. I'd always appreciated how Joe and I seemed to be on the same page in this regard.

However, in our current state, the prospect of spending the next few hours together seemed to make us strangely awkward around each other. Like a bad first date. Although I believe first dates seldom include discussion of how you will raise your baby together and almost never touch upon your date's mysterious parentage.

"Are we going to talk about . . . your dad?" I asked eventually through a mouthful of garlic dough balls.

Joe stiffened ever so slightly. "In all honesty? I'd rather not. But if you need to, then we can."

"OK, how about we talk about your mum then?"

That earned me a wry smile.

"Have you spoken to her?" I asked.

He sighed. "Not yet. I don't really want to have to tell her that Pilkington's dead. Just in case he is . . . you know. And I really don't want to have a conversation with her about who else she might have been shagging at the commune thirty years ago."

This seemed fair enough.

"I can't believe she never mentioned any of this to me," I complained; I was more than a little put out. I considered myself pretty close to Laura (or should I say Flora). With my parents living so far away in Spain, and my mum being, well, like my mum, I'd turned to her a lot during my pregnancy. And yet, she had never so much as hinted, even when we moved to Penton. "I spoke to her just last week. She never said anything."

At least one thing made sense now. No wonder she wasn't keen on coming down for a visit. She might bump into Joe's dad. And this made sense of her weird comments on the phone about someone saying something to upset Joe. She had been talking about his dad.

"I wouldn't feel too bad," said Joe. "She's barely mentioned it to me, and it's my dad we're talking about."

"She's going to have to speak to you about it at some point."

Joe shrugged. "Maybe."

This was such a Joe response. I opened my mouth to argue that there wasn't any "maybe" about it, but at that point the pizzas arrived. In a book or a film, the protagonist wouldn't be able to eat because of the fear and worry eating her up inside. Me? I was bloody famished.

"I just don't understand why you didn't tell me you were trying to find your dad," I mumbled through a mouthful of large stuffed crust pizza, washed down with quantities of garlic and herb dip. "We're supposed to be family. We're not supposed to have secrets."

It's just possible I could have phrased that a little more tactfully.

"I think if there's one thing we can agree on," said Joe, "it's that families keep secrets from each other."

Touché.

At least there were no further secrets between Joe and me. I didn't have to worry anymore about what he was up to. It was out in the open now, and it was nothing more sinister than a bit of dad-hunting.

Of course I hadn't been totally honest with him. I would probably never admit to him that there had been a point at which I had wondered if he was involved in the deaths of two of his fatherhood candidates. I had barely articulated the suspicion to myself. And I wasn't ready to irreparably sabotage our relationship, not yet.

CHAPTER 56

I'D OPTED FOR an early night. My head had been spinning with everything we knew and—more crucially—everything we *didn't* know. My stomach was spinning with pizza and baby.

I was barely an hour into an uneasy sleep, however, when my phone pinged, waking me from an anxiety dream in which I had lost the baby in Central London. At the point I jerked awake, I'd finally found him, toddling around Leicester Square wearing a Tesco plastic bag as a bandanna and drinking Special Brew. Lying there in a cold sweat, I congratulated myself upon realizing that it had, in fact, been just a dream. What a relief. Then I realized I had set the bar for parenting incredibly low.

I scrabbled for my phone. It was a message from Ailsa.

> I said I'd get you into the commune.

> Elowen is in labor. Birthing ceremony now.

> See you at the car park in the woods.

> Don't bring Helen.

I HAD to sneak out to avoid waking Joe—I knew he would kick off big time if he caught me sneaking out to the woods at midnight so near my due date. I left him a note and tried not to feel too guilty as a small inner voice whispered that maybe he had a point. Even Helen gave me a suspicious glare as I tried to open the front door as noiselessly as its ancient hinges would allow.

Ailsa and Poppy were waiting for me by the gate to the commune. So, to my surprise, was Hen.

"What are you doing here?"

"Nice to see you too," she replied. "Antoni's working late, so I thought I'd tag along. It's not like I'd be getting any sleep anyway." She cast a look at the baby who, despite Hen's aspersions, was fast asleep in her car seat. Hen picked the seat up and slung it over one arm with difficulty, like an unwieldy grocery basket.

"You can't lug her along in that," said Ailsa.

"Why not?" bristled Hen.

"Because you'll dislocate your arm after five minutes. Why don't you sling her? Look, we can use my scarf."

Ailsa pulled off her enormous batik scarf and started wrapping it round Hen's waist. Hen flinched, but Ailsa snapped at her to stay still, and within a few minutes had fashioned a passable soft sling and was inserting the still sleeping baby into it with surprising gentleness and skill.

"Are you sure about this?" I asked dubiously. The baby was, what, two weeks old, and I'm no expert on these things, but the kid seemed to be spending more time than was normal investigating murders and being dragged round woods in the dead of night. But then what did I know; in my dreams my kid drank Special Brew and wore plastic bags. I was falling somewhat short of the ideal parenting mark—and technically I hadn't even started yet.

"Well, she's not going to be the youngest baby there, is she," said Hen briskly. "Come on, let's go."

We headed off toward my second birth in as many weeks. As we stumbled along the dark tree-lined path, tripping occasionally over erratic roots, I felt a hand slip into mine. It was Poppy's.

"This feels weird, right?" she whispered.

I nodded, forgetting she wouldn't be able to see my face in the dark. We'd been trying to get back into the commune for so long. And now we finally were. We were heading for the place where Jasmine Pan had died nearly ten years earlier. Had she lived, she would have been the same age as we were now. It could have been her child's birth that we were hurrying toward. But that whole future had been cut short. How?

I squeezed Poppy's hand slightly. "It was a long time ago," I said, trying to sound reassuring. "I'm sure the commune is a very different place now. And we're all together. It'll be fine. It'll be more than fine, it'll be wonderful."

But as we hurried through the dark and silent woods, it felt ominous. The contrast felt too stark, heading toward a new birth, but thinking of an old death.

When we reached the commune itself, however, it was blazing with light and activity. People bustled back and forth, in particular congregating around one of the yurts, which was brilliantly lit with hundreds of candles and lanterns all around it. The sound of a gong reverberated from within. That sounded like Sandra's handiwork. There was an energy and excitement in the air that felt infectious. I risked a glance at Poppy, and she gave a half-smile.

"That's the birthing yurt," whispered Ailsa, dragging us toward the building that shone like the Blackpool Illuminations, making the woods behind it an inky pit in comparison. "Let's go."

"I should have known you ladies would turn up." We were halted partway across by Rowan. He was smiling, but it looked strained, and he wouldn't meet my eye. But then again, I was avoiding his, so I couldn't be entirely sure.

"What are you doing here?" Ailsa asked antagonistically. "No men allowed in the birthing hut."

"I'm not going in the birthing hut, wouldn't dream of going where I'm not welcome. I'll be with Dad and the other guys in the woods."

"In the woods?" I was surprised.

"Yep, ladies' night. We're all getting kicked out."

Ailsa sniffed. "Quite right too."

Rowan looked a little hurt. "You'd better get a move on. I think things are moving pretty quickly." And with that, he hurried off.

"Awkward," I whispered to Poppy.

"Just a bit."

"Do you really think he . . ."

". . . shagged his sister? Dunno."

"What are you two whispering about?" asked Ailsa sharply.

"Nothing," I lied. Now probably wasn't the time to bring up her ex-boyfriend's possible incest. It had been bad enough the first time.

Ignoring Ailsa's suspicious glare, I bustled toward the birthing hut, a mixture of eagerness and trepidation swelling inside me (although it was possibly heartburn), unsure what I would find inside.

At the entrance to the yurt we were met by Sandra, who looked flushed and excited. She held out an arm to stop us entering.

"Undo that baby sling," she whispered. "And undo your laces, if any of you have shoelaces. There must be no knots inside the birthing yurt or they could impede the opening up of the vulva."

That was a new one on me.

We hastily kicked off our shoes, and Hen untangled the baby from her makeshift sling. Then we crept inside.

It was dim and warm in the yurt, like crawling into a womb. I wondered if the baby would be able to tell the difference once they were out. Although it was rather busy for a womb. A very pregnant, very sweaty woman was squatting on a low stool in the center. I could tell exactly how pregnant she was because she was entirely naked. It was strangely shocking. I mean, I know I see a naked pregnant woman pretty much every day when I shower, but her belly looked inhumanly large. Perhaps it's just a perspective thing. Two women stood either side of her, clasping her hands, and another twenty or so were gathered around the walls of the yurt. Open flowers were scattered around the birthing stool, no doubt to encourage the uterus to "open like a flower," as hypnobirthing would put it. I hoped we weren't in for another round of positive affirmations—but the vibe seemed a lot quieter and stiller than that, embodying the ancient cave-like calm that the hypnobirthing lady had talked about a lot, but somehow never managed to manifest with her sparkly upbeat T-shirts and chirpy affirmations.

Sandra took up her place next to an enormous gong in the corner, which she began to beat softly, giving off a shimmery sound that was actually very pleasant. The women around the walls began to sway gently. A few were chanting softly—a variation on the one-chant-fits-all that we'd done at the gong bath. What with the flickering candles and the muggy warmth of the yurt, it was extremely soothing. I leaned back against the yurt wall and yawned.

Some time later, I was shaken awake by Poppy.

"It's crowning!"

"What? Who's being crowned? What the—" As wake-ups go it was one of my more confusing ones. A guttural yell from the woman on all fours in the middle of the room brought it all rushing back.

The circle of women contracted around the central scene, blocking our view of the action. I wasn't altogether sad about this—there were scenes from Hen's birth that were burned on my retina like a migraine. And I was very aware that I still had to do all this myself.

There were some muffled groans, a protracted yell and then the squall of a baby.

"Volunteers to gift wrap the placenta," whispered Hen quietly. I tried not to laugh.

CHAPTER 57

EVERYONE SEEMED VERY busy. Doing what, I couldn't say, but there was a general air of "bustle." Ailsa had gone over to congratulate the new mother—and to look at the baby. People like doing this, I've noticed. Personally, after a few seconds I find it creepy. Hen was involved with her own baby, who was feeding. Yes, again.

Poppy sidled over to me.

"The women all look pretty busy, and the men are all out of the commune," she muttered. I gazed at her blankly.

"It's the perfect opportunity to have a poke around," she hissed.

"Now?" I glanced around. "Isn't that, I don't know, bad karma or something?"

"There's no such thing," said Poppy briskly, starting to shepherd me toward the exit.

"What are we even looking for?" I protested weakly.

"They're hiding something here," she replied. "Like what happened to Jasmine, for a start."

I doubted there were going to be any clues lying around relating to a ten-year-old death, but I let Poppy pull me out of the birthing yurt. I still felt I owed her one.

We paused uncertainly. It was a proper, witchy full moon. I imagine this was terribly auspicious for the birth. Or possibly inauspicious. Having spent thirty-odd years with only a hazy awareness of the moon's presence, I didn't feel qualified to decide. Over to our right, the moonlight glinted off metal. The padlock.

"The dispensary's unlocked," I nudged Poppy. "They must have opened it for the birth."

We affected a weird sort of nonchalant creep over to the stone cottage, the door of which stood ajar, the padlock hanging open.

Inside the dispensary was dark and a little bit sinister. Our phone torches shone spotlights directly ahead of us, but cast the surroundings into even deeper darkness. The twin dancing lights picked out a jumbled assortment of images that it took my brain a few moments to jigsaw together.

In the center of the room was a large wooden table, on which sat a number of pestles and mortars in different sizes and variously made of wood, stone and what looked like marble. There were also several chopping boards and enough knives to make me uneasy. The walls were lined with shelves that were crammed with a haphazard assortment of containers. Some looked appropriately apothecary-like, big ceramic jars with waxed stoppers, those old-fashioned glass chemist's jars and woven baskets, but mixed in among these were old plastic ice-cream tubs, stained Tupperware, a jar that still had its Hellmann's Mayonnaise label. The contents of the more transparent containers were visible—roots and mosses and dried flowers. The usual apothecary's wares, which is to say the sorts of things I would tread on during a walk without a second thought.

"We can't search through all this," I muttered to Poppy. "And we wouldn't know what we were looking at anyway."

She nodded, her torch playing across the shelves.

"Wait!" I grabbed her hand and traced her light back along the shelf it had just scanned. A couple of pristine white boxes had caught my eye. I strode over and pulled them off the shelf. They were standard pill packets, the sort you might get from any pharmacy.

I flipped one over. "Camran Pan," I read. "Amias. Eight milligrams, once a day."

I looked at Poppy, who shrugged. "Never heard of it, I'll google."

"This must be what he was collecting at the pharmacy the other day," I mused.

"Here," said Poppy, leaning over to show me her phone screen. "Amias is a brand name for the drug candesartan, which is prescribed for high blood pressure."

"Oh," I said, feeling a little deflated. "So he takes blood pressure meds. So does half the population these days, it's no big deal."

"No," said Poppy thoughtfully. "I'm a bit surprised he hasn't opted for some sort of natural remedy though."

"Perhaps he doesn't have quite the faith in ground-up tree bits that he pretends to have," I said sagely. "When your own health is at stake, I wonder if you don't discover a newfound respect for pharmaceuticals. Given he runs this place, though, he might not want his fellow communites to know."

My mind flashed back to the burning article in the woods. Pieces were slotting into place. Although I couldn't be sure . . .

"It was just on the shelf though," Poppy was saying. "Anyone could see it."

"You saw the padlock," I said absently. "Didn't Mr. Oliver used to be the apothecary? I guess Camran took over when he left; maybe he's the only person with a key to this place?"

"Yeah, I guess . . ."

I slotted the boxes back onto the shelf.

"Well, there's nothing criminal about taking blood pressure meds. Come on."

We stepped back out, glancing around nervously, but there was no one about.

I started to head back toward the birthing yurt, but Poppy grabbed my arm.

"We should check Camran's yurt."

"What? No!"

"This might be our only opportunity."

"Poppy, wait—" But she was already disappearing inside the tent where we had taken tea with Camran and Hazel about fifty million years ago. I groaned and followed her—reluctantly.

"I'll take this side, you take that side," Poppy ordered me, already sifting through the debris scattered across a side table. For a small yurt, there was a lot of clutter. The center of the tent was taken up with a large double bed, overflowing with brightly colored throws and cushions. Yet more cushions made up a small seating area around a low table, which held a samovar and a stack of chipped and mismatched crockery. All round the walls were rickety cabinets and bookcases, filled with trinkets and knick-knacks and dog-eared paperback books.

"What are we looking for?" I asked, tentatively picking up an ornamental spoon and putting it back down again.

"Anything suspicious," came Poppy's voice, slightly muffled, from inside a railing of Hazel's brightly colored clothes. Featuring, no doubt, a lot of hemp.

I sighed and began my search.

It felt wrong, rifling through someone else's possessions. I opened one drawer and found it full of underwear. I closed it again, untouched. I know in detective stories people always find things in the suspect's underwear drawer but there was no way I was pawing through Camran's unmentionables. I still had standards. Of a sort.

Poppy was shaking books on the other side of the tent, in what looked like a pretty professional manner, so I decided to give that a go. The first seven paperbacks yielded nothing. But when I shook out the eighth (*The Complete Works of John Clare*, natch) a folded-up piece of paper fell out.

I bent down to pick it up and froze as a shadow fell over me.

"Anything I can help you with?"

Rowan stood in the doorway.

CHAPTER 58

"WHAT THE HELL do you think you're doing?"

Poppy and I stared at Rowan guiltily. Poppy was holding one of his mum's kaftans, her hand still in its pocket. I wished she would put it down. Rowan looked pretty mad, which seemed understandable.

"I asked you a question," he said, in a slightly more menacing tone. My bad—I'd thought it was rhetorical.

"We were just . . . looking," I said in a small voice. I shoved the scrap of paper into my pocket and straightened up.

"Through my parents' private belongings?"

"We just want to know what happened," Poppy chimed in, finally putting down Hazel's kaftan. "We want to know what happened to Jasmine all those years ago, because it might have something to do with what's happening now. And no one will talk to us, so yeah, we took a look around."

"You have no right," began Rowan, but I snapped.

"Look, I lied to the police for you!" I butted in. "So don't get all high and mighty on me. You owe me."

Rowan looked taken aback.

"What? Why would you lie to the police for me? What about?"

"They found your press pass at Nature's Way," I said. "We know you were there the night Mr. Oliver died. And the police will work it out, too, it's just a matter of time. Your fingerprints are probably all over it."

Rowan paled. "That's not—I didn't—"

I shrugged. I probably should have felt scared. Rowan was in the frame for murder, he was potentially dangerous. But mainly I felt pissed off. I wanted answers out of this boy or I was ringing Inspector Harris the minute we were out of the tent. Assuming we made it out of the tent, that was.

"So before you start having a go at us for being where we shouldn't— want to tell us what you were doing at a murder scene?"

Rowan sat down heavily on his parents' bed. He looked up at us. "I didn't kill him, I swear."

My expression didn't change. His denial meant nothing. I doubted a murderer would feel any compunction when it came to lying about their actions. "So what were you doing there?"

"I just wanted to talk to him. About Jasmine."

"On your first night back here?"

"Not exactly."

After a pause, I pressed him. "Want to expand on that?"

"I wasn't there the day he died . . . I was there the night before."

"But you didn't arrive back until . . ."

"I'd already been back for a week when he died," he said flatly. "I'd been staying in town, trying to get my head together before I went to see Mum and Dad. And I wanted to . . . ask a few questions before coming back here." He pulled a hand down his face. "I was looking into what happened to Jasmine. I was going to write a piece on it for the *Bugle*. You know, investigative journalism."

I tried, and probably failed, to keep the incredulous look from my face. I mean, the *Penton Bugle* wasn't exactly the *Guardian*.

"You were writing a story on her? On your—" I broke off. I genuinely wasn't sure where I'd been intending to finish that sentence. Lover? Sister? And now she was, what, his journalism project?

"Yes. Look, I wasn't entirely straight with you. I kind of knew Jasmine—"

"We know," I interrupted. "We know all about that."

He flushed.

"Ailsa told you?"

"Of course."

"And did she tell you that it just happened once? And that it was the only time I ever even met Jasmine?"

I didn't say anything. We hadn't pressed Ailsa for details. I doubt she'd have given us any.

"It was the night I came home from my first term at uni," went on Rowan—not that we'd asked. "It was the solstice party. Ailsa hadn't come back from Wales; she'd decided to stay there over Christmas, some kind of sit-in protest. I was upset. I met Jasmine at the party—she'd just joined the commune. And she was nice."

I snorted. Rowan had the decency to look a bit ashamed. If he said "one thing led to another" I was going to punch him.

"Then one thing—"

"Yep. Yep. We get the picture," I cut in. "So then what, you shagged her, left, never spoke to her again?"

Rowan closed his eyes briefly.

"I was going to speak to her," he said eventually. "But when I came back the next summer, Dad said . . . she'd died. He wouldn't say what had happened."

"So you ran away," I concluded. "You didn't even ask any questions."

His eyes flew open. "I did!" he protested. "I did! But you've no idea what my dad is like . . ." He trailed off, but my brain filled in the gaps. Of course, he hadn't really wanted to know, not when it involved his commune family, his dad . . .

"But I came back," he said quietly, as if he knew what I was thinking.

Ten years later and after the interested party is dead was the epitome of too little, too late if you asked me.

"Why now?" I asked. "After all this time, what's the point?"

He blushed a little.

"Well, it wasn't exactly about Jasmine. That wasn't why I came back, not in the first place."

I kept watching him, waiting for more.

"I heard about, you know, I heard about . . ." He gestured vaguely.

"Sorry, what?"

"I heard about Ailsa. Having a baby. So . . . I came back."

I opened my mouth to say—I'm not sure what—when the tent flap was pushed open and—oh good. Ailsa entered. Her timing was incredible. I even wondered briefly if she'd been lurking outside the tent, waiting for the most awkward moment to make her entrance.

"Talking about me?" she asked dryly. Rowan looked like he wanted the earth to swallow him. Or possibly Ailsa. Possibly everyone.

"No," he said shortly. For a guy who lied a lot, he was a shit liar.

"I heard my name."

"These two were just showing an unnecessary interest in my personal life," he said shortly. I felt this was a little unfair. We hadn't asked for the details of his shag-and-run, he'd very much volunteered that.

"Oh yeah," said Ailsa. "Were they asking you about shagging your sister?"

Rowan's eyes popped like a cartoon character's. "What the fuck now?"

Next to me, Poppy put her hands over her face. God, this was a farce.

"Yeah, they think you shagged your sister," continued Ailsa. "They're about to start the birthing breakfast outside, you guys coming?"

"Wait, wait, wait." Rowan held both hands up. "I don't even *have* a sister!" He looked around at us.

Ailsa gave her trademark shrug. "I don't care. It's none of my business who you shag."

Ouch.

"Likewise," Rowan retorted with a meaningful look at Ailsa's bump. OK, so that was below the belt. Well, literally above the belt, but metaphorically . . . Anyway, Ailsa looked murderous. Although that was not a term to be bandying about these days.

"OK," Poppy stepped in. "Rowan, calm down."

"I will not calm—"

"You've got a bloody nerve," Ailsa cut over him coldly.

"Maybe we should just get breakfast," I suggested. Three pairs of eyes turned on me with incredulity.

"Just a thought," I backed down.

"So does anyone want to tell me where these batshit accusations are coming from?" asked Rowan, his lips tight, his eyes furious.

"They think Jasmine was your sister," said Ailsa in an almost bored tone. I didn't know whether I wanted to hug her or punch her. On the one hand, what the fuck was she doing? On the other hand, these were the exact questions I wanted to ask and was too cowardly and/or prudent to ask.

Rowan turned to look at me. "Seriously? Why? Why would you think that?"

"You have the same surname, and it's not exactly a common one," I said.

Rowan looked confused. "What? What was her surname?"

"Pan," I said. "Same as your dad. And, I presume, you."

Rowan's face cleared slightly. "Right. And the same as half the commune, probably."

It was my turn to look confused. "What?"

Rowan actually laughed, although there wasn't much humor in it, and it sounded more like a bark. "Pan isn't a surname. Or I suppose it is, of a sort . . . We don't use surnames at the commune, but some people take on the name Pan when they join. It's a way of becoming part of the commune family, part of nature's family. It's after the old god Pan."

He looked at me, a condescending sort of amusement on his face. "And you thought it meant we were related?"

Some embarrassments are pink and fluffy and crawl across your face. This embarrassment was red and hot and flooded my whole body. I'd been wrong. I'd been *so* wrong.

"So . . . she definitely wasn't your sister?" I asked, slightly desperately. "Like, a long-lost sister you might not have known about?"

"No! She had her own family—her mum and her dad lived like two villages away. And a brother or a sister, I think, maybe both. She definitely wasn't my dad's daughter, and she definitely wasn't my sister."

"Huh."

There was silence for a bit. I couldn't look at Poppy and Ailsa. What a monumental cock-up.

"I'm sorry," I mumbled eventually, risking a glance at Rowan. The fury had gone from his face, to be replaced with a hurt expression that was potentially worse.

"Whatever," he muttered, and he turned and left the tent.

"Well," said Ailsa. "That's cleared that up then. Now—breakfast?"

"I FEEL like such a tit," I moaned as we stepped out into the pre-dawn light.

"I'll bet," said Ailsa unsympathetically.

"It was an honest mistake," said Poppy kindly. "And to be fair, we all went along with it."

"I didn't," pointed out Ailsa.

"Why didn't you say something?" I asked Ailsa, rounding on her. "You must've known about the surname thing!"

"I don't think you actually told me that was what was behind your theory," she said thoughtfully, seeming supremely unbothered by the morning's dramatic events. "Or yeah, I'd have put you straight. And for the record, I did tell you that you were way off the mark with this one."

With a flush of irritation, I realized she might actually be right. Yet I couldn't help feeling a slight lingering resentment. It seemed to me that even if Ailsa had never outright lied to us, she hadn't been exactly helpful.

"So what *were* you doing in Camran's yurt?" she asked.

"Looking," I said tersely.

"Find anything?"

My hand curled around the piece of paper in my pocket.

"Nope."

People were streaming out of the birthing yurt now, heading for two long tables that had been set up outside. Hen was waving to us from one of the tables, where she'd saved a couple of spaces.

"I'm going home," I said morosely.

"Look," said Ailsa, "Rowan will get over it. Sure he's pissed off right now, but that's just Rowan for you. Anyway, if he'd been straight with us from the start, we wouldn't have had to poke around like this and make wild guesses."

I had a feeling this was Ailsa trying to be nice. I wasn't sure I was in the mood for it though.

"Stay," she said. "Have some breakfast. We need to fill Hen in. We need to talk about what we do next. And we need food—it's been a long night."

She was definitely right about the food. And her offer to discuss next steps sounded suspiciously like an olive branch. I wasn't sure about "nice Ailsa" though, it was disconcerting.

Poppy's arm slipped through mine. "Stay for just one vegan omelette?" she asked. I half smiled.

I looked around. The sun was just beginning to show its face. Maybe Penton was rubbing off on me, but I had to say the commune was looking really quite magical. The air had that wonderful fresh morning taste, and the just rising sun was sending those shafts of light streaking across the sky that always make me think of that scene at the beginning of *The Lion King*. Perhaps we should hold the new baby up to the sky to a rousing chorus of "The Circle of Life." To my alarm, I realized that if I started belting out a few lines, everyone would probably join in. Unironically. Guaranteed a few people would sing with their eyes closed.

"Fine," I said to Poppy. "For a bit."

"I THINK I might have a naming ceremony for her," announced Hen on our way back to the cars. "Maybe even up at the commune." The baby was staring up at the trees overhead, seemingly entranced.

"Oh!" said Poppy. "You've picked a name?"

"Well, no," admitted Hen. "But when we do, I think we should have a naming ceremony."

"How long are you planning on waiting?" I asked. "Until she can choose her own name?"

"We'll wait as long as it takes," said Hen in a dignified tone.

Hen had taken the news about Jasmine in her stride. She seemed really quite buoyed up by spending a night in a tent watching a naked woman give birth. For someone who was essentially the polar opposite of the commune, she seemed pretty at home there.

Me, on the other hand? I felt like a half-melted jelly baby. I was going to go home. I was going to drag my duvet down to the sofa. I was going to watch minimum five episodes of *Queer Eye* and I wasn't going to think about any murders or deep dark Penton mysteries. I was *done*.

As I pulled my car keys out of my pocket, the folded-up piece of paper fluttered to the ground. I picked it up and unfolded it absent-mindedly as I slid awkwardly into the driving seat. I'd probably stolen an ancient shopping list, or something equally incriminating.

It wasn't a shopping list. It was a letter. A very short one, dated 19 May 1989.

> *Camran,*
> *I wanted to let you know that your son is earthside. His name is*
> *Joe, and he's perfect.*
> *Love, Flora xx*

Oh for fuck's sake.

CHAPTER 59

IT WOULD BE nice to get through one day without a birth, a murder or the arrival of a long-lost family member. Of late, some days appeared to contain all three.

I probably should have felt more. I'm not sure more of what, but just *more*. It was a pretty big deal—confirmation of the identity of Joe's dad. But mainly, I just felt relieved. For a start, this meant that Joe's dad was still alive—a pretty major bonus. I just really hoped that it wasn't because he'd killed the other two candidates.

By the time I got home the sun was well up. The couple of hours' sleep I'd sneaked in the birthing tent had well and truly worn off. I hoped that Joe would still be asleep and I could put off the next hideous conversation.

Ha. I'd be lucky. Joe was awake and up, and boy was he pissed off. He was making eggs in his special "I'm really annoyed" way, which involved a lot of clattering of utensils and bits of eggshell going supernova.

"Do you have any idea how worried I've been?" he began before I'd even got my shoes off. "Oh my God, you're making me sound like my mum." He threw his hands in the air in a dramatic gesture that was even more like his mum.

I stared at him.

Your dad is Camran Pan. A hippy who may or may not have killed two men.

There had to be a better way to tell him.

"Sneaking off to the commune in the middle of the night?! When you're about to give birth any minute now! What were you thinking?" Two more eggs—*crack! Crack!*

Your dad is Camran Pan. Your dad is Camran Pan.

"Hello? Al? Is there anyone in there?" Joe waved his spatula in front of my face.

"I, um, I actually need to talk to you about the commune."

"What you need to do is sit down. I'm making you eggs. And then you're going to sleep—you look absolutely done in."

"I know who your dad is."

The egg pan smacked onto the hob. Joe didn't turn around. He didn't say anything.

I took a deep breath. "I found a letter up at the commune."

JOE SAT holding the letter. The eggs had long since congealed in the pan. I was trying really hard not to mention them—it felt like the wrong moment. But the smell seemed to encircle the whole kitchen. My stomach turned.

"Shall we move into the sitting room?"

Joe didn't move.

"The hippy guy up at the commune is my dad."

"Yeah, looks like." I really wished there was something more helpful I could say.

"You're sure?"

"The letter seems pretty clear," I said. "And that is your mum's handwriting. Also, you look kinda like Rowan. The nose, especially. I can't believe I didn't see it before."

"Great. I have Rowan's nose. Now who the fuck is Rowan?"

"Er. Your brother."

"*My brother?*"

"Yeah, he's nice. Well, actually, he's a liar and a cheat, but I kind of like him anyway." This much was true. And at least it looked like he wasn't a murderer. Unless he was lying about that too, of course.

"You met him, actually, he was at the pub the other night."

Joe stared at me. "Curly-top? He doesn't look anything like me."

I refrained from comment. This was happening to me a lot recently. I felt it showed unprecedented levels of personal growth and tactfulness. I should get a small trophy.

"So let me get this straight. You know my . . . brother?" He stumbled slightly over the last word.

"A bit," I said awkwardly. "But he's not really talking to me right now because I kind of accused him of having sex with his sister."

"His sister? His *sister*? *My* sister? Do I have a sister?"

"Oh wait, no. Sorry. She's not your sister, or his, as it turns out." I paused and took in Joe's horrified face. "I'm not doing a very good job of this, am I?"

I tried to fill him in on my toe-curling mistake about Jasmine. In hindsight, it was probably too much for him to deal with at that particular moment. By the end he was looking slightly wild-eyed.

"So in conclusion . . . I don't have a sister who died mysteriously ten years ago?"

"No."

"And my brother hasn't slept with the sister we don't have?"

"No. Wait, yes. Hang on . . ."

"But I do have a dad who worships the moon and a brother named after a tree."

"Er . . . yeah."

CHAPTER 60

JOE HAD GONE for a walk with Helen. He said he needed to get his head together. I was prepared to accept that my explanation of the situation had been lacking in finesse. As dramatic as the morning's revelations had been, my concentration hadn't been a hundred percent on the matter in hand: there were still a minimum of two unsolved murders, and I felt sure that I now had all the necessary information to unpick the deaths of Jasmine, Mr. Oliver and Ronald Pilkington. The problem was, I was going to fall asleep, I could feel it . . . Pregnancy had turned me into an insomniac narcoleptic, and to be quite frank, a murder case didn't stand a chance against an ill-timed midmorning snooze . . .

My head whirled with images; Joe and Camran and Rowan held hands and danced around Jasmine's tree, while Sandra rang a host of gongs hanging from its branches; tiny bottles labeled "drink me" rained from the sky; Helen and Ronnie walked solemnly through the prancing figures, wearing Druid robes . . .

There are worse ways to be woken up than a phone call from Inspector Harris, but I'm struggling to think of one right now.

She was halfway through barking a load of information at me before I'd got my brain in gear. But having the murder investigation thrust into the forefront of my still waking brain had a similar effect to mainlining three espressos.

The gist of Harris's call seemed to be confirmation that Mr. Oliver had indeed been poisoned with wintergreen oil. But this was playing second fiddle to her need to inform me that my prints were found all over the bottles of oil and had completely obscured and destroyed any useful evidence that might have otherwise been on them.

When Harris paused to draw breath from outlining the cretinous depths of my idiocy, I broke in—after all, it didn't seem like I had anything to lose. "Did you see the coroner's report for Jasmine?"

There was a pause. Then, "And how would you know about that?"

"A hunch. What did it say?"

"Once again, I'm only telling you this to stop you running round asking inappropriate and potentially damaging questions."

I held my breath.

"She died of natural causes. Absolutely no question about it."

Well, that blew every single one of our little theories out of the water. Except, of course, it also made perfect sense.

WHEN HARRIS had rung off, I flopped back onto the bed. My head was too full. I had a feeling that all the pieces of the mystery had come together while I was sleeping; it was just still ever so slightly out of focus somehow.

I glanced down at my phone again. What the—Twenty-three texts from Hen?

The baby shower.

The goddam baby shower.

The party to meet the baby with no name whom I had already met like ten times. Christ, I'd seen her *born*, it was a bit late for a handshake and a formal introduction.

Hen's messages were increasingly irate. It appeared Poppy had been supposed to help set up for the shower, but had pulled out at the last minute. Which meant there were napkins to be folded, salads to be dressed, balloons to be inflated.

The murders would, apparently, have to wait.

Ping! Twenty-four.

> Alice, I wouldn't ask you unless I were desperate!

That could be read in a less than flattering way. But who was I to turn down a distress call from a fellow mother in need?

I'm on my way!

As I left the house, adrenaline pumping, ready to prep the shit out of this baby shower, my phone pinged one last time.

Don't bring Helen.

When I pulled up at Hen's, I was still feeling wired, but not in a good way.

There were a lot of balloons tied to the gate. Mainly pink. I prodded them, making them dance.

Everything looked pretty ready to me. Clearly there was nothing I could do to improve on the already perfect scene. The back garden was of course idyllic, and two laden tables were already heaped with Instagram-perfect salads, breads and dips. There was a whole side table for drinks—alcoholic and soft—and even glass-bottled sparkling water, which I do consider to be the height of sophistication.

Hen, however, answered the door looking just a little bit less pristine than normal. Sure, she still looked more put-together than I do on a good day, but she was definitely a little blurred around the edges.

"Thanks for coming over."

"I'm kinda flattered you asked me," I said truthfully.

"Well, Poppy bailed on me—I think Lin had a rough day yesterday—Ailsa is at a scan this morning, even Dot couldn't make it—knitting circle. So I had to call you, there wasn't anyone else."

"Sort of like a last resort, you mean?"

"Exactly like that."

I shrugged. I wouldn't be my first choice to help set up a baby shower either.

"Where's Antoni?"

"Out."

"Out where?"

"Just out."

"Oh, OK."

There was a slightly awkward pause. "So what are we doing?" I awaited my instructions.

"I'll deal with the mini quiches, you get the extra champagne flutes. They're in the spare room upstairs. They'll need a rinse and polish."

I made my way upstairs, wondering ominously what Hen was intending to do with the mini quiches. The upstairs hall was tastefully decorated in pale gray and had not one but *two* vases of fresh flowers. In a *hallway*. I was also confronted with more doors than one house should decently possess. The first room I peered into was the nursery. It was beautifully decorated in pale yellow and cream. A crocheted blanket was stylishly draped across the bars of the very trendy Scandinavian-style crib. Gold star wall stickers had been painstakingly plastered in an artful spray up the wall and across the ceiling. On the shelf above the cot sat a Montessori rainbow, its inverted smile beaming out over the room. An adorable fox-shaped book cart was already fully stocked with a number of no doubt highly educational and improving baby books, like *Baby's First Shakespeare* and *Calculus for the Under-Ones*.

I'm only mocking because clearly I was extremely jealous. It was the nursery of dreams.

Unfortunately for me, however, it did not contain the "extra" champagne flutes. I moved on to the next door.

This room had Hen written all over it.

The bed was neatly made. There were no clothes anywhere on the floor. There were flowers in a vase. In short, it wasn't my idea of a bedroom. On the bedside table there was a stack of parenting books, all of them bristling with colored Post-it notes. There were *three* laundry baskets, handily labeled "WHITES," "COLORS," "DELICATES" (this blew my mind). I had already mentally awarded Hen the trophy for "World's Most Adult Adult," and this was just confirmation.

There was no sign of Antoni's presence in the room. I wondered if they were at the separate rooms stage. No judgment on my part—Joe and I would a hundred percent have been in separate rooms if we could've afforded a house which actually had another room.

The third door I tried confirmed this. It was clearly Antoni's room. I am confident of this because yes, I did open the wardrobe and it was full of suits. Like, more suits than any one guy needs, surely. I think I speak for womankind when I say all men's suits look the same.

I'm not entirely sure what I was looking for in Antoni's wardrobe. It just struck me that, since I was there, I might as well have a quick peek, and if I were to stumble across evidence of his affair—say a rumpled Costa uniform in the corner—then I would have no choice but to tell Hen. There was nothing. Not so much as a discarded sock.

Relieved, I closed the wardrobe door and turned to leave. And that was when I saw it.

On the bookshelf there were two photos. One of Antoni in a suit with Hen looking outrageously stunning in a very dramatic wedding dress. And the other showed Antoni and—was that the Costa waitress with him? I snatched up the photo. Yes, there was Antoni, looking significantly younger, and beside him was the Costa waitress. But it was the other figure in the photograph that caught my attention.

Because that? That changed everything.

CHAPTER 61

"ALICE! WHAT ARE you doing up there? Get down here, the guests will be arriving soon and we haven't even sliced the fruit for the Pimm's!"

Hen's voice echoed up the stairs. I was still standing there in Antoni's room. Still holding the photo. The facts dropping into place, slotting together like little cubes of ice in my mind. Cold and clear and horribly transparent.

"Alice? Alice? Can you bring the napkins down with you as well? They're on the bed in the spare room. The ones with the fern pattern, not the floral ones!"

I couldn't respond.

I heard Hen bustling around downstairs. With shaking fingers, I took the photo out of the frame and shoved it in my pocket, barely registering the few lines scrawled on the back. Then I went downstairs—pausing to pick up the napkins from the spare room. The fern ones, not the floral ones. I deposited them on the kitchen side. Then I walked straight out of Hen's door and out to my car, Hen's frustrated shout echoing after me.

I had to go to Costa. And God knows I needed something stronger than a coffee right now.

IN JUST under an hour, I was pulling up at Hen's again. I scanned the faces in the garden as I walked through in a daze. There were a number of women with that posh girl hair that makes them all look identical. They were accompanied by variations on Antoni—men who looked as though, even if they weren't wearing suits right now, had formal dress practically tattooed into their skin. When they were older they would almost certainly wear colored chinos. I saw Joe peering nervously over the garden gate, wearing his ratty old Ramones T-shirt, and felt a surge of affection for him.

The one person there was no sign of was Antoni himself.

Panic was starting to build up inside me, like a shaken bottle of Coke. I made a beeline for Joe.

"What's happened?" he asked immediately upon seeing my face, his voice sharp with worry.

"What's going on?" Poppy and Lin appeared on my other side, with Ailsa in tow.

I told them.

There was silence. Lin closed her eyes and looked as if she might pass out.

Eventually, it was broken by Ailsa. "But what are we going to do?" she asked, and there was an edge of panic to her voice that I had never heard before.

"I think . . . I think we need to call your sister," I said in a small voice. "We need to tell her what we know."

"But poor Hen," whispered Ailsa. "We can't do this to her."

At that point Hen came over.

"Alice! What on earth happened to you earlier? That was completely unacceptable! Can you put the napkins on the table by the salads? And we need more—" She broke off. "What's got into you guys?" she asked, switching the baby to her other hip and glaring at us suspiciously.

"Where's Antoni?" asked Poppy, sounding worried.

"And don't say he's in London," I added urgently.

A frown made a crease line between Hen's eyebrows.

"Of course he's not in London. He wouldn't miss the baby shower! He actually went up to Stricker's Wood, which is weird, because I didn't think he knew the woods existed. He should be back any minute, though. He promised he'd be back in time to start up the barbecue and he's already late."

We all stared.

"Stricker's Wood?" I said in a strangled voice.

"Did he say anything before he left?" asked Poppy.

"No. Yes. I can't remember . . ."

"You have to remember!" Perhaps the urgency in my voice triggered something in Hen.

"He said . . . he said something about making a mistake. He had to go and sort something out. I don't know, I was distracted, I still had to make the potato salad and the decking was—"

"He made a mistake," I cut across her hollowly. I was horribly sure I knew what that meant.

"Sort something out," echoed Poppy.

In a detective program we'd probably have broken into a purposeful sprint. But we were a bunch of overly nosy pregnant women who didn't really know what to do.

"Camran . . ." I said, looking meaningfully at Poppy.

She'd gone pale. "You don't think he'd . . . ?"

"I think that's what he meant to do last time . . ."

"But he made a mistake . . ."

"What do we do?"

"We need to get up there now!"

There was a confused thirty seconds of bustling while Lin and Joe tried to protest, and Poppy and I flapped around, and Hen asked in an increasingly strident tone, "What the hell is going on?"

I didn't want to answer that question, even if I could have, so I pretended I couldn't hear it.

As I headed for my car, dragging Joe after me, I heard Ailsa saying to Hen, "Come in my car, I'll explain on the way," then as Hen protested I heard, "I've already got the car seat installed. Yes of course it's an Isofix base. What kind of mother do you take me for?" And then, as I wrestled with the car keys, I heard her on her phone. "Jane? I think you need to get up to Stricker's Wood now . . ."

Again, in a detective drama, at this point there would be a cut scene, immediately transporting us up to the woods and the big showdown. Whereas in reality we had to endure an agonizing fifteen-minute drive up to the woods, including interminable waits at red lights and a frustrating three minutes when Joe wouldn't overtake a cyclist "until it was safe to do so."

"This is your *dad* we're going to rescue!" I kept saying.

"He's not my dad, he's my unconfirmed potential biological father," Joe would reply each time, in an annoyingly calm voice. "And let's not jump to conclusions. I know what you think Antoni did, but we have no reason to believe he has any intention of hurting Camran."

Nonetheless, I saw his hands tighten on the steering wheel, and he finally overtook the cyclist. He was also glancing in the rearview mirror constantly.

"Ailsa's car is behind us, isn't it?" I said in a tight voice.

"Mm-hmm," he said.

I risked a glance. Ailsa appeared to be talking, her face a mixture of anxiety and desperation. Hen sat, staring forward, her face giving nothing away.

WE WERE halfway down the path to the commune when we heard the commotion up ahead. I tried to find some extra gears but my cumbersome body was really letting me down. The noise was coming from one of the yurts. Camran and Hazel's yurt. As we approached it, a figure in a somewhat rumpled suit burst out of one of the yurts, dragging another figure whom he appeared to have in a headlock.

"You're all mad, the lot of you," Antoni shouted. "Madmen and criminals. You should all be locked up."

The figure under his arm was Camran. He was purple in the face and seemed to be struggling to breathe. Rowan came running out of the yurt after them, and Hazel's terrified face peered around the tent flap.

"Antoni, let him go, we can talk about this," Rowan tried, holding his hands out placatingly. "I know you're angry but—"

"You don't know anything," Antoni roared. "Where were you when she needed you? Running around, chasing some other girl! You're just as bad as the rest of them!"

Rowan paled, and Antoni turned and began to drag Camran toward the gate again. He snarled when he saw Poppy, myself, Joe and Lin standing at the path entrance. "Get out of my way. This is nothing to do with—" He pulled up short.

"Hen? What are you doing here?"

Hen had appeared on the path behind us, clutching her baby to her, Ailsa hovering protectively by her shoulder.

"Antoni, what's going on?" she asked in a small voice, quite unlike her usual tone.

He seemed to shrink inside his suit. His grip loosened and Camran dropped to the ground. He gave a great heaving breath and began to scrabble away from Antoni, clawing through the dirt, his breath still rasping.

Rowan was beside his father in an instant, helping him to his feet.

I heard a small noise next to me, something between a gasp and a choke. Joe was staring at them, and now they were in the same place, the family resemblance was unmistakable. Through something of a haze I registered that this probably wasn't the ideal circumstances for his first face-to-face meeting with his biological father.

Camran was on his feet now, leaning heavily on Rowan.

"What's—" His voice came out as a croak. He coughed and tried again. "What's going on? Why—" He broke off when he saw who was standing next to me. His eyes flickered from Joe to Rowan and back again. An unreadable expression came over his face.

"Do I . . ." he whispered hoarsely. "Do I know you?"

Joe nodded, but didn't say anything.

Camran raised his hands, then they dropped to his sides again. He looked suddenly very helpless.

My head whipped back and forth like I was at a tennis match.

"I—" began Camran—and I wonder what he would have said. Would he have gone all Darth Vader, "I am your father," or would a simple "I'm sorry" have slipped out? But Joe cut him off.

"Now's not the time," he said tersely, and he turned back to the scene unfolding behind us.

"I don't understand," Hen was whispering, her eyes fixed on Antoni. "Ailsa said you . . . Antoni, what have you *done*?"

He didn't say anything, but spun on the spot, staring wildly around at the circle of people surrounding him, like a trapped animal.

Eventually, Poppy spoke up. Someone had to. "She was your sister, wasn't she? Jasmine?"

"That wasn't her name!" he snarled.

Another piece clicked into place.

"It was you, wasn't it? Erasing her name on the plaque at the tree."

"Nathalie." He almost howled it. "Her name was Nathalie Connell. Jasmine Pan was some stupid new name she took when she joined this . . . this *cult*, run by that *madman*."

I felt Joe flinch, next to me.

"What happened to her, Antoni?" Poppy asked, her voice level and calm.

Antoni's face screwed up. He looked incapable of speech.

"She got sick, didn't she," I said quietly. "I spoke to her friend in Bridgeport this morning. Sarah. The one you visited the other night. She told me you'd been in quite a state when you spoke to her. That you kept saying they'd murdered Jas—sorry, Nathalie. That's what you needed to think, wasn't it? After what you'd done."

"It was cancer," he said at last. "Nathalie was diagnosed with breast cancer when she was twenty-three. But it was operable. It was treatable. If she'd had the right medicine. Chemo, radio, the right drugs. But no, she said they could treat it up at the commune. That ridiculous apothecary had the right elixirs, she said. It was Crispin Oliver thinks this and Crispin Oliver says that. He brainwashed her with his lies and his witchery. She was just a scared child, and he took advantage of that to play out his sick experiments. He was going to treat it 'nature's way.' There was no force more powerful than nature." He spat on the ground. "Well, look how that worked out. Six months later and she was dead. Poisoned, by their crackpot ideas. It was criminal. *That* was murder. They murdered her. What I did was justice."

"When you poisoned Mr. Oliver?" I asked quietly.

Antoni's face twitched. "I didn't mean to," he said, so quietly I could barely hear him. "I didn't mean to kill him."

Hen's face was a mask of horror.

"What happened?" I pressed.

Antoni closed his eyes. He looked exhausted. Haggard.

"I knew he ran that shop. Even the name of it was an insult to her memory . . ." He took a deep breath. "I'd been keeping an eye on him for a while. But I wasn't planning on doing anything. I honestly wasn't. But then Hen went into labor and it was too soon! And I was scared for the baby—and for her. And when she said Mr. Oliver had given her some herbs or something, some oil, that might have induced labor, I just saw red. He was still at it. He was still messing around with these things, with people's lives, even after what had happened to my sister. I had to get some air. And as I was going outside I saw his tea on the desk, and all those little bottles. And I swear I didn't know it would kill him, but I tipped a couple of bottles into his tea. I just wanted to make him sick . . . I wanted him to suffer like he made my sister suffer . . ."

There was silence across the commune.

Hen stood frozen, completely gray-faced. She clutched the baby even tighter to her, until she began to squawk in protest. Ailsa stepped forward and took the baby from Hen, who continued to stand there. Staring. Silent. Her empty arms dropping to her sides.

"Why didn't you tell me?" she whispered, her eyes never leaving Antoni.

He ran a hand down his face. "I wanted to, Hen. I can't tell you how much I wanted to. But I couldn't. My parents never even mentioned her after the funeral. Everything fell apart. It was easier just to . . . pretend none of it had ever happened. But then coming back here. Seeing that man . . . still peddling his—his *poisons*."

And then Hen turned to where Poppy and I stood.

"How did you know?"

It was the question I had hoped she wouldn't ask.

I cleared my throat. "I caught a glimpse of the article they wrote when she died. It was just a glimpse. I saw something about 'unconventional treatment,' but I didn't think anything of it at the time, and I suppose it could have meant several things. Then I saw a picture in Antoni's room. Her graduation photo—Nathalie, with her best friend Sarah, and her brother." I barreled on before she could point out the obvious—that this meant I had been snooping around her house. When I was supposed to be there as a friend. Supporting her. "I recognized Nathalie from the photo in the paper when she died. I suppose it would only have been a couple of years later . . ."

Hen had tears in her eyes. "And Pilkington?"

"Ronald Pilkington was a mistake, wasn't he?" I said quietly to Antoni. A desperate look flared in his eyes.

"I thought he was . . . I thought . . ."

"You thought he was Camran." I completed the sentence for him. Antoni nodded. "I suppose you thought Camran was almost as responsible for Nathalie's death—he was supposed to be in charge up here, after all," I continued, feeling horribly ruthless—but it had to be said. It all had to come out now. "So he had to die too."

"You overheard Camran and Pilkington arguing in the woods." Poppy picked up the thread. "You heard Pilkington shouting that it was his commune, and you thought he was Camran. So you followed him and pushed him into the quarry."

Antoni closed his eyes and nodded. "I didn't realize until Hen told me the next day. I didn't know . . ."

"And then you realized the job wasn't finished."

Antoni looked down and didn't speak. He looked broken. As did Hen.

I turned to where Camran stood with Rowan and Hazel, huddled against the side of their yurt.

"That's what you fell out about, wasn't it? You and Mr. Oliver? It was over how he'd treated Nathalie."

Camran nodded curtly. "It should never have happened," he said quietly, one hand rubbing his throat. "Jasmine—or, sorry, Nathalie—was too young. She didn't understand the decisions she was making. And Crispin should have realized that. But he was too wrapped up in what he was doing, in his alternative medicines. He really thought he could cure her, I'm sure of that. But when it became clear that his treatment wasn't working . . . We begged her to seek medical advice in other quarters, but she was adamant Crispin knew what he was doing. Then, of course, it was too late . . ."

"It broke the heart of the commune," said Hazel quietly.

"No," said Antoni, loudly and harshly. "It broke the hearts of my family. And it was all your fault."

"You're right, it was all of our faults. But Crispin's most of all. And he would never see that. He moved into town and began his shop. I would never set foot there; I couldn't believe he was still . . . So we stayed away. Like cowards. And Crispin turned bitter toward all of us, thought we'd blamed him unfairly . . . He never could see that he'd played a part in her death."

"Have the decency to call it what it was," spat Antoni. "He murdered her. And you were all complicit."

Camran hung his head. "I'm so sorry," he whispered.

The stretching silence was broken by the chink of the gate, as Inspector Harris let herself into the commune, accompanied by a uniformed constable.

It was all over.

Except, of course, that it wasn't. Because as Antoni was led away, handcuffed, head low, shuffling steps, the credits didn't roll. We were all still standing there. And Hen. There stood Hen. Tears pouring silently down her cheeks. And there, nestled in Ailsa's arms, was the baby, wide-eyed and unaware. In so many ways, it was just the beginning.

ONE MONTH LATER

STRICKER'S WOOD HAD been washed with an early-morning April shower, making the spring growth glow even brighter. The sun was barely up, filtering through the trees, painting weak shadows across the ground and glinting off the rain-speckled leaves.

I met Poppy and Lin by the gate leading down to the commune. Lin had baby Noah in a sling. Jack, too, was in his sling, nuzzled sleepily against my chest. It had been two weeks now, and I could barely remember a time when he wasn't attached to me like this. Helen stuck close to my legs. Ever since Jack's arrival she had been glued to the pair of us, like an overbearing, furry mother-in-law—competing, in fact, with my actual mother-in-law, who had arrived for a visit a few days after Jack was born and was yet to leave. Even Maya had been lured back to Penton by the arrival of her godson, whom she was besotted with—much to my surprise, and even more to her own.

Poppy looked tired but happy. I imagine I looked the same. The events of the previous month had taken their toll on Lin, and her usual energy was still subdued. But she smiled and stepped forward to hug me, trying to navigate the babies strapped to our fronts.

"Hey, Alice, it's good to see you."

It was good to see her, too. I would never tell her that there had been times I had wondered about her involvement in everything that had taken place. Because I had. But in the intervening month, she had grown from a new acquaintance to a valued friend.

Talking of which . . . "No Ailsa?" I asked.

"She's already there with Hen."

Ailsa had been spending a lot of time with Hen recently. Understandably, after the events of the baby shower, Hen hadn't wanted to see either Poppy or me for a while. In fact, we hadn't seen her since that awful afternoon. Not to mention that both Poppy and I had been rather busy in the interim. When I'd got Hen's text inviting me today I'd been pleased, but more than a little apprehensive.

When I had told Hen I would certainly be coming, her follow-up text had made me smile. Just two words:

Bring Helen.

"Nervous?" asked Poppy, apparently reading my mind.

"A touch," I admitted.

"No Joe?"

"Not today. He's kind of avoiding the commune. Him and Camran are still . . . working things out. And he said today wasn't about him, or Camran. Best to leave the day to Hen."

"Things are going well with him and Rowan, though?"

"Yeah, they've been to the pub a couple of times. I think there could be a good thing there." I smiled slightly. "It's weird for him, suddenly gaining a thirty-year-old brother . . . But good weird, I think."

Poppy smiled. "No more family secrets."

"Well, I don't know about that," I admitted. "We've agreed never to tell Rowan we thought he might have been a murderer."

"Noted."

"But today isn't about their family, whatever the hell that may be, so Joe thought he'd sit it out. He's excited to find out what the name is, though."

Hen's baby was six weeks old now and today, finally, she was having her long-awaited naming ceremony.

THE COMMUNE was looking beautiful in the early-morning light. Calm and still. We passed through the almost deserted cluster of yurts, heading for the small knot of people gathered around the young silver birch tree that stood just outside the main commune. Hundreds of brightly colored ribbons had been tied to its slender branches. It looked festive and vibrant and alive. Jasmine's tree. Or possibly Nathalie's. It was the perfect place for the naming ceremony.

In front of the tree stood Hen, holding her baby close to her chest. In the month since I'd last seen them, the baby seemed to have doubled in size. She made Jack look like a doll. Hen, on the other hand, seemed to have shrunk. Her clothes hung off her already tiny frame, and her face looked drawn. But she was smiling. A small, tense smile, but a smile nonetheless. When she looked up and saw Poppy and me her smile faltered, but she pulled it back.

"Thanks for coming," she said, a touch awkwardly.

"Wouldn't have missed it for the world," said Poppy.

"Thanks for inviting us—really," I said. "I'm so glad we're here."

"Me too." And her smile looked a little more genuine.

"How are you doing?" I asked tentatively.

"Oh, you know." She shrugged. "Husband in prison, single parenting. You know how it is."

"I'm so sorry," I mumbled.

"Don't be," she said. "You did the right thing. Anyway. We're here because we're moving on. New beginnings, and all that."

THE CEREMONY was beautiful. Camran led the ritual, which was short and simple and just right. He welcomed the baby to our world, which I couldn't help but feel was a mixed bag right now. But he spoke, briefly, about the power of the earth to heal herself. And about the power of the dawn, every morning, birthing the world anew. Two months ago I would have scoffed at it, labeled it "hippy shit," in the words of Maya and Joe. Now, it still made me uncomfortable; I was still so far out of my comfort zone I practically needed an oxygen mask. But I was a new parent now, so that feeling appeared to be my daily reality. And I was learning that it was a big old world, and there was room for plenty of opinions and beliefs beyond my own.

Throughout the whole ceremony, Ailsa was right beside Hen, holding her hand for most of it. Her pregnancy bump looked unnaturally big, so much more so now that I no longer had mine. Ailsa was the last of us, still whole, still waiting to be split into two people. Lin, Poppy and Noah stood by me, Poppy and Lin clutching each other slightly tighter than seemed necessary. I had a feeling they would never let go.

Then came the moment that we had been waiting six weeks for. The naming.

"Welcome to the world, Arora Nathalie Jasmine Lee."

It was the perfect name.

Arora stretched in her mother's arms and focused her tiny eyes on the beribboned tree above her—eyes that were already so much more aware, that were already gaining the tints and shadows of the world.

I looked down at my own new little person, feeling the mingled awe and fear that I was learning constitute the daily life of a parent. Every day would be terrifying from now on, and every day would be magical.

"Welcome to the world, small one," I whispered. "It's a shitshow. But it might just get better now you're here."

ACKNOWLEDGMENTS

AH, I'VE BEEN looking forward to this bit! So many people to thank, so many tears of joy and gratitude and sheer bloody exhaustion to weep. First and foremost, hi reader! Thanks for buying/borrowing/stealing this book—I hope you enjoyed it!

On to business. To my agent Jemima Forrester—thanks for being such an excellent companion on this voyage! Enthusiastic, tireless, ever-optimistic and excellent at agenting—all I could possibly ask for in an agent. To my editor Kelly Smith, who immediately got the book, got the tone, the humor—thanks for being a forensic, intuitive and sensitive editor. Both of you immediately understood the importance of snacks and dogs, and also saw exactly what this book needed to make it step up. Between the two of you, you really shaped this into something I hope we can all be proud of. Thank you also to my copyeditor Sandra Ferguson (I do feel slightly awkward for claiming in the book that Sandra is not a cosmically enlightened name, sorry), and proofreader Jenny Page.

Thank you to the wonderful team at Minotaur Books who have produced this beautiful American edition—and most especially to my editor, Catherine Richards, who has been so spectacularly enthusiastic and supportive. I couldn't have dreamed of a better home for my book. (And you basically put my own dog on the jacket, for which I will love you all forever.)

Of course, a huge thank-you to the team of the Comedy Women in Print prize, and especially Helen Lederer, without whom this book would not exist. I submitted a total mash of words to the prize, written in haste over an extremely hazy three-week period, but you saw potential in it! Thank you for celebrating women and writing and humor—three of the best things in life.

To my real-life NCT pals, Carly, Lisa, Sophie B and Steph, I can't imagine a better bunch to investigate a murder with. Yes, our experiences did provide some of the inspiration for this book, but I promise none of the characters are based on you or your partners! That said, Sophie, I will always feel responsible for sending you into labor so early—*take note: clary sage is bloody potent.* And Carly, thank you for not walking away the minute I produced a cold omelette from my pocket on a dog walk. To the extended Stroud Motherhood, especially Alice, Kate and Sophie L—thank you for letting me tag along; you'll never shake me now. The lot of you have made moving to Stroud a blimmin' delight. And finally, I know you can't read this, but to Jazz, Rupert and Katie (RIP), of whom Helen, Ronnie and Sultan are shameless rip-offs, cheese and sausages for you beauties; you know I really wrote this book for you. And for the record, I do not actually think Rupert looks like a badger mated with a croissant—he is a very handsome hound (but I do think Jazz is out of his league, sorry not sorry).

A heartfelt thanks to Fran, Indira, Liz and Matt, who read the hopeless early drafts and are my real-life Mayas. Thank you for sharing a warped sense of humor, a belief in the importance of snacks, and too many bottles of wine to count. To my beloved Lakes crew, thank you for being such endlessly supportive and loving pals who were so enthusiastic about this book. And to my Reading pals, old friends are the best, thanks for sticking around.

To my cousin Alice, it didn't occur to me I had pinched your name. I also somehow failed to realize I had initially called Alice's boyfriend Paul, your brother's name, and yeah, that was a weird moment when we realized that . . . Sorry!

Mum and Dad—thanks for bringing me up in a house full (too full, really) of books and for being so apparently genuinely enthusiastic about my weird early writing attempts as a child (I haven't forgotten the Mole People, and I'm sure you haven't either). Especial thanks to you for the serious park hours you clocked up with your grandson so I could write in peace—this book would never have been written without you. And to my in-laws, for endless patient childcare and being so wonderful when I disappeared for extended periods on a long-awaited, much-postponed family holiday to write.

Caleb, the greatest squish in the universe. To be honest, you haven't actually contributed a huge amount to the writing of this book . . . Other than possibly 3 A.M. breastfeeding fever dreams. But you're the best. Love you, stay squishy.

Jamie. I have saved you for last because this is one thanks that it is impossible to write. I actually think you genuinely always believed I would publish a book. Your faith in me, in us, is truly what got me to this point. Our adventures have been many and strange, and excellent book fodder; long may they continue. I love you.

Turn the page for a sneak peek at
Kat Ailes's new novel

Available Spring 2024

Copyright © 2024 by Kat Ailes

CHAPTER 1

THERE USED TO be an advert for Boursin herby cheese that showed a couple enjoying a picture-perfect picnic in a meadow—only to zoom out and reveal a combine harvester heading straight for them. Picnicking with babies—and my dog—is very much the scene of devastation *after* the combine harvester has passed through.

We'd gone for a picnic because it seemed like a "new mum" thing to do. I wasn't sure if calling us new mums when the babies were now one, and therefore possibly no longer babies, was stretching it a bit, but I definitely still felt new to the job—that morning I'd managed to put Jack's nappy on back to front and had been forced to use some of my moderately expensive face cream on him because we'd run out of baby lotion.

But picnics are what you do on maternity leave—I've seen the pictures on people's social media. You and your new-parent friends sit around drinking rosé, smiling and laughing and swapping comical stories about how little sleep you're getting and how many bodily fluids you've dealt with in the last twenty-four hours. All while gazing adoringly at your gurgling, content offspring, who smile adorably for the camera. You imagine a sun-soaked meadow, maybe one of those wicker hampers with actual genuine crockery in it, and probably a fancy French cheese wrapped in cloth. You lounge gracefully on your tartan rug, laughing elegantly as the summer breeze gently ruffles your hair.

Yes, picnics are one of those charming fantasies/lies. The reality is an hour-long search to find a large enough cow-pat-free area, grass that is *weirdly spiky* and gives you a disconcerting rash, and an ensuing war of attrition to keep the dog from gnawing through your Tupperware and eating Babybels with the wax still on. And that's before you add children into the mix.

I had to admit though, the general setting for this one was pretty decent at least. It was unseasonably warm for May and the sun had that early summer glow—before the burn really sets in. We were in an honest-to-goodness meadow, the grass still lush and long from spring. It looked like the whole blimmin' scene had an Instagram filter on it (if you didn't look too closely, that is).

The new-parent friends were all right too: Hen, Ailsa and Poppy, whom I had met the previous year at antenatal class and gone on to solve two murders with (or possibly three, depending on your take), the first of which had actually taken place at our antenatal class. There had been, let's say unforeseen consequences for several of us, following our sleuthing debut, but we were moving past that. I think. We were joined by our five babies and three dogs. This did a lot to undermine the perfection of the scene. While Poppy's greyhound Sultan was posing exquisitely at a slight distance, casting us the occasional look of mild disdain, her other dog Ronnie was alternating between pinching sausage rolls and mounting my dog, Helen. And as for the babies . . .

"I still can't believe you didn't tell us you were having twins." I shook my head at Ailsa, watching her twins Ivy and Robin rolling back and forth, rubbing jam in each other's hair.

Ailsa shrugged. "I'm sure I mentioned it."

"I think we'd have remembered."

"I knew," interjected Hen. Ah yes, well, the Hen–Ailsa relationship defied explanation; I had never met two more opposite people. In looks alone they were chalk and cheese, Ailsa's ruddy dreadlocks and patched dungarees in stark contrast to Hen's sharp black bob and actual branded maternity wear. Then there was Ailsa's commitment to all things natural, organic, and preferably made from hemp, set against Hen's apparently pathological need to douse every surface, including her daughter, in industrial-grade cleaning products. Ailsa performed sun salutations and was on first-name terms with the moon goddess; Hen worshipped at the altar of Baby Boden and Petit Bateau. But they'd gone for that whole opposites attract thing and were alternately best friends and arch nemeses. It seemed to be working for them.

Hen smoothed imaginary wrinkles from her daughter's white frock and adjusted the parasol over her. Arora, just over a year old, was eating strawberries with impeccable daintiness. Next to her, my own son, Jack, was solemnly posting hummus down his nappy. Other than the nappy, he was entirely naked, because babies.

My dog, Helen, escaped Ronnie's clutches and came trotting over, one ear inside out and a crazed look in her eye. She gave Arora's face a hearty licking. For some reason, best known to her, she adored Hen's baby. She was broadly indifferent to Jack, whom she lived with and, I hoped, regarded as part of the family.

"Has she eaten any cowpats?" asked Hen sharply.

I shrugged helplessly.

"It's Helen," said Poppy, who was lying on her back, eyes closed, face to the sun. "If it's just cowpats you'll be lucky." I felt this was a tad unfair, as Ronnie posed almost as much of a hygiene risk as Helen. I didn't say anything though—Poppy had seemed . . . subdued of late.

Out of the corner of my eye I saw Hen sanitize Arora's face.

"Weaning's going well then." Ailsa nodded toward where Jack was now stuffing a fistful of grass in his mouth. I sighed and removed it from him. He gave me a deeply hurt look.

"It's good for his gut bacteria," I replied. Behind me, Poppy snorted. Her own son, Noah, was curled up next to her. He had inherited Poppy's Afro, but whereas hers was small and neat, Noah's was wild and filled with grass seeds—probably courtesy of my own son, it has to be admitted. Mother and son were snoozing idyllically in the shade of an enormous gold umbrella. I watched them covertly. Poppy had always had a driving force behind her, a dynamism that I quite frankly envied. But over the last few months it seemed to have drained out of her. Of course, she was tired—we all were. Noah and Jack had just turned one, meaning it was one whole year since either of us had slept properly. I just hoped that was all there was to it; it felt as though as distance had opened up, not just between Poppy and myself, but between Poppy and the world. She had barely spoken during the picnic, rousing herself only infrequently to liberally suncream Noah. Then again, it was hot—like is-this-really-England hot—too hot for conversation, really. The day had that peaceful heaviness that covers you like a warm blanket of sunshine and invites one of those half waking, half sleeping naps. I wondered whether Jack and Helen would manage not to destroy the picnic/meadow/themselves for a full five minutes if I closed my eyes.

In a swift response to this thought, Helen flopped down heavily in the middle of the picnic, flattening several unfortunate sausage rolls and spraying Arora with guacamole.

Hen squealed, immediately produced an enormous pack of wet wipes and began dabbing at her daughter, who now looked like she was splattered in avocado bogeys. Arora simply giggled and shared a conspiratorial look with Helen.

Luckily, I was saved from Hen's wrath by Poppy, who had half opened one eye at the commotion.

"Oh look, people," she said drowsily.

I squinted through the sun to where two figures had emerged from the cluster of ancient trees that grew in the center of the meadow. I couldn't see so well because I had lost my sunglasses—by which I mean I was pretty sure either Helen or Jack had buried them—but even blurred . . .

"Are they naked?"

At this Poppy rolled over to get a better look. It was the first time she'd moved in an hour.

"Ooh, I think they are you know."

"Nothing wrong with that." Ailsa sniffed.

"I didn't say there was," I pointed out. After just over a year of life in Penton, a town on the further end of the hippy spectrum, I liked to think it would take more than a couple of nudists to faze me. My first year living here had introduced me to such Pentonic delights as gong bathing, ritual aura cleansing and a plethora of herbal, crystal and chakra-based remedies. While I seldom dipped more than a toe in the more alternative side of Penton life, I enjoyed watching it from a distance with mild amusement and cynicism.

"No wait, I think they're wearing *something* . . ." Poppy narrowed her eyes. "Or maybe it's paint?"

"I think they're coming over," I said. "What should we do?"

"Take our clothes off," suggested Ailsa. I wasn't sure if she was joking. In many ways, Ailsa remained as much a mystery to me as she had before a year of enforced mat-leave friendship. Which, by the way, I had greatly enjoyed, although I sensed Ailsa was still on the fence about me.

The two figures were close enough now that even my sun-dazzled eyes could tell that yes, they were naked, and yes, they had words painted across their torsos.

"Save our . . . corpse?" read Poppy hesitantly.

"Copse," corrected Hen automatically, although she hadn't appeared to even glance at the figures. "Means a small group of trees."

"I know what it means." Poppy sniffed. "It's my eyes that don't work, not my brain."

I kept quiet—it was entirely possible I'd never heard this word before.

The figures waved as they approached. At which point Helen erupted from the picnic blanket, catapulting crisps and Fondant Fancies over the assembled babies, and greeted the newcomers in her own special way—a maelstrom of tail wagging, high-pitched chicken squeals and, in this case possibly inappropriate, licking.

"Sorry! Sorry!" I scrambled to my feet, accidentally sending Jack flying into the hummus, and fumbled to get Helen under control before she washed off all their body paint.

The newcomers were a man and a woman—very definitely so—and both, I couldn't help noticing (I mean, I really couldn't), impeccable physical specimens. They looked like those Roman statues you see in museums, all toned abs and chiseled jaws—although with more limbs than your average ancient statue. The man had a mane of glossy black hair with an oil-slick feather braided into one side. The girl had close-cropped hair, also black but with a blue sheen that suggested either a dye job or a hint of petrol in her genetics.

"Hi!" they chorused as I finally managed to restrain Helen.

"Lovely day for a picnic," said the man, looking disproportionately serious about the fact.

"Beautiful," I agreed, making aggressive eye contact to avoid my gaze falling anywhere else. I sought for a suitable conversational gambit—they'd already commented on the weather, which left me fresh out of ideas for polite conversation.

"Er, would you like some sunscreen?" I asked, noticing a pink tint already burnishing the man's milk-white body. Not that I was looking. Just—there are some places you really don't want to burn. "It's kids' sunscreen," I rambled on, as is my incredibly socially engaging way. "But, I mean, what difference can that really make? Other than adding an extra four quid on the price. It might blur your body paint though, that could be a problem."

"Lovely day for a naked stroll," interrupted Ailsa, which was probably for the best. "Soaking up some sun?"

"Do you normally slogan yourselves before nude sunbathing?" I added, before I could help myself.

"Oh we're not nudists," laughed the woman, slightly derisively. Well, you could've fooled me.

"No?" Hen raised a skeptical eyebrow.

"This is just for the protest," said the woman, gesturing to her slightly Helen-smeared body paint. "We're protesting against the desecration of this ancient meadow and copse by the building of a wind farm."

I glanced around, unsure exactly who they were protesting to. Far off on the horizon, a handful of cows seemed unmoved by their searing political statement.

"This is just a preliminary photo shoot," explained the man. "My brother's a photographer. He's coming up to photograph us for the protest website."

Ailsa had propped herself up on an elbow looking interested. "What's this about a wind farm?"

Hen, I noticed, had flushed slightly and was fiddling with the straps on Arora's pinafore dress.

"It's a local green energy company, you might have heard of them," said the woman. "Aether? They're based just over the hill in Bishop's Ruin."

"So-called green energy," broke in the man. "If you can call the complete desecration of a thriving, delicately balanced ecosystem 'green.' Just to serve our endless greed for more energy, more power."

Ah. Aether. No wonder Hen was looking so awkward. This was going to be interesting.

"Anyway," continued the woman, "they've somehow managed to buy the lease on this meadow and are intending to build a wind farm here—including cutting down the sweet chestnuts that have been here for over five hundred years." She gestured toward the copse of ancient and gnarly trees that hunkered in the center of the meadow and which I knew well, having sheltered there during many a rainy dog walk. I felt a twinge of sadness that after so many centuries, and having sheltered many thousands of dog walkers, the trees were fated to be cut down.

"How have they got permission?" asked Ailsa, now fully sitting up. "I did some fieldwork here a few years ago—it's Jurassic limestone, there are all sorts of rare flowers up here. There was Cotswold Pennycress growing last I looked. That's incredibly rare, and it's a declining species—they can't just destroy an endangered habitat like this!"

"Cotswold Pennycress?" The man looked interested. "A rare species?" He turned to the woman. "We should make a note of that."

She nodded and her hand moved involuntarily toward a pocket—and presumably phone—that wasn't there. She looked around vaguely as if a notebook or scrap of paper might appear. I was going to suggest she use some body paint to make a note on a blank stretch of thigh, but the man was talking again.

"Companies like Aether have no time for the environment—oh, I know they say they're a green energy company," he cut across himself as Hen opened her mouth to speak, "but it's a classic case of greenwashing. Would a company that really cared about the environment be prepared to bulldoze a meadow and tear down an ancient copse of trees?"

"All they really care about is the bottom line," chipped in the woman. "Raking in the profits while presenting a respectable environmentally friendly face to the world."

They both had the slightly over-bright eyes of the true zealot.

"It's a fair point," said Ailsa. Hen shot her a look.

"I'm sure that's true of a lot of companies," said Poppy soothingly, before Ailsa could say any more or Hen could throw a cake at her. "But what makes you so sure that's the case with Aether?"

The man and woman exchanged a dark glance. "We have evidence," said the woman shortly.

"So what are you planning to do about it?" I asked. "Naked photoshoot aside?"

"The photos are just a small part of it, we're a whole movement," said the man earnestly, his eyes practically glowing now. "We're part of the Earth Force protest group. We've been trying to expose Aether's green-washing for the last year. I'm surprised you haven't heard about us—it's been in the news quite a lot."

I had last read the news about twelve months ago, before parenthood had reduced my available mental capacity to approximately that of Helen. Ailsa, however, was nodding. "I think I've heard about it. Didn't some of you naked gatecrash an Aether press conference the other day?"

Oh good, more nudity.

The not-nudists nodded enthusiastically.

"Yes, that was Raven and couple of others from the group," said the woman earnestly.

"And you would be . . . Raven?" I asked the man.

He nodded. "And this is Leila." He gestured to the woman. It had been a good ten years since I only found out someone's name *after* I'd seen them naked. I noticed Hen start slightly, shooting Leila a sharp look, almost . . . accusatory?

"It's nice to meet you," I mumbled. I was about to announce my own disappointingly ordinary name, Alice, but Ailsa cut across.

"So what's your plan to halt the wind farm," she asked, sounding genuinely interested. This kind of thing was right up her street. Since meeting Ailsa she had introduced me to such eco-friendly delights as reusable nappies (yep, it's a thing) and reusable wipes, and treated me to several lectures on the perils of junk food (my main food category) and in fact eating anything that wasn't organic, local and sustainably sourced. For my birthday she signed me up to Greenpeace.

"We're on our final chance," said Raven somberly. "Aether have construction vehicles coming in on Thursday to take down the trees."

"And lay concrete foundations in place," cut in Leila angrily. I had to admit—it did seem a shame.

"So we'll be staging a sit-in protest on Wednesday night," continued Raven. "Chaining ourselves to the trees."

"If they want to take the trees out, they'll have to take us out with them," declared Leila defiantly.

"I thought protestors mainly glued themselves to things these days," I said absent-mindedly.

"We did think about that," said Raven earnestly. "And we had a lot of success gluing ourselves to the Aether company headquarters a few months ago. But we were worried the glue would harm the trees, so we're going old school and using chains."

Idly, I wondered how they'd eventually unglued themselves, because I'd recently glued one of Jack's toy trucks to my hand while trying to fix it, and it turns out the slogan "The bond that never breaks" is terrifyingly accurate. I'd had to soak my new Transformer-hand in a weird hand-bath for nearly an hour.

"We're having a meeting on Monday evening to plan the sit-in," said Leila. "You should come along, find out a bit more about the proposed development and the untold harm it will cause. And how we're going to stop it."

"Um—" I began.

"Sure," broke in Ailsa. "We'd love to."

"Would we?" I asked blankly. She ignored me.

"Eight o'clock, Monday," said Leila. "At the school hall in Bishop's Ruin."

"Sorry, where?" I asked.

"It's a village in the next valley," said Ailsa.

Of course it was. I'd never get used to the weird names they had for villages in these parts—personal favorites being Petty France and the un-forgettable Upper and Lower Slaughter. With my track record for finding bodies in the Cotswolds, I was steering well clear of the latter.

"I think that's Sam," said Raven, shading his eyes with his hand and peering at a figure (possibly clothed, possibly not) that had appeared on the horizon. "My brother," he added to us.

"How come your brother is called Sam, and you're called Raven?" I asked. "I don't mean to be rude, I'm just saying, there's a bit of a discon-nect."

"Raven is my chosen name."

I didn't have much of an answer for that.

"Well, we should get on with the photos," said Leila, sounding slightly less enthusiastic all of a sudden. "I think your dog might be trying to get involved."

I yelped and looked round; Helen was indeed making a determined beeline for the distant newcomer, presumably in the hope that his pockets were inexplicably full of cheese and sausage. This rarely happens, but she never gives up hope.

"Helen!" I shouted, without much conviction. "Helen?"

"Your dog's called Helen?" Raven asked curiously.

"Yes, why?"

He shrugged. "That's an unusual name for a dog, that's all."

I stared at him—was he serious?

"It's her chosen name," I said flatly.

CHAPTER 2

THERE WAS A slightly awkward silence after Raven and Leila left. I wondered who was going to be the first to bring up the elephant at the picnic.

"Did you hear what he said to her as they left?" asked Poppy. Ah good, we were avoiding the subject.

"Yeah, he said, 'Play nice with Sam now,' or something like that," Ailsa replied.

"Neither of them look the playful sort, if you ask me," I said. I've always struggled with earnest people; as someone of few moral convictions and the ethical depth of a spoon, I tend to have very little in common with them. This was one of my many moral failings that Ailsa was working hard to correct.

Hen still hadn't said anything. She was avoiding meeting any of our eyes.

Eventually, Ailsa went there—she was usually the bravest.

"So, did you know about the wind farm?" she asked Hen. I felt myself tense involuntarily. Ever since Hen had started her job as PA to the CEO of Aether, she and Ailsa had been clashing more than ever. The two of them had been almost inseparable since Hen's husband had . . . left. Like Hen, Ailsa was also going it alone—with the added challenge of twins which, let me tell you, is *more* than twice the work. Or perhaps that was just Ailsa's particular brand of twin. I knew Ailsa stayed over at Hen's several nights a week, pooling resources, as it were. But they also bickered worse than an old married couple over everything from whether to give the twins jam to the environmental costs of certain types of green energy.

When Hen's new status as a single parent had forced her to find a job after just six months of maternity leave, Ailsa had initially been enthusiastic and entirely supportive of Hen's new job at Aether. But there had been growing whispers in the community of late that Aether was not quite the wonder-solution people had initially hoped, and Ailsa had fast turned skeptical. This latest news promised to deliver a real doozy of a row between the two of them.

Hen met Ailsa's eye defiantly. "Of course I did, they've hardly talked about anything else at work all month. It's going to be a major project."

"You never mentioned it," objected Ailsa.

"It never came up. I didn't know you'd be interested."

"You thought I wouldn't approve," needled Ailsa.

"That's not true," said Hen hotly. "If anything I thought you *would* approve. It's renewable energy! You'd rather we burned fossil fuels? Or chucked particles at a nuclear reactor and flooded the area with radiation? You'd rather have fracking until the whole valley caves in?"

"I'd rather," said Ailsa, rather coldly, "not flatten an ancient copse and destroy a thriving and biodiverse ecosystem. Do you know how fast meadows are vanishing across the UK? I can't believe this isn't a protected site! Especially with the Cotswold Pennycress, and the ancient chestnut grove."

Hen threw her hands in the air in exasperation. "There's no perfect solution, Ailsa! Aether have done their due diligence—the environmental impact of building here will be minimal. All the reports said so. When it comes to balancing the impact of one relatively small area of grassland against the ongoing *catastrophic* impact of fossil fuel energy—"

Ailsa snorted derisively. "Come on, Hen, the habitat degradation alone . . ."

"Did you recognize Leila?" I broke in to ask Hen, hoping to head things off before they went nuclear.

"No, why?" she said curtly.

"I don't know, you just looked at her a bit weirdly, that's all."

"Your imagination is running away with you, Alice."

I have to admit, I do have a pretty active imagination, though in this case, I wasn't so sure. But when Hen clammed up you'd have more luck persuading an oyster to spit out its pearl, to mix my sea metaphors. The argument mutated into an impassioned debate as to whether Cotswold Pennycress could still be found in the meadow, and this time I left them to it, turning my attention to Jack and Noah, who were peacefully smearing mayo on Sultan's nose, as the regal greyhound lay motionless, possibly content, possibly utterly defeated.

HEN AND Ailsa eventually returned from a fruitless search to see if they could spot any Cotswold Pennycress. They appeared to have made up—I saw Ailsa hip-bump Hen affectionately as they made their way back up the slope. Poppy and I sat up and made some effort to look like we had been actually minding the babies, as requested. I smeared some suncream on one of the twins—probably Robin?—where it mingled with his jam body paint to create quite an appealing Müller Corner effect.

"Find anything?" asked Poppy, draping a wet muslin over Noah's head. I had done the same thing over Helen—partly to cool her down, partly because a blanket over her head appeared to switch her off, which was to everyone's benefit.

"Too hot to look properly," huffed Ailsa, after chugging from her water bottle. "It must be six thousand degrees out there."

"Ailsa's dedication to the cause couldn't take the heat," teased Hen. They clearly *had* made up, because Ailsa's only response was to flick water over Hen, who turned her face to the spray with an expression of bliss.

I rolled onto my stomach and rummaged through the detritus of the picnic, looking for any remnant that wasn't melted, squashed, or covered in dog hair. It was slim pickings.

"Can you not?" I said to Ailsa through a mouthful of reconstituted meat and egg, without needing to look round.

"What?"

"I'm trying to enjoy my Scotch egg and I can feel you glaring at me."

"It's disgusting, that's all," she said matter-of-factly. "When are you going to go veggie, Alice?"

"I have low iron," I retorted.

"So eat some spinach."

I ignored her and continued trying to enjoy my Scotch egg of doom. Around me, Hen had started bustling, tidying away rubbish and putting the remains of food into Tupperware and beeswax wraps, muttering about the sun getting too hot for the babies—which was probably true; it was definitely getting too hot for me. With a sigh, I sat up and began wiping Jack down—a thankless and ultimately pointless task. Helen lent a hand, or rather a tongue, with considerably more enthusiasm and, it has to be said, more efficiency than me.

The walk back to the cars, laden with now very hot and grumpy babies, and almost certainly inedible picnic remnants which, as always, seemed to have exponentially expanded from the amount of food we'd actually brought, seemed much longer than the walk out. The meadow still looked idyllic—grasses shifting ever so slightly in a barely there breeze, the occasional flash of color from a wildflower—but seemed to have stretched into a savannah.

In the distance, we could hear faint voices floating across the still air from the copse, and I could make out the pale, naked forms of Raven and Leila draped across various trees, as a third figure ducked and weaved around them.

"Are you still staying over tonight?" I heard Hen ask Ailsa in an unusually small voice.

With an exasperated sigh, Ailsa put her arm around Hen—which seemed a sticky move in this heat, in my opinion. "Of course I am, you idiot. I'll cook. We can watch a movie and not think about—y'know. Him."

This, of course, was why we'd been picnicking today. Not that we'd mentioned it. It was one year since the door had closed, finally and dramatically, on Hen's marriage. We didn't talk about it much, but it had felt important to all be together today. I was glad Ailsa would be with Hen tonight—it wasn't a night to spend alone.

"D'you think Hen will be OK tonight?" I asked Poppy, as we loaded the children and dogs into her car to be ferried home.

"Hmm?" Poppy sounded distracted—which seemed to be the case more and more these days, as though she wasn't fully there.

"Hen," I repeated, wondering anxiously whether Hen wasn't the only one I needed to be worried about. "Do you think she'll be all right?"

"Oh, right. Yeah, of course she will," said Poppy vaguely. "She's got Ailsa to look after her."

I wasn't sure whether this was a positive or a negative; being looked after by Ailsa sounded a bit like how I viewed exercise—dubious bordering on painful at the time, but ultimately extremely beneficial.

"Makes you grateful for Joe and Lin, huh," I prodded Poppy gently, as I buckled Jack into his car seat and drew the straps so tight he squawked—I wasn't taking any risks. Joe was my scatter-brained, haphazard and deeply irritating partner whom I was nonetheless extremely fond of. Lin was Poppy's capable, efficient and all-round lovely wife.

"Hmm, yeah," said Poppy, her mind still clearly elsewhere.

I eyed her worriedly as she drove us back toward town. I made a few attempts at conversation around our nude picnic-crashers—surely a rich topic—but Poppy remained withdrawn, an unusual state for her, although I reflected that it was becoming increasingly common of late. I lapsed into silence, an unusual state for me. Of course, I could always make up for this when I got home and filled Joe in on every minute detail of my day.

Indira Birnie

KAT AILES works in publishing as an editor and freelanced for several years to allow her to take a couple of belated gap years, which included hiking the Pacific Crest Trail from Mexico to Canada. She now lives in the Cotswolds with her husband, their young son, and their beautiful but foolish dog. *The Expectant Detectives* is her debut novel, the first draft of which was written largely (and frantically) in three weeks after she submitted the first few chapters to the Comedy Women in Print prize and was unexpectedly shortlisted.